Why it's bad to spy on the wee folk . . .

Looking straight at the elfin Dola, all Carl could see was a storeroom, dimly lit by bare bulbs hanging on cords. Concentrating very hard, Dola made the image of a great, black spider walk across the floor. Carl gasped, then realizing he had spoken, clapped his hand over his mouth. He turned and began to feel his way back up the corridor. As Carl passed the younger elves, Moira squeezed Borget's hand.

"Eeeeeeeeeah!" shrieked Moira at the top of her voice.

"Hmmhmmhmmhmmhahahahaha . . ." laughed Borget in as sinister a tone as he could manage.

Carl straightened and bashed his head on the ceiling. There was another burst of ghostly laughter. Clutching his head, Carl felt his way out of the tunnel, hotly pursued by his banshees. He screamed curses back at them, but the elves only laughed. An elvish trick!

"I'll get you, too," he swore, as he ran up the stairs. He wasn't going to get his evidence this way, that was sure . . .

● ● ● ●

MYTHOLOGY 101

JODY LYNN NYE

POPULAR LIBRARY

An Imprint of Warner Books, Inc.

A Time Warner Company

POPULAR LIBRARY EDITION

Copyright © 1990 by Jody Lynn Nye

Popular Library®, the fanciful P design, and Questar® are registered trademarks of Warner Books, Inc.

Cover illustration by Don Maitz

Popular Library books are published by

Warner Books, Inc.
1271 Avenue of the Americas
New York, N.Y. 10020

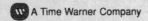 A Time Warner Company

Printed in the United States of America

First Printing: February, 1990

10 9 8 7 6

For Bill,
who believes in me.

• Chapter 1 •

"Are all now present?" the Master inquired, squinting over the top of his gold-rimmed spectacles. The light of two dozen burning lanterns hanging around the huge room flickered off the lenses and metal of his glasses. It glinted almost as brightly from the Master's coppery red beard and hair. Even his pointed ears had tufts of red hair sticking out of them which caught the quivering light.

On the benches around the wooden meeting table, the Folk shifted to position themselves comfortably. It wasn't often the whole Council attended a village meeting, so though the benches were long, the regulars had to suck in their sides to make room for their more erstwhile companions. It was a sign of the seriousness of the situation that there was no banter, no friendly arguments between the young Progressives and the older Conservatives.

"Gut. Then I declare that the meeting is open." The Master continued familiarly, "I recognize the Archivist." He nodded to Catra, a young female who wore her long brown hair in a severe braid.

Catra stood up and shook two sheets of paper at the assembly. "These I borrowed from the very desk of the Big Folk chancellor himself. They detail a proposal to demolish our very home! They wish to build on this site a new library building of great height and size. It will have a new foundation made

1

by filling in all the lower levels with concrete." She shuddered at the image of a wave of concrete rolling over their village and handed the document to the Master, who blew on the wick of a lantern to ignite it, and read the decree through by the light. He nodded affirmation to the others.

"We're lost!" Keva shrieked. For all her hundred and seventy-eight years, she had a voice that carried shrilly to the distant walls and echoed off them. Her fellow villagers looked around cautiously as if the chancellor and his minions might hear her. "We must flee!" Her fellow Conservatives nodded solemnly.

"It's only a proposal at present," Aylmer said in a calm voice. He was a Conservative, too, but didn't approve of alarmism.

Holl, a chunky young fellow with thick blond hair, scratched thoughtfully at one tall pointed ear. "I think we should call in the help of the Big Ones who are our fellow students."

There was a general outcry. "No! You can't trust the Big Ones. They're too stupid." "They wouldn't help us. It's their own chancellor and his administrators who seek to put us out of our home." "Yes, ask them!" "Progressive! You want us to be annihilated; to have our culture swept away."

"The separation of aur folk fro' theirs must an' will continue," Curran, Holl's white-haired clan chief, told him severely.

"I think there are some that can be trusted not to do more than we ask," Holl insisted. "Ludmilla. No question of her, I hope. Fair Marcy, for example. And there's always Lee."

"Yes," agreed Enoch, a more somber-faced youth with black hair. "I know these well, and there are others, but I am not sure I would involve the young folk even if I trusted them."

"What of those peculiar walkings-about we keep hearing? Who's responsible for those cloppingly clumsy footsteps? One of your trustworthy fellow students? You don't know either!" Curran snapped at Holl.

"I put it to a vote, then," the Master said, signalling for silence. "Those in favor uf asking for help vrom the Big Ones, raise your right hands." He counted. "Hands down, please. Those against, the left." There were no surprises. The Progressive voted in favor of Holl's suggestion. The Conservatives voted against the Progressives, whom they outnumbered two to one. He and Catra abstained. The Master felt that the Headman must remain neutral. Catra often declared that an archivist could not take sides or it would ruin her objectivity. "Very vell. The motion is defeated at present. I adjure all uf you to put your minds to a solution, or ve may truly be homeless."

"I must return the document to the chancellor's office before dawn," Catra reminded him.

"Qvite right. I must haf a copy to study the details." The Master blew out his lantern. He picked up a sheet of handmade parchment slightly larger than both pieces of paper and laid it over the document. Stretching out both hands palm-down above the parchment, the red-haired leader closed his eyes to concentrate. Under each of his hands, a shimmering blob of black print appeared and spread across to meet the other, then the joined mass rippled outward to perfectly straight squared margins. No one made a sound until he was finished. It was a difficult task for one of their kind to work from paper that had been printed with iron and steel.

"There," he said, examining the big sheet. "Vell enough. It vill do."

"Master," Catra chided him gently. "I could have used the Xerox machine."

▪ Chapter 2 ▪

"Mr. Doyle?" inquired Dr. Freleng, holding a thesis paper in the air with disgusted thumb and forefinger. The teacher's grey mustache lifted on one side as his lip curled. "This is Sociology 430. Don't you think this paper should better have been submitted to your fiction writing teacher instead?"

"Well, I'm not taking that course this semester," stammered Keith Doyle, scrambling to sit upright from his comfortable slouch behind Mary Lou Carson, the fattest girl in class. He met the teacher's eye and drooped back again. The student's narrow face turned red, only a few shades darker than his hair. "Um, no, sir. What's the matter with it, sir?"

"Or perhaps this is Introduction to Mythology? What is the matter? 'A Study of Human/Alien Interaction'? This paper was supposed to be on a documented facet of human behavior. Would you mind telling me when we made contact with extraterrestrials? I'm sure the government would be more than interested to know." Dr. Freleng opened his fingers and let the paper fall to Keith's desk, covering up the *Field Guide to the Little People*, which luckily the professor hadn't noticed. The other students snickered. Freleng dusted his fingertips together and eyed Keith with an air of doubt.

"It's a study based on theories I formed, speculations on the probable behavior of mankind when faced with alien cultures more technologically advanced than ours," Keith explained with patient resignation. "Older extraterrestrial cultures. I based it on my research into recent Western contacts with older civilizations, such as the Chinese."

"Of which you seem most disparaging," Freleng said, gesturing at the paper, on which a circled red F adorned the title page. Keith stuck out his chin determinedly.

"I think non-Western cultures suffer because of the overeager come-on that they get from Western anthropologists. Think of the business of the desert tribe religion that believed in planets it couldn't see, just because those researchers asked 'em leading questions. Look," Keith said earnestly, "when zoologists are observing rare animals, they're so careful not to interfere with their natural behavior. It's almost like people don't get the same privilege. It's as if, well, because they're different they're told they have to change to conform."

Freleng turned away from Keith's indignant stare, fluttering a dismissive hand at him. "Preservationist poppycock. Field anthropologists act with more responsibility than that toward their subjects."

"Yeah, sometimes, but what about Peace Corps volunteers? Missionaries? We make change look too attractive, too imperative, and play down the importance of the society's own, diverse cultural facets," Keith went on, his voice loud with conviction, quoting phrases from the Sociology textbook, which Freleng ignored. It was one of the professor's own favorite tricks, and he hated to have students use it back to him. "They've done without Coca-Cola for centuries. They don't need it either, but we dictate to them, the times when we don't collapse at their feet and shout 'teach me,' instead. We impose our impressions of how they should behave on them. Our opinion molds them."

"Yeah," added a girl with brown-black hair, seated two rows ahead to Keith's left. She had clear, pale skin with just a dusting of dark freckles across her nose and cheekbones, and Keith had been watching her avidly all semester. "Like Little—I mean, short people. Tall ones tend to treat them just like children. They react to an unspoken assumption that if someone is smaller than you are, he must be younger, and not as mature. Or if they're obviously older, they must be senile, or something less than mentally competent."

Keith was amazed. Usually the majority of his fellow students sided with the teacher on how they felt about his peculiar essay topics. As a rule, they all thought he was crazy. He felt much encouraged by Marcy Collier's unsolicited support. Not only was she beautiful, but she was a fellow philosopher.

"Yes, Miss Collier, I have your paper here," Freleng turned on her. "You expressed your opinions on paper with *somewhat* more coherence than Mr. Doyle, though you failed to identify most of your research sources. I require clearer footnoting than that, as you are aware. It is worth 15 percent of your grade on any paper." Her paper fluttered down, marked with a circled C.

"Um," Marcy Collier echoed Keith's discomfort of a few minutes past. The teacher's cold gaze made her writhe. Her eyes dropped, and she addressed her reply to her desk. "They were field-study subjects. They asked me not to identify them by name."

"I see. In those cases, it is traditional to supply a pseudonym with the actual age, sex, profession, and social condition, so that we can judge as much by the subject as by their statements. However interesting such statements may be, they offer only half of the data we use in our studies. Your essays each constitute 10 percent of your grade for this course. The final exam carries more weight, 30 percent, but displayed application of skills learned in class is 20 percent of your grade. Please bear that in mind."

"Yes, sir. I'll do that next time, sir." Red-cheeked, Marcy shoved the paper into her bookbag. Keith glimpsed lots of red ink through the last page before it vanished. Old Freleng had taken her bibliography to pieces. Hah. His own paper probably looked like a Rorschach test. He felt sorry for her. He felt sorry for himself. He slumped back into obscurity behind Mary Lou. Her paper had an A on it, as usual.

At last, the bell rang. "That one was really dumb, Doyle." Burke Slater jabbed Keith with an elbow as he jostled past the others out of the classroom. "Real comic relief."

"I think you're wonderful to stick up for the primitive tribes," offered Abby Holt, a brown-haired girl in blue jeans who tended toward mystical topics herself.

Keith smiled and pushed past them into the hallway, running after Marcy as she maneuvered through the crowded corridor of Burke Hall. "Hey, wait! Marcy?"

"I've got a class in McInroe next period," she said curtly, her eyes narrowed at him. Keith thought it sounded like she cleared tears out of her throat. She wasn't the type who usually got C's, he decided, and she was taking it hard. He pulled his own crumpled essay out of his nylon backpack.

"I got an F," he said, smiling at her winningly. "Wanna trade?"

She looked at his paper, and then met his eyes. The sullen mask broke. "Oh, God, what am I going to tell my parents?" Marcy wailed, tears dripping down her cheeks. "I've never gotten a C in my life. Dr. Freleng is a fiend. It's too late for me to drop the course now. I've had all A's all my life. My parents expect it. They just won't understand. I'm failing."

"I wouldn't call a C failure," Keith said, jumping forward to open the door for her and following her out into the brisk October air. Leaves swirled away from their feet as they dashed across the narrow streets toward McInroe Hall. "I'm a B-man myself. I do get A's but I don't expect 'em. If you're not in the front line you don't get shot at as often."

"Get what?" Marcy shouted, avoiding an ancient Volvo which screeched backward into a suddenly available parking space on the curb.

"Shot at!" Keith yelled. "Teachers love to pick on A-seekers. Besides, we're Freleng's favorite victims because we're not seniors or grad students. We're making it look like it's too easy to take his class. He considers it a putdown. I can't blame him.''

"I wish I'd never taken it," Marcy said miserably.

"It isn't a total loss," Keith soothed her. "It's your only C, remember? Would you like to join forces against the evils of Sociology? We can study together. Misery loves company, you know." He fished around in his pocket for a folded wad of tissues and wrapped her fingers around it.

"Well, I'm in a study group already . . ." Marcy dabbed at her eyes, but her voice had steadied again.

"Oh, come on. I know about Honors study groups. They sit around and compare Daddy's tax returns or talk about interesting atoms they have met."

"It isn't an Honors group. This is a different kind. Hey," she said, changing the subject in surprise, "how'd you know I'm an Honor student?"

"It's written all over you. Places you can't see." Keith waggled his eyebrows wickedly. "Besides, I've been watching you. Haven't you noticed?"

Marcy shook her head. "I'd rather study alone. I get more done that way."

"Well, just Soc., then." Stairs, and then another door, opening into another echoing tiled hall full of hurrying figures. "Say, can I read your essay?" Keith asked, suddenly. "It sounded really interesting to me. You can read mine, but I guess you'd probably think it was fiction, too," he finished, suddenly sounding disgusted. "Nobody respects a scientist anymore."

"Sure you can," said Marcy, thrusting the paper into his hand. "Now I'm going to be late. Thanks for the Kleenex. See you."

"See you." Keith watched her dash away.

Level Fourteen of the Gillington Library stacks was quiet in the afternoon. Unlike the system most buildings used, the library stacks were numbered top to bottom, so the uppermost of the eight half-high floors above ground was Level One, and the lowest, in the third sub-sub-basement was Fourteen. The library itself was numbered normally, its four full-height floors numbered from the bottom to the top. It confused a lot of freshmen the first week of classes, but since there were separate elevators for the two sections, students got used to the concept in a hurry. They put it down to typical baloney from the Administration. One more thing to be ignored.

This level was devoted mainly to historical archives, a comprehensive collection of Americana of which the university was appropriately proud. Rare books were stored down here until they were called for in the usual way by users of the reading room upstairs. On occasion, master's degree candidates could get a special pass to peruse the shelves themselves, but they were rarely here during the afternoon. The archives librarian took advantage of the silence and pushed the bookcart through the rows of tiered shelves, listening to the sounds of the building as it settled, replacing returned books. She was a thin, pinched-faced woman who looked right with her salt-and-pepper hair tied into a tight bun. Fallen books she straightened up in their slots with a scolding expression as if they should have known better than to tip over.

With her narrow hands, she deftly sorted through a sheaf of old newspaper folios. The yellow-brown pages in their transparent folders were crisp and fragile. As she stacked them gently into a library box, she heard footsteps coming swiftly toward her, and turned away from her task to see who was running. Probably a student who had forced the stairwell lock with a plastic I.D. card. "This level is restricted," she said sternly. "No one is to be here without authorization. Did you hear me?"

No reply. She heard high-pitched giggles coming from that direction, shut the storage box with a snap, and started off to dispense some discipline.

Suddenly, the librarian heard the same giggle from behind her. She spun and ran back that way, her shoes flapping on the floor. No one was visible at that end of the aisle. She stopped. Again she heard running footsteps, the soles of the shoes grating with a sandpapery hiss on the concrete floor.

"Stop that!" she cried. "This is a library, not a racetrack. Who are you? Show yourself. Leave this building at once." Her voice rang in the hanging metal beams. "I will call Security if you do not leave NOW!"

The giggles erupted echoingly into the silence. She ran toward the dancing sound, but it dissolved into silence before she found the source. "Hello?" she called softly.

"Helloooo," came a whisper from behind her. She jumped and let out a small scream of frustration. The falsetto laughter bubbled up again as the footsteps ran away. This was not the first time she thought she had heard students chasing themselves around in the dark. They thought it was funny to flaunt their disobedience and startle her. They wanted to use *her* level in place of the back seats of their decrepit cars. "Horrible brats." In all her years, she'd never been able to catch the miscreants, or even see who was making the noise. Gremlins, that's what it was.

Looking this way and that, the librarian walked back to her cart to resume her task. The cart refused to roll forward. She kicked at the brake on the left front wheel, but to her surprise, it was off. She leaned all her weight against it. The cart would not move.

She pulled on it from the front. It wouldn't come forward an inch. Neither would it move to either side. It was as if the cart was cemented to the floor. She stacked all of the books from it on the floor and tried to shake it loose. Nothing. The librarian was ready to sob with frustration. There was nothing physically wrong with the cart, no reason why it should not roll normally, but it was firmly rooted where it stood. She stacked the books back onto it, somewhat less neatly than before. Her hands were shaking.

Dealing the cart a final disgusted shove, she headed for the elevator to get the janitor. He would have to oil those wheels before she could continue. When she had turned around the head of the row, there was a loud creak and rumble. The woman scrambled back to see the cart rolling away by itself. For a moment, she thought about running after it, but a blast of mocking laughter sent her scurrying into the elevator instead, fleeing for the safety of the faculty lounge. Years ago the dark and dusty cubicle had been designated a Civil Defense Fallout Shelter, and that gave her twitching nerves a sense of security. No one would question her spending a few hours lying down on the couch. The old library was widely believed to be haunted. She would feel safer if she could finish up later, preferably with another librarian for company.

But when she would return, the books would be on their shelves and the cart empty, and she knew it. It had all happened before.

* * *

"Well?" asked Pat Morgan, glancing unsympathetically at his roommate, Keith, who staggered across their dorm room and dropped with a melodramatic thud facefirst onto his bed. Pat went on watering houseplants. "So, tell Uncle Pat. What'd you get on the Sociology essay?"

"F," groaned the voice, muffled in a pile of laundry. "F for Freleng. He hates me."

"Fair enough. You hate him."

"How can a sociologist be so closed-minded?"

"Those who can't, teach." Pat was an English major, and he loved one-line cappers. He was tall and hollow-chested, and had a tendency to stoop over, so he seemed to be perpetually out of breath. His long, lank black hair made him look like a repertory company Richard III out of makeup.

"And what about those who can't teach?" Keith said, shaking the twisted sheaf of paper at him. Keith's looks tended to make people think he was jolly or bad-tempered, depending on one's predispositions about red hair. He was short, straight-backed, and thin. His eyes were hazel, and changed color with his mood. Right now, they were blue. He buried his head in the laundry again.

"Oh, hell, maybe you can fix it up and ask him to regrade it. Say you didn't understand the assignment. It's only the first paper. Here, give me that." Pat dropped the plant mister in the sink and snatched the essay out of Keith's hands. "That stuff's clean, by the way." He tilted his head toward the pile of clothes upon which Keith was lying. "Your turn to fold. No creases this time or you'll eat 'em."

Keith rolled onto his back, broadcasting socks across the floor. "I can't tell him I didn't understand it. I made a big deal about its social importance right in the middle of class."

"You've got a death wish," Pat said without looking up. He detoured around their shared wooden coffee table and sat down at his desk. Unlike Keith's, which had fantastic towers of books and papers teetering around a central cleared workspace, Pat's was a uniform level of possessions about ten inches high on which the current books and assignments lay. "You know, I read this once before. I still think there's nothing wrong with it. It's an interesting theoretical examination without any actual field study. He's probably insulted because you told him through this paper that you consider all the other sociological studies, like inner city and Appalachia, boring and not worth considering.''

"Well, they are boring. Every other social scientist has studied them to death. I can't find anything new to say about one. Even the minor stuff I'd explore has been overdone by everybody else.''

Pat considered for a moment. "True. But I think he gave you an F because you piss him off. Why don't you turn this one in to Mythology or Fiction, the way he suggested?''

"Because Mrs. Beattie has heard it all before, too. Wait until he reads my next one, on leprechauns. I told you about Marcy, the girl in my class?''

"Oh, yeah? She noticed you yet?''

"No. Ah, unrequited love. But she's very shy. That's one of the things I love her for. She doesn't throw herself at me.''

Pat blew a raspberry at him. Keith shrugged it off.

"Anyway, I think she's got a boyfriend, somewhere, one of those guys who's 'above reproach,' and all that garbage. The way she's been acting, I think she's afraid of him. What she really needs is someone charming and harmless, like me. I've got her paper here, from the same assignment. I want her research materials. I think I can use 'em.''

"Harmless. Oh, God,'' Pat groaned, shaking his head. "And the good Lord forgive you the lie.''

"Never mind that. I've got this terrific theory about why the Little People only appear to drunks and other unreliables,'' Keith began, spinning a towel in the air and catching it so it folded in half neatly over his extended forefingers.

"That's because you are one, jerkface.'' Carl Mueller came in the door, warding off flying laundry with one hand. He wore his thick light brown hair in a modified crewcut that, with his typical sour expression and healthy muscular build, made him look like an angry marine.

"A leprechaun?'' asked Pat.

"Sure,'' added Keith. "Viewed only by drunks and other unreliables. That's why you can see me, Carlitos.'' He whirled a towel like a bullfighter's cape. Carl and Keith had a Spanish class together, which he hated and Keith loved. Anything that Keith loved, Carl hated.

"Don't call me that, asshole," Carl said, staring belligerently at Keith.

"I never call you 'that asshole.' Dónde está la pluma de mi tía? How's things in Track?" Keith innocently changed the subject, gauging that the last ounce of tolerance left in Carl had just evaporated. "Want a beer?"

Carl grunted. "Okay. But cut the Carlitos shit. I'm dropping the class anyway."

"Too late," observed Pat, who always knew the course schedules. "Last day without penalty was Thursday."

Keith opened the little refrigerator under his desk and pawed through it, emerging with three beers and a box of vanilla wafer cookies. "Here, peace offering. See you later," he told Pat.

Keith took his snack, Marcy's essay, and the *Field Guide* out into the hallway. He hated to concede the territory to Carl; it was his room, after all; but there was no point in starting another argument. There were just some people who were automatically and irrevocably rubbed the wrong way, and Carl was one of the ones he'd so rubbed.

It was all a matter of attitude, Keith had decided a long time ago. Carl was too serious about life. He wanted so badly to do something important that it affected everything he did. He needed a cause. The guy was born to be a senator or Albert Schweitzer. Keith felt sorry for him. Of course, that didn't help him where Carl was concerned, who still reacted to Keith as if he was a flea: hyperactive, bothersome, and just out of reach.

Keith shrugged and opened Marcy's paper.

In the library, Marcy waited between the tall rows of bookshelves until no one was in sight. It was late afternoon, so there were few people around, but she could never be sure she was unobserved. With infinite care, she eased open the door that led to the fire stairs. It creaked loudly. She winced, but the sound drew no one's attention. The building was old, and everyone was used to its assorted settling noises.

She descended flight after flight in the darkness, her whispering footsteps confident, intimately familiar with her surroundings. At the bottom of the last concrete step, she halted and drew the smooth steel door open just wide enough to permit her passage. It slid shut behind her, and Marcy felt rather than heard the boom as it closed.

Two more flights of steps, another door, and she passed inside, crossing the floor, with its hulking shadows of more shelves darker than the darkness. From her pocket, she took a key, which gleamed a brilliant green. With the aid of its light, Marcy found her way to the hidden keyhole, inserted the key, turned, and pushed the door open.

Light flooded out upon her, throwing a long shadow back between the bookcases. She threw up a hand against the glare until her eyes adjusted, and spoke apologetically to the circle of Little Folk and the tall human students seated at desks in the low-ceilinged room. They regarded her expectantly.

"Vell?" asked the Master, laying his pointer down on the easel.

"We got a C," Marcy said.

"If you examine your stated principles as an objective observer," the Master stated, reviewing Marcy's essay, "you will see that you are relying upon your reader to furnish his own mental pictures of your subjects. In order for your reader to come to agree with your premises, you must provide accurate images from which he can draw his conclusions, which if you have been skillful will agree with yours."

"I didn't want to say too much," Marcy said in a low voice, feeling ashamed. "I couldn't draw accurate pictures." She stared at her desktop. "I probably shouldn't have attempted the subject. But I did want to try."

Her fellow college students present exchanged sympathetic glances. The Little People favored her with friendly gazes, but said nothing, as usual.

"Mees Collier, there vas nothing wrong with your attempt of the subject," the Master said gently, setting the paper on her desk and looking up at her. "Nor with your conclusions. It is merely that your audience vas not prepared for it."

▪ Chapter 3 ▪

A dorm hallway was by no means the quietest of places to read. It smelled strongly of sweatsocks and mold, and the carpet was perpetually damp. There seemed to be an unwritten rule for residence halls that the areas with the most traffic should be the worst lit, so Keith was left trying to read by the feeble brownish glow of dying fluorescent ceiling lights. Nobody ever seemed to look down toward the dimly lit floor while they were walking. He was kicked a few times by passersby who didn't see him. One student fell over Keith's legs, spilling a heap of fresh laundry halfway down the hall. After apologizing and helping to refold it, Keith fled to his resident advisor's room for sanctuary.

He poked his head through the doorway into the R.A.'s suite. "Hi, Rick. Can I borrow a corner?"

Rick MacKenzie looked up from his desk, a black crewcut over lightning blue eyes and a lantern jaw which twisted around a grin. "Sure, Keith. C'mon in."

"Thanks. There's no room back at the inn."

The R.A.'s eyes narrowed dangerously. "Rubber band on the knob?" That was the signal that female company was being entertained by the other roommate, and disturbances would be unappreciated. Rick maintained an unspoken rule that no one was to band out their roommates on weeknights on his floor.

"Oh, no," Keith assured him, folding up like a grasshopper on Rick's ancient green tweed couch. "Just a friend of his who isn't a friend of mine. Our pal Carl."

"Uh huh. What've you got there?"

Keith handed over Marcy's paper. "I think I've got research material for my next essay in Sociology."

Rick thumbed through the pages. "You're going to rip off one of your friends?"

14

"Heck, no! I'll give her credit for it. Look, she analyzed the stresses brought to bear on people with a racial tendency toward dwarfism. The whole thing about being treated like children because they're small. But by the internal evidence, these people aren't circus midgets, or African pygmies, as you might normally assume. In fact, they seem to have come from a temperate climate, with almost Arctic winters. And their oral tradition comes from pretty far back, suggesting resistance to technology."

"Isolation?" asked Rick.

"Well, yeah. It would have to be. We don't have much of an oral tradition anymore. Not since we learned to write and use movable type. What do you do when you want to remember something?"

"I write it down."

"Right. Now, our ancestors just recited their notes over and over again until the information was memorized. Once in, never out. And they could pass on the recollections from generation to generation. That's why those family feuds lasted forever. Take the Hatfields and McCoys."

"So? That doesn't mean these people had the same kind of background, or even that they're from this hemisphere."

"But I think they did. Look, if it wasn't for the part about the racial dwarfism, I'd have said they were Irish, or at least from one of the great islands in the northwest of Europe. Naturally, I have a preference for Ireland."

Rick threw the essay back with an expression of disgust. "Oh, I get it. You and your little people. You know, they lock up people with your kind of mania."

"Just consider it a need to know. The evidence suggests that I'm not the only one with this mania."

"Don't go reading something into that paper. Probably she came upon a village of short people in Scotland who got tired of hearing 'How's the weather down there?' "

"I want to talk to these people. They might have oral legends of Little People that I can use. It's the legends that I'm interested in. I've read all the fairy tales and junk. I want information that hasn't been through thirty publishers. I want hard evidence."

"Oh, come on. What makes you think she would believe your wild ideas, let alone pass you on to her subjects? That's the last thing they'd want to talk about with an outsider. They're ordinary people, and they want to live their lives in peace. They'll probably think you're another one of those 'look-at-all-the-funny-people' journalists. Or just a nut. Which you are.''

"Hmm," said Keith, thinking deeply. "I don't want them to think I'm crazy. All I want is their recollections. Fairy tales. Local legends.''

"What makes you think that just because they're short they have any more knowledge of legends than Joe Schmoe up the street?''

"Just a hunch." Keith shrugged. "Something about the way she states her facts. She's leaving something out, and I want to ask what it is. She's usually so quiet in class. Perhaps she'll be more talkative over dinner." He rose and scooped up the paper, then started for the door.

"Whoa!" The R.A.'s voice halted his headlong departure. "Dinner? Aren't you coming to the Student Government meeting tonight, Doyle? You're our best speaker. I think this'll be the night we can get a deciding vote on the library issue. If you don't come, I guarantee we will lose.''

Keith bashed himself in the side of the head with Marcy's paper, further crumpling it. "I'm sorry, Rick," Keith apologized, instantly changing plans again. "Yeah, I'm coming. I'll just drop this in my room and be right back with my notes. We can discuss strategy.''

Of the forty-five official senate members representing the fifteen residence halls on campus, only a third or so usually attended the meetings held every two weeks in the Student Common. Keith had been elected to represent his dorm, C. V. Power Hall, on a nomination moved by Rick, who, as the representative resident advisor from Power, had to be present at meetings and liked to have his friends around. Pat had seconded the nomination, since it was the most likely way to keep himself from being chosen. Keith, who hadn't been present at his election, was upset for about two weeks, until he discovered how much fun it was to make hay out of Robert's Rules of Order. Thanks to Keith's enthusiastic support, there was now a college regulation on the books forbidding walking your zebra on the streets after dark. The actual wording of the rule banned any animal not specifically domestic in nature, and its proven intention was to prevent attacks or escapes by those animals after nightfall, but the committee which had proposed it to the Dean's Council called it the Zebra Crossing Ban.

The other delegate from Power Hall was clear across the room, chatting with one of the girls who lived in Bradkin. Carl never sat with Keith and the R.A.; he seemed to think it spoiled his dignity. He had actually volunteered to serve in student government, which made him the legitimate object of derision by those who had been shanghaied into office. For once, though, he had a legitimate excuse for separating himself from the rest of his dorm mates. They were on opposing sides of an issue.

To Keith, issues weren't life-or-death matters. The girls from Edison were proposing another formal letter of complaint to ARA Suppliers, concerning the poor quality of dorm food. The senate sent at least three of those a semester, and they hadn't done any good yet. The food was still just barely edible. On the other hand, Carl took his role as the voice of student opinion very seriously, and offered his support to matters he believed in. He hadn't the same gift of gab Keith had, and was regularly out-debated whenever they disagreed. For that reason and very little else, Keith made sure he and Carl were opponents, no matter how trivial the issue. If Carl supported it, Keith was out to undermine it.

"Quiet, please! Hey, can it!" yelled Lloyd Patterson, president of the Inter-Hall Council. "Let's get this going, huh? I've got an exam tomorrow. I don't want this to drag on. Venita, will you take the roll?"

Venita March, recording secretary and R.A. delegate, rose, tossing her head. Venita was a friend of Rick's from his class at high school, and she taught self-defense part-time at the University Women's Center. Her kinky black hair, swept up into a tall, superbly styled natural decorated with a plume, swayed for a moment after she had stopped moving. Rick stifled a snicker and Keith elbowed him. "Shut up. She'll cream you."

"I know, but I can't help it. That style almost touches the roof." He sketched height over his head with a hand twitching with mirth.

"*If* we may have some order," Venita asked icily, a quelling glance aimed at Rick. He lowered his arm, smiling with mock innocence. She shook her head at him, slack-mouthed, tapping a long-suffering foot on the floor. Rick folded his hands studiously before him and sat at attention. Raising one eyebrow at him, she read down the list.

"You can tell she likes you," Keith told Rick sardonically.

"Okay," Lloyd said, after Venita sat down, hairdo aquiver. "Any old business to take care of?"

"Dean's Council has ruled on the matter of student parking," a girl clad casually in blue jeans and a leotard spoke up. "All spaces will be allotted first-come-first-served to dorm students first, frats and apartment dwellers second, and night school gets what's left. The areas will be divided into three zones, and students are supposed to apply to the zone center closest to their residence. The center lot will still be set aside for medical plates and visitor. Those with school stickers caught parking there will have their cars towed and privileges revoked, no refund." There was a chorus of groans from both sides of the room. "I'm sorry!" she snapped defensively. "That's the best I could get. At least the people who live in Barber won't have to park all the way over near the frat houses."

"That's something," Venita said, encouragingly. She lived in Barber.

"Okay. That'll help," Lloyd acknowledged, making notes. "Anything else?"

"Yessir," Keith said, springing to his feet. "Doyle, Power Hall. I want to bring up the subject of the proposed library renovation project." He smiled triumphantly at Carl, who was just raising his hand. There was a great deal of movement in the room, as the student delegates, recognizing the signs of a debate, separated themselves into three rough groups, showing their support or opposition to the issue, with the center delegates undecided or uninvolved. Dividing up depending on one's opinion on an issue let them know who else was actually interested, and gave them something to do at meetings. Several pushed their chairs over to Keith's side of the floor, the Pro-renovation side, and settled down.

"You have the floor."

"Thank you." Keith moved into the center of the room,

and assumed an orator's pose. Rick sat back to watch with obvious pleasure. "There is a proposal before the Dean's Council for replacement of one major building on the Midwestern campus. Dean Rolands has cut the choices down to two: a new Phys. Ed. building, or a new library. To me, the correct choice is obvious.

"My question to the assembled senate is this: why did you come to college? To run laps? To cheer at Big Ten games? Well, you're at the wrong school to begin with." Some uneasy laughter; Midwestern had pretensions toward national college football, but the team simply wasn't good enough. Carl glowered, and Keith continued. "But since you are here, it's to learn, isn't that right? To pick up skills which will be of use to you after graduation. I for one can't think of anything I'll ever do that involves vaulting over the horse or hand-walking on parallel bars. Can you?"

"How about weight lifting?" someone asked.

Keith gestured at his narrow frame. "What weight?"

More laughter. "What about physical well-being?" Carl demanded. "That's real important, too. And how about leisure sports?"

"P.E. in high school or grade school is good for learning about things like that. You get a whole selection of different sports and exercises. Variety. At the university, physical education is too specialized, too competitive. It's great if you're interested in playing volleyball or practicing aikido, but you can just take an exercise course to keep fit, and that doesn't need any special space, or specific environment."

"The hell it doesn't," one of the opposing delegates sneered.

Keith went on, ignoring the outburst. "In fact, if you insist, you could keep fit by exercising in your dorm room. Why not?" He pantomimed doing jumping jacks, athletically at first, then bowing over more and more in mock exhaustion. "Your roommate asks, 'What are you doing?' and you say, 'I'm doing my homework for Gym.' " Laughter exploded around the room.

"Now, except for the one gym course we're required to take to graduate, fewer than 40 percent of the students at Midwestern ever set foot in the P.E. building again, and most of those are specialists. On the other hand, over 90 percent use the library. Why, even a few of the jocks do." More laughter.

"It's crowded in there during midterms and finals," one of the girls on Keith's side complained. "There's never enough carrels, and they lock the classrooms."

One of Carl's backers, Maurice Paget, a tall black student, raised a hand. "Couldn't that be negotiated with Library Services? If there was more study space available in the present structure, they wouldn't need to build a bigger building."

"The trouble is that those classrooms are used all year round, especially during finals," Keith said. "At maximum capacity, the student need exceeds the available space. Library Services wants to bring more study aids in, but there's nowhere to put 'em. And audio/video aids, records and tapes, works of art, even," a forefinger was raised on high, "*National Geographic*. All of these things are to be available for study, to give you the, well, wisdom of the ages, to prepare you to be whatever it is you want to be when you leave Midwestern. But wisdom dictates two things cannot occupy the same space at the same time."

"That's physics," Rick put in.

"Whatever," said Keith. "Wise men discovered physics, right? The need for a better building to house books and study-aids, and provide more room for their users, in my opinion, far outweighs the wishes of a few jocks for a fancier field-house."

"Very alliterative," called Lloyd from the center section. He never took a side. There was some applause as Keith sat down. Rick grinned, and they both looked to the other side of the room. Carl rose to his feet.

"What about the kids that come here on athletic scholarships?" he demanded. "Don't they get a voice?"

"Don't they have to earn diplomas?" Keith asked, counterpointing his question. "Just like anyone on a math scholarship, the idea was that by the one outstanding talent they displayed, they were awarded a sum of money to continue their education by being more deserving than anyone else with that talent. In the opinion of the judges, of course.

"But I see what you're asking, Carl." Keith put on a reasoning expression that he knew particularly irritated the other. "Don't they deserve to have a forum in which their particular talent can be brought to the attention of such people as football scouts?" He paused. "Well . . . no, not really."

"What?" Carl sputtered, starting to speak. "Why not? It's . . ."

Keith neatly cut him off. "The job of the college is to educate students and fit them to seek out their fortunes afterward. Having them available for scrutiny by scouts is a side benefit. Too bad there isn't a place for kids who are not dumb, but not academically inclined either, just to go and offer themselves for professional sports teams. Like theater auditions. As it is, this is the way the system works. Why should the academically inclined, for whom this campus really exists, suffer for the ten or so who will go on to earn six-figure salaries in pro ball?"

Rick poked him sharply in the ribs from behind with his toe, and Keith clamped his jaw shut, remembering too late that Rick was a P.E. major, and had hopes of one of those big breaks. "What Mr. Wizard here means, of course," growled Rick, "is that the needs of the many outweigh the needs of the few. To coin a phrase."

"Where have I heard that before?" Carl asked, sarcastically. "What you're saying is that the athletes don't deserve a good place to practice their skills. I disagree with you! You do need a particular place to do gymnastics or play football. The gym is too small. The pools leak. The lights are bad, and there aren't enough of them. The old building needs to be replaced, and a modern one with good lights, good floors, good plumbing, has to be built."

"Aha," Keith crowed triumphantly, jumping up. "Old? You call a gymnasium only twenty years old, old? Gillington Library is a hundred and sixteen. It had a minor facelift in the forties, when there was a lot of new construction here, but not a thing since. Haven't you ever heard the floor creak when you were looking for a book in the stacks, and wondered if it was going to collapse under you? Those of you who've been in the stacks for books, that is. The rest of you won't care if the building moves," a michievously deferential bow to Rick, who had mentioned earlier a quiet corner he and his girlfriend frequented. Dodging a kick this time, he went on. "If they ever have to make emergency structural repairs to Gillington in the middle of midterms, you'll wish you had voted to renovate it. You can prevent that disaster by voting for the reconstruction now."

Recognizing the need to rally newly awakened support, Rick swallowed his pride and exclaimed, "Think about it. I'm studying business, for the years after I don't want to play soccer any more."

"Or can't," Carl put in.

"Watch it, Mueller," Rick snapped, becoming serious. Carl acceded sullenly to the warning, and fell silent.

"Where would the new library be built?" Francine Daubiner wanted to know. She was one of the undecided.

"The dean says that it would be built on the foundations of the old one, just as the Sports Center would go up where the P.E. building is now." Keith had all the facts handy in his notebook. "Neither one could cost more than three million dollars, nor less than one million. Dean Rolands insisted on a reasonable range for the project. The other structure would follow in three to six years, depending on need and availability of cash."

"Part of that money would go for several computer terminals," Venita said, after examining the list Keith had submitted to the secretary. "Sounds like they've got some other projects tucked in there."

"All part of information retrieval," Keith pointed out, cheerily. "So, why don't we make it offic . . ."

"Okay." Lloyd stood up, cutting him off. "We don't have enough people here for the vote, so it'll have to wait. In two weeks, we'll have a mandatory meeting, full Student Senate, and finalize what our recommendation to the Dean's Council will be, and who gets to take it there." Everyone groaned. "Now come on. Is there any other business? No? Well, then, I declare this meeting adjourned . . ."

"Seconded," Carl said, still glaring at Keith, but warily, because Rick was looming behind the skinny student. The gavel fell, and the room cleared quickly.

▪ Chapter 4 ▪

Ludlow heard a banging sound coming from the little cluster of administrative offices at the head of the hall. His eyes narrowed and he stopped swabbing the floor to listen more closely. Yes, it was definitely the noise of metal on metal, like a sliding drawer in a file cabinet. There it was again. Maybe one of the old lady librarians working late. He could complain to her about not reporting the leak in the ceiling that was sending a dribble of rusty water down the pale tan tiles of the floor.

The sound repeated itself, this time more frenzied.

Ludlow crept closer to have a peek around the edge of the doors through the narrow pane of glass that ran the length of the knob side, carefully still mopping so it looked like he was working, not spying. No one in any of 'em, and the lights were all out.

The banging ended with a frustrated rattle practically under his ear. It was coming from the supply room. An intruder, certainly a thief. He tried the solid wooden door, shaking it gently. It was locked. The deadbolt boomed ominously in the doorjamb. As soon as whoever it was heard him, operations within the supply room ceased. He unreeled the heavy ring of keys from its retractable lead on his belt and shouldered open the door, levelling the mop handle like a shotgun.

With a gasp, the intruder whirled, opening wide green eyes on him. Ludlow was disgusted. It was a kid. A little kid, with a head full of wild red curls, wearing a short, shapeless dress and socks but no shoes. She had her hands full of Xerox paper reams and felt-tip pens, some of which cascaded to the floor in her surprise.

"What are you doing here?" he demanded. "How'd you get in here? Never mind. You're coming with me. I'm calling the police."

The child didn't speak. Instead, clutching her booty, she lunged under his arm toward the door. Ludlow blocked her exit easily with the mop handle and reached for her. She backed up, her solemn gaze remaining fixed on his face.

"Where do you think you're going?" Ludlow asked. He felt not unkindly toward the child. After all, he had five of his own at home. But you had to teach 'em what was right and wrong. And why the hell was she stealing office supplies, of all things? Didn't look like the usual college thief. Was she one of the teachers' kids? They'd have to come and get her from the Campus Security office. He opened his mouth to ask.

Swiftly, the red-haired child darted around his other side. Ludlow flung the mop away and grabbed for her with both arms. Squealing, she twisted free of his grasp, danced a couple of paces away, and pointed a hand at him.

Ludlow started after her, but found he was restrained by his belt, which was attached to the retractable keyring. The supply room door key, on the end of its tether, was still inserted in the doorknob. He pulled at it, but it wouldn't come free. He shook the knob angrily. The little girl, watching cautiously, started to back away up the corridor, the boxes of pens and paper still in her arms. He snatched at the buckle of his belt, seeking to undo it, but unaccountably, the buckle tongue seemed to adhere solidly to the frame. There was no way for him to unfasten it or wriggle out of it.

The child turned around and fled. Ludlow, relinquishing the hope of catching up with her, twisted and pulled at the key. It wouldn't budge. In fact, now it wouldn't even turn. He attempted again to undo his belt. The buckle held itself fast.

With a groan, Ludlow sat down on the floor, and wondered whether it would be more humiliating to unfasten the hinges and drag the door with him until he could find a way to dislodge his key, or to sit there and wait for someone to come along with a pair of shears and cut him loose from his belt.

▪ Chapter 5 ▪

When Keith returned to the dorm room later that evening, Pat was there alone. Crumpled wads of waxed paper and foil from the college deli were piled up on the coffee table next to a fat biology textbook. "Do you have a test, Pat?" he asked. "I would have brought dinner in for you if you'd have mentioned it. Or at least kept you company."

Pat grinned wryly and rubbed his eyes. "Thanks. I'd rather study by myself. It's quieter without you."

"Everyone says the same thing." Keith threw a pillow at him.

Pat caught it dexterously with one hand, and pitched it back, catching Keith in the middle of the chest. "How'd the meeting go?"

"I think Carl went away to bury his shame or something. I was a big success. The assembled were overwhelmed by the thought of all those poor, homeless books with no place to go, evicted by the evil football team. The jocks'll scream, but the other appointees will be on our side. Lloyd cut the meeting short before we could call for the vote. I suspect him of being a secret athletic-supporter. I think the motion'll carry next time, when we do vote on it. Required attendance by all delegates."

"That'll be popular," Pat said, cynically. "You'd have to drag me there in chains. Well, anyway, here," he said, and tossed some papers in his direction. He gave Keith an apologetic glance. "I went over that Sociology paper of yours again, and unless you can convince Freleng that your idea is a radical new theory based on existing data, I'm afraid you'll have to rewrite it completely with real facts. It's okay the way it is, if he'd go for it, but he won't. That's just my opinion, of course."

"Terrific," said Keith, dropping his notebook on the bed. Then a memory struck him. "Hey, Pat, where's that paper I showed you earlier?"

"I just gave it to you."

"No, the other one. Marcy Collier's paper. Had a C on it, not an F. I thought I left it right here before the meeting." Keith pointed to his bed.

"Sorry," said Pat. "I haven't seen it. Are you sure you didn't take it with you?"

Keith struck the side of his head with the heel of his hand. "Right. That must be it. I left it in the meeting room. What a mind. If medical science could locate it . . ."

"Get it tomorrow, and shut up."

"Yes, my leader."

"I owe you an apology," Keith panted, catching up with Marcy the next day after Sociology class let out. "I have looked everywhere, but I can't find the essay you lent me. It isn't like me to lose things like that. I'm usually trustworthy, honest."

"Oh, no, don't worry about it," Marcy assured him. "I got it back. It's in my apartment somewhere."

Keith dashed a hand across his forehead melodramatically. "That's a relief. I think I must have left it in the Inter-Hall Council. My brain is deteriorating in my old age. But you got it back, for sure? Some kind soul brought it back to you?"

"Uh huh. Thanks for caring. I always throw out essays when I finish with the course anyway. And I'm sure not going to want to keep that one."

"Yeah, I know what you mean. Would you like to study together this evening?" Before she could refuse automatically, he rushed on. "How can I whisper sweet nothings in your ear if I never have it all to myself? Lend me an ear. This approach worked for Marc Antony. On the other hand, look what happened to him."

She giggled, no longer nervous. "Oh, all right. I think I have an extra ear around here someplace."

"No, I'm sorry," Marcy said, meeting Keith's eyes seriously. They were studying at the kitchen table in the apartment Marcy shared with three other girls. "I can't give you any of their names or tell you where to find my subjects. I promised. Freleng asked me the same thing for my essay. I finally made something up. I'd rather sacrifice my grade than hurt my . . .

friends. I don't want to do the same for you; you'd know I was lying.''

Keith's shoulders collapsed in disappointment. ''Well, look, maybe if I told you what I want to talk about, you'd arrange for me to meet one man or woman.''

''Go on,'' said Marcy, opening a bottle of Coke steaming with frost. She took two glasses from the yellow rubber dish drainer, shook out their droplets of water, and filled them with soda.

''I have a theory about legends, that they have a base in reality. One of the most interesting things about them is that . . . thanks . . . they're everywhere. And they have a uniformity that intrigues me. Before mass communication came along, something got into the storytelling around the world that has little or no variation wherever you go. Dragons, for instance. On whichever side of the planet you ask, dragons are big, intelligent lizards. Most of them can fly. They eat meat. They hoard treasure. Chinese dragons are like Celtic dragons, and so on.'' He took a long swallow of Coke.

Marcy giggled. ''You want to ask my people about dragons?''

''Nope,'' said Keith, warming to an interested listener. His smile seemed to wrap most of the way around his thin face. ''I read your paper pretty carefully. Your subjects aren't pygmies, are they?''

''No.''

''Caucasian?''

Marcy thought for a minute, then decided that one piece of information wouldn't reveal anything extra. ''Yes,'' she said.

''Terrific! I'm Irish, you know,'' Keith began.

She looked critically at his hazel eyes and red hair. ''I would never have guessed.'' He certainly had the gift of gab. She found that there was something appealing about him, in a face that exclaimed ''egghead'' instead of ''jock.'' She probably wouldn't call him handsome. To her, handsome implied square jaws and athlete's muscles, not sinews and those slim, cleverlooking hands. Maybe ''cute'' was a better word. But he looked like he would be a lot of fun to have around. Not her type, but not not her type.

''Sarcasm will get you nowhere, *ma petite*,'' said Keith.

The ruddy eyebrows bobbed up and down. "I want to know about the little people. The Fair Folk. I'm trying to figure out where they went when they disappeared. *If* they disappeared. Another legend says that all the Irish are related to the Fair Folk. You can say I'm just doing a genealogy of the Doyle family. No, don't say that. I want to know if they died out, or if they went underground, or what?" He drank deeply from his glass and set it down with a satisfied sigh. "Is there anything unusual about your subjects that you're not telling me?"

Marcy was taken aback. Did Keith really have that kind of perspicacity, or was he just guessing? "*I* don't think so," she said at last, her fingertip drawing rings around a minute puddle of spilled Coke. "Please don't be offended, but I think they'd think your paper's frivolous."

"So does everyone else," Keith admitted without rancor. "But it's not just a paper to me. My R.A. says I've got a mania. Okay, so I'm very interested in writing a paper on it for Sociology class, but I don't have to. Your subjects have a strong genetic tendency toward being short, right? Is it mixed fairy blood, or just recessive genes with no place else to go? Who knows? You pay more attention to stories with a personal application, you know. Some people are proud of the idea that they might be related to the Fair Folk. Like myself, for example. If they'd just talk to me about legends, the things they heard while they were growing up . . ."

"I don't think they would," Marcy interrupted hastily.

"Well, answer me this: are they all from the same village, or county?" Keith persisted.

"Yes. Maybe. Their coloring's alike. It's like yours."

"Are they Irish?" Keith leaned forward.

"I think so, but . . ."

"Great! Please, please ask if I can talk to any of them. I care. I won't publish anything if they don't want me to. It's to satisfy my own curiosity," he finished earnestly. "If they say no, well, I'll respect their privacy. If they say yes, I'll respect their privacy. Either way. The fact that you haven't thrown me out yet or called me crazy encourages me."

"Okay," she said reluctantly. "I'll ask."

"Blessings on you. I owe you a soda or something else wholesome. How about tonight?" She turned her head shyly away from him. "Aw, come on," Keith coaxed. "Is it your boyfriend? I'm no threat. I'm just a friend."

"No, it isn't that," she insisted, louder than necessary. "I have to meet with my study group."

"Hey, you mentioned that yesterday. Tuesdays and Thursdays. Can I come, too? I'd like to study with you. Get to know you better."

She bounced out of the kitchen chair, as if spring-loaded, and started to rinse out their glasses at the sink. "It's a closed group."

"You said that before, too, but they have to get members from someplace. Is it a sorority club? Women only?"

"No. Are you kidding? I'd rather have *real* friends."

What brought that confession on? Keith wondered. He studied her face. No, she wouldn't fit in with sororities. She was the right kind of pretty and the right kind of smart, but her skin wasn't thick enough. All of his predatory instincts had been knocked on the head once he'd started listening more carefully to her. Instead he found that she aroused his natural protectiveness. Keith felt himself to be more effective as a big brother than a boyfriend. Not that Marcy was falling all over herself for him. As much as he hated to concede the field to the virtuous unknown boyfriend, whoever he was, Keith hoped the guy was worth it. But she was darned good at changing the subject. "I'll be your best friend," he volunteered.

"Oh, cut it out," she snapped, her back to him. "I don't need pity."

"I know; I'm sorry. Look, do you want to go for a walk, or to a movie, or get married, or something?" he asked in desperation. "I can't leave until you're not mad at me anymore."

She turned around to retort, and he clasped his hands under his chin in supplication. He rolled his eyes up. So did she. "Do you always offer to marry everyone who's mad at you?" Marcy giggled.

"Only the women," Keith answered, animated again, like a jack-in-the-box. Marcy shook her head, and glanced at the clock. Keith felt hope returning. "It's not an Honors group," he said impulsively, "or a sorority group, so if you sponsored me, could I join you? Maybe just once. I'll even sponsor you to Student Council, although I'm not so sure that's a favor."

"Okay," she said. "I'll ask."

"Two sodas!" Keith exclaimed. "And a movie. They're showing *Attack of the Killer Tomatoes* tomorrow night. You'll love it." With a start, he noticed the flowered clock over the sink. "Oops, I'm late for my next F. See you in Flunking with Freleng tomorrow."

"Don't remind me."

Keith appeared at her apartment the next evening clutching a bunch of daisies before him. A tall blond girl in sweatpants let him in. She gave him a disinterested once-over, left him on the threshold, and walked back into the hallway.

"Marcy!" she called, and Keith heard her go on in a lower voice through the thin wooden walls, "your nerd's here." He chuckled, noticed another girl, one with brown hair, watching him from the kitchen table, and favored her with a toothy Archie Andrews grin. She clicked her tongue in disgust, and went back to reading her magazine. Keith flashed a wink in her direction, and surveyed the rest of the apartment.

There was a war of styles going on in here, and it looked like Modern Pop was going to win by accumulated clutter. Posters, mostly those of Wham! and Duran Duran, were taped over the dusty green walls everyplace but the light switches and windows. Boxes of records flanked a mighty stereo system and a VCR. One of the girls who lived here had money. By comparison, the basket of skeins of yarn, the spinning wheel and embroidery frame in one corner, and the modest bookshelf under the windows took up scarcely any space at all.

"Thanks a lot," came Marcy's voice, faintly.

Another mumble from the other girl, of which Keith could only discern, "trouble with . . ."

"Look," said Marcy's voice, growing louder as she came out of her room, "I don't care what he says." She emerged into the foyer checking the fit of her dark green sweater and pale green slacks in the hall mirror. "Hi."

"Hello, there," Keith said, appreciatively. "You look very nice."

The sweater was embroidered with roses and the slacks were very flattering to her figure. He gave her an encouraging grin. She looked down self-consciously, as if the combination was accidental. "Oh. Thanks."

"Shall we go down to the Student Union first? *Attack of the Killer Tomatoes* starts at eight."

"As long as it isn't *Reefer Madness* and *The Groove Tube* again."

Keith held open the door, and they stepped out into the bitter cold of the night. "It all depends on the vagaries of the studio distributor. Don't you know that's their subtle little way of telling us that the feature didn't show up?"

When the film ended, which did after all turn out to be *Attack of the Killer Tomatoes*, they walked over to a little bar and grill on the corner not far from the auditorium called Frankie's, which was heavily frequented by the student population of Midwestern. Keith was enjoying her company enormously. In spite of her shyness, Marcy made conversation easy. "Sorry I can't take you anywhere classier," Keith said apologetically. "My roommate borrowed my car. I agreed to let him have it before I remembered we were going out this evening."

Marcy flinched. "Don't call it 'going out,' okay?"

"Whatever you want. It doesn't mean anything." Keith was upset at her discomfort. "I'm just your friend. Say," he demanded, with a lightning change of subject, "is Marcy short for anything?"

"No." Marcy stopped, and hopped uncertainly onto the new train of thought. "It's my whole first name. I think it's out of one of those cutesy comic books my mother used to read when she was little. It was almost Barbara, or Barbie for short, except my aunt had a daughter three months before I was born, and they named *her* Barbara. Thank God."

"Sounds terrible. You were lucky. My full name's Keith Emerson Doyle, because my folks are big Emerson, Lake & Palmer fans. My dad was heartbroken when I didn't want to take piano lessons. Or guitar. Or drums."

"Did you take anything?"

"Yup. Clarinet. For a year and a half I sounded like leaky plumbing, and then suddenly, I could make music. Dad forgave me, and started listening to more jazz."

Marcy giggled. "Do you play anymore?"

"Just to annoy the neighbors," Keith said with satisfaction. The waiter, a graduate student, stood next to the table with pencil touching order pad. "Order anything you want," Keith said expansively. "I pawned an old family heirloom for our . . . outing tonight."

They settled on Cokes, and bacon-lettuce-and-tomato sandwiches. As soon as the waiter went to put in the order, Keith leaned across the table and whispered in a conspiratorial tone to Marcy, "Well?"

"Well, what?" she asked in surprise.

"Well, don't keep me in suspense. What did they say?"

"Oh!" Marcy turned red. "They said they'd think about it."

Keith made a face. "They have to think about it? It must be the most exclusive study group in the world."

"Oh, the study group. I thought you meant . . ."

"Yeah, your subjects. Well, let them think about it, too. I've got all the time in the world. As long as they didn't say no. So I can come to the study group? Great! When's your next meeting?"

"Tomorrow . . . but you can't come to that either," Marcy said, lamely.

Keith blinked. His nonexistent whiskers twitched. To him, that was a sure sign there was something interesting going on here, though he didn't know what it could be. He rubbed his chin thoughtfully. There again was something she was keeping hidden. And the more she held back from him, the more curious he became. She was doodling with her nails in the condensation on the side of her glass, avoiding his eyes. "If it's in your boyfriend's dorm room, he might get suspicious as to why I'm there," he guessed slyly.

"No, it's in the li—" She bit off the word. The library, Keith deduced. He smiled, pretending not to notice her verbal slip.

"It's just my week to get blackballed," he said, cheerfully. "Don't fret about it. If anyone at all wants me around, you know where to find me." The sandwiches arrived then, to Marcy's evident relief, and Keith allowed the subject to drop entirely. "Food," he exclaimed, happily. "I have to go out to eat now and again, so that I don't start believing what they feed us in the dorm is really edible. It sure couldn't be nutritious." He chewed a toasted sandwich corner.

"It is pretty disgusting. That's why I moved out of the

dorms. Only it turns out my roommates are terrible cooks, too.'' Marcy attacked her sandwich with zeal, grateful that he had the tact to let go of an uncomfortable topic. Keith was nice and nondemanding. It was too bad she couldn't tell him what he wanted to know, but it wasn't her secret to tell. If she could have, she would have. Keith seemed easy to trust. ''Um, how's your paper coming?'' she asked.

''Oh, my research? Fine. Maybe I'll write a book some day. For example, did you know that the places where belief in the supernatural has been holding on through modern times are mostly agrarian or third world nations? It looks like as soon as a country or civilization goes industrial, stops being so close to the earth, those beliefs disappear. There's something scary about machinery, that you lose sight of the fact that it isn't sentient. The only 'Little Folk' you have left are the malign ones, like gremlins getting in and gumming up the works.'' Keith made a face. ''A long way from the kind little guys who sneaked in and made shoes for you while you were asleep. Since man can make shoes for himself while he sleeps, with machines, what do you need the fairies for? I guess the need for 'em dwindles when what was once considered to be impossible to do yourself became possible with technology. Either that, or blame the iron in steel. Very few things of magic could bear the touch of cold iron.''

Keith let himself prattle on, his conversation only occupying a small portion of his mind. He could tell Marcy had something to think over, but didn't know what. She was uneasy about having him encroach on her private activities; that was obvious, and understandable. The library. Well, since she couldn't enlighten him further, the only gentlemanly thing to do would be to follow her there and see what was going on for himself. He took a last satisfied bite of sandwich.

On the way back to Marcy's apartment, they had to huddle together against the sharp winds, now blowing almost parallel to the ground. Marcy discovered that her thin coat had an unexpected cold spot where she guessed the worn-out lining had finally given way under the arm. Keith had on nothing but a windbreaker, and was cheerful despite the fact that he must be freezing. He clutched her around her cold side steering her around puddles riming over with thin, crisp ice. She huddled gratefully into his arm.

A boy with a wool cap pulled down firmly over his ears marched out of the gloom toward them, aiming his path directly between them. They dodged him, but ended up parting to dive for opposite edges of the sidewalk to make way to avoid the enormous knobby shopping bag the boy was clutching to his chest. Marcy gasped as a freezing gust went up the legs of her pants. As the boy passed, he glared at both of them, as if to blame them for the bad weather.

From under black brows, his dark-eyed stare met Marcy's, and she flinched. She knew him. It was Enoch, one of the Little Folk from the hidden room. He shouldered away from the two of them and went on, heading in toward the campus.

"Boy, what's his problem?" Keith asked, glancing over his shoulder. Marcy looked a little dazed, and he held out an arm to her. "Forget him. Probably sore because he had to go grocery shopping in the cold."

To Keith's surprise, Marcy waved away the arm. "Thanks. I'll be okay now." She huddled into her jacket, pulling the spare folds of cloth around to the torn side, and lowered her chin to protect her throat from the wind. The boy's glance had disturbed her. She leaned into the wind, ignoring the puzzled expression on Keith's face. "Come on. It's late."

"Right," Keith agreed, hurrying after her.

▪ Chapter 6 ▪

It wasn't much warmer the next day. In the shelter of a brick gatepost across from Marcy's apartment, Keith was congratulating himself on remembering to wear two sweaters under his coat, but regretting that he'd left his hat behind. Other students brushed by, some glancing his way, but most of them ignoring him, not wanting to turn their necks in the cold wind. A girl gave him a sideways look, and he smiled. "Hi, there," he offered. She turned away quickly, dismissing him. He sighed. "Cold-shouldered again. Nice day for it, though."

Overhead, the heavy sky was turning slate and dark purple. The National Weather Service had suggested that the first flurries of snow might be on their way; if not now, then certainly before the end of the month. Keith shrugged, huddling his ears into his collar. There was no such thing as an easy midwestern winter. One just hoped the inevitable wouldn't be too early in coming.

Broken brown leaves swirled through the iron tines of the gate, and collected, rustling, in the shelter between Keith and the corner of the wall. The wind increased in velocity, whipping the students from a walk to a run between the class buildings. Keith felt his nose and ears growing frosty and numb, and tried not to think about them.

White sheets of paper cartwheeled down the sidewalk, pursued by their owner, a honey blond-haired girl in a pink aviator's jacket, waving an empty folder and yelling over the howling chorus of the wind. A few of the pages swirled in behind him, and he managed to trap them against the wall without crumpling them too much. He stepped out of his hiding place to help her gather up the rest.

"Thanks," she gasped, brushing her hair out of her eyes. "It's my research paper." Keith held the portfolio open while she shuffled the fluttering pages together. From the depths of a pocket full of oddments, he found a large paper clip which he offered to the girl. She secured the paper to the folder, flipped it shut, and smiled up at him. Her eyes were blue-green, and very pretty. "Thanks again."

"No problem. You know us Boy Scouts," Keith said, interested in pursuing the conversation until over her shoulder he caught sight of Marcy emerging from her apartment. He had to make a rapid choice between duty and pleasure, and curiosity won. " 'Scuse me. Duty calls." He dodged out of sight behind the gate, and waited until Marcy had passed, heading toward the library. The girl in pink gave him an odd look, and went away without further comment.

Keith stayed outside the library until he could see which direction Marcy was going through the glass doors. The heavy bronze frames creaked as he hauled one of them outward into the wind. Two other students behind him caught the metal door's edge, which burned their bare fingers with cold, and together they pulled it open. The wind shook it in fierce protest as they struggled inside.

Keith kept to the edges of the foyer until Marcy showed her pass and entered the library stacks. He found his own stack pass, and went in behind her.

He almost lost his quarry on the ground level, until he noticed the fire stairwell door hissing shut. No one was allowed to use those stairs except the librarians. The general-use staircase was in a different place. With a quick glance around to make sure no one was watching him, he followed.

Marcy's footsteps sounded out below him, and he trotted down the stairs, taking care to stay a flight above her. Either this study group met down in one of the conference rooms in the stacks, or he was probably going to interrupt Marcy and her boyfriend, having a private "study session." Keith made a face. He decided he didn't want to think about the latter, and stifled the little whine of jealousy in his mind.

It was dim in the stairwell, and the echoes sounded about him. Even his faint footfalls threatened to drown out the distant clatter of her steps. He was descending into no-man's-land, the private realm of the librarians. Keith felt as if he was on a safari, passing into dangerous territory. Did the library staff know that Marcy's group met here? The very secretiveness of her group honed Keith's already sharp curiosity. But what would Marcy think if she caught him following her?

Another set of footsteps joined the echoes in the hall. Keith stopped, wondering if it was the boyfriend, or someone else from her group. No, the sounds were too definite, too deliberate. It was not another student sneaking up the stairs. Someone with authority. Keith straightened up and let his shoulders swing in a nonchalant attitude, pretending he belonged here.

"Young man!" A tall dignified woman with a coil of black hair on her head swam out of the gloom. "What are you doing here?"

"Um, going to Level Eleven, ma'am," Keith said, blanching. He started around her, but she clenched his upper arm in that powerful grip peculiar to librarians engaged in administering reproofs.

"This area is restricted from students' use except during emergencies," she said coldly. Her scrawny neck and full cheeks made her look like an angry turkey. "You are to use the north stair only.'' Keith nodded politely, and tried to catch the sounds of Marcy's footsteps, but they had disappeared. The librarian escorted him forcefully to the eleventh level and pushed him into a waiting elevator. ''Your privileges will be restricted to the study rooms for tonight.''

''But my project . . . ?'' There was no chance of catching Marcy now.

''Your project will have to wait. You students must learn that you cannot break rules without punishment.'' She flipped his stack card out of his fingers and brandished it at him. ''You may reclaim this from my secretary tomorrow morning. I'm Mrs. Hansen, the head of Library Services.'' The elevator closed with a snap on his protests.

Keith wandered around the reading rooms, keeping an eye on the stack entrance, until the teaching assistant on duty threw him out. After that, he sat in the lobby, wondering if he should try to get into the stacks another way. He dismissed the idea, realizing that he would probably miss Marcy if he left his watch-post. Nine o'clock closing came, and the other students drifted out of the stacks. Marcy was among them, and she was alone.

''Hi!'' Keith hailed her as she appeared.

Marcy smiled at him curiously. ''How long have you been here?''

''Just a little while,'' he assured her. ''I had nothing else to do. Thought I'd just wait and find out what your study group had to say.''

''How did you know . . . ?'' Marcy exclaimed.

''You almost said it last night,'' Keith said, apologetically. '' 'The li—' Sorry. It's the bloodhound in me. And the rest of my face isn't so good, either. How about it?''

''I . . . they still say they'll think about it. Please. I'm doing what I can. Don't rush me. They're kind of . . . funny about having people join.''

''No problem,'' Keith said, stretching as he rose from the marble bench. ''Want to go for some coffee?''

''Sure,'' Marcy said, relieved. ''I'm glad you're being patient.''

''That's me,'' Keith said, taking Marcy's arm. ''Patience is my middle name. Right after Emerson.''

* * *

The next Tuesday, Keith spotted Marcy walking alone across the common, and hurried to catch up with her. His mouth was open to call out a greeting to her, when Carl Mueller appeared from between two concrete posts on the edge of the parking lot, and matched his stride to hers. She smiled shyly and tilted her head to one side, responding to a remark Carl was making with a satisfied smirk on his face. Keith was too far away to hear what they were saying, but it was obvious from the body language what he was seeing: *this* was the above-reproach boyfriend in Marcy's life. Carl fell neatly into that sort of pigeonhole. He considered himself to be a cut or so better than most of the other students, and had somehow persuaded Marcy to agree with him. Poor kid.

Keith had an impulse to run up and start a conversation with her, which would infuriate Carl, but Marcy would probably get upset if he annoyed her boyfriend. He assumed that Carl must be in the mysterious study group, too. That would explain perfectly why Marcy was uncomfortable about having him, Keith, around. Not only was Carl a snob, but he was a jealous snob, too. The guy probably monogrammed the flowers he gave her. He wondered if Carl knew he knew Marcy.

He followed them down the street, trailing about a hundred feet behind, until they came to Gillington Library. Hanging back so they wouldn't see him, he paused at the top of the steps, squinting through the double glass doors until he saw which way they turned. Ah. Left. The stacks.

Feeling like a private detective on the scent of an adulterous divorcée, he flashed his I.D. card at the librarian on duty at the entrance to the stacks. Marcy and Carl had disappeared, and Keith heard the bang and whirr of the elevator. He ambled down the aisle toward the double metal doors, idly fingering the spines of books, as if looking for something to read.

Out of the corner of his eye, he watched the indicator drop. Either this study group met in the basement of the stacks, or the lovebirds were just looking for somewhere dark to neck. Not Marcy! he chided himself, right hand slapping his own left wrist. She wasn't that type. Campy, but true.

The librarian, a thin woman of middle age who looked like a failed actress, glanced at him oddly. "Black widow spider," he explained solemnly, holding up his wrist for her examination. "The bite is usually fatal."

"Oh," she nodded, and then looked away, her forehead pulled into a puzzled frown.

The indicator stopped on Level Fourteen, which was the lower half of the third sub-basement. He was on Level Eight, the ground floor. The library stacks were half-high levels, eight above ground, and six below. As far as Keith knew, there was nothing official that went on in those underground levels. They were archives; locked floors to be entered by library personnel only.

Unless Carl and Marcy had keys, they must have exited the elevator before then. And yet, he hadn't noticed the indicator stopping before it showed the basement numbers. Something most definitely was going on here. Hastily, he found the stairs, and started down to search the floors one by one.

Weaving his way through the low-ceilinged, narrow aisles of the stack levels, Keith put on a show of bored nonchalance flavored with the attitude any harried student had toward trying to find an obscure book out of which some teacher threatened to construct the entire final exam for his course. The first four underground levels were a snap. The lighting was good, and no one paid him much attention. The heavy thrum of the heating system spread a blanket of white noise throughout each floor. Maybe ten students occupied each floor in various isolated carrels, cramming for one course or another, with heavy heads full of knowledge cradled in supporting hands over textbooks. But his search was frustrated. None of the meeting rooms on Twelve was occupied, and Marcy was nowhere around.

Maybe he had mistaken another number for fourteen. No, he was sure he had seen the indicator change from a one and a round number before the elevator stopped, and he was certain it wasn't ten. Capturing the elevator, he held the door open with one hand and, leaning in, punched the last two studs in the double column. They refused to light up, obviously waiting for the key to be turned in the locks below to activate them. The door surged under his hand, and from somewhere in the bowels of the mechanism, the elevator emitted an imperative *BEEPum BEEPum BEEPum*. Petulantly, Keith gave the door a sharp shove before letting it slide closed. It thrummed away, the beeping fading into the floors above.

Carl and Marcy weren't on any of the four floors. That left the two security floors. What was so special about this meeting that it had to be held down there? Of all the inconvenient locations! At this hour of the evening, 90 percent of the classrooms on campus were empty. Maybe he was about to stumble into a communist satrap, or a weird religious cult. He mentally scratched the latter option; he couldn't really see Carl dancing around in a pastel muslin robe.

How about a spy ring? he speculated, as he stood in the stairwell, prying at the locked door to Level Thirteen. Keith loved a mystery, especially one that he didn't have to take seriously. He could see through the edge of the door that the lock wasn't quite latched, but that there was no knob on this side. With the tips of his fingers, he dragged at the painted metal door, pulling it a quarter-inch out from the jamb. The hinges groaned and scraped, echoing deafeningly in the dim hall. He scrabbled at the emerging edge with one hand, but it slipped back flush. It was simply too heavy for him to hold open with just one set of fingers.

He needed to get something between the door and the frame to keep it from slamming shut until he could get his hands free. A pencil was the only thing he had on him that was light and strong enough. It went between his teeth, eraser-end outward, and he pulled at the door again. The rubber eraser skipped across the paint, jabbing the point of the pencil into his tongue. "Aagh," he mumbled around it, and then winced at the sound.

Carefully, he maneuvered it into the tiny opening of the door. It took him four tries before he could pull the door wide enough for the pencil to go through the opening. It occurred to him too late that the point would have helped him widen it. Never mind. He let go of the door when the pencil was in place. It snicked shut onto the wood, and Keith stepped back, spitting out graphite.

Dusting his tingling fingertips together, he levered the door open and let himself through. A crumpled candy wrapper pressed into the latch socket was what had prevented the door from locking automatically. Keith deduced in his best consulting detective method that someone else without keys wanted access to these floors. In the pitiful light of a wavering fluorescent bulb high up in the stairwell, nothing out of the ordinary would have been visible.

Checkout cards lay strewn on the floor with scuffed footprints and dust on them; here and there the end of an internal shelf had slipped, letting the books on it fall sideways, as if they were reclining. Just as in the twelve levels above, carrels and study nooks occupied two walls, and the elevator descended down a shaft drilled straight through the middle of the level, visible over the metal bookshelves. The room was surprisingly cold. They must have all the heating ducts closed, since no one used this floor much. It didn't have to be fit for human habitation, or for librarians, either.

Nothing here, anywhere on this level. That left Fourteen.

Once beyond the security door between Levels Twelve and Thirteen, there were no more barriers. Keith trotted down the last set of stairs, listening to his footsteps reverberate in the hall like ping-pong balls bouncing. He thought for one breathless moment he could hear other feet on the stairs, but guessed that the echoes were playing tricks on his ears.

Fourteen was, if anything, more deserted than Thirteen. There were no emergency lights down here at all. He felt his way to the elevator, wishing he had brought a flashlight. Not that he was afraid of the dark, but what if something jumped out at him? The light switches were somewhere on the central pillar. There was a groaning hum under the floor that raised the hair on the back of his neck, but that was from the furnace blowers. It was nice and warm down here, but not inviting. He decided he had to be wrong about Marcy being down here somewhere. It was dead quiet. There was no one down here but himself.

He touched the wall, found his way to the switchplate. The slots were empty. They required the insertion of a switchkey, something impossible to duplicate without a screwdriver or a paperclip, and Keith had neither. He felt for the elevator call button. He wondered where Marcy and Carl could have gone. This was an old building. Maybe there was a secret passage around here somewhere, and they lost him on Level Eleven, right under the librarians' noses. His imagination drew up pictures of a spy sect, something to do with the CIA or communism, melded with the weird religious cult that worshipped IC chips. Men and women wearing gray business suits under sackcloth robes and chanting from mystic flow charts. He'd be intruding on a bunch of mindless hulks who would beat him up, and spread his guts out across Anthropology through History in the name of electronics.

"C'mon, I'm scaring myself," Keith said chidingly. His throat was dry and tight.

A click sounded behind him, a heel scraping against the concrete floor. Keith spun, just as the blinding beam from a flashlight hit him square in the eyes. His heart pounded, threatening to jump out of his open mouth.

"What are you doing down here?" a man's voice boomed.

"Uh," cried Keith, goggling. His voice had abandoned him. The beam moved closer, dazzling him with the sun-bright circle of yellow light at the center of the white, and passed, brushing the wall until it came to the elevator indicator. The flashlight turned vertical, as the hand holding it shifted to punch the call button. The light turned horizontal again, and stayed on Keith's face until the elevator arrived. Keith shrank back against the cold, rough stucco wall, trying to avoid looking down the hot torch-beam. He felt like a rabbit caught trying to cross a road. The other hand appeared now, reached up, and shoved him into the car.

"Don't come down here again without authorization," the voice grumbled. As the doors closed, Keith caught a glimpse of a bearded man in a security uniform, and the flashlight, as it turned back toward the floor. Something about the guard's proportions seemed wrong, but before he could be sure, the elevator doors closed.

He posted himself in a Level Eight study carrel that was handy to the elevator and the stairwell, and waited for Marcy to reappear. The scrawny librarian kept staring fiercely at him, willing him to sit still and study. Keith smiled sweetly, and went on jumping up every time the elevator stopped near him. After an eternity of false starts, the elevator doors opened, and Marcy and Carl emerged, chatting. Keith raised himself up, and waved over the carrel wall. Marcy noticed him, and involuntarily started toward him, shaking her head, signalling a frantic "no." Carl noticed him then, and glared hotly, pacing ahead of Marcy. If Carl had been Superman with heat vision, Keith would have been a little crispy smudge on the floor. He ignored Carl, and smiled brightly at Marcy. "Hi!"

"Uh, hi," Marcy said, her voice barely audible.

"Good to see you," Keith said. "Marcy's in my Sociology class," he explained.

"I know," Carl glowered. He tugged at Marcy's arm, and she turned away too quickly, banging her knee against an exposed I-beam. She gave a soft gasp and nearly dropped her books, but she kept moving. Carl didn't seem to notice that she had hurt herself, and virtually pulled her out of the stacks. The last Keith could see of her was an expression of wide-eyed appeal. Or desperation.

"I'll see you later," he called to her.

"Please, just leave me alone," she breathed, clutching her books tightly. Keith subsided into his chair, puzzled.

"Shhh!" hissed the librarian, triumphantly.

▪ Chapter 7 ▪

Keith spent most of Monday night in the company of his R.A. and several other members of the Student Government, on an act that required the utmost secrecy. It was a mission of mercy on behalf of Dan Osborne. He was a member who was attending the university on an athletic scholarship, and he had won the first-place medal in the regional swimming competition for the 440-meter race. Danny was ecstatic over his victory, and had been seen all day walking as if on air. The other members decided that it was up to them to keep him from getting a big head over his success, and maybe walking right out of the atmosphere before he noticed. It was for this reason that they were engaged in transporting his Volkswagen Scirocco from the parking lot to the bottom of an empty swimming pool at one o'clock in the morning.

They decided it was worth it to help him out, since the chances that the administration would blame Student Government for such a prank were suitably small. Pat, shaking off his lethargy for once, decided to help. He was a friend of Danny's, too.

One of the guys in on the joke was an Engineering major. With the help of an Architecture student, Sharon Teitelbaum, they had constructed a pair of jointed ramps that hung over the edge of the pool like a set of badly broken skis. Mere Business and English majors, like Keith and Pat, were delegated to be pallbearers and help carry the car out of the lot.

Once in the loftily named "natatorium," Rick sprang the door lock, and took off the emergency brake. With four men on either side, the car was eased down the ramps.

"There," said Rick, with satisfaction. "It'll take him hours to figure out how we did it."

"Let's leave the ramps in the office," Keith suggested, "so it won't be too hard to find them later."

"That doesn't mean a thing," Pat sniffed. "People who are intelligent enough to understand machinery don't become gym teachers." Rick hit him solidly between the shoulder blades, and he choked.

"Knock it off, Shakespeare," Rick growled in mock ire, "or I'll put you through the goalposts."

"Spoken like a true snob," Keith accused Pat cheerfully.

"Of course," Pat answered, airily. "P.E. majors stand right ahead of us English majors on the unemployment line."

It was quiet and dark in the hallway of the dormitory. There were a few students still awake, but they had their doors closed to keep the noise from stereos, TVs, passionate discussions, or other activities from annoying people who would rather sleep. This floor was nearly empty. The figure sneaking toward Keith's room had seen everyone leaving over an hour ago. There would probably be time enough left.

With a look over his shoulder to ensure that no one was watching, the figure set down his bag and bent over the doorknob. A quick gleam of metal flashed, reflecting the safety lights at the hall's T-intersection, and the door creaked gently open. The figure stepped inside the dark room.

* * *

When they tramped back to their dorm room, fortified from Rick's personal store with beer and potato chips, Keith popped open the door, flicked on the lights with a flourish, and stopped short on the threshold.

"Oh, Pat," he chided his roommate. "You didn't tell me you were going to redecorate."

"Huh? Oh, shit," Pat said, pushing in past Keith. Books were scattered all over the floor, and papers lay in a chaotic snowstorm on the bed, the desk, and the dresser. A broad map of sticky brown film spread on the wall had obviously issued from the empty bottle of Coke on the coffee table. But the carnage was limited to Keith's side of the room. There could almost have been a line drawn down the center. Not a scrap of paper or a drop was on Pat's side. "What happened?"

"Well, if it's Santa Claus, he's two months early. And I really woulda preferred coal in my stocking. It's a lot more subtle."

"My man, you've been pimped. Who have you ticked off lately?"

"I bet it's Carl. Why else would your stuff be left completely alone? I'm going to go talk to him."

"Enough," Pat commanded, blocking Keith from leaving. "It's after midnight. Carl thinks you're a royal pain but not worthy of the trouble. Believe me, I've heard it all from him at length."

"But who else could it be?" insisted Keith. He eyed the mess. "I'd better clean it up now. I can't sleep with that Coke dripping off the wall onto me all night. I'd dream of Chinese torturers."

"You'd drive them nuts, too. I'll go tell Rick, then I'll come back and help," Pat offered.

"Thanks." Keith wrung out a washcloth and set to work, grumbling. Pat slipped out of the room. In the stillness, Keith could hear him knocking, and then the low hum of voices. In a moment, Rick appeared at the door.

"Honest to God, Doyle."

"In the immortal words of Han Solo, Rick, it's not my fault."

"It never is. I'll ask around. Come and talk to me after

dinner, okay? I'll tell Jackson and they'll change your locks tomorrow. It's the best we can do.''

"Yeah. Thanks." Keith went back to work on the wall. " 'Night.''

His nocturnal activities left Keith feeling worn-out all Tuesday. Only anticipation of solving the mystery of Marcy's study group kept him from declaring a mental health day and cutting Sociology.

When he got to class, he wished that he had cut. Dr. Freleng, in full knowledge that a holiday break was coming, and that all the other teachers were loading the students up with work, issued instructions for a new term paper, worth the usual 10 percent of the grade. Keith walked out of the room reeling with exhaustion and irritation. Marcy smiled at him sympathetically as she left. "See you later," she called.

"Absolutely," Keith promised.

This time, Keith made certain that he was invisible. He had positioned himself in the stacks on Level Eight, thumbing through boxes of crumpled periodicals when Marcy appeared right on schedule, and stepped into the elevator. After a suitable interval, Keith shoved his handful of magazines back into the box, and slipped behind the fire door.

He crept down the stairs in almost total darkness and into the bottom-most level of the library. His mother used to say that if there was justice in the world, he would have been born with cat whiskers as wide as his shoulders to prove that one day his own curiosity would kill him. He wished for those whiskers now, as his head rapped against several metal bookshelves which laughed hollowly at him in the gloom. Odors and fragrances familiar to him tickled his nose in the thick warm air: concrete dust, moldering paper, and library paste.

A humming white line of light grew down from the ceiling and stopped noisily at the floor. Steel doors clashed open, and Marcy appeared out of the book elevator clutching her green notebook. She felt around her head for the nearest bookshelf and started forward, guiding herself with her free hand. The elevator closed behind her, cutting off the light. The confident tap of her shoes on the concrete floor passed Keith and went on down the row. He prayed that he could follow her without bringing down Dewey Decimal System numbers .3440 to .785 on top of himself along the way. He sank catlike to all fours. Maybe he could crawl after her. Maybe not. It always looked easier when babies did it. He struggled along the floor, trying not to make any noise.

His movements stirred up a fair amount of dust on the floor, which he promised his twitching nose he would sneeze at later. His knees informed him that he was too old for this manner of locomotion, but his ears informed him that he was doing a pretty good job of shadowing without making noise or being noticed. Marcy was keeping a slow pace ahead of him. A sudden light gleamed in her hand. Keith's heart jumped. If she had a flashlight she wasn't using until the last moment, Keith was going to have to do some fancy explaining. Certainly he was at a disadvantage: what could he say? "Hi, doll. Of all the library stacks, in all the universities, she walks into mine. Oh, what am I doing on the floor? I dropped my next line."

She stopped. Keith could see at last that the light she held came from a key. It shone faintly green against the keyhole of a low door behind the last row of bookshelves. Probably one of those key-lights. A miniature flashlight would be vital down here, but the sure way she had found the door spoke of long familiarity. The door opened inward, and Marcy disappeared into a sudden riot of light and noise. It boomed shut behind her.

"Nuts," he said to himself. "Now what do I do?"

On hands and knees, he crawled carefully over to the door and felt over its surface for the keyhole. He found a polished square with a slot and put his eye to it. He could see nothing. It was as black as the room he was in. They, whoever *they* were, must have blocked it to keep light from leaking out and betraying the presence of the room on the other side. And what was that room anyway? Keith didn't know of any further excavation or construction in Gillington Library. The perimeter of the stacks stopped where he was standing, or rather, kneeling, right now. This must be really top secret.

He could feel the bass hum of conversation vibrating the door under his fingertips. Leaning close, he set his ear gently on the rough wood, and closed his eyes to concentrate. Several people were talking, though their words were no more distinguishable than if they had been speaking under water. One tenor voice, its tone proving its owner to be seething with irritation, overpowered the others, and then went on alone somewhat more calmly.

Definitely the faculty advisor, Keith decided. But for what subject? Or purpose? There was something about this situation which made his imaginary whiskers bristle out. Why meet in the sub-sub-basement of the library when at this hour three-fourths of the classrooms on campus were empty? And what about that key Marcy had? Its green light was unlike that of any phosphorus or LEDs he'd ever seen. Must be some really neat mechanism. He was intrigued. Something very interesting was going on here. His thin nose twitched with curiosity.

And dust, Keith discovered in a panic. He was going to sneeze. His eyes watered as he pinched his nose to hold back the explosion. He rocked back on his heels until the impulse passed, and then hunkered down once more against the door. The room on the other side of the wall had fallen silent. Keith blinked in the dark with surprise. No voices, not even the faculty advisor's. Had everybody left through some other door? he wondered, holding his breath and straining for any telltale sound. No, if that place had a second entrance, Marcy wouldn't have to come down through the stacks, risking the librarians' wrath. No, he reconsidered, it was probably all set up with the librarians. Maybe he could coax one into telling him all about it, later. He gently cuddled his ear closer into the rough wood, leaning his weight inward.

A second later, he was measuring his length on the concrete floor of a brightly lit room, shaking stars out of his head. Marcy was halfway to her feet, about fifteen feet away, fingertips over her mouth, staring at him in shock. Right now he felt as surprised as she seemed over his unexpected appearance. Her books sat atop the kind of wood and metal desk Keith called an "iron maiden," for its deserved reputation of discomfort comparable to the medieval torture device. From his undignified vantage point, Keith also recognized Carl Mueller. Aha, you scum, he thought. There were other college students there, but most of the rest of the class were adolescent kids, and they were all gawking at him. If this was the "study group," what were *they* doing here? Were they what the mystery was all about? Was Marcy ashamed to admit that she talked about her homework with a bunch of genius midgets? Or was it something more sinister, like a government think tank?

A figure introduced itself between Keith and the rest of the room. Keith's eye travelled upward—not too far—past a pair of short legs, a protuberent belly, and a barrel of a chest, to a round face bethatched and bewhiskered with hair of bright carrot red going white over the ears. Pointed ears! Keith's jaw dropped open. He blinked and twisted his neck to change his angle of view. An optical illusion? No, they were pointed, all right, and about four inches high. That was impossible! They must be made of latex, like theatrical artists used. And then again, maybe not. He opened his mouth to say something, but the man stopped him with a curt gesture of his hand. A pair of gold-rimmed spectacles sat on the bridge of a pugnaciously turned-up nose behind which iris blue eyes regarded him icily. By all that Keith knew or imagined, there was a living leprechaun standing there looking down at him. "Top o' the morning to ye," he cried, cheerily.

"Gut efening," said the leprechaun. He was the owner of the tenor voice Keith had heard through the door. "Vould you care to get up?"

▪ Chapter 8 ▪

Keith rose to a sitting position and dusted his scraped chin with a bemused hand. There was some self-conscious tittering from the bigger youths, his fellow college students, and Keith remembered that he and the leprechaun weren't alone in the room. In the softly lit, stone walled chamber the others, the children, stared at him in silence. His head felt like it was spinning. What were ordinary human beings doing hiding out in a library basement with a leprechaun?

The Big Folk were surprised when Keith catapulted through the door. Holl and the other Small Folk were not. In fact, they were expecting him. Keith's footsteps had been audible for some time in the silence on the other side of the wall. He looked as surprised to be discovered as his classmates were to see him.

The Elf Master closed the heavy door with a thud, and turned to Marcy, whose face was beet red. Holl felt sorry for her. "Zo, Mees Collier, your friend has joined us. Not efen waiting for his infitation. Zit down zomvere, Meester Doyle." He crossed his arms patiently and stepped back to let Keith get to his feet. In control as usual, the Master was taking this blatant invasion of his domain nonchalantly, as if it was not the first time such a thing had occurred.

Holl and Enoch sat back at their ease in the shabby maple-topped desks and watched with amused pleasure as the young man clambered up off the floor. His jaw was hanging agape. Though the other students usually waited to be asked to join the group, one and all they had started out disbelieving in their surroundings. Right now, Holl's classmates were regarding the intruder with sympathy. They all remembered what it was like to walk in. Sourpuss Carl, with his shoulders bunched up around his ears, was the only unfriendly face, and he looked furious to see Keith. He too, however, kept his seat. Soft-spoken Marcy had dropped her gaze to her books and was refusing to look up at anyone. Lee was tightening and unclenching his fists. Holl glanced over at Enoch, who was obviously trying to judge Marcy's reaction to the intruder. It boded ill for Keith Doyle if he was Marcy's enemy.

The red-haired intruder was trying to speak. Squeaky noises like unoiled door hinges in the wind issued from his throat, eliciting nervous giggles from the others in the room, so he stopped trying to talk and stared instead.

This boy had better recover soon, Holl realized. The Master's patience wouldn't last long. Holl snickered, watching Keith as the young man's eyes turned to him and Enoch. He smiled at them, and then started, like a shying horse.

"I know what he's thinking," Enoch whispered sullenly through his teeth. "The ears."

"They all do it," Holl murmured back good-humoredly.

Keith still stood in the center of the floor, apparently dumbfounded. The Master cleared his throat and regained

Keith's attention. He pointed to the empty iron maiden between Holl and Enoch. Obediently, the boy made his way over to the desk, still glancing over his shoulder again and again at the little red-haired man.

"He looks as if he thinks the Master's going to vanish if he takes his eyes off him," Marm commented, fingering his beard, leaning over toward Holl.

"He'll be wishing it before the semester's out," Holl confided.

With one hand on the back of the seat, Keith swung the desk under himself. Its legs screeched painfully across the concrete floor. He dropped into the chair, too fascinated by his surroundings to notice the noise. He smiled around at everyone, then subsided into a pose of attentive interest, fingertips drumming an excited tattoo on the battered maple desktop.

What was going on here? Who was this little guy? Was he a midget? Keith looked at him again, trying to work what he was seeing into some kind of reality.

Marcy wouldn't meet his eyes. Keith knew he had some explaining to do for her later, but he had hundreds of questions to ask. The teacher looked for all the world like Brian O'Connor, the Little People, legend of the Celts, the Irish— his own background. So how come he sounded like Bela Lugosi? And what were all these children doing here? With a start, he realized that they had on pointed ears, too, and two of the young faces wore beards. Were they in on the gag, or was there something here that was beyond his furthest expectations? Magic? Was there magic in this place? If so, there was no one so ready to appreciate it as was Keith Emerson Doyle, scholar of legends.

"Hi, I'm Keith Doyle," he said to his two seatmates, and waited for a response. "Um, do you speak English?"

The black-haired boy cleared his throat with disgust and looked away. He had a fierce glower in his dark eyes that made Keith feel as though he'd been scrutinized by the genius kid-brother of a girl he was dating for the first time. Keith had seen the light of blackmail on many a similar face in his time.

The blond lad was friendlier, and favored Keith with a real grin before going back to his carving. He had dishwater blond hair and the sort of chubby cheeks that one of Keith's aunts would have loved to pinch. The narrow, sharp-pointed knife dug in to the partially whittled stick, and a splinter of wood leapt away from the minute pattern.

He was good. His skill level was way above average for his age, which Keith judged to be eleven or twelve. Keith watched him work for a moment, then indulged himself in a good stare at the profile turned to him. The ears were pointed, all right, and just a bit outsized for the boy's face, but if they were fake, the guys in Hollywood would fall all over each other to meet the makeup artist. The whorls seemed exaggerated, and the tip swept backward, continuing perfectly the lines of cheekbone and eyebrow up and toward the back of the head. The elfin girl on the boy's other side spoke softly, and the boy brushed little wood shavings onto the floor and turned his whittling over in one hand. He scratched at the ear with his little finger, thinking. The skin reddened where the nails touched. The little girl caught his eye and smiled up at him over her friend's head. She had a thick ponytail of red-brown hair, shockingly green eyes, and looked about ten years old. Her own ears, poking coyly out of the ruddy mass, went rosy when she blushed at Keith's wink. He glanced around at the rest of the group, suddenly aware he was being stared at.

Those ears were real. *They* were real. Keith's smile widened. There were several people with ears down here. It was one thing to want to have a dream come true, and entirely something else to have it happen to him in daylight. Not one Little Person, but a whole group! The Little People were alive. Keith's heart raced with joy.

Carl looked ready to explode. This so-called study group was obviously something he had wanted to keep to himself and a few select friends. Keith eyed him witheringly.

He was brought back to the present by the sound of a throat clearing imperiously. The red-haired teacher was gesturing at a slate perched on the bed of an easel. *My God*, thought Keith, *it really IS a study group*. "May ve continue mit today's discussion? Mr. Mueller, you had made a fery gut point regarding the exchange of ideas between different cultures. There is likely to be more interaction, more exchanges, including admiration, between peoples in positions of equal or mutual security. As your example, the British und the Americans."

Distracted from his study of Keith, Carl smiled smugly, and

settled back in his chair, tapping the eraser end of a pencil on his desktop to suggest that the question had been a snap for him. He was at home here. Probably he had been coming down here a long time. Keith felt like exacting instant retribution, but "King Brian O'Connor" was way ahead of him. The teacher peered over the tops of his lenses at him, looking like a frog about to surprise a fly.

"Vould you suggest that the exchanges are permanent societal incorporations, or rely upon ephemeral trends? How are they accomplished?" Carl stopped tapping, and sat up a little straighter.

"Uh, what do you mean, sir?"

"Vhat makes one culture accept facets of another?"

Keith raised his hand. He was awed by his surroundings, envying the other Big People present their privilege, but the teacher's question inspired a reply. The little guy sure knew his business. Keith had to admit that he was also determined to one-up Carl, so he might as well participate rather that just sit admiring the scenery. "Sir?" The little teacher swung away from Carl.

"Our new addition, Meester Doyle." He pointed a forefinger at Keith.

"I would suggest, uh, sir, that most permanent exchanges start with trends, and depending on its quality of positive acceptance or nonacceptance, and reassertion, say, through channels of mass communication, they may get incorporated permanently."

One thick red eyebrow arched up, wrinkling the teacher's forehead. "Examples?" He pronounced it "exahm-ples."

"Umm. Hair styles. Slang expressions. They go both ways across the Atlantic."

"There is no need to prove your knowledge of geography." The other students tittered, including Marcy. Keith was relieved to see that she was relaxing. He must be doing all right. "Very vell, you haf an opinion. That is gut. I vould like to see three to fife pages from you on the subject, to see if you can support your thesis. Bring it mit you in fife days."

"Yes, sir," said Keith, elated. He had been accepted! He was part of the mysterious group, associating with, well . . . elves! Well, the old guy might be one. Otherwise this was some sort of weird group that met in costume. No, he had made a legitimate discovery; he felt it to the roots of his hair. These other pointy-eared people were probably the old guy's kids. He counted them. Seven. Prolific old bugger, wasn't he?

On the other hand, they might not all be kids. None of the others besides the teacher had any lines on their faces. They could all have been under fourteen, just judging by size. But what about the ones with the beards? He'd have to find out; if not the next time he joined the group, the time after that. That one sexy girl across the room was a perfect miniature Marilyn Monroe, with waves of thick blond hair and a body to match. If it wasn't for the fact that her feet didn't touch the ground from the seat of the desk, he would have to swear he was looking at a fully grown woman. As it was, she seemed more on the order of a little girl playing dress up with mommy's clothes. Her face was round and perfectly smooth, no makeup.

She noticed him looking at her and raised an eyebrow coyly, the corner of her mouth smiling an obvious invitation. Real live jailbait. He grinned. The blonde grinned back. Keith blushed, and she giggled silently into her hand.

And then it dawned on him that he had just been assigned to do a research paper, and that it was due on Monday. The smile melted off his face, and he groaned, settling his elbows on his desk with a thump. The blond boy on his right snickered. "You'll learn to keep your mouth closed," he told Keith in an undertone, watching the teacher's back cautiously. "He gives extra work to`the *schmartkopfs*."

"Thanks too late," Keith muttered back, slouching over his elbows. "Teachers are all alike." Then he realized the boy had spoken to him. Funny, he didn't look German. Or sound German. Except for the one word, he could have been the kid next door. Well, well, well . . .

An hour later, the teacher rose from his stool and nodded to the class. Without a word, the group dispersed, the humans heading out the door through which Keith had made his spectacular entrance. There was no knob on this side, but the door seemed to adhere to the fingers of the first person to touch it, and stayed obediently open until everyone had passed through.

The Little Folk were moving toward a lower wooden portal, which opened onto a hallway about four and a half feet high. The blond boy shot him a friendly glance, and scrambled out of the desk after his fellows. "I'll see you, widdy," he said.

Keith watched after them for a moment, trying to decide whether or not to follow them, and then looked around for Marcy.

She was already gone. Keith dashed out into the library after her, but the elevator at the end of the dark aisle was already on its way up with a load of students. Behind him, the classroom door hissed shut, closing him out in the dark. The line of white light cast between the elevator doors shimmered upward and was swallowed by the invisible ceiling. At best, the library elevators could only hold four people comfortably. Three human students, all strangers, their shadows deepening as the light disappeared, waited in the dark for the car to return. Carl and Marcy were probably in it now. Even though it required a key to operate the elevator down here, he refused to doubt anything if the . . . if THEY were involved.

Casually, Keith sauntered over to the others and asked out loud, "So, how long have you been coming down here?" He tried hard to keep the excitement out of his voice, but he could tell he wasn't succeeding.

For a time, there was no reply. Then a female voice, which Keith guessed to be attached to the fashionably dressed girl with *sorority* written all over her, said uncomfortably, "Oh, a while."

"Who is the red-haired guy? What's his name?"

"He's just the schoolmaster," she said. "I don't know what his name is. That's all I've ever heard him called, Master."

"And the kids?"

"Fellow students," one of the young men said shortly.

"What class is this?"

"Sociology," the other man said. His voice was thunderously deep.

"Sociology?" Keith shouted. The others shushed him. "Sociology," he repeated in a whisper. "I'm failing that now with a *real* teacher."

"No," said the girl firmly. "*He* is a real teacher." The others all murmured assent. There was no question as to whom "he" was. "Last year, he was teaching Mathematics. I was failing Calculus miserably, and my boyfriend took me down here. It was the one course I had to take for my major that I just couldn't pass on my own. I understood it after the Master explained it. He's teaching those kids anyway, and the more the merrier, I guess. The other teacher was just no good. I'm grateful.''

"Me, too," said the first young man. "Before Math it was Greek."

"Where does that other passage lead?" Keith asked, thinking of the low door.

"We don't know."

"*What* are they?"

"We don't know."

"Elves?" the girl volunteered uncertainly. No one scoffed at her.

"Where do they come from? Why are they here?"

"We don't know."

"Aren't you curious?"

"Oh, sure," said the second young man. "But they don't answer any personal questions. They're good at ignoring 'em. After a while, you stop hitting your head against the wall and just do your assignments."

"Not me," said Keith. "I have a very hard head. By the way, I'm Keith Doyle."

The elevator's light reappeared in the ceiling and crept downward. He could see silhouettes now, as the two other young men stuck out their hands. "Lee Eisley," said the first, his cap of black hair glinting in the light. "Barry Goodman," said the second. "Teri Knox." Keith shook hands with them all.

The elevator door opened, and disgorged a librarian with a cart. She stuck a key into a wall panel. Fluorescent lights flickered on over the aisles. Keith's eyes stung from the sudden brightness. The woman shrieked when she saw them waiting there, but recovered her composure quickly.

"What are you all doing down here?" she snapped suspiciously, in a voice like her cart's. "This is a restricted level."

"We, uh, came down the stairs. They were unlocked," Keith lied, waving vaguely behind him, thanking the unseen that it wasn't Mrs. Hansen. "We got lost." He gave her what he hoped was a melting smile.

She was unimpressed. "That is impossible. No one is allowed down here without a pass." Elbows out, she pushed the cart into their midst with typical librarian arrogance that they had better get out of the way or be run over. Its wheels squealed an earsplitting protest. Keith, with assiduous politeness, bowed her past him. Teri giggled.

The woman gave them a sour glance over her shoulder. "Stay off this level unless you get authorization from the head of Library Services," she said firmly, and stalked off behind the squeaking cart.

"Yes, ma'am," Keith said, buoyed on his joy. "Uh, you need to oil your axles. That way you won't squeak so much."

Her back stiffened, and she turned to make a suitably quelling retort, but the elevator door slid closed on their grinning faces.

"By the way," Teri said, just before the elevator stopped on the ground level, "it's very important that you don't tell anyone about . . . the class. No one else knows it's there."

"How can the librarians miss that door?"

"Believe me, they just don't see it. Nothing's visible when the light is on," Lee said adamantly, his long curly hair bobbing as he talked. "I've tried, and you have to know what to look for."

"The Master doesn't want to be bothered by just anyone," Barry said, belligerently. "You're in on something special. Don't ruin it for the rest of us."

"Of course not," Keith assured him with all his heart. "I know how special it is. I'll keep it very quiet."

"Please," Teri begged. "He's already threatened once to exclude . . . Big Folk. I really value the class, and I don't want to stop going. It's like, well, touching a fairy tale. That sounds dumb, I know. But it's really helping me in my regular classes, too."

"I understand. Believe me. I promise," said Keith. It seemed to him the other three heaved a sigh of relief. He smiled placidly at nothing. Touching a fairy tale . . . He might have phrased it that way himself. Keith decided he was going to enjoy this class.

Keith was still determined to get the most pleasure that he could, but it was much harder work to enjoy it, now that he was a functioning member of the secret class. His paper had been dissected during the second session by the Master, and Keith was made to endure a grilling on his facts and opinions that left him sweating. To his surprise, no one laughed at him, even though he was fumbling over words. In fact, he noticed real sympathy on more than one face, both from Big People and Little People.

None of the Big People, now all friends of Keith's except for Carl, voiced their thoughts on the origin of their fellow classmates. None of them dared to make a guess. Keith called them elves, for their empirical resemblance (awaiting more data, he would say), and the handle stuck, almost as if the students were thankful that someone had suggested one.

He wanted to ask Marcy what she thought, but she was still avoiding him. He felt a little guilty, realizing that he was avoiding her, too, but consoled himself that he had a lot of new information to assimilate, and she would understand—if she ever spoke to him again. He promised himself that he would apologize to her at the next opportunity.

Keith watched his new classmates with fascination, a little taken aback by how natural and ordinary the Little Folk were. They seemed to be just short people with funny ears, though he felt there was more to them. He was also exasperated by the distance the two groups put between one another. He was held back from making his own overtures by the worry his own fellows exhibited that somehow he would spoil their special haven. More than ever, he was determined to make himself goodwill ambassador from the Humans to the Elves. After that, it should be easy for the others to follow his lead.

Marcy, after listening blank-faced to an impassioned, melodramatic apology on bended knees from Keith in the middle of the parking lot blacktop, unexpectedly broke up into hysterical laughter. "It's okay," she told him, clapping her palms over his mouth to halt the torrent of apologies. Keith's big, sad hazel eyes regarded her over her folded hands. "I forgive you. The Master was going to let you come in anyway. You just didn't know. I wish I could have told you, but you would probably have thought I was out of my mind. If I had trusted you, you might have understood, but sometimes you seem so crazy. So I guess I owe you an apology, too."

"Thanks," Keith said, and then paused. "I understand. I'm having a little trouble believing in it, too. But I'm working on it! Say, I didn't know you were going out with Carl."

"What business is it of yours?" she snapped suddenly, circling around him and walking away.

"None at all," Keith admitted cheerfully, getting up and following at her elbow. "I'm a business major. Professional curiosity, you know."

"I'm sorry," Marcy said, her anger dying away as swiftly as it rose. "It's just that we're fighting. Mostly about you, I'll have you know."

"Good," said Keith. "I've decided that what I want to do in life is be Carl Mueller's nemesis. It would make my life complete if I could drive him bananas. To think he knew where I could get . . . *research material*, and was keeping it to himself. I mean, what was he saving it for? I had to believe in magic on sheer faith." He shrugged. "I'm sorry, too, if you really like him."

Marcy was silent for a long time, staring at the ground in front of her feet as she walked. "I'm not sure any more. He's nice enough to me, but he's so—he's so *ambitious*, I think. It isn't healthy."

"The man without a cause," intoned Keith, sounding like a television movie announcer.

"Yeah, exactly." Marcy's thoughts seemed to be carrying her far away, to a place she didn't seem to care much for.

"But he's an A student. What's he doing in the Elf Master's class?" They walked up the stoop in front of Marcy's apartment building, and he held her books while she searched for her keys. "It's for dopes like me, who need tutoring."

"You're not a dope, Keith. Teri brought him in." Marcy looked up from her purse at him. "Didn't she tell you?"

"Nope. Probably ashamed of herself."

"Oh, come on. He's not that bad."

"Maybe not," Keith admitted, changing the subject with admirable tact. He still felt he owed Carl a grudge. "Remember the paper I told you I was researching for my Mythology course? I got an A on it. Without using any . . . material from class."

"Congratulations," said Marcy, spilling her purse and books onto the kitchen table. "It sounded pretty good to me."

"Thanks. I've been wondering if I ought to check my theories out with some of our little classmates."

"I don't think that's such a good idea," Marcy insisted, with a trace of her former reluctance.

"Why, just because they dodge 'personal questions'? Well, maybe I could take one of 'em out to dinner. I bet it's all peer pressure. If I can isolate one, maybe I can get him to talk. Or her," Keith said, thinking of the little blond girl. Then he noticed the look on Marcy's face. "Oh, no. You're not going to tell me no one's ever tried to socialize, are you? You are," he accused, before she could open her mouth. "I could see it in your face. And everybody else's, too. Why not? My God, Big People on this campus have been associating with them for how long now?"

"Five years," Marcy said in a cautious undertone, listening for her roommates.

"Five years, and they're still strangers. Some neighbor you are."

"Well, what about you? You're just curious," Marcy pointed out defensively.

"Downright weird, my roommate says," Keith added, unabashed. "But sure! Here you are with an incredible opportunity, to talk to legends, and you hold them at arm's length."

"It's not like that at all," Marcy said, getting excited. "They wouldn't like being called legends. And, it's more like, well, I'm too shy . . ."

"But not everyone is," Keith said, more gently. "I'm not. Wait and see. I'll get to know them better, and then I'll introduce you."

Marcy giggled. "But I know them already."

"No, you don't. But that's okay. You've already got a nodding acquaintance going. That's a good start."

▪ Chapter 9 ▪

At the next class meeting, Keith decided to begin making friends. He sat down deliberately between the blond kid and an older, bearded elf that he hadn't seen before. The boy winked at him again before going back to his customary whittling. Keith watched for a while with close interest, and then noticed the other fellow was watching, too. When the Elf Master was called away to attend to something at the other end of the mysterious tunnel, Keith struck up a conversation.

"Good, isn't he?" he asked the bearded one, who seemed surprised to be addressed by a Big Person. He grunted.

"Needs practice. He's too showy. That pipestem'd break the first time it got a look at a set of teeth."

The boy lifted his head from his work. "Now, Marm, you know that's not so," he said patiently, laying down the blade.

"It is so. You want strength in a bitty piece of work like that, you need a harder sort of wood, or you need to work across the grain."

"Here," said the boy, thrusting the tiny thing past Keith, and into the other's hands. "Look for yourself. It's not wood. It's bone. I suppose your eyes are getting too old to tell the difference."

"Well," said Keith, "for bone, that looks pretty good, I think. His wood carvings are really fine, aren't they?" he added hopefully. The older elf grunted his approval.

Marm turned the little stick over in his hand. Keith could see that its length was covered with a pattern of interlocking broad-leaved vines. It was astonishing that anything that small should be so perfect. He couldn't tell what Marm was complaining about. Probably just jealous. "Yah, you're right. Must be a goat's bone, now that I see it closely. Yah, a goat's bone. Fine work, Maven."

"What did he call you?" Keith demanded of the young elf, astonished.

"Maven. The Maven. That's what everyone calls me. It's a Yiddish word, means 'expert.' My name is Holl. And by the by, thanks for the compliment."

"Sure. I meant it. Where on earth did you get a Yiddish nickname?" Keith asked, not to be diverted. Jewish elves? Holl started to answer, but stopped, and held up both hands to shush him. "Why . . ."

"Quiet, you widdy, can't you hear him?" He puffed out his ruddy cheeks and blew bone fragments off his desk, then sat up straight.

"No . . ." But in a moment, the clicking of a pair of heels on the tunnel's concrete floor floated up over the rest of the noise. The Elf Master was returning. Abruptly, all the voices ceased, and everyone sat at polite attention.

"Quiet," the Master said wearily, though there was no noise. "Ve vill continue. Tay," he gestured at the second bearded elf, a pale blond with sharply tilted eyebrows, "has briefly outlined the development of modern agrarian society. Vhat, Mr. Eisler, vould you say vere the primary social changes brought about by the Industrial Revolution in the agrarian countries of the vorld?"

Keith hung back when class ended, and tapped Holl on the shoulder when he got up to leave. He kept his voice low as the other students passed by. "Listen, I think your work is really good. Do you think I could come over sometime, and see other things you've carved?" Keith tossed his head casually toward the low doorway. "I could never do that stuff. I'd cut my fingers off."

Holl cocked an eyebrow, and peered at him a good long time before answering, knowing full well what Keith was asking, and giving it honest consideration. "You're a different one, Keith. I'll see. Maybe you can come for an evening meal. The older ones won't gripe so much about a visitor while they're eating. And I don't mind an audience for my work."

"Terrific!" said Keith. "In exchange, I hereby invite you to be my guest in the dining hall. Only you probably won't think it's much of a favor when you've tasted the food."

"A good guest never counts the dishes served, nor spits out the mouthful he's chewing."

"Right. Always eat every meal as though it was your last."

"Wait here. I'll ask now." Holl vanished down the echoing hallway.

After a while, he returned. "You can come. Wait by the big sycamore outside the back of the library building in an hour and a half. I'll find you there. You'll need to be on your best behavior, boy."

"Yes, sir!" Keith saluted. His voice rang in the classroom, picked up tones from the concrete floor.

"Shush," said Holl, turning back into the tunnel. "You'll make them change their minds."

Keith held his jubilation until he reached the ground level of the library. When the elevator door slid open, he could contain himself no more. He danced out, and let go with a wild, "Yahoo!"

"Shhh!!" a librarian hissed sternly.

Following instructions, he waited, concealed behind the library building. About two hours had passed since the end of class, and Keith felt that if he had to stuff in one more particle of excitement, he would explode in a shower of sparks. The Maven—boy, what a name—told him to keep out of sight of the path and sit tight. They would have to wait for the right moment to let him inside. Keith had no objections. If they had managed to keep themselves hidden for this long, he wasn't going to be the one to blow their cover. What would Marcy say if she knew where he was going? He did a little dance, which he quickly converted into jiggling around for warmth in the chilly evening air as a couple of students passed him. He smiled at them, and craned his head after them as they walked away.

He heard a grating noise from behind him, and spun around to see where it was coming from. A whole four-foot-high-section of the stone wall, beginning an inch or two above the grass, had sunk back, leaving a deep, black opening. A hand extended through and beckoned to him. With a quick glance around, Keith dove for the hole and skittered to the side as the stone facade grated ominously back in place. He found himself standing in a passageway so narrow he had to press his shoulders together to turn around. He put out a hand to feel for the mechanism, but found nothing but the back of the stone wall. On his other side was rough brick.

"Keith Doyle," said a voice in the dark, sounding ominous. He jumped.

"Y—yup?" he affirmed.

"Welcome, then. You're just in time." A lantern flamed alight, and Holl was there looking up at him. "Follow me."

A short while later, Keith found himself sitting on a low bench, surrounded by a host of miniature humans; adults and children both. He kept his elbows very close to his sides, which meant he had to dip his head every time he wanted to take a bite from his miniature fork. *Now I know how Gulliver felt,* he thought, ignoring an itch along his ribs for fear of knocking over the tiny old lady on his left. Gingerly, he extended a hand to pick up the jug of milk, and poured some into his wooden cup.

Holl sat across the long table from him, occasionally studying him with a humorous twinkle in his eyes. He was aware how ridiculous the big youth felt, but it was a lesson in humility to watch how well Keith handled himself in adverse conditions. Holl could also see that old Keva was wearing her pincushion on her belt, and it was undoubtedly sticking into Keith's side. To his credit, the big fellow wasn't complaining. She had probably left it there on purpose, spiteful old hen. Good for him. He was a fair guest.

The others of Holl's people were not demonstrating themselves to be hosts worthy of such a guest. More than once, Holl had heard an unfavorable comment, fortunately inaudible to Keith's less sensitive ears. "What's he want to come in here for? To gawk, I'll bet." "Dey neffer let us alone vonce dey know. How ve know he has any discretion?" And from the oldsters: "His kind've been faithless before, for sure, darlin'. What difference will only a few generations make?"

"Uh, you know," said Keith, "this pitcher looks just like the kind we used to have at my summer camp. They're really indestructible. I oughta know. I used to shoot off bottle rockets from one."

Keva stopped chewing with a shocked intake of breath. She stared at the human balefully.

"Oh," Keith continued, misinterpreting her ire. "No one was hurt. I did it out next to the lake."

"Are you after suggesting that we took this pitcher from your summer camp?" Keva demanded.

"Now, Keva," Holl chided her, but the old lady ignored him. The other diners fell silent, listening.

Keith regarded her with puzzlement, his narrative dying away to silence. "No, not at all. The camp was up near Chicago. They're mass-produced. There must be thousands of them around the state. It just reminded me of camp. Sort of homey. I'm sorry if you thought I meant anything by it."

Keva nodded warily. "Well, all right then."

"If camp was something you enjoyed," Holl interjected,

shushing Keva. "Otherwise, perhaps we should apologize to you for reminding you."

"I didn't mind camp," Keith acknowledged cheerfully. "I think my parents only lived for the day when they could send all of my brothers and sisters to camp at once."

There was another susurrus of whispers around the room again. From Keith, there was no sign that he could understand or even hear any of it, but Holl's attenuated hearing translated them clearly. "Does he accuse us of stealing?" Hmmph, you old frauds, thought Holl, grinning to himself. And where did you think our things come from these long years? Do hens lay plates? Or curtains?

Keith looked around at the tables of elves, most of whom were glancing at him openly or covertly while they ate. He guessed there must be eighty or ninety of them. The little old lady had gone back to her own meal, pointedly turning her back to him as best she could in the limited space available. Keith made a mental note to apologize to her later. He sent a questioning glance to Holl, and received an amused gesture to go on eating and ignore the old lady. He figured that she must be the local equivalent of his great-aunt Martha, a woman who enjoyed bullying her relatives into believing that they had really offended her so she could demand apologies for the imaginary insults. He took another sip of milk and turned his attention to his surroundings.

The planked wooden tables were dark brown and polished smooth on top, but carved prettily around the sides. A few of the chairs at the ends were made to match, as were the benches, but a number of chairs were obvious refugees from a kindergarten. Keith had noticed one, occupied by an extremely dignified elf with silver-templed black hair, that had the alphabet and a teddy bear painted on the chair-back. The dishes were mostly ceramic, hand-thrown with a great deal of skill. Blue, green, and yellow were their favorite colors; the elves made their clothes in the same hues they painted their dishes.

At each long table sat a few elderly elves, others that he would term *middle-aged*, and an assortment of younger ones that he guessed were up to twenty years old in Big People terms. By the common resemblances, each group represented one extended family. It was touching to see that little silvering-blond grandmother feed the tiny infant on her left to give the tired brunette on the child's other side a rest and a chance to feed herself. There weren't too many babies in the room. Each table had two or three, rarely more. The one behind Holl had four toddlers, all of which looked exactly alike, and each of whose little bottoms could comfortably fit on the palm of Keith's hand. His classmates were scattered among the clans, as he called them to himself, so they probably weren't all sisters and brothers.

The Elf Master occupied the head of a table to Keith's left. Next to him sat Enoch, the young elf with black hair. Enoch had met Keith's glance on his way in, and apart from that one glance, ignored him. Keith decided not to think about him, and just smiled at anyone else whose eyes he met. On Enoch's other side was the pretty, auburn-haired elf girl whose name was Maura. She smiled sweetly back when he grinned at her, and looked down again at her plate.

The food was good, what there was of it. The servers, elves of both sexes, trundled over with big (to them) steaming crocks of stew, baskets of bread, and bowls of vegetables, and then sat down to serve themselves and their families. Keith prayed his stomach wouldn't grumble as he filled his doll's-dish with stew from the crock and took a piece of bread. He promised it the pound cake he kept sealed in a tin under his dorm bed for emergency midnight snacks. He even promised it extra breakfast if it would keep quiet for now. In his excitement over the coming meeting of the study group that afternoon, he had forgotten to eat any lunch, and he was embarrassingly hungry now. He tried to eat slowly, but in a few small bites, the plate was empty.

The crock thumped to a halt in front of him. "There's plenty," Laniora, his pretty brown-haired classmate, coaxed him from two seats down to Holl's left. With a grateful smile, Keith dished himself another helping.

The bread was something special. It was soft and fresh-baked, with a crisp, thin brown crust. The aroma made him sigh and lift his eyes heavenward, which drew laughter from his tablemates.

"Dinna worship it," snapped Keva. "Eat it!"

Obediently, he ate. It was delicious, and he said so. A moment later, an extra portion of bread plumped down next to his plate, and the sharp pain withdrew from his side. He had forgotten all about it until it disappeared. Holl grinned at him suddenly and Keith grinned back.

At the meal's end, Keva gave him a frosty little nod and smile, and walked away. Keith rose and bowed to her, scratching his side. Then he bowed to the elders clustered at the end of the table. The old man at the end inclined his head and went back to his own conversation. Since Holl showed no inclination to hurry away, Keith sat down again.

"You've flattered Keva," Holl told him. "It was her bread. She's the baker. It was her pincushion in your ribs, too."

"Oh," said Keith. "She your aunt?"

"She's my sister. I'm the middle one of three. Right now three, that is," Holl said blithely. "That was my baby sister down there at the end of the table. Three is considered a big family with us. My folks are a progressive pair."

"Sister? Hmm, hah, uh, how old is she?" Keith asked, amazed. "Never mind that; how old are you?"

"Old enough, my lad. In terms of this world, forty years have passed since my birth."

"Forty? Of course you look about twelve. I should have guessed. Wow, I would have thought you were more my age. I'm twenty."

"Let's shake." Holl extended a hand. "I'm considered a young adult to my folk, too. We'll call that common ground enough to build on."

Keith shook the hand, engulfing it in his own. Looking around, he discovered they were nearly alone in the big room. "Where'd everyone go?"

"To the living quarters. Some call it the village, but that's a fanciful title. It's a big place like this one, only divided up according to the clans. Come and see."

They walked through another low tunnel similar to the one that led from the schoolroom, though this one sloped down at a slight angle. The passage was dimly lit high along each side, though Keith couldn't see the fixtures from which the flickering light issued. "You don't get many . . . er, human . . . visitors down here, do you?"

"No, indeed not," said Holl. "You're the first in a long, long time."

"Then why me?" Keith asked, walking stooped-over, with his hand running along the ceiling checking for rafters and bumps. "Ouch. I feel like Quasimodo."

"The Hunchback of Notre Dame. Because you asked, Keith Doyle, and I trusted you, so you were allowed to come. I'm taking a chance on you. It's my nature to take chances. The others think I'm too progressive, but I call it a hereditary failing. My parents don't mind."

"You read a lot of classics?" Keith inquired, ducking to avoid an electrical conduit.

"What else is there to do in a library?"

"I guess I never thought what it might be like to live in one." Keith had a sudden vision of the secret door in the wall opening, and thousands of elves pouring out into the library, pulling books out of the shelves, using the slide projectors, calling up articles about leprechauns from PLATO, and stern little elf librarians hissing "Shhh!" He chuckled.

"Come on, then," the young elf called out, disappearing around a sharp bend in the hall. Keith hurried to catch up.

"When this building was built, back along, they made this floor to be a maintenance-way, to take care of the pipes and the foundation," Holl said, stopping to point out the sheaves of conduit that ran along the ceiling here and there. "Only it was never used that much. The one below it *was* the foundation itself. You can see that no one your size could walk down here for long without giving himself a good backache. As long as nothing went wrong with the pipes, they had no reason to look for a way to get at them. And we make sure that nothing goes wrong with the pipes. They've forgotten about it, see, and the parts of the blueprints describing this level and this part of the steam tunnels were destroyed, all by accident. They kept them in this very same building," Holl said, innocently. "We had a friend who warned us to get rid of access-ways and plans when we came here . . . but she's no business of yours." The elf's tone was a definite warning.

"A good friend," Keith said, tactfully not pushing for details. By the direction they were walking, he guessed that the rounded passage must run directly below the Student Common.

Feeling satisfied with the number of questions Holl *was* answering, he was content to let him talk. "How did you get here, Holl? And where did you come from?"

"Ireland, wasn't it?" Holl shot him a sideways glance full of mischief. Keith's theories were well known among Holl's folk, and they considered them most entertaining.

"Yes, wasn't it?" Keith asked, not letting the jibe penetrate. "I heard your relatives talking up there. I've got cousins that really do look like you. Not the ears, but the rest of your features. The cast of them, as my grandmother would say."

The Maven shrugged. "Your legends may have some truth to them. I'm not saying how much. You don't think we get pleasure out of saying we're kin to the enemy, now, do you? Simmer down, boy," for Keith was getting red-faced and waving his arms preparatory to a verbal explosion. Holl poked him in the midsection with a forefinger. "*You're* not an enemy yourself. At least I think not. But there'd be many more of us if there weren't so many of you. What normally becomes of highly interbred racial mutations under your typical intensive, impersonal scientific scrutiny?"

Keith's color faded slowly as he thought about it, and then he spoke. "Extinction."

"Uhuh . . . but fortunately among the characteristics we maintain are camouflage and silence. My kin have had much practice on their way across this continent. I can steal the eggs out of a duck's nest if she'll lean forward a mite."

"I can scare one silly and get the eggs that way," Keith volunteered. "I failed woodcraft in Boy Scouts."

"And can't I tell that? It's part of the quality of being obvious that makes me want to trust you. You were making quite a racket in the stacks that day. Any one of us could tell there was someone out there, though the rest of the Big Ones couldn't."

Keith opened his mouth.

Holl forestalled him. "And we heard you two days before that, when Bracey tossed you out. He's one of us, too."

Keith shut it again.

"This is where we live," Holl announced, stepping aside so Keith could stand up out of the low hallway. Rubbing his back tenderly, Keith squinted down the length of the room. "We lowered the dirt floor several feet. Used to be just a few feet high, but we like our head room. It makes for a far more congenial living space.''

Keith certainly would never have suspected its existence. It covered an area the same size as the large library levels above, but without partitions. The illusion of size was enhanced by the height of the ceiling, somewhat loftier than that of the dining hall one-half level up, and the size of the structures within, which were perfect small-scale models of the ones he was used to.

They were undeniably houses, though of a peasantish cottage type that he associated with woodcutters and Little Red Riding Hood. The roofs, solid and slanted, were, naturally, not needed underground to keep off the weather, but they served to give the illusion that the village was in the upper air. Groups of cottages were scattered throughout the vast room. Neighborhoods, Keith realized with delight. He could see his tablemates going about their business in the knot of houses nearest the passageway.

The same flickering light that illumined the passages lined the ceiling between bare rafters, though it was much brighter here, almost as bright as spring sunlight. It was as warm as springtime down here, too. The elves carried on life as usual with less noise than Keith would have thought possible for such a large number of human beings, but as Holl pointed out, he was probably mistaken about that, too.

A group of five or six children were playing tag around the corners of the small shelters, giggling as they managed to elude "It." It was a nice, quiet little village scene, but one that reminded Keith more of a Bronze Age enclosure than something that could exist in the twentieth century, especially within a hundred feet, albeit straight down, of a modern university.

In front of the cottage doors, here and there, a woman in a long skirt and blouse, or in the same straight-legged pants the men wore, sewed, usually patching clothes, and humming to herself or chatting with a neighbor. The floor was packed earth, hoed up here and there to make way for tiny flower beds and herb gardens. Bunches of greenery hung in nearly every doorway, scenting the air, and adding to the springtime atmosphere. You'd never know it was October—a cold October, too— upstairs. And everywhere was the same ornamental woodwork, the sort of fine carving that Keith watched the Maven do during class for the last couple of weeks.

He fingered a small polished square panel set into the upper part of a wall, admiring the design of intertwining ivy leaves carved upon it. "Did you do this?" he asked.

"No." Holl smiled. "But you have a good eye for a pattern. My father's work, that one is. That panel keeps the house together."

"Oh?"

"Aye. Cohesiveness. Knits its bones. I learned my skill from him. Scrap wood's one thing that's available in plenty, so I never lack for practice pieces."

Keith leaned close to the wall, trying to see joins between the tightly fitted slabs of wood. No two pieces were exactly the same size, grain, shade, or quality. They looked as though they had been puzzle-cut together with a very sharp knife. Particle board clung to oak between bits of plywood, balsa, and pine. These elfin builders could have given precision lessons to Pharaoh's architects. "So what's wrong with using nails?" Not that he could see any in the construction.

"They rust. They bend. Also, we tend to be a wee bit sensitive to having too much metal around."

"I heard that cold iron dispells magic," Keith said, teasingly. "Maybe that's why you don't use it."

"And maybe the effect is more like heavy metal poisoning, Keith Doyle. Call it an allergy. Don't look for foolish explanations unless no others suffice. There's plenty of common sense to go around. Even you could find some."

"I believe in magic," Keith said, softly.

"But do you know it when you see it?" Holl demanded.

"Probably not," Keith admitted, cheerfully. A fragrance of spices and baking tickled his nose, and he changed the subject. "How do you do your cooking here? I never smell anything out of the ordinary in the building."

"Oh, the chimneys over the fires are all vented together to the outside, toward the Student Common. We tried electric stoves once, but the cooks protested one and all that they couldn't control such an impersonal element, so that was the end of that experiment. They know where they are with wood-burning, and we left it at that. The steam tunnels run by here, and we make use of them. It's also from them that we get our heat. If you ever smelled any of the good cooking upstairs, you probably thought it was coming from the delicatessen in the Common.'' Holl wrinkled his nose. ''Or, if bad, from the Home Economics department. We don't eat fancy, as you see, so it's never anything unusual enough to bear investigation. Strong smells linger, so we're careful never to eat fish unless it's fresh, or any cabbages at all.''

Keith wandered between the shelters, nodding as nonchalantly as he could manage to any elf that met his eye, and most of them did, nodding back and smiling, as he tried to believe that he wasn't doing something unique and extraordinary in just being near them. But they preserved the illusion for him, and he allowed himself to make a full tourist's ramble of the big room.

He watched a handful of elves, male and female, folding sheets from a big wicker basket and gossiping over their work. Young ones played a complicated pretending game with toys on the ground. Keith saw a jointed toy horse clopping across the floor with an elfin toddler in pursuit.

''Electronic?'' Keith asked Holl.

''No, it's all wood.''

''Magic . . .'' In delighted disbelief, he watched the horse look back over its shoulder and change direction just as the little one would have reached it. It was alive! The baby gave a crow of glee and turned to pursue his toy. Holl broke his reverie by tapping him on the shoulder.

''There's more,'' he said, beckoning him along.

''How's that work?'' Keith asked, pointing at the horse, wanting to go back and investigate.

''Just a toy,'' Holl shrugged offhandedly, pulling Keith along. Keith took a quick look back before following him around a corner. The child's mother had seized the toddler up and was washing his face with a wet cloth. It was not a task the baby enjoyed, and he kicked and cried under her ministrations. She shot an apologetic look toward Keith, who smiled at her. The brown wooden horse stood at her feet and regarded its master with glass-eyed sympathy.

A thin pipe ran between the patterns of light on the ceiling, and divided into several smaller pipes, which descended along the wall and floor under the back of each house. Keith glanced over to Holl, eyebrows raised.

"Water," the elf explained. "We've run a tap pipe from the fire sprinklers. The pressure is kept constant, and again, no one notices."

"You think of everything." Keith looked around admiringly. "I wouldn't be able to work all this stuff out, even if my life depended on it. And yours do."

Holl looked pleased. "We've had time to work it all out. It wasn't so comfortable at first. But there's more. Did you know that there's a small river running under this building?"

"No," said Keith, astonished. "I've never seen sign of anything like that. The nearest river is way down the road."

"Well, you're wrong; there is one. It's the way towns were always built. Underground rivers make a natural disposal system. And we take water out of it upstream. Look here." He led the young man to a broad patch of growing greenery. Tay, the blond-bearded fellow from the Master's class, waved to them and went back to pulling up carrots and tossing them into a slatted bin. The bright orange vegetables were of unusually good size, and looked amazingly alive in the artificial sunshine. Holl appropriated two from under Tay's slapping hand, broke the greens off into a pail, passed one to Keith, and snapped a crunchy bite out of his own. "Hydroponics," he explained as he chewed. "These have their roots dangling in the river. It's right under this end of the building."

Keith brushed the water from the carrot, and took a bite. It was crisp, cold, and sweet, and even tasted healthy. "Why would they have built right over water? That's asking for trouble with the foundation."

"Well, it didn't start out that way. The river has changed course over the years. One more thing the university doesn't suspect is in its basements. And it makes a perfectly viable hydroponic garden. The water's always fresh. Waste goes in downstream."

"Wow." Keith didn't hide his interest. "How do you know so much about a river no one's ever seen?"

"Oh, well, one of our folk has an earth-wise way about her. She asked it, and she knows."

Keith nodded, trying to picture an elf-woman talking to a river. It sounded plausible as far as he could tell. Though there was a quiet buzz of conversation, and the occasional *click-zizz!* of a saw or *tap-tap* of a hammer, the loudest single noise in the place was the sound of his own shoes thudding along on the hard-packed floor. Most of the elves' footgear was a kind of soft-soled sock-shoe, sewn of suede or leather, and pulled on without lacings. The children generally wore a ribbon tied around each ankle to keep their shoes from falling off, but a slower form of locomotion than running wouldn't dislodge them. Holl was watching him speculatively, noting Keith's study with silent approval.

"It's peaceful here," Keith said at last.

Holl smiled wisely. "It is that."

Nothing seemed ever to be wasted by the Little People. Keith saw the same stiff flowered fabric used over and over again in different applications. Two little girls' dresses, several window curtains, an old woman's apron, and a gaudy young man's shirt had obviously all come from the same bolt. "And bed coverlets, too," Holl affirmed, after Keith mentioned it to him. "There are no looms in this place. That much wood we cannot spare, so textiles are some of the hardest things to come by. You'll see the same scrap of cloth recycled a dozen times before it's too badly worn to mend. It's a sure sign that fabric's on the way out when it becomes curtains. No wear to the body of the cloth, you see."

"Sure, I see," said Keith, musing. Now that he was aware of it, he saw that most of the fabrics here were well cared for, but old and worn, including his friend's clothes. Patches were skillfully blended on trouser-knees and jacket-elbows. Probably re-dyed, too, for camouflage. "Textiles, huh?"

"Huh. What we can't grow for ourselves, or make, or . . . er, find, we do without. Now, Lee Eisley, in the class, has a handy job as an assistant in the Food Services. He has been known to drop packages of meat our way, and a few other feats of kindness, after . . . well, when we lost another source of supply."

"Don't you ever buy stuff you need?" Keith asked impetuously, and then wished he hadn't.

Holl gave him a pitying look. "How and with what, Keith

Doyle? Shall I go out and get a job selling cookies? Or maybe helping out Santa Claus at a shopping mall?''

"Well, why not?" Keith had a sudden delighted vision of dainty point-eared elf helpers escorting hulking human children to Santa's throne. "No one would believe you were real, under the right circumstances. Nobody knows who Santa's helpers are.''

"Why not?" Holl echoed. "Because these nameless workers have backgrounds, backgrounds that your government knows about, and takes for granted. Maybe you don't know who they are, but they are known. It's a casual thing for you to have a job. It's your world. You've got a *Social Security Number*. Everyone knows where you came from. An adult, especially one that looks like me, popping out of nowhere prompts questions, questions that we don't want answered in public, starting with 'where did you get them ears?' " His eyebrows drew together, and his voice took on the tone of a moronic teenager.

"I'm sorry. I feel awkward asking such dumb questions, but I don't how else to ask what I want to know.''

Holl's face relaxed, and he slapped Keith companionably on the back, catching him solidly in the kidneys. Keith winced.

Holl said, "The trouble with you is that you have a basically honest heart. Haven't you heard it said to you by a thousand professors, Keith Doyle, that there are no dumb questions?''

". . . Just dumb people," Keith finished, self-deprecatingly. The curious illumination in the ceiling was dimming, shading more toward a sunset finish: reds and oranges on one side, and already blue-black on the other. Some special effects. Whoever did the programming on that ceiling was good, Keith thought. It had been cloudy and rainy all day outside, and it was already long past dark up there, but here he was watching the sun go down in a perfectly clear sky. He envied the elves for being able to delay sunset as long as they wanted. They sure knew how to live. The little children were being called in by their parents. "Look, I'd better go," Keith insisted. "I've got some homework to finish tonight.''

"Mm-hmm. Late for us, too. You're welcome here. I'll ask you to guest again some time. You've not met my family, yet.''

"Yeah, I'd love to. Thanks for asking me! When would you

like to come to dinner in the dorm? The food's not much to brag about, but there's lots of it.''

A broad smile lit Holl's face. "I'll come with joy anytime you like, if only to see how you explain me away to your friends, Keith Doyle.''

"I'll think of something,'' Keith promised, smiling down at him.

"That's what I'm looking forward to.''

▪ Chapter 10 ▪

When Keith left the library complex, he ran all the way back to the dormitory and seized the phone. Pat was out, probably at play rehearsal. Keith felt that if he didn't share his experience with someone, he would explode. He dialled Marcy's number and counted the rings impatiently until she answered.

"Hello?" She sounded irritated, probably interrupted in the middle of a good television program, or sleep, or something. Keith realized at that moment he had no idea what time it was.

"Hi,'' he sang, his voice sounding heady even in his own ears. "It's Keith. I just had dinner with *them*. You know. Them.''

"What?'' Marcy demanded, sleepily. "Which them?''

"They, them. Holl and Tay and Maura and . . . I was right there, where they live. I *saw*. I just had to tell someone. You. I wanted to tell you. And, Marcy? Thanks for getting me in there. You don't know what it means to me. Well,'' all his breath came out in a rush on that one syllable, and he forced his tone to assume false casualness, "see you in class.'' He hung up the phone.

"Wait!'' came a shriek out of the receiver. "Keith—?''

Keith threw himself around the room for the next few hours, unable to settle anywhere in his excitement. He waggled a finger chidingly at the *Field Guide* and the other books on legendary creatures stacked every which way on his shelves, feeling pleased with himself that he now knew something none of them did. "I've got your numbers, guys." Real elves were more interesting than any of the pipe dreams and fictional illusions he'd ever read about. And how did those lights in the ceiling work? There were no wires or even *fixtures* . . . More unexplained data, and he had to know.

The ringing of the telephone disturbed him, so he took the receiver off the hook and threw the whole instrument under the bed.

The arrangement he had seen in the library basement amazed him. To do as the elves had done, to have created a viable living environment inside a dark concrete box without letting anyone ever see them, or know what they were doing, and to continue to exist—even prosper, to a certain extent—surpassed all means or vocabulary Keith had for expressing admiration. They were survivors. They ate, slept, cooked, made clothes and houses and tools, played, and raised children, all in a space the college had forgotten, and would have dismissed as unimportant and unusable if reminded of it. What were discards to his spoiled generation became raw materials in the hands of those concealed craftsmen. Look at what they did with scrap lumber and used curtains . . .

It troubled him that all their skills couldn't disguise the poverty of their situation. True, they could create beauty and function out of garbage, but it was still garbage. Now that he thought about it, there probably wasn't a whole two-by-four in the whole village. Then, too, there was the clothing. It was all of an old-fashioned, loose, comfortable cut, intended to wear for a long time. None of it was way out of the ordinary, but it remained far from fashionable. Just about every garment sported a patch, sometimes more than one. Keith thought guiltily of jeans he owned that had patches embroidered on them just for show. He would help supply his new friends with donations of fresh raw materials, anything they needed. He was good at finding things. What those elf seamstresses could do with pretty new fabrics—! It would take all his ingenuity to come up with a way to get what they needed; he certainly didn't have an unlimited money supply. Keith scowled impatiently out his window at the night, wishing it wasn't too late an hour to start on his resolution. Textiles, food, lumber, kitchen utensils, tools . . .

The list was beginning to form in his head when it occurred to him that he wasn't alone in his eagerness to help out the Little Folk. Lee Eisley was already doing it, though he had never let on when Keith grilled him about their classmates. He would have to find Lee and talk to him, and find out what needed doing most.

"Very vell," the Master said, leaning over the head of the table. "I declare that the Council of Elders is open, and all who need to speak vill be heard." He sat down and looked around, waiting for someone to speak.

The old folk around the table glanced at one another, but no one opened his mouth. With a rueful shake of her head, Catra got to her feet. "I would speak, Master."

"Gut. Vhat haf you to say?"

"You must already know, for I have not made a secret of my discovery." She turned to the others, holding up a small, neatly trimmed piece of newsprint in the lantern light. "As archivist, it is my duty. I found a story in one of the weekly newspapers that leads me to believe we are in grave danger of discovery." The room erupted into a hubbub of worried exclamations. "Now, wait. It doesn't go so far as to mention any of us by name. All it says is that folk answering our general description have been seen frequenting the streets of the Midwestern campus and town."

"Frequenting!" Curran exploded. "There's a bare few who go 'round and about, and no' often. Do we keep them from gaeng out, then?"

"No. Ve cannot keep them from their tasks. Ve need to haf them done."

"Huh!" Dierdre, Catra's clan leader, seated to her right, was glancing at the slip of paper. " '. . . As if Santa was setting up shop right here in the Midwest.' 'Tis an insult!"

"Stereotypes," Ligan agreed. "Too few stories for to choose from here." He was the eldest of the Master's clan, though it was the Master who spoke for the whole of the village.

"But who can have written this? Why now?"

"Is there no one new in the village class, now?" Ligan wanted to know.

"Just the vun, Keith Doyle," said the Master.

"You met him the other day at dinner," Catra reminded them, venturing a cautious opinion. "I don't think it could be he."

"And why not?" Curran demanded.

Catra shrugged her shoulders. "He doesn't seem the type."

"Ve must be more careful," the Elf Master said, peering at them all over the tops of his gold glasses. "Only at night shall the scavengers go forth, and hats worn. Approach no new Big Folk. If this is a security leak, ve shall stop it here and now." The others sadly nodded their approval. "Now, is there any more business to bring to our attention?" None of the others raised a hand or stood up. The Master rose heavily to his feet. "Then the Council is closed."

• Chapter 11 •

"Lee Eisley?" Keith inquired into a cloud of hot steam billowing out of the maw of an industrial dishwasher. A burly man dressed in a greasy white uniform levered his torso upright from the conveyor belt he was trying to fix, and peered at Keith.

"Nope," he boomed. "Back there." He gestured over one shoulder with a rubber-gloved hand, and went back to banging on the control box with a wrench. "Dammit."

Keith scurried past as the dishwasher belched out another blinding burst of steam. He shuffled by a column of white-enameled stoves and stainless steel work tables, where a dozen or so white-clad workers were making up huge batches of soups and salads. There was an incredible racket in the kitchens, the clanking and hissing from the dishwashers harmonizing with the growling mixing machines that were churning vast quantities of sweet-smelling dough. The yeast floating in the air made Keith sneeze on his way past.

He found Lee, also dressed in white, beyond the next row of machines, loading fifty-pound sacks of flour and rice from a pallet into storage cabinets. He waited until Lee's hands were empty before attempting to attract his attention.

"Um, Lee?"

The older student started, obviously surprised to be addressed. He peered at Keith without recognizing him.

"It's me, Keith. From the class?"

"Yeah, hi." Grunting, Lee hoisted another sack to his shoulders and staggered it across the room. "What can I do for you?"

"If you have a minute, I want to ask you a couple of questions."

"Sure. Shoot."

"Um," Keith looked around. "It's about our mutual classmates."

"What?" The sack landed on its mates with a thud, and Lee spun, looking around for eavesdroppers, and seized a handful of Keith's shirt. "You crazy, asking me about that *here*? Get out, you jerk."

"They told me you've been, well, helping out." Keith went on, wondering if he was wise to have confronted Lee here.

"You heard wrong," Lee said, a little louder than necessary.

"Come on. I want to help, too." Keith said persuasively. Lee's expression told him nothing. "I know you're helping. They told me. I'm sure there's things I can do, too. I've got some ideas. But there's stuff I need to know."

"I told you before. I don't know anything."

"But that was before . . . before I knew you were taking supplies to them from Food Service stocks . . ." Keith lowered his voice to a confidential whisper.

Lee clamped a hand roughly over Keith's nose and mouth. "Shut up," he hissed. "All right, I have. So what? I still don't know anything."

"How long have you been doing . . . that?" Keith asked, more tactfully. His nose hurt. He rubbed it ruefully.

Lee went back for another sack. "I started doing it as a favor. I'm a grad student in Journalism. I did my undergrad J-school work here, too. Five years. I took over when old

Ludmilla asked me to help out her 'little ones.' Hell, I thought she meant feeding her cats.'' He scowled at Keith as if he resented his good deeds being found out.

Keith took a deep breath. "Who's Ludmilla?"

"She was a university cleaning lady. She retired four years ago. She still lives in town. If anyone knows about . . . them, she does.''

"Do you know her address?" Keith held out a notebook and pen. Lee snatched them, and scribbled a few lines.

"There. Now beat it.''

"Don't worry. I'm gone. Just your basic good samaritan, doing my annual good deed. No point in intruding on other good deeds.'' Keith looked meaningfully at the food storage units. Lee seized a fifty-pound sack of rice threateningly, and Keith scurried away.

▪ Chapter 12 ▪

Along one side of the campus ran rows of collapsible brown-stone six-flats that were used mostly by students who preferred, and could afford, apartments to dorm rooms. The other tenants consisted of older people, couples just getting started, and people who worked at the university. The rent was cheap, so most didn't complain about the condition of the buildings. The address he was looking for turned out to be only two doors down from Marcy's place.

The crumbling concrete and brickwork were original issue, and in the dimly lit, redolent plaster hallways, Keith was sure he could trace some inscriptions hitherto found only in caves in prehistoric France. Heavy, varnished wooden doors hung at angles in their frames, allowing triangular spears of light to shoot out from under them onto the worn runners. He could hear television soap operas blaring, muffled behind the thick walls, and distant footsteps, followed by doors slamming. Two giggling children, a sister and brother both aged five or so, heels slipping, dashed down the flight above just as Keith rounded the landing. He moved himself out of their way against the bannisters. "Hey, watch it," he complained.

"Sorry," the little girl called back, and broke into playful shrieks as her brother caught up and started tickling her. "Stop that! I'm telling! *Momma*!" Keith shook his head, grinning, and kept climbing.

On the fourth landing, Keith found the faded card that read "Hempert." He knocked.

A slender old woman with yellow-white hair opened the door. "Yes? How may I help you?"

Keith cleared his throat nervously. He was face-to-face with Ludmilla Hempert. Now how did he begin explaining what he wanted? "My name's Keith Doyle. I'm a . . . friend of friends of yours, Miss Hempert."

"Mrs. Hempert, but mein husband is these many years dead," Ludmilla told him, looking up at him with startlingly kind, flower blue eyes. She wasn't much taller than the Elf Master, and she had the same kind of summing, patient expression. "Vhich friends?"

"Your . . . the little ones."

"Ach!" She caught her breath, and gestured him to cross the threshold. With a cautious look over his shoulder, she shut the door. "Dey sent you?" she asked in a low tone. "Is someting der matter?"

"No," Keith hastened to reassure the old lady. She was already reaching for the limp wool coat hanging from the hook behind the door. "Really. Nothing's wrong. Truthfully, they don't even know I'm here. They're kind of . . . protective of you."

Ludmilla smiled, her cheeks lifting, and all the tired wrinkles disappeared from her face, making her look many years younger than the seventy or so she must have been. Her hand fluttered down to her side, straightened her dress. "My kinder, like them they are. Zit down, please. Tea?" She darted ahead of him, hastening to dust off the top of a spotlessly clean, flowered sofa cushion.

"Um, sure. Thanks." Keith sank onto the couch, and found it so soft he was all but swallowed up in its embrace. Ludmilla rushed out of the room, and Keith could hear clinks and rattles coming from the kitchen. She returned in a moment, pushing a narrow, brass-bound tea wagon, on which was set a steaming pot, two cups and saucers, and a plate of sliced sponge cake. Keith sniffed appreciatively, and accepted tea and a generous serving of cake.

"You know," said Ludmilla, sitting down opposite Keith in a deep upholstered armchair, "it is just today I am thinking of my little vuns. It is forty-two years since first I met them."

"What?" Keith exclaimed, interrupting her unintentionally. "*How* long have they been here?"

"I am tellink you, young man." Cutting him another section of cake, the old woman began her story.

In the years during and after the Second World War, Mrs. Hempert had worked the night shift cleaning the University buildings. She and her husband were raising a family of three children, taking opposite shifts so both of them could hold jobs. The post-war shortages made food and clothing more expensive for five people than one income could cover, so the Hemperts divided the duty. One parent remained home in the daytime, and the other at night.

The Midwestern University neighborhood was a pleasant place to live. The old woman smiled as she described the big apartment building as it had once been, a community with every door open, and the corridors full of the smell of cooking and laughing children.

The night shift, considered less desirable than day work, paid a higher scale, which was felt by some to be hazard pay. The buildings were connected together by a series of dark, underground steam tunnels. At first, Ludmilla was afraid to walk through them, for the light switches were far inside the echoing metal corridors, and the lights themselves were spotted irregularly throughout their lengths nearest to the manholes and maintenance hatchways, leaving huge pools of darkness spread across the floors and walls. She learned to identify each tunnel and section by the number of lights. The longest lay between the Science building and the library, containing just fourteen lights. The next longest was between the Liberal Arts building and the Student Common, where most of the night shift employees ate their midnight meals.

It was forbidden by the Administration for anyone to use the tunnels without authorization. At one time, they were intended to be Civil Defense shelters, but the CD decided that the pipes packed along the ceiling in asbestos fibers would probably fall down in the event of an aerial attack, so the tunnel walls were never finished beyond sealing the concrete, and the system was ordered off limits except for the maintenance and cleaning crews.

Because the steam system generated a great deal of dust in the conduits, Ludmilla needed to clean them at least once or twice a week. The thrumming of the ventilation system sent a thrill of terror along her skin. She fancied that it sounded like the beating of a giant heart, trapped in the darkness. She kept to the middle as she scurried from building to building, keeping to the middle of the skirts of light, and staying in the dark as little as possible. All the other cleaners followed the same custom, so she left her equipment, such as mop and pail, and her lunch in the shadows, to keep the others from tripping over them. Her allotted meal time was only half an hour, too short to go home and eat, so she was careful to bring a lunch every night, or go hungry until dawn. She worked alone most of the time, but sang or hummed to herself to keep from feeling lonely.

There was always scuttling sounds in the depths of the old buildings. Insects and rats scratched in the darkness, which disturbed her. There were never enough traps or insecticide to go around the large campus. Ludmilla had always hated rats, and grew deft at killing them with the end of her broomstick.

One night, she heard a scratching sound coming from a part of the tunnel, and like a spear, she hurried back along the passageway, ignoring the looming darkness on either side. Those rats! They wouldn't get her food if she could help it. It was a wonder she didn't break any of the hanging light bulbs.

There was a small hulking shape crawling among her things. She swooped in on it, striking it away from her bag with a triumphant cry. It slid across the rough floor, tumbling against the wall. If it was a rat, it was the largest she had ever seen. The figure had to be over two feet long. But it didn't behave like a rat. As she raised the stick to crush its head, it flung up its two front paws.

"No!" it cried out.

Ludmilla stopped, shocked. "It speaks? What are you?"

She put the stick down, and the small figure sprang away, turning to run, but her reactions were quicker. She put out a hand and dragged the little figure to her. "Now we will see what you are."

Taking it into the light, she discovered that her prize was a black-haired child, clad in a shirt and trousers. The clothing was ordinary, but the child, the child was amazing. His cheekbones were sharp and wide, making his face look like that of a little wild animal, and its ears were pointed, like a cat's laid back. It weighed almost nothing in her arms. The only force she felt was its struggle to free itself from her grasp. Ludmilla was instantly reminded of the little house spirits, legendary in her home country, who would do good deeds or bad, as it suited them. What else but magic could account for this child's appearance?

But it was still a child, however strangely it might appear. It cried out its distress in a language Ludmilla didn't understand. Its face was dirty, and under the loose shirt, its ribs were thin. With a wrench, she thought of her own children. This poor little thing was probably hungry.

"Easy, now, little one," Ludmilla crooned to it, moving gently to where her lunch basket lay. "I vould not harm thee for all the world. Lie easy. This is what you sought. You shall have it."

Carefully, she lowered the little creature to the ground. It regarded her with suspicion, staring meaningfully at the broom. Opening her hand, she let the broom lean against the wall, and stooped to her basket. The child had already opened it, but she had caught it before it had taken any of the contents. With a sorrowful glance at the child's thinness, she laid out in a line the items she had brought for her lunch: apples, sandwiches, a pint bottle of milk, and a wrapped slice of cake, baked by Ludmilla herself with proud skill from her mother's recipes. She smiled gently at the trembling mite, to show it that she meant no harm, but it stood where she had left it, and trembled.

"Small wonder you are frightened. I vould be, too, if I had been plucked up like a rabbit by a hawk."

It said nothing, but it let out a sudden gasp, pointing open-mouthed over her shoulder. She sprang up, spinning around to see what had alarmed the child. Had one of the large male janitors appeared in the corridor behind her? Nothing was there. She turned back, just in time to see the child dashing away, with all of her food in its arms, and laughing heartily.

"You have all your wits about you!" she called after it. "An old trick, and I fell for it!"

In seconds, the child had disappeared into the darkness. Ludmilla went on with her work, feeling blessed for having seen it, and even more for having done it a kindness, because it was good fortune to do favors for the magical kind.

When she returned home that morning, she told her husband that she had seen one of the Little People in the school buildings.

"What?" he laughed, disbelievingly, pouring himself coffee. "You work alone in the darkness, so you make up little friends for yourself to talk to? Fairy tales, that is all."

"I know what I saw," Ludmilla insisted stubbornly, putting away her cleaning supplies and sitting down avidly to her own breakfast. Her exhilaration didn't change the fact that she had worked a long, hard night without any food.

"Don't be silly. The New Learning in the University would keep away any of the old superstitions."

"But what if it is not a superstition, but reality?" she demanded.

Her husband regarded her with fond amusement. "If the Old Ones are real, then the New Learning would teach about them, too. It does not, therefore *they* are not."

Ludmilla sighed. He had closed his mind to the possibility. She thought of bringing him to see the child, but decided against trying. If he was afraid to believe in the good folk tales, it was because then there was as great a chance for the evil ones to be true as well. It would only upset him more to find out she was right. She never mentioned the subject again, to him or their children.

The next time she went down to clean the tunnel between the Science building and the library, she could see a glint of light far down the passageway. Hoisting her bucket, she hurried down to see what lay there. It was her milk bottle catching the light. It was sitting on top of the folded napkin in which her sandwiches had been wrapped. Both were perfectly clean; the bottle gleamed as if it had been polished. Ludmilla smiled.

"This is how you say 'Danke', eh?" she called into the purring echoes. Gratified, she left behind a quart of milk, more apples, and a loaf of homemade egg bread flecked with bacon, from an old family recipe she had brought from her village. It had occurred to her that the child must have parents. If she herself would starve to let her sons and daughters eat, in what pitiful state must this thin one's parents be? This food would be sustaining.

She stretched out her cleaning tasks as long as she dared, waiting to see if the child would appear again. At last she left for another part of the campus, after placing the food carefully under a hanging light. There was no sound or movement.

The next day, the bottle and cloths were sitting in the light near the entrance to the tunnel. After that, she brought them food every day. It niggled at her conscience that she might be taking food out of her own children's mouths for people she had never seen, but her mother had always said that hands were made open so they could give. Fruit was cheap, and meat and produce could be had from her sister's husband, who had a farm not far away. If she was thrifty before, she became even more so, supporting those three desperate little ones hidden in the steam tunnels.

She knew she wasn't their sole source of food. Her fellow workers complained that the rats were getting into their lunches. Her little ones must also have been responsible for the occasional disappearance of supplies from the dormitory kitchens. No one else mentioned seeing a strange child, for which Ludmilla was grateful.

She fell into the habit of saving the library passageway for last. It had been so long since she had seen the little child that she was half beginning to believe her husband, who felt she had imagined it. She wanted to see them, to prove to herself that it had happened. This time, when she spread out her offerings of milk, bread, and fruit, she sat down beside the food and waited.

After a time, the smell of good bread must have attracted the little folk, for Ludmilla could hear low conversation not far away in the dark. They were surprised to see her, and were evidently discussing whether or not to reveal themselves to their benefactress.

"Come out," she called, her heart in her throat. "I will not harm you." She held out her empty hands so they could see. "I have no weapons. Even my broom is over there."

There was more hasty conversation. Ludmilla strained, but she couldn't decide how many voices she could hear. At last, there was movement in the shadows. Her elf-child stood forward, and behind him came two more, a man and a woman, perhaps a foot taller than the child. Her hair was the same shiny black as the boy's, but the man's was orange-red. Their clothes were much mended, and they looked thinner than Ludmilla felt was healthy for any living creatures. She comforted herself by gazing at the boy. He was less thin than before, and for a wonder, he was clean. His shirt was neat, and his face had been washed. Ludmilla smiled.

"You knew even before I, that I would wait for you this night, did you not?" she asked. His expression didn't have the hunted fear of their first meeting, nor the hard defiance. He reminded her more than anything else of her younger son. He had a formidable will, into which, with care, he would grow one day. She felt sympathy with the parents. There was more here to deal with than making their child stay presentable.

The parents commanded her attention next. Their well-worn rags reminded her of refugees, who suffered because of war not of their making. But from where had they come? Why were they hiding here?

"How do you do?" Ludmilla asked slowly. At first, they didn't seem to comprehend her speech. She tried English and German, but there was still no response. Uncomfortably, she began to talk. She talked about her husband and her children, about her childhood, and how she came to America. They listened closely when she described how she met her husband and when they got married. And how, when she was young, she heard stories in her home village of people like themselves, the Wise Old Ones, the craftwise, who did good or evil as it pleased them. When she finished one of the tales, the little man spoke for the first time.

"Are there of them any left?" he asked, with hope.

"I do not know," she admitted. "I never did see them myself."

She could see that he was disappointed. He didn't pursue

the subject. Instead, he asked her sternly, "Why do you offer charity to us?"

Ludmilla wanted to smile, but knew that he would be hurt. He was so proud. She was keeping his existence and that of his family a secret, and still he was challenging her as an equal. Instead, she drew her head up as if offended.

"It is not charity to give gifts to new neighbors. I am a good neighbor."

For the first time, the little man laughed. It made his face brighten, and she could see a glint of humor in his blue eyes. "Even so," he said, smiling. "But it must not be unreturned."

The first thing they presented her was a plate upon which she could set her newly baked goods to protect them from growing mouldy or stale. Even uncovered, a loaf of bread remained fresh and soft. When she protested that a gift of such magical virtue was too great a gift for a little milk and meat, they only smiled.

They told her how they had come to central Illinois, and how they found this place of shelter, which was warm and sheltered from the winds, and yet not filled to brimming with big people. They felt that here they could be safe. It had been many years since they crossed the ocean, but never told her how, or where they came from. They knew nothing of the World War, or anything of the news of the day. It seemed they had isolated themselves well from the influence of their bigger neighbors.

Midwestern University was at its lowest enrollment and had the fewest professors in the school's history. Anyone who could had gone to fight in the War. As a result, there was little attention paid to goings-on in the half-empty buildings. Ludmilla promised to help them establish a home there, and the little man and his family took her to meet the others.

"Others?" she asked, but heard no answer. The little man beckoned her after him.

It had been easy to go from believing in a single needy child to encompassing its family. It was quite another thing to go from a single small family to a crowd of thirty or more of the poor beings. They were huddled together in one of the abandoned basements of the library, fearful of discovery. They had travelled together under the cover of night, facing dangers, avoiding cities, and eating crops from the fields. They resembled a host of refugees from the European horror, as she had seen in the newsreels, and her heart went out to them.

"But where did you come from?" she asked the small crowd. Either they didn't understand her or didn't want to tell. In any case, she never found out. But they became good friends to her, and she helped them to make a home in a safe, secure, warm building which no one else seemed to need.

"And so, it was my insistence that they close off the lowest level of the library in which to live. This place was here, in the heart of the generous farmlands, and it seemed made for them, so they intended to stay. The ceiling was too low for any classes to be held there. I think perhaps it was built by the government to use as a secret office, but it was too old; the government felt a closed door was enough, then. Tens of years had it been neglected. All that remained there were boxes of rotted wood, containing old books and other school property. The janitors were all old men, and they forgot that the place was there. Here I suspect magic, for one of these was Franklin Mackay, and Mr. Mackay had never forgotten one thing in his long life. I believe that after a time only I and my little ones knew there had ever been a lowest floor." Mrs. Hempert placed her tea-cup into the saucer with a resolute click.

"I sure didn't," Keith admitted. "How did Lee get involved?"

"The same way you have. A kind heart and a willingness to help. Since I retired, he has done all that which I used to do. He orders extra goods. No one notices the missing supplies, ever, for there is always so much wasted. But he was never closer to them than he is now. He trades food for education. They were eager to exchange what they had in plenty— knowledge—for that which they needed. I helped to work that out. Their pride I could circle around, once I knew that. Lee vas doing poorly, now he does very vell. But he vill soon graduate; then he vill be gone. You vill take his place. I am glad you are here."

"Me, too," Keith said, thinking deeply. "Tell me, where does their light come from? I mean, on the ceiling?"

Mrs. Hempert was amused. "I do not know. If I say magic, and you believe me, you do not know more than if I said nothing at all. Now tell me, how did you find your way into their home? I know it is well hidden. I watched as it disappeared."

"Well, there was a girl . . ."

The old woman smiled. "One whom you like a great deal?"

"Yes, as a matter of fact. She has another guy who is interested in her . . . except that might not last too much longer. He's bullying her and she doesn't like it."

"A bully," she repeated thoughtfully. "No, that is not right. But I tell you I am glad you have found my little ones, and that you are friends."

"Why are you telling me all this, Mrs. Hempert?" Keith asked earnestly. "I'm really grateful to you, but . . . I'm a stranger. I could be a fraud, or a reporter who just happened to hear something. Why are you trusting me?"

"Are you not trusting me?" she asked, a twinkle lighting the blue of her eyes into sapphire. "If I went to a reporter and told him, I have seen elfs, he vould tell me I am a crazy old voman, yes? And I trust you. At my age I have learned something about character. You are honest. I can tell. I can tell."

"Just one thing: what are they doing here?"

"Just living, like you, or like me."

Keith nodded, and got up to go. "Thanks for talking to me. Um, may I come back again?"

"Of course." She smiled, also rising. "And bring your young lady, too. Ve are in one another's confidence now. What vill you do now mit your new knowledge?"

"I'm not sure. Help out if I can. I won't tell anyone else." Keith stuck out a hand. Ludmilla put her right hand into his, and enfolded both of theirs with her other hand. She had a strong, warm clasp, and he realized that she had plenty of residual strength from years at her job. However fragile she may look, she was not feeble. "I'll tell 'em you said 'hi.' Hmm," he scowled, as he remembered Holl's warning. "Maybe I won't."

"If you can, you vill. Good-bye, Keith."

Catra continued paging through the weekly Midwestern gazette. Nothing new had caught her eye since the first article, even though she had been especially vigilant. She was relieved. However time-consuming her task was, it was easier to bear than the fear of discovery once their presence was suspected in the basement of this big building. Then, as she was passing up the advertisement pages for used cars, she found a two-inch column with the headline, "Circus Midget Colony?", that went on to describe "miniature adults in a midwestern Illinois town."

This article was still reasonably vague. Probably it was just an echo of the one from the time before; these little journals read one another's copy; it was clear from week to week where the sources were found. It had no detail, only rumor, but it would still worry the elders. With a deep sigh she marked it with a sharp fingernail and put the newspaper back into its folder. Later on, she could make a Xerox of it, when the librarians had gone home for the night.

▪ Chapter 13 ▪

Keith leaned conspiratorially over the Secretary's desk at the office of the School of Nursing. "Hiya, Louise, baby," he purred, twitching one eyebrow, à la Humphrey Bogart. "We're goin' over the wall tonight. I need your help."

"What do you want?" Louise Fowler demanded, pushing Keith's hands off a pile of carbon paper. "Keep your paws off my desk. I'm going to search your pockets before you leave."

Keith bounced off, and dashed around the desk to kneel beside her. She deliberately cultivated a starched-stiff attitude in her duties as administrative assistant to the Nursing School, but Keith had a way of disarming her, and to her it usually meant trouble. He took her hand in his and said mournfully, "Such a lack of trust."

Louise pulled her hand back. "I don't have time for this. Do you want something?"

"Of course!"

"Well, what?"

"For a start, sheets. Gotta have something to tear up for rope ladders," he said, going over a list he had rehearsed in his head.

"Why? Haven't you ever heard of doors?"

"Whose jailbreak is this, anyway?" he insisted. "Maybe I'll use the surplus for my Halloween costume."

"A ghost, right?"

Keith shook his head in mock dismay. "You're too quick for me, baby. I'll have to take you with me. Wanna be a moll?"

"Nope."

"Look, I'm serious. What happens to the medical center's old sheets and pillowcases when they get worn out?"

"Well, they go to the school, for nurses' training."

"And they come in like that whenever the Med Center gets new ones? Have they had any recent replacements?" Louise nodded. "Can I have some of them?"

"No!"

"Oh, come on. Please. It's to make some kids happy."

Louise stared at him suspiciously. "Are you serious?"

"Honest. May I never go to Mars if I'm not. It's a . . . Junior Achievement group," Keith announced, after a moment's pause.

"Okay," she sighed. "Come back this afternoon, and I'll see what I can find."

"May Allah bless you and all your children. And all the ones you don't know about, too." He departed, kissing his fingertips and bowing low to her as he backed out the door. Louise groaned and drew out her inventory card file.

"Sure, I have fabric left over from earlier semesters," Mrs. Bondini said, accepting the can of cola from Keith. She slid the plate containing her tuna melt and french fries off the tray. Keith set down his fries and a pair of turkey sandwiches, and put the plastic tray out of the way on an adjoining table. He had headed Mrs. Bondini off from the entrance to the faculty lunchroom, pleading the need for a personal audience. Amused, she had accepted his invitation to eat with him in the University Deli. Evidently, she had memories of the course she had taught in three-dimensional sculpture in which he'd enrolled a couple of semesters back. "Why?"

"It's this Junior Achievement group I'm working with," Keith said, popping open his own can, and unwrapping a sandwich. "As I'm not too familiar with this kind of project, I thought I'd come to someone who is."

"And 'this kind of project' is . . . ?"

"Um . . . Cabbage Patch Kids' clothes. It'll be a big hit. They've something really different in mind. Costumes. Ethnic dress from other nations. That sort of thing." Keith smiled politely at her. After all, he was *almost* telling the truth.

"Well, aren't they supposed to sell shares and get their operating capital that way?"

"Well, first they need money to print the shares with. And I remembered you also taught the costuming course, so . . ."

". . . So you figured I might be a soft touch," Mrs. Bondini finished cynically. "Remembering, of course, that the college owns those bolts of fabric."

"Mm-hmm," Keith agreed, innocently, tucking a quarter sandwich into his mouth. He tried to talk around it, struggling to swallow quickly. "And the thing is, I'm sure there's some, well . . . undesirable prints, or something, hanging around, that you might be willing to throw to me instead of to the dumpster."

"Maybe." Mrs. Bondini rolled up the cellophane from her lunch and dusted her hands together. "Well, come with me, and we'll see what I might have for your future tycoons."

With an innocent smile, Keith followed her.

He had one more stop to make. In the History Department, he spent a little time going through the local archives. Everyone was away from their desks at lunch except a student aide, so he was able to root through the drawers undisturbed. Satisfied with his findings, he used the phone in one of the empty offices to put through a couple of calls, all the time looking around nervously to make sure no one was overhearing him.

Keith was in such a good mood that he didn't even flinch when Dr. Freleng handed out a new research assignment that threatened to cut into his dwindling free time. When the other students in the class moaned, groaned, and griped about the heavy assignment, he smiled vaguely and maddeningly. Even to Marcy, who knew, or thought she knew, the reason for

Keith's behavior, he seemed oblivious to reality. He had never failed to complain about such a time-consuming project before.

"What is wrong with you?" she hissed in his ear as they left the classroom.

"Wait and see, my pet," he smirked.

That evening, he was late making his way to the class. The bags he carried were obviously heavy, and full of slippery bulks that showed a tendency to slump to one side. The librarian on duty at the entrance to the stacks was not convinced when he told her that his two huge plastic-wrapped bales contained drop sheets for the painters that were coming in the morning.

"You can not bring those things in here! Absolutely not!" she insisted so vigorously that her glasses slid off her nose. They dropped to the end of their tether, and bumped against her chest on every stressed syllable, especially the *nots*.

Keith sighed, trying to look patient and martyred, wishing he could carry the bundles in through the elves' back door, though it would spoil the surprise. "I told you, Mrs. Hansen wants these on Level Ten. They won't be in anyone's way. I'll just put 'em where she told me to."

The librarian seemed taken aback by his evocation of a higher authority than herself. "Well, we'll see. I'll go ask Mrs. Hansen myself!"

Keith waited until she was out of sight, and then rushed himself and his two bundles into the stairwell.

It was far less harrowing, but no less clumsy, an entrance than his first one into the hidden classroom. Both bags wouldn't fit through the doorway at the same time, so he had to hold one in his arms and propel the other before him with a foot. The session had already begun. With a newly developed awareness of what to listen for, he could hear voices long before he ever got into the room. Carl Mueller was on his feet, red-faced, with one hand in the air. Keith had most likely interrupted him in the middle of another spate of deathless prose. He kicked the two bags into a corner and sat down. They sloshed against each other, and subsided.

Holl glanced over his shoulder, and looked curiously at Keith, who gestured for him to wait. The Elf Master favored him with the same expression, but Keith sat up attentively, hands folded, and displayed ingenuous interest in class proceedings. The Master was not distracted. He turned away from Carl and came to lean over Keith.

"Vhat haf ve here, Meester Doyle?" he inquired, eyebrows raised.

"Um, nothing much," Keith answered, shrinking back in spite of himself.

"If it is nothing, then why is it so large?"

"Well, I *brought* them . . ."

"Obviously."

". . . to see if you wanted them," Keith finished, his mouth dry. Suddenly his attack of generosity didn't seem like the good idea it had been the night before.

The thick red eyebrows climbed nearly all the way into the hairline.

"Vhich 'you' do you mean?"

Keith swallowed. This was not going at all the way he had wanted it to. He had hoped to bring the matter of the parcels up quietly at the end of class, when he could fade away without making a big fuss. And why was the old guy being so touchy? "Well, you all," he gestured, indicating the elves, then flipping the hand and shrugging uncomfortably, his carefully prepared speech deserting his memory. He had been positive the Master would be pleased. "Just some things I picked up here and there. Thought you could use."

He knew he was saying all the wrong things. After listening to Ludmilla explain to him how touchy they were about accepting favors, he had just spat out every buzzword in the lexicon. The other students remained silent. The young elves were expressionless, but the humans looked positively irate. Lee had a bloodthirsty light in his eye that made Keith very nervous. He smiled hopefully at everyone. Whatever he had interrupted, it was a dilly. The others just watched him uncomfortably. Seeking to diffuse the tension, Holl got out of his seat, clearing his throat loudly, and dragged the bags into the center of the room. The young elves were around him in a moment, leaving the Elf Master pinning Keith to the back of his chair with a needle-sharp gaze of disapproval. There were exclamations of interest and approval from the Little Ones as they opened the bags. Holl made a great show of presenting the contents to the others.

"Look how useful these'd be," Holl said, championing Keith. He held up a white hospital sheet and tested its strength. "Still in the best condition. The Big Ones are always tossing out things with life left in them."

"That's a truth," said Catra, tossing her long, taffy-colored braid out of the way. She rubbed the fabric between her thumb and forefinger. "Ah, percale. Nice fabrics. The one thing I've been wishing for. I'll have that. My mother will be able to do much with a sheet that big."

Her sister, the little blond elf, reached for the sheet's edge, a sour look on her face. Holl reached into the bag, and found it was full of sheets. He put another into her hands. "Candlepat, here's one for you." She beamed, tucking the bundle under one arm.

"Ahh." The others were sorting through the plastic sacks. The sheets were counted and divided up. Candlepat and Catra unfolded bolts of fabric and tried them together for style. Most of them were Christmas materials, red stars on white background, white stars on red, blue and white stripes, green and white, red and green. When they came to the green fabric decorated with small white stars, it looked like the two sisters might come to blows.

"I want that," Candlepat wailed a protest, holding onto the bolt. "You bully me because you're older. It isn't fair."

"It'd look better on me than it would on you. You have fine clothes in plenty because you're the prettiest. And you have a whole counterpane, the newest in the household. I do not. This will do me well. You can go without, for a change."

Marm pushed his way between the two of them. With a reproachful look at each, he unwound the bolt, found the midpoint, and tore it into two equal pieces. Eyeing each other like a pair of angry hens, they accepted their halves from him, and went on pecking through the contents of the sacks. Marm himself nodded pleasantly over a short piece of tweedy brown, and tucked the end into his tunic belt.

The floor was soon strewn with lengths of cloth, most of them loud and gaudy from the humans' point of view, but obviously attractive to their smaller classmates. Laniora was cooing over a length of white-starred blue. Maura had out the lone bolt of blue denim fabric and was holding it up against herself, mentally measuring for an outfit. She skillfully twitched the end out of Catra's hand when she reached for it, and appeared to be entertaining some pleasant thoughts on decoration. Catra looked up only once to see that it wasn't her sister competing for the piece of cloth, and went back to her own browsing. Holl, after exchanging an unspoken communication with Maura, draped the blue cloth over his arm and approached Keith with it.

"What'll you trade for this one, eh?" Holl asked, rescuing him from the Elf Master.

Gratefully, Keith broke eye contact and nervously edged out of his seat. "Ah, I hadn't thought about it, really. It was supposed to be a gi—umm," he paused, responding to his friend's obvious prompt for more diplomacy, and rubbed the corner of the cloth between thumb and forefinger. "What would you like to trade?"

Maura whispered in Holl's ear, and he nodded, fingering the fabric speculatively. Keith watched him with respect. He didn't look too keen or too disinterested: a natural garage-saler. "I'd say it might be worth a small lantern, or a toy, or a carved wooden box this big." He sketched a form in the air about six inches wide. "There's more than a single garment's length here, you see."

"Sounds fair. How about the lantern?" Keith asked quickly. Holl nodded and rerolled the bolt around its flat cardboard core. Maura took it and the two men shook hands. Patting Holl's arm for thanks, she disappeared down the tunnel, waving the bolt happily. Taking their friends' cue, the others spoke up at once with offers for their prizes.

"Look," Keith said, holding his hands palms out to the others. "I'm no good at this sort of thing. You take what you want, and we can figure it out later, okay?"

There was a general chorus of agreement, and the elves simply bundled the bags up and carried them away toward their home. In the echoing passage, Keith could hear the shrill voices of the elfin sisters, arguing about *who* would wear *what*. Holl had a satisfied grin on his round face. Keith felt pretty good himself. Everyone seemed happy. This was more like what he had in mind. The other students' ire seemed to have dissolved.

They had arisen from their seats to watch the bartering, and now came over to praise Keith for his generosity and thoughtfulness. His idea seemed to have gone over well with them all.

Except the Elf Master. He still stood by Keith's desk, radiating disapproval. Keith tried not to look his way. He felt himself cringing away from the stern little man. The other Little Folk were reappearing out of the tunnel and taking their seats. Keith appeared to have broken the ice, and the students, all of them, were chattering to one another, relaxed, the cultural barriers down at last. Marcy distracted him at that moment by grabbing his face between her hands and kissing him right on the mouth.

"You doll!" she said. "So this is what you were being so mysterious about. I've been wanting to do something like that for months."

"Well, why not do it again?" Keith leered, slipping an arm around her waist. He caught a glimpse of Enoch who had a shocked expression on his face. Keith winked at him over Marcy's shoulder, and was rewarded with a cold stare. Oh, well, the little sourpuss never liked him anyway.

"No, not that," Marcy corrected him, playfully but firmly turning her face aside. "You know what I mean."

"Yup," he acknowledged. But he kept his arm around her, and she didn't protest or move away. This was a reward he hadn't expected for his efforts, and he was enjoying it. There was a thundercloud building up over Carl's head, and Keith enjoyed that, too. He was a hero. In everyone's eyes but Carl's, the Elf Master's, and Enoch's, that is. What was eating them?

"What are you going to do with the jeans fabric?" Teri Knox asked Maura shyly. It was probably the first direct question she'd ever asked one of the others.

Maura seemed just as timid. "I don't really know. I would like to make an outfit like the one in green wool you wear."

"Oh, my pantsuit? Well, I could bring it around, and you can copy the pattern." She eyed Maura, estimating her size. "It's too bad they don't make tailored styles that small."

"That's no matter. I'm good at fittings. I can copy almost anything, but there are no books of patterns in all of Gillington. I'd be most grateful." Maura, just as shy, was warming to Teri's friendliness.

"No problem," Teri said. "I'd be happy to. You'd look really good in a blazer, too. You're built just like a Barbie doll. Did I ever wear this outfit down here? I think you'd like it." The two girls bent over a sheet of paper, and began discussing designs.

"Great fellow, this Keith," Marm said, in an aside to Carl, who was sitting at his desk, staring at nothing. "He's a friend."

"He's a phony," Carl growled.

"Not in my books, laddie," the elf retorted, testily. "In my view he's thoughtful, not like some other people who think only of themselves, and scoring off the other man."

"I don't do anything like that," he snapped.

"And you don't do anything else," Marm flung back.

"You think I'm lying?"

"If you say that about Keith Doyle, you must be."

"Marm, bring your voice down," Holl said, glancing over his shoulder at the Elf Master.

"But, Maven, do you hear this fool? Listen to him," Marm said, indignantly.

The Elf Master sat by himself, watching, saying nothing himself. He appeared to be thinking deeply on some subject, one that disturbed him. Everyone else seemed to be pleasantly chatting. It was the most relaxed class meeting the Master had ever witnessed, especially one that had started so badly. But it boded to end ill.

Marm's and Carl's argument was getting louder, and some of the others were joining in, mostly on Marm's side.

"You really must be dumb if you believe that." Carl had a finger levelled, and was jabbing out for punctuation.

Keith was still talking quietly to Marcy, and seemed unaware that there was a battle going on.

"After what I've told you?" Carl continued. "He's not your friend. He's nobody's friend, except his own."

"And why else would he bring us things?" Marm demanded, ignoring Holl's attempts to bring the argument to a close.

"Yes, vhy?" the Elf Master spoke at last, making himself heard over the din, and addressing Keith directly. "For vhat reason do you bring us gifts?"

"Um," Keith was distracted from his private chat with

Marcy, and had to think how best to phrase his answer. "Just because I wanted to. No good reason."

"Eh, I told you," Marm said, triumphantly.

"They're bribes," Carl shouted, pushing his way into the middle of the crowd, and sending a forefinger thudding into the center of Keith's chest. "So when you lose your home you won't blame him. But it'll still be his fault. He's the one behind the movement I told you about. He's trying to get the Administration to tear down the library!"

Keith's mouth dropped open in amazement. So that was what was up. The vindictive creep!

The chatter and noise died away without an echo, and Keith found everyone staring intently at him. "Is that true?" Marcy demanded, a hurt expression in her eyes. "He said that at the beginning of class."

"Well . . ." Keith began, his voice dwindling to a squeak. "Not exactly. The vote hasn't been taken yet."

"*Is* it true that you've been working toward it?"

"It was," he said, uncomfortably. "I did it to annoy Carl. But that's all over. I looked up some facts on the library building today, and I called the Historical Society. They might be able to declare it an historic landmark. If they do, it can't be torn down."

"And if they cannot so declare it?" the Elf Master inquired frostily.

Eyes on the ground, Keith mumbled, "Then I guess it'll be torn down. But I'm sure I can get them to reverse the vote."

"Meester Doyle," the Master said, very slowly and distinctly. "I think you should leaf now." Keith gathered up his books in silence.

"I'm really sorry," Keith said from the doorway. No one looked up, but Holl gave him a little wave from behind his back. Enoch and Carl had identical grim smiles on their faces. Keith sadly pulled the door closed behind him.

"See," crowed Carl, breaking the silence. "He didn't deny it. For the sole purpose of bugging me, he threat—"

Tears were overflowing Marcy's eyes. "Shut up, Carl."

He whirled on her, angrily. "Hey, he's been a pain in the butt as long as I can . . ."

"I said, shut up," Marcy blurted, sniffing. "I don't want to hear it. I don't want to hear anything you have to say. Big hero. We're through. You can leave me alone from now on."

"Marcy!" Carl looked astonished, then angry.

"Didna you hear what the lady said?" Enoch hissed, springing up and glaring into Carl's face. "Leave her alone."

"Back off, shorty," Carl snapped. "I'll say whatever I feel like." His face went red and his hands tightened into fists. The slightly built elf stood up to him.

"Did your mother teach you no manners, Carl Mueller?" Enoch sneered.

Holl watched the three of them absently, his fingers playing with his whittling knife. He was bitterly disappointed in Keith, not because he had admitted to backing an issue that would inadvertently evict them, but he found his methods shy of sense. If I'd been out to even a score with this big stinking fool, Holl thought, I'd've made it more personal. His clan friends had a lot to think about, by the looks on their faces. Poor Marm, getting straight into the middle. He never had more sense than to start a fight without all the facts in hand.

Keith had a good idea, thinking of having the library declared a historical treasure, though the others didn't give him time to explain how it would work. Holl had read about such things in the library books, and in the periodicals, too. At the very least, it would make for all kinds of delay. His people could find a place, given time. They all liked Keith, but now they were confused.

He knew the older ones believed that the Big Ones were dishonest, two-faced. After all, they had history to back up their opinions. A setback like this one could get them all believing that Keith was one of those, but Holl himself understood the boy's impulses, and that made all the difference. The younger ones might share Holl's perspective. He'd have to discuss it with them later.

Holl realized that the only person in the room who had not voiced his views one way or the other about Keith's seeming treason was the Master. He was holding himself aloof from the situation, refusing to pass judgement or make comment, in much the same way he handled village meetings. Holl watched him curiously, wondering what was in his mind. He strongly suspected the old one liked Keith Doyle, but was very protective of the Folks' way of life. Holl drew himself up attentively as the Elf Master raised his arms for attention. He'd say something now.

"Class dismissed," the Master said, at last.

▪ Chapter 14 ▪

When he opened the door of their dorm room, Pat found Keith sitting on his bed with all the lights off. "Now what?" he demanded.

"Did you ever have a case of really classic bad timing?" Keith asked unhappily.

"Yes," Pat answered, turning on the lights. Keith not only sounded miserable, he looked miserable. The black arcs underlining his eyes made him look like a red-haired raccoon. "There was this girl in Kankakee once, well . . . And so, I repeat: now what?"

"I've made a big fool of myself," Keith said. He seemed truly worried. "I meant to do something nice for someone, and it backfired."

Pat pulled Keith's chair around and sat down. "It happens," he responded sympathetically. "What did you do?"

"Some uh, friends of mine may be getting . . . evicted. They literally have no money," Keith said, since it was the exact truth. "And I walked into the middle of it today with a bunch of presents for them, and they threw me out."

"So? You hit 'em in a sensitive place. You're a have and they're have-nots. You ought to pay more attention to all that sociological research you're supposed to be doing. It's not your fault."

"But it is! And I've got to fix it somehow." Keith dropped his head into his hands.

"No way. You're not responsible for their problems. Injured pride's a tough thing to deal with. You can help, but don't try to do it all for them."

"But they have nowhere to go."

"Bullshit. Everyone can find someplace to go. And you'll just have to curb your generous streak for now, my boy. If they want something from you, let 'em ask."

"I wish I could win the Lottery. That'd solve the problem. I could buy a place for them to live. Or," Keith caught a glimpse of Pat's face, utterly exasperated, "lend them the money to buy one."

"That won't help," Pat said seriously. "Remember self-respect? It's tied to self-sufficiency. Charity is given by those above to those below. Let 'em be your equals. Give a guy a fish, and he'll eat today . . ."

"I know . . . teach him to fish, and he'll eat for the rest of his life. You've got a cliché for every occasion, but this time I think you're right. Unfortunately, I don't have any skills to teach them that'll help. Not in time, anyway."

Pat patted him on the top of the head with a fatherly hand and rose from the chair. "Don't worry about it. Maybe they won't be evicted. That'd be the end of the problem."

Keith mumbled through his hands, "I'm not counting on that."

"What choice have you got?" Pat asked, reasonably, picking up the glass carafe from their Mr. Coffee. "Say, have you had dinner yet?"

"No. Not hungry." His stomach felt wrung out with worry.

There was a tap on the door. "I'll get it," Pat said. Keith heard the door open. "It's for you, Doyle. It's some kid."

He looked up. Holl stood on the threshold, in a coat and knit cap, clutching a bag under one arm. "Hi, there, widdy. I've come for dinner, as you asked," he said, cheerfully.

"Sorry. He's not hungry," Pat told the boy.

"Come on in," Keith said. "Welcome. Am I glad to see you."

"It's a long, cold walk from the bus station," Holl said, with a meaningful sideways glance at Pat.

"Sure is," Keith nodded, catching on. "How was your trip?"

"Okay." Holl pulled off his coat and hat. Keith took them from him and hung them up in the closet. When he turned back, Pat was staring with open interest at the elf's ears. Holl stared back, blue eyes innocent.

"Trekkie," Pat announced.

"Yup," Keith agreed.

"Huh?" Holl asked.

" 'Scuse me a minute." Pat walked out of the room brandishing the coffee pot. Holl started to speak, but Keith held up a hand to forestall him until Pat was out of earshot in the washroom across the hall.

"What?" Holl demanded in a hiss.

"Too long to explain now. It's harmless. Look, you're my nephew, okay? And when Pat comes back, just say 'Yeah, I really like Mr. Spock.' "

Pat came back into the dorm room with the sloshing pot of water.

"Yeah, I really like Mr. Spock," Holl said, obediently.

Pat smiled and plugged in the coffee maker. "Aren't you going to introduce your guest?"

Keith sighed, and waved his hands between the two. "Pat Morgan, my roommate, meet my nephew."

"Holland Doyle," Holl said, extending a hand.

"A pleasure," Pat said, taking the hand with a courtly salute. They shook.

"Say, let's eat," Keith said. "I just remembered I'm starved."

Holl walked wide-eyed down the buffet line behind Keith and Pat. "Do you eat like this every day?" he asked Keith in a whisper.

"No," Keith muttered back. "Sometimes it's even worse."

Dozens of Big People were filling trays in the serving room, and hundreds more were sitting out in the vast dining hall beyond the door. Most of them smiled indulgently at the little blond kid in the cap who was sticking so close to Keith Doyle. Possibly they were remembering their own first visits to a college. The sheer number of human beings was sometimes just plain overwhelming. Certainly the boy seemed impressed.

The abundance of food impressed him, too. Not one, but five main dishes, with several steaming pans of vegetables, and a basket of fresh-smelling rolls. Holl sniffed. Not as good as Keva's bread. But everything else wafted enticing aromas his way. It was hard to choose what to take to eat. At least in the clan kitchen the decision was simple. You ate, or you didn't.

Aware that other diners were waiting patiently behind him, Holl pointed to one of the steaming pans at random. A shining white plate appeared, and a heap of small, golden chunks was shovelled onto it. "Potatoes or fries?" asked the white-uniformed woman behind the counter.

"Fries?" Holl said, uncertainly. A scoop of fries joined the entree.

"Peas and carrots?"

"Yes," Holl said automatically, mesmerized by the deftness of the woman's hands.

"No!" Keith exclaimed, overhearing him and turning around. "No. String beans. You want string beans, right?"

Holl shrugged. "Sure." The hand dropped the scoopful back into the cauldron of green and orange, and dipped the spoon into another filled only with green.

"The peas and carrots are left over from the First World War," Keith said out of the corner of his mouth. "At least the beans are fresh."

"Oh," said Holl.

Somehow the plate passed unspilled over the top of the counter, and Holl went on to secure a carton of milk and a piece of cherry pie in a bowl. Balancing the heavy tray uncertainly, he followed the other two through the dim dining hall to a table near the window, and sat down across from Keith.

"These are good," he said, tasting one of the golden chunks. It was a small piece of chicken, covered in batter and deep-fried.

"What's he got there?" Pat asked, peering over his own plate.

Keith was struggling to cut a tough slice of beef with a dull-looking knife. He glanced over. "Chicken McNuggets. At least those aren't regular army issue." The meat slid, pushing his potatoes off the plate. Pat snickered, picking up a forkful of a thin grayish stew with crisp brown noodles and rice.

Holl filed the name and the expression for future use, and attacked his meal. He had started out using a fork, but careful side glances showed him that all of his fellow diners were eating the chicken and fries with their fingers. Nonchalantly, he followed suit. The food was as greasy as it looked, but it tasted good enough. Keith looked up and gave him a wink.

"What's that there?" he asked, indicating Pat's meal.

"Pork chow mein," Pat said.

"Go on," scoffed Holl. None of the library's cookbooks had an illustration for chow mein that looked like that.

"Honest to God," Keith vowed. "That's what they think it is."

"Want a taste?" Pat offered.

"No, thanks," Holl said. "I know when I'm well off."

"Oh, by the way, the ladies sent to tell you that they all think you're very kind." Holl pushed his empty plate aside and leaned forward on his elbows.

"Ladykiller," Pat leered at Keith, who blushed.

"It's not what you think, Pat," he said, with a long-suffering grimace. "What else did they say?"

"Mostly, it degenerated into an argument about whose point of view served the community best. Naturally, I'm of the opinion that mine does. Most of your younger cousins side with me. It's all the aunts and uncles who disagree. And, as a result, I'm temporarily declassified, myself."

Declas—? Out of class? "That's not fair," Keith protested.

"Not fair, but also not permanent. The same is true for you, if you manage to redeem yourself with them."

"This kid is a genius," Pat declared. "I can hardly understand a thing he says."

"Yeah. He's going to college next year," Keith added.

"This one?"

"Not a chance," Keith said. "He'd meet too many weirdos like you."

"Worse yet," Pat told him, "like you." He put his tray aside and stood up. "Enough of haute cuisine. I've got to get to rehearsal. Don't wait up for me, dear."

"Don't worry, sweetie," Keith said, sourly.

"Live long and prosper, kid." Pat waved.

"The same to you," Holl called back.

"You know," Keith mused, when they were back in Keith's dorm room, "it's kind of ridiculous to call you my nephew, when you're twenty years older than I am."

"Not at all, cousin," Holl corrected him, airily. He snatched off his wool hat and threw it on the bed. With both hands, he rumpled up his blond hair into a comfortable bird's nest. "Much better. In our family, it's nothing unusual for a grand-dad to have a forty-year-old nephew. Or a two-year-old great-aunt, for that matter. Keva's grandson, Tay, is in that very position right now, with his aunt Celebes, our baby sister. Who, by the way, is dressed in a natty new gown of red and white, courtesy of you. Many thanks."

"You're welcome, I guess. I didn't think it would cause so much trouble," Keith admitted, remembering the source of his troubles. "All I wanted to do was supply a little raw material where I thought it was needed."

"And it was needed. Don't let the old ones distract you from the truth of that. Tonight there're a lot of blessings being showered on your head. Though the main opinion is that in your case, the heart is greater than the head is."

"I know," Keith groaned. "I'm working on my new strategy to swing the Student Senate's vote the other way again. I hope they'll go for it. Everyone wanted a new Sports Center before Pat, Rick, and I started our campaign."

"I surely won't bring *that* news home," the elf said, shaking his head with wry amusement. "If they thought you were a widdy before . . ."

"But if I *can't* fix it, what will you do?"

"What we can." Holl's shoulders sagged. "We don't know, and that's the truth of it. There was a fine free-for-all in the village after class broke up, with nearly everyone crying for your head on a pike. I tried to explain to them that you made your mistakes before you knew about us, but I didn't get much of a hearing. Curran and Keva were the loudest, as usual. They consider that you're giving us presents as a sop for your own conscience."

Keith reddened. "It isn't like that."

"Oh, I know that, you widdy. But you must understand their fears. What would they do if they had to leave here? Where would they go? I was born here; I've never lived any-where else, so I haven't a real grasp of what it was like for the older ones to find their way here. They're all terrified by the idea of moving on. Small wonder: the world's changed a lot in forty years."

"Didn't you explain historical landmark status to them?" Keith asked, clenching his hands between his knees. "That'd stop the problem, and then your folk wouldn't have to worry anymore."

"Oh, I did bring up your scheme. And then they turned on *me*, complaining that you've seduced me with your Big ideas," Holl said bitterly. "It did me no good to protest that I knew my heritage and would protect it, nor to assure them that you had nothing but their best interests in mind."

"So why were you tossed out of class?"

Holl's voice hardened. "Until I remember who I am and where I came from, the Master has ordered me to stay away from you Big Folk. It's dangerous to absorb too much of your culture."

"That's unjust!" Keith protested.

"Well, he said he decides who he'll teach and who he won't," Holl sighed. "A pity he won't decide who will learn. Starting with himself."

"Pat suggested that I teach you how to fish," Keith said, after a thoughtful pause.

"What do you know about the *Art of Fishing* that Isaak Walton didn't?"

"He doesn't mean real fishing. He meant I should use my considerable skills to teach you how to solve your own problem. But there's nothing I know that you don't know how to do better."

"It's a good idea your roommate had, though. You're both kind for caring," Holl said, kicking his heels against the legs of the desk chair. "Truly, it isn't your problem. It could have happened at any time before this."

"Are you sure you haven't got some pots of gold hidden somewhere?" Keith asked. "It sure would help."

"Of course we do," Holl answered, sarcastically. "Which we carried from the old place to here on our backs. Have you ever hefted real gold?"

"No. I wish I could win the Lottery or something for you. I'm not rich. Far from it. I'm here on scholarship, myself."

Holl saw that Keith was falling into a depression. "Cheer up, Keith Doyle. Here you go, then." He retrieved the bag he had arrived with, and tossed it toward the youth's hand. "Your payment."

"My what?" Keith caught it and drew out the contents of the bag. It was a wooden lantern about a handspan high, rectangular in shape, with sharply peaked roof surmounted by a stiff ring, and lattice-carved sides as fine as filigree. Inside was a spiral-carved wooden candle topped by a white cotton wick. The bottom panel was one of Holl's 'cohesiveness spells.' "It's beautiful."

"All my own work," Holl told him proudly.

Keith turned the lantern over and over in his hands, stroking the polished frame. "There's no opening. It's just ornamental, huh?"

"No! What good would it be if it didn't light? I promised you a functional lantern."

"I don't get it. I mean, how would you light it?"

"How do you think?" Holl answered the question seriously. "Blow on the wick."

Obediently, Keith blew. The wick ignited. Astonished, he dropped the lantern. It hit the floor with a THOCK! but the flame didn't go out. "That's incredible," Keith exclaimed. "How does it work? Magic! Is it magic?" he demanded.

Holl regarded him patiently. "Old skills, like carving," he said, picking the lantern up and holding it out. "It's stronger than it looks. All good hardwoods. Go on, blow it out."

Keith screwed up his face like a little boy with a birthday cake. The flame vanished, and the wick showed white again in its wooden cage. It wasn't even hot. "I don't believe it," he said, cradling the lantern reverently in both hands. "This is mine to keep?"

"Of course. We made a bargain. Value given for value received. I'm satisfied. Here, there's more. These are from the feuding sisters." From his coat pockets, Holl produced a pair of wooden spoons, a small painted marionette, and a flat-hinged box. "From Marm, who still believes in your innocence," he said, indicating the last. "Good work, but nothing fancy."

"Nothing fancy, he says," Keith echoed, mockingly. "It's professional quality stuff. Even better!"

Holl turned the box so the lock was facing Keith, and took hold of one of his hands. "Put your thumb here, widdy." Puzzled, Keith allowed his thumb to be pressed to the lock plate. "Now it'll only open to your hand. Good for things you want to keep private. You might keep the key to the classroom in here, if you choose."

"A magic lock! I love it. Eat your heart out, CIA."

"Will you stop? A simple charmed lock is nowhere near so important as full-blown magic."

Keith flushed. "Sorry. I'm not used to getting anything that's charmed or magical." He picked up the marionette and admired its glittering glass eyes. "What's this do?" He made it dance a few steps, whistling a few bars from the "Beautiful Blue Danube." The joints turned smoothly, and the painted wooden shoes beat a delicate tattoo on his coverlet. But when he let go of the puppet's strings, it did a step of its own before dropping nervelessly to the bed. Its bright stare was reflected in Keith's own astonished eyes. He was speechless.

Holl cocked an eye at it. "You've got a bit of energy of your own," he said enigmatically. "It wouldn't work like that for everybody. Amazing."

"You guys are amazing, not me," Keith exclaimed, poring over his treasures. "I know people who would pay anything for stuff like . . . That's it!"

"What's *it*?"

"How you could earn money."

"And why do we need money? We don't live in a cash economy; strictly barter."

"Well, don't you understand? If you made enough toys, like these," he held up the box and the puppet in one hand, "and like *this*," the lantern in the other, "you could sell them and earn enough to buy your own home. Then you wouldn't have to worry about jerks like me trying to tear it down around your ears." Keith blushed, having made mention of those very obvious attributes. Holl didn't notice. He was thinking it over. Keith didn't have to. It was obvious—it was right.

That, of course, was the answer. Marketing was one of his skills. Hadn't he just been demonstrating it to his present disadvantage in Student Senate? Had he not done a thorough selling job on Marcy to get him in to meet the elves in the first place? Was he not, after all, a Business Major? He was.

"Come on, Holl," he said, jumping to his feet and shouldering into his coat.

"Where to?" The elf looked up from his meditation in surprise.

"To redeem myself, and maybe you, too."

▪ Chapter 15 ▪

Getting through the concealed door in the side of the library building unobserved was the easy part. The sun had set behind a skyful of rain clouds, and very few students were out on the common. A few lonely streetlamps draped their beams on the shiny wet pavement, and the tired brown grass lay flat. Keith and Holl crossed through the gloomy pools of light and eased in behind the paving stones as simply as shadows. The hard part was trying to convince the elders that Keith had a rational point of view to which they should listen. Most of them were for throwing him out on the spot. Holl, who had had the whole concept explained to him on the way over, was not entirely convinced himself. He had to concur, at least, that it was a darned good idea, and had managed to convince the clans to give Keith a hearing.

"But why not sell handcrafts?" Keith insisted to an assembly of the Little People. "Bored housewives make a bundle on color-by-number tole paintings at craft fairs. You could clean up on your creative skill alone."

"Exploitation!" one of the white-haired men shouted.

"Not by me," Keith said, frankly. "I can't tell you how sorry I am about my mistake. But apologies won't really help you. I know I blew it, I'll admit, but that was before I knew anyone was living here."

Strangely, it was the Elf Master who came to his rescue, speaking up from among his fellows. "Is it any wonder, when we haf gone to so much trouble to prevent detection?"

Keith was grateful for his teacher's intervention. "Right now you can't afford to buy a new place if you lose this one. The least you can do is consider making it easier to find a new home. If you exploit your own talents, you help yourselves."

"We have no wish to expose ourselves. You have already done enough to jeopardize us," one of the Little Folk growled.

Full of excitement, Keith threw his arms out toward the little man. "But that's where I come in. You won't be exposed. *I'll* find buyers for you. I'll deliver the merchandise, and I'll handle all the external negotiations. All you have to do is make things."

"What *things*?"

"These!" Keith seized the handful of wooden toys out of his pocket. There was a general outcry.

"You're ridiculous! Toys!"

"You want to stereotype us to your foolish folktales. Santa's little helpers. Big Ones are all alike!"

"Meester Doyle," came the Elf Master's sadly patient voice, "Meester Doyle, where did you get the impression that ve are eager to take up handicrafts as a means of supporting ourselves, however covertly, in your society?"

"Well, I . . . you know, that's how . . . In fairy tales, like the elves and the shoemaker, they . . ." Keith sensed the ridiculousness of his words and broke off, bright red. "I'm sorry. Myths and legends are the only stuff I have to go on to know what's in common between your culture and mine. You know, like the story that unicorns are only attracted to virgins."

"And supposing the unicorn hasn't read the story?"

Keith took a deep breath. "I assumed that maybe legends were based on observations that had been distorted over time. I'm sorry. I just wanted to be helpful."

"Don't help. Don't get involved. You haf already done enough. Just go."

"Ye should never ha' come in the first," Curran, Holl's clan leader snapped out, stepping forward. "I was agin it, and still I am."

"Wait," Holl said, holding his hands up for silence. "Curran, there are others with opinions. Can we consider it?"

"Ye're too progressive, lad," the old man growled, shaking his white head doubtfully.

"And what choice have I got?" Holl demanded, addressing not only the old man, but all the elves. "The world's not the same as it was. When was the last time that any of you were ever able to walk about in honest daylight? We younger ones can because we look like Big Ones' children, and we can tell you that this fastness into which we've dug ourselves has become surrounded by *city*.'' He looked around, searching for understanding in his friends' faces. ''Have none of you wondered why scavenging parties take so long to return? The farmland has receded away from our door. The natural ways are drifting out of our reach, and a colder way is taking their place.'' His voice sank to a choked whisper, but the room was silent, aware, listening. ''There's no magic out there now, just machines and money.''

A plump, elderly woman spoke up. ''Then we've trapped ourselves like coneys. Is no open land left?''

Holl looked at Keith, passing on the question, and the tall student cleared his throat. ''Sure, outside of the cities. Ironically, this one just grew up around the University because the Agriculture School is so good. It's big, but there's plenty of farmland and forests beyond it.''

''Perhaps we should consider it, then,'' she suggested. Her daughter, or granddaughter, a child with flaming red curls, nodded vigorously. The elders wrinkled their foreheads, muttering among themselves. ''Look you,'' the woman exclaimed, ''time was when there was plenty and enough for a'. I do not want to live in a maze we canna find our way out. If we must *buy* a home on a day soon, we'll have to have the gold in hand before then.''

''Um, we don't use gold any more,'' Keith put in. ''Not since the twenties. Just dollars.''

''How much will we need?'' Dinny, a younger elf, inquired. His black eyes were in marked contrast to his ice-fair hair and beard.

''Depends on the land,'' Keith said, frankly. ''I don't know anything about real estate.''

''Ach!'' spat Catra. ''Don't you read the newspapers, Dever? There are advertisements in, every day.''

''I don't read them,'' Dever admitted, shamefaced. ''I only read the comic strips and the columnists.''

The room broke up into a dozen arguments.

''I say, do it!''

''No, it would be selling out.''

"We could try . . ."

"Do you know another way? I don't."

The argument got louder and more forthright, shifting into a language that Keith could not identify. There were German words thrown in here and there, and he was positive he heard some slang, too, but the body of the discussion was nothing he'd ever heard before. There really were three distinct sets of accents in the room, when they spoke English. The old ones sounded Irish, or something like it; the middle-aged ones exclaimed their opinions in middle-European; the young ones in midwestern American, complete with slang. Right now they all sounded exactly alike.

"I dinna trust him," Curran growled, and Keva nodded in sour-faced agreement.

"What about those newspaper articles?" one of the others demanded.

"He wrote them," Enoch speculated blackly. "He deserves none of our confidence."

"Not at all," Holl interrupted. "He offers to help us."

"He offers to make a spectacle out of us!"

"Why not discuss it?" Tay said, dropping back into English and thrusting himself forward into the middle of the group. Keva waved a dismissive hand while making a sound like she was spitting and turned away.

"The Maven has been rarely wrong," a burly, dark-haired elf said in English with a thick accent like the Master's, stroking his beard thoughtfully.

"He's becoming too like the Big Ones, Aylmer. Best to stick to what we know, and make our own way," Keva said forcefully. She glared over his head at Keith.

"Yes! Why do we need this Big One?"

"Yes, why?" "Why does he have to come into our lives?" "Ask him!"

Aylmer turned to Keith, and fixed him with a stern brown eye. "And vhat do you get out of all this hard vork for yourzelf?"

"Nothing," said Keith, earnestly but firmly. "You're my friends. I just want to help."

"No," the Master said, chopping a hand downward to forestall debate. "That is more of your charity."

"What charity?" Keith demanded. "Even if it is my scheme,

you'd be earning your own way. It will be hard work. Like Holl said, value given for value received. Okay—you can give me a commission for being your business manager. Ten percent is fair. Check it out in the business law texts. That's standard.''

''I haf,'' the Master admitted, showing a small glimmering of humor at last. ''The usual percentage is thirty to forty.''

The young man turned red again. ''Maybe. I'd be happier with ten, myself. You're going to need all you can save to buy land. How about it, then? I'll take care of the shipping and you just fill the orders. What more could you ask? You could have a cottage industry with real cottages!'' Keith demanded triumphantly. ''That's a degree of reality you rarely find today in business.''

''It sounds too easy,'' Marm complained.

''It vill not be easy,'' the Elf Master said, considering. ''But perhaps it should be done.'' He turned a piercing eye on Holl. ''Ve can *learn* at least if it is practical.''

Holl bowed acceptance. It would be the closest thing he'd ever get to an apology from the imperious teacher. ''Thank you, Master.'' He turned to Keith. ''The floor's yours, widdy. What do you want us to do?''

Scratching his jaw, Keith considered. ''The obvious market is gift shops, and places like that. I think we'll need at least a dozen to fifteen items to start off with for the buyers to choose from. What else can you make besides these?''

Several of the elves ran for their homes, and came back with armloads of wooden implements. ''See this,'' one said. ''That's half worn-out,'' another scoffed. ''See this!'' Tay and a woman, probably his wife, came back pushing a small wheelbarrow.

Holl sorted the crafts into piles. ''Cook's tools,'' he pointed to one group. ''Musical instruments. Toys and puzzles. You'll never figure that one out, Keith Doyle, so you may as well put it down.''

Keith set the puzzle box back and helped sort out the most attractive items.

''What about the lanterns?'' Marm asked. ''They're useful.''

''Easy to make, too. It's only a case of strengthening the natural characteristics and uses of the wick,'' Dever explained. He would have gone on, but Keith shook his head in wonder.

"I don't understand."

"His brain's got enough to do, moving that big body," Holl said, cynically. "He'd need years of instruction."

Keith held up a regretful hand. "I don't know. How will I explain magic lanterns to the shop owners? It might seem perfectly natural to you, but they don't believe in magic."

"That's not a magic lantern," Marm said. He picked up a little box which had a round window on one side that was covered by a thin cloth screen. "This is like your televisions. Here, look."

He shoved the screen-side at Keith, who peered closely.

"I don't understand," said a finger-sized Keith, looking stupidly at a thumb-sized Dever.

"His brain's got enough to do, moving that big body," an image of Holl repeated.

Keith goggled. "I don't believe it. That's impossible."

"But there's nothing to it," Holl insisted. "It's made with the heartwood of a tree. That part can hold memories forever. Not too lengthy an event, but you can make records over and over until you've got one you want to keep. Keva's got one of Tay taking his first steps."

"Sugar," spat Keva, who was ostentatiously not listening to the progressive Doyle and his cohorts, and hated to be considered sentimental. Tay blushed and stroked his beard. Holl smiled.

"Well, I can't take that," Keith insisted, putting down the magic lantern. "I don't think the Midwest is ready for it."

"Well, then," Holl said. "Will these do?" He pointed out his selections.

"Yeah," Keith said, kneeling before the display appreciatively. "All of it is beautiful. These things'll sell themselves." He considered, fingering the little wooden boxes. "I'll need about three samples of each item, in case I have to give some away. Just let me know when I can come and get them."

He had plenty of volunteers among the younger elves who were ready to show off their skills. Some were openly disappointed that their work hadn't been chosen. "Why not these?" Dinny asked, sounding hurt, as he retrieved a hand-sized harp.

"I only need a small representative sample to start," Keith explained soothingly. "I don't want to blow their minds on my first visit. Plenty of time for expansion later on when we see how big our market is. These are so terrific, my big problem is figuring out where to tell people this merchandise is produced. No one would ever believe I made 'em.''

It was a popular answer. They redoubled their offers of help. The middle-aged set joined in less enthusiastically, but they were convinced of Keith's sincerity, and flattered by his admiration of their work. The eldest elves still held themselves apart, refusing to participate.

Curran, the white-haired Elder, remained unconvinced, even though most of his clan were involving themselves excitedly with Keith's plan. "But what if the inevitable does not happen, lad?" He rapped Keith smartly on the top of the head with his knuckles to get attention. "What be the point of setting ourselfs to earn this money, if we may not need it?" He said "money" as if it burned his tongue. "The resolution to tear down may be dropped."

"If you *don't* have to move?" Keith rose, frowning thoughtfully. "Well, what if the day comes when you *decide* to move, of your own free will? You could. If it were me, I'd rather have the means available than have to scratch for them in a hurry. It would keep your options open."

"A valid point," the old man said. "I will gi' conseederation to it. Whether or not we follow your scheme."

"Thank you, sir," said Keith. "Well, I'd better go now. I've still got some studying to do before tomorrow." He gathered up his coat and other possessions. Waving his good-byes to the others, he disappeared into the dark stairway, his heels pattering happily on the floor. Curran gathered up the other elders with a glance, and they drew together in conference. The argument began again.

"Um, there's just one more thing," Keith said, reappearing around the doorjamb and addressing the Elf Master. "Sir? Can I come back to class?"

"Yes," the Master said, rounding austerely on him. "Next week. You are still suspended for causing a disturbance. You must understand that a classroom is no place for theatrics. Others are there to learn."

"Yes, sir!" With a wink to Holl, Keith vanished again.

▪ Chapter 16 ▪

Behind the protective bulk of Mary Lou, Keith bent over his plan of attack for marketing the elves' work while Sociology class went on without disturbing his calculations. Jewelry boxes. Penny whistles. Puzzle boxes. Miniature marionettes, fully articulated, using nearly invisible dowels. Love spoons. Spice bottles with the herb leaf carved into the side or forming part of the lid. He smiled, thinking of the magic lanterns which were undoubtedly his favorites.

Holl assured him that it would be only a few days before his samples were ready, and he could get going. There was an old sample case in the Business Major office, but he had been unable to convince the secretary to let him borrow it. He retreated, and found an old briefcase for two dollars at the Salvation Army store. With a little waterproof shoe polish and a lot of elbow grease, it cleaned up admirably. No sense in letting anyone see what he was doing until the merchandise was on the shelves. Besides, it would look more professional.

There wasn't time to get official business cards printed up. Keith had spent some time with the school computer and a graphics program running up a few sheets of personal cards on sixty-pound bond that had his name, address and "Sales Manager," printed on them.

The presentations shouldn't be too hard. He'd meant it when he said the pieces could sell themselves. Wooden things had a sort of charm completely absent from identical items of plastic. He composed a separate pitch for each that would dovetail with any other. Good technique for selling: be friendly, brief, and eloquent. He rehearsed each speech to himself, muttering them quietly under his breath. Piece of cake; he should know them all by the end of class.

There was so much to do that missing a week's worth of

Elf Sociology didn't bother him much. And he was keeping discreet notes on all the preparations he was making, so when the time came to get his M.B.A., he'd have all his marketing research in the bag. The hardest part of his preparation was finding the single iron the dormitory owned to press out the dark blue suit he now wore.

Marcy found herself glancing over her shoulder at Keith. For someone who had caused as much trouble as he had, he didn't seem too repentant. In fact, he winked at her the one time she managed to catch his eye. She was confused. There was no doubt that he had jeopardized the Little People's safety and privacy, but she didn't agree with Carl that it was this malicious mischief that would get the Big students tossed out of the Master's class.

All of the humans felt the same way. Ever since Keith had been suspended, nerves were taut at each class meeting. They were afraid of sharing his punishment, though the Little People, even the Master, didn't show any signs of ire. If anything, they seemed positively enthusiastic about something. Even Teri, whose friendship with little Maura was blooming, had no idea what was up. Lee in particular was nervous. He was in the first semester of his master's program, and he cursed Keith fluently whenever his name came up, yet he refused to side with Carl. Marcy continued to defend Keith, but she was clearly in the minority.

Most incredibly, Lee reported having seen Keith and one of the Little People in the dormitory cafeteria after the classroom debacle, on obviously friendly terms. He didn't feel happy about it, being deeply superstitious on the subject of the elves, as if mentioning them would make them go away. He'd known them the longest, and he seemed to resent Keith's easy familiarity with them. Marcy had scoffed at Lee then, but with Keith, who could tell? Keith's persistent good humor over the last week made her uneasy; it meant he wasn't taking his expulsion seriously. And why was he talking to himself?

Keith was grinning at her again. She turned her back on him, but she fancied she could still feel his eyes on her.

Dr. Freleng made his way down the aisles, passing out the latest graded papers. She received her B in silence, content to be maintaining a standard with Freleng. He had a reputation for being very tough, and she acknowledged his right to it.

"Mr. Doyle," Freleng was saying, "I am puzzled but most pleased as to your improvement in style and quality of research. Your surprising thoroughness is most gratifying, considering your earlier shoddy efforts. My congratulations."

Keith, surprised out of his reverie, accepted his paper with a tongue-tied mumble of thanks. Marcy peeked back. There was a circled A on the title page. She started to mouth her own compliments to him, but he was already absorbed again in his clutter of papers.

"Congratulations," she said in an offhand voice, as the class broke up.

"Huh? Oh, thanks, Marcy." Keith was obviously off in another world. He was gathering his work together, and Marcy caught glimpses of phrases like, "one of a kind," and "quality, handmade," before the papers were swept into his bookbag.

"What was your paper on?" she persisted, trying to guess what he was working on.

"Rural farmers," Keith said, faintly. "I got into Compuserve on the library computer, and I collected about fifteen articles. Hashed something together. I guess he liked it."

"He liked it," Marcy assured him. "You really weren't listening today, were you?"

"No," Keith admitted. "I've had a lot on my mind."

"It is like pulling teeth to get any information from you. Is all that stuff for an Advertising class?" She poked his bookbag.

"Not exactly. I didn't know you were talking to me."

Marcy paused. "I'm not really. I just wanted you to know I'm still mad."

"But I didn't *do* anything," Keith protested. "By the way, can I ask you a favor? Will you give this to the Maven? I'm suspended."

"I know you're suspended," Marcy said with some asperity. "You've got a fat lot of nerve asking me to do anything for you. He probably won't want to talk about you at all. And, besides . . ."

"Oh, I forgot," Keith smacked himself in the head. "*He's* suspended, too. Please ask Maura if she'll take it to him? I'm beggin' ya. It's important."

Marcy opened and closed her mouth, too overwhelmed by his chutzpah to say no. "How would you know that?" He didn't seem to hear her. He dug deep into the bag, and produced an envelope, which he tucked into her hand. "And why are you wearing a suit?"

"Thanks," he said, ignoring her questions and giving her a quick hug before she could avoid him. "I've got to go. Oh," he added, almost as an afterthought, "I never got to tell you what happened when Holl asked me to dinner, and you made me promise. Would you like to go out tonight, and hear it all?"

"Oh, you! . . . Why not?" Marcy said, peevishly. "I'm not saying I forgive you yet for misleading me."

"Aagh!" Keith yelped, anguished. "For the last time, I didn't mislead anyone, especially not you. My only crime is one of bad timing. As soon as I became aware I was making trouble, I began to undo it. Ask anyone. Ask Carl. No, don't ask Carl. Ask Rick. Ask Pat."

"Never mind," she sighed. "Pick me up after class."

"To hear is to obey!" Keith shouted over the rush of traffic as he pushed open the door for her and trotted off down the street, kowtowing in the rain. She shook her head and put the envelope in her purse.

As he was finishing the seven *salaams* one makes upon departing the presence of royalty, Keith bumped into something, or rather, someone. "Oh, sorry," he apologized, turning around to see whom he had inconvenienced. His feet were swept out from under him, and his books went spinning into the water-filled gutters. He hit the wet pavement with a painful splat. Scrambling on his knees to retrieve his possessions, he saw Lee Eisley hurrying away. "Wait," he called out, but Lee paid no attention to him.

"Nobody loves me," he grumbled, fishing his papers out of the water.

▪ Chapter 17 ▪

Voordman's Country Crafts & Gifts was at the top of Keith's list of good prospects. It was in the middle of the shopping district in town, good sized, well lit, and it had all sorts of wicker and gingham knickknacks on display. After a few minutes of perusing the contents of the show windows, he pushed in through the glass double doors.

A little bell suspended from an arm jingled furiously, and a dark-haired woman behind the counter raised her head. "Be with you in just one moment," she called, pointing to the telephone against her ear. Keith nodded, running a hand through his rain-drenched hair to make it lie flat, and browsed the aisles until she was through.

"What can I do for you?" She smiled, coming over to him. Then she saw the sample case. The smile dimmed and hardened. "Oh. A salesman. Did you call for an appointment?"

"I did call earlier, Mrs. Voordman," Keith began, placatingly.

"*Ms.*" Her fluffy hair stiffened into black glass filaments. So did her eyes. Keith put on a determined smile. A New Woman. His very first words put him at a disadvantage. She was going to be tough to sell. He wondered what Andrew Carnegie would do in a case like this.

"My apologies," he said, trying to look competent and penitent at the same time. "*Ms.* Voordman. Do you have a moment right now so I can talk to you?" He took a look around. The shop was empty except for them.

The woman noticed his surveying glance and the raised eyebrows that followed it. She was on the defensive, but she could choose only to listen or to tell him to go away. "Very well. Come this way."

* * *

Keith stood poised over his sample case, his prepared speeches ready, waiting for the shop owner to make herself comfortable in the swivel chair behind the desk in her tiny, cluttered office. He opened his mouth to speak, but Ms. Voordman held up her hand.

"Before you start, I just want you to know that I've seen it all already. There's nothing you can say I haven't heard. This business has no surprises. That's one of the reasons I'm in it. I'm not interested in anything you have, and I'm only giving you this time because I'm not busy. Understand?"

Keith swallowed. She was a tough cookie. "Sure," he said. He reached into the case and drew out the items one by one. "I always say, a good product will speak for itself." Ms. Voordman leaned forward, and began to handle the individual pieces, eyeing them critically.

"Good workmanship," she said. "Is that adze-mark hand-done or artificial?"

"These pieces are made by a sort of commune. No electric tools at all."

"Um-hmmm. The cookie cutters are nice. Unusual shapes and designs. I don't mind telling you I'm tired of the same gingerbread men, angels, and Pennsylvania hex symbols. This one's a little deep. Shortbread mold?" She turned it over in her hands, ran a finger around the chiseled inner rim.

"Um, yes," Keith agreed, hoping it was true. His two great scratch kitchen accomplishments were scrambled eggs and fudge. He was pleasantly surprised to see her gaining more interest the longer she looked, and he began to hope for a small order.

"And what's this?" she asked, holding up the lantern. "Wonderful screens. To think something this precise is all handmade."

"It's a sort of toy," Keith explained. "But it makes a good reading-lamp, too." He blew on the wick, which ignited. He was almost used to the wonder, but his prospect wasn't. Ms. Voordman's eyes went huge. Her hand fluttered away from the screen, but returned when the part of the frame she was clutching didn't grow warm. "Never needs batteries. Patent pending." He blew it out.

"That *is* something else. What's it run on?"

"Can't tell you that, but I promise it's harmless. See?" He turned it upside down so she could see the inside of the lid. "No scorch marks. All fireproof."

"I've got to hand it to you," she said, after trying it herself a few times, more relaxed than before. "I've never seen anything like this. Ever. And I've been in this business twenty years. I've got customers who furnish in Early American who'd go for these in droves. They're a little miracle. I want a few myself. They'd make a hell of a party gag."

"Ms. Voordman," said Keith, solemnly. "We're *serious* about our knickknacks."

She threw back her head and laughed. "You've made a sale, mister. What's your name?"

Keith felt his face burning. First law of salesmanship down the drain! "Keith Doyle," he said, extending a hand. "With, um . . ." He remembered at that moment that they hadn't picked a company name yet. Desperately casting about for inspiration, his eye fell on an eight-inch-high painted porcelain statue of an elf peering out of a stump. The ceramic imp's red hair and glasses reminded him of the Elf Master. On the tag was printed the same little face. "Hollow Tree Industries," he finished, mischievously. "Yes, you never would believe where those cookie cutters come from." From his case he took one of his ersatz business cards and the list of prices he and Holl had worked out.

The woman shook his hand and glanced over the price list. "I'll take a half-dozen of everything here but the lantern. *That* I want a dozen of."

"Yes, ma'am!" said Keith, seizing his notepad and scribbling.

"And when can I expect delivery?" She was watching him write.

"Uh, we're a small, new firm, just tooling up." Keith chewed on his pencil-end. "I'll turn the tables on you: when would you expect delivery?"

Ms. Voordman moved everything off her desk blotter, and drew an invisible line down the calendar with a cookie cutter. "Four weeks from today. Absolutely no later than that. I've got to stock the store fully for Christmas by the second week of November."

Keith counted in his head. "Okay. Can I get a deposit? Terms are twenty-five percent down and net thirty days."

"Twenty-five and net sixty. I'm a small firm, too." She looked at his card. "There's no telephone number on this."

"Well, we're relocating," he explained, jotting his room phone down for her. "This is my home number."

"Hmm," she said sympathetically, watching him pack up the sample case. "Moving is a bitch in winter." She wrote out a check for him and they shook hands. "First-time salesman?"

"Sort of. Does it show that badly?" Keith asked in dismay and surprise.

"You haven't got enough of the paraphernalia. No orderblanks. No receipts. Oh, don't worry about it. You're a refreshing change from the usual polished hustlers. See you in four weeks, Mr. Doyle." She stood up, dismissing him.

He smiled uneasily at her as he slipped on his coat and gathered up his case. On his way out, Keith surreptitiously plucked the tag off of one of the porcelain statues.

By the end of the afternoon, Keith's feet hurt, his back was sore, and his palm had three small blisters starting where the stitching on the sample-case's handle rubbed, but he felt good. Inside the sample case were three orders with checks from three gift shops, along with business cards from two other storekeepers who promised to think it over. He was astounded how easy it was to convince the shop owners to buy. On the weekend, he planned to drive to a few nearby towns and pick up a few orders at the gift shops there. In the meantime, he needed to get into dry clothes and find something to eat. He was starved.

Marcy was waiting for him in the lobby of Power Hall. She got to her feet and came over to him as he walked in the door.

"Hi," he greeted her. "Just a minute, let me run this up to my room, and I'll be ready to go."

"No," she said, holding him back with a hand on his arm, "I want to know what's going on. Now."

"What's the matter?" Keith asked, stripping off his wet raincoat.

"Everyone's acting so mysterious. I gave Maura your message. And she gave me one to give you. *Sealed.*" Aggrieved,

Marcy thrust an envelope at him that was addressed to "Keith Doyle" in flawless copperplate calligraphy. "I don't like playing carrier pigeon."

"I'm sorry. I didn't expect . . . I don't want you . . . Oh, well." He hoisted the case and escorted her to the door that led to the cafeteria, wincing at the tenderness of his palm. "After you."

It was getting late, and the cafeteria was nearly empty. Half of the lights had already been turned out, lending the room a dim, intimate character. Food-service employees gathered dirty dishes and banged them into plastic trays that resounded like tom-toms. Keith and Marcy picked out an isolated corner-table. He tried to slide in next to her, but she gave him an apologetic look and stayed put in her place on the bench. "I'm sorry, Keith," she told him. "I just don't feel like being close today."

"No problem," Keith sighed, taking his place across from her. "I hope nothing's wrong."

"N-no," she replied, uncertainly. "At least I don't think so. Now, wait a minute. You have some explaining."

"I sure do. Here goes."

Between bites, she chewed over his recounted adventures, and he skimmed Holl's note. It was brief, just to let Keith know that the vote to go along with his plan hadn't merely succeeded, or even just come close. It was a *landslide* for progress. He could pick up more kinds of sales samples later on outside of Gillington. They would be in a plastic sack behind the bushes. Keith felt like a bagman for a numbers runner. He looked up at Marcy. She was still digesting his story. He hadn't told her anything about Ludmilla yet, but he remembered the old woman's words. Why would Marcy need to know about the elves' history? He had no doubt Ludmilla had a reason, but he couldn't guess what it was.

Marcy spoke up at last. "I feel so bad. Why couldn't they be left in peace?"

"At least this way, we have some warning. See, if it wasn't me, it could easily have been a bunch of bureaucrats, and we'd never know about it until it happened. Anytime the university wanted to get rid of Gillington, it could. Are you still mad at me?"

"No. I suppose I never was really mad at you. I'm just so frustrated that there's nothing I can do to help."

"That is where the nimble brain of Keith E. Doyle comes into play," he said, and explained his plans for Hollow Tree Industries. After a careful look around to make sure no one was watching them, he opened the case and slid it over to her side. Marcy's face lit up as she poked through the wooden gifts.

"These are adorable," she said. "And you're terrific. Who else would think of something like that?"

"Only another deranged mind," he assured her.

"No," Marcy waved that away. "You're not deranged. A little weird, yes. Can I do anything to help out?"

"Not really," Keith said, considering. "Wait. There is one little thing. You could tell me what's going on in class?"

Marcy giggled. "Fashion is happening in class. The Master is using the phenomenon to demonstrate his favorite principle of cultural adaptation to customs. Today, Maura showed up in a blue denim pantsuit. Catra wore a patterned skirt and a blouse made of old sheet material, and Candlepat had on a sundress and headband straight out of a Vogue magazine that Teri brought for her." She grinned impishly. "It is sort of startling in star-spangled green, but the line is good, and it is *very* form-fitting. The guys really noticed. Quite a contrast, since the rest of us are all in winter clothes. How old is she, anyway? Fifteen?"

"She'd be a lot more likely to tell you than me," Keith said.

Marcy smiled. "It's been very quiet this week. I think everyone misses you. The Master is being very patient with us. Now that I know we're not going to be tossed out of the class, I can relax, and maybe the others will, too. Though I was stuttering so much today that he stopped me and promised he wouldn't bite me even if my ideas were farfetched. His kindliness frightens me more than his gruffness does."

"I know what you mean. He's a great teacher. I respect him, but I'm scared of him, too," Keith said, earnestly. "I would never deliberately want to make him mad at me."

That evening, he met Pat coming toward him in the hall, looking furious. Keith started to dodge past him with a pleasant word, but his roommate grabbed his arm, turned him around and marched him back toward their room.

"All right, Doyle," Pat snapped. "This is getting to be a habit."

"What is?" Keith asked, trying to free his arm, but Pat's long fingers had embedded themselves in his biceps.

"The room got trashed again!"

"You're kidding!" Keith pulled free and broke into a run in spite of the weight of the sample case in his hand. He dashed through the door, and a deluge of water splashed down on him from above. The case crashed heavily to the floor. "Wa-wa-water balloon," he gasped.

"That's weird," Pat said, coming in behind him. "I've been through that door already. Twice." He squinted over the bridge of his long nose at the lintel, and at the empty scrap of rubber on their rug. "Why didn't it fall on me? There's no tape or anything on the wall."

"I don't know," Keith said, dabbing at his face with a towel. "Maybe it was balanced funny. Or maybe our culprit just planted it. Someone from this dorm, like Carl, for instance! What is it with everyone and water today?" He surveyed his half of the room. Once again, there was cola on everything, but this time he saw pieces of a book that had been slashed up and stuffed into the plughole of the sink. It was the *Field Guide to the Little People*. He ripped the soaked coverlet off his bed, and found that it had been short-sheeted. "Thorough job," he commented.

Pat snorted. "Why would you think it was Carl? Plenty of people want to kill you. I want to kill you myself. I was planning to get to sleep early tonight!"

"I'm sorry, Pat," Keith said, but his roommate wasn't listening. "I'll keep it down. This'll probably take me all night." Sighing, he went in search of cleaning supplies.

Two hours later, leaving a snoring Pat behind, he sneaked out of the dorm and crossed the campus to the library building. A security patrol-car shone its spotlight on him but drove on, disinterested in a single student.

Keith found the plastic sack without difficulty, and pulled it out of its hiding place, brushing drops of water and wet leaves from its surface. As he was walking back toward Power

Hall, a knot of drunken-sounding frat brothers turned the corner and started weaving their way toward him. A group that large, especially in their uninhibited condition, spelled trouble for a lone dormie out by himself. They'd probably stop short of beating him to a pulp, but there were other kinds of trouble they could make for him. He didn't want to have to explain his presence or his burden to the security force.

He froze, looking for a place he could conceal himself and his bag of magical toys. The path was lined with high, thick thornbushes that had once been part of the college's formal gardens. He could force himself between the leaf-bare branches, but he wouldn't be able to pull free again without help.

To his surprise, the frats streamed around him as if they couldn't see him. They passed so close he bet that he could guess the brand of beer they'd been drinking, but not one of them touched him. As soon as they were gone, he unfroze and tore down the path toward Power, refusing to question his good fortune, miracle though it seemed. He found that his pulse was racing.

He sneaked back into his dorm room without turning on the lights. A quick peek inside the bag with his miniature flashlight told him that everything promised was there. The white wicks of the lanterns gleamed faintly from their dark cages. "Ha-*HA*," he cackled under his breath.

"For God's sake," Pat yelped from the other bed. "Go to sleep!"

• Chapter 18 •

The New Accounts officer at the Midwestern Trust Bank explained the whole system again patiently to the eager red-haired teenager. He looked as though he had been explaining the same thing to dim customers for the past sixty years or more. "If you want a business checking-account, you have to maintain a balance of a thousand dollars, or there's an eight dollar service-fee each month. If you want my advice, young man, just open a personal checking account. The bank doesn't care what name and address you have printed on the checks.''

"Fine," Keith said, appearing to understand at last. "That's what I want.''

"Good," the man said, passing a hand over what was left of the thin brown hair on his head. His round face folded into the semblance of a Parker House roll as he smiled at Keith. "Now, if you'll just fill out these forms, we'll get you your temporary checks.'' The man swept Keith's three deposit checks away, and took them over to a teller's window. In a few minutes, he was back with an important-looking slip striped in blue and tan. "Here's your new account number.'' Keith looked up from it at him.

"Um, I want my nephew to be a cosigner on this account, but he hasn't got a Social Security Number yet. He's twelve.''

"That's no problem," the banker said. "Only one of you needs to have one. I assume you do. What's the account for, if I may ask? Boy Scouts?''

"Junior Achievements," Keith said.

Three days later, two boxes arrived for Keith from the student print shop. Cackling happily over the contents, he hurried down to the elf village, the cardboard boxes cradled in his arms. The stone door opened for him, showing him that some changes had been put into operation since he was there last. He smiled and greeted everyone, but didn't explain his presence until he reached Holl's hut. Holl lived alone at the edge of Curran's clan. Like the others, the cottage was built of odd pieces of wood, but they seemed to be arranged in a handsome and subtle pattern that used both color and texture as motifs; most appropriate for a woodworker who was the son of a woodworker. The sloping roof was incised with a pattern of rounded slates. There was no need to keep out weather, so its builders had concentrated on form, rather than function. Its door stood open.

The young elf was at home, poring over a thick leather-bound book with print so small that Keith couldn't read any of it from his distance of three feet above the pages. A carved shelf was fastened to the wall just underneath the glassless window. It was full of books, all borrowed from the library upstairs. Beyond a partition wall, from which a curtain was drawn back, lay a simple frame-bed covered with a patchwork quilt and pillow, and a chest with the lid thrown open. The windows were hung with curtains in a filmy-thin red-and-blue weave through which the village's curious lighting shone almost unabated. Holl's woodworking tools were neatly placed on a worktable against the wall between the two rooms. The cottage was a neat little bachelor's apartment.

Holl looked up at the gentle tap on the doorframe, and gestured his friend inside. Keith ducked under the lintel, laid the boxes down on the low table and opened them up.

Behind him, anyone who wasn't busy had followed him from the entrance, and milled around outside the low doorway, speculating on what the daffy Big One was doing now. Even some of the elders, without abandoning their poses of disinterest, found a reason to hang around the neighborhood.

Holl closed his book and pulled the boxes across the table to him. Examining the contents, he paused to peer up at the tall student. "An appropriate conceit, though bold," he said, tapping the letterhead and the accompanying line-artwork with his fingertips, "but has he seen it yet?"

Keith had no doubt as to which "he" his friend meant. "No," he admitted guiltily.

Holl rose from the backless wooden bench that served as his desk chair. "Well, we'd better go right away, before someone else tells him."

Desperately, Keith threw up a hand to stall him. "Um, there's no need to do that right now. I've got some other things for you, too." Maybe it hadn't been such a good idea to use the face from the tag for the logo. He was embarrassed at his own audacity. But it had been almost like an omen to see it there in Voordman's Country Crafts, the little man in the tree, smiling out at him. Looking so much like the Elf Master . . .

"Oh, no," said Holl, enjoying Keith's discomfiture a little, but also serious about making his point. He waved the orderforms in Keith's face. "Now, you can't use them if he doesn't like them. The cooperation would end before it fairly began. You'd have to have them done over. No sense in prolonging the situation." He grabbed one of Keith's wrists and pulled.

The blond elf was amazingly strong. "Oh, and bring the stationery, too."

Keith shifted from foot to foot as the Elders passed copies of the order-forms around. "It's an insult," Aylmer said, thumping the paper with the back of one hand. "Using a likeness. Has he no respect?"

"It was available as stock art," Keith protested uncomfortably. "Cheaper than a custom drawing." He towered over them, waving his arms for attention, but they ignored him, as they would ignore a tree swaying overhead. "We're on a pretty tight budget."

"What happened to all his easy promises for our privacy?" Curran asked, acidly.

"Ah, go on," Holl said. "Nobody knows any of our faces."

Most of the younger folk were looking over the Elders' shoulders, pointing and laughing. Keith felt like an idiot. His fellow students came in to ask what the joke was, and they, too, had a chuckle over Keith's slyness. The room divided into two parties: the Keithites, and the Anti-Keithites. The groups were similar though not identical to the Progressives and the Reactionaries. Holl and all the younger elves who were on his side made up the first group. They thought the idea of using the village schoolmaster as their logo was funny. The Anti-Keithites, the Elders and those against the scheme, were all for disemboweling him on the spot. Both parties were loudly vociferous about their opinions, and Keith ceased to try getting anyone's attention. There was no way he could be heard over the din. Suddenly, someone let out a piercing whistle, and the whole room fell silent.

The Elf Master appeared at the mouth of the tunnel. Curran called to him. "The Big One has brought something you must see."

"It's just business stationery, and cards, some with my name on 'em, and some blank so anyone can use 'em. And these are the order-blanks. Really nothing to look at. Not important." Keith pulled the boxes away as the Elf Master came over.

"May I see them?" the teacher asked, holding out a hand to Keith. The boy blanched, swallowing hard.

"Oh, you don't need to . . ." he protested weakly.

The Master deftly slipped the box out of Keith's arms, opened it, and his eyes narrowed. "Hmmm." The Anti-Keith-ites smiled with vindictive satisfaction. This time the Master wouldn't be so eager to defend the irresponsible, irreverent Big One. Keith shifted his gaze from the stationery to the Master's face and back again. Had he managed to alienate his newfound friends yet again? He wished passionately that he would learn to consider consequences before he acted.

The Elf Master didn't say anything for a long moment, and then croaked out one sentence. "Appropriate for the marketing strategy." Keith almost fainted with relief. The Keithites cheered.

But that was not the end of the Master's thoughts. "And a fine likeness, as vell," he said.

▪ Chapter 19 ▪

Lloyd Patterson slammed his gavel on the desktop. "Order! Order, dammit!" The roar of conversation quieted, and Lloyd cleared his throat. "I declare that this meeting of the Inter-Hall Council is in session. Venita, take the roll."

Keith sat in his place next to Rick, staring at a spot in the middle of his desk. He responded with a halfhearted "here," when Venita read his name, but was otherwise silent. The room was so full that some of the student delegates stood near the walls and others leaned against the door for lack of seats. Rick had his feet on the chair of an empty desk, and his expression dared anyone to come and take it away from him. He had no takers. The general consensus among those present who followed college sports was that if Number 41 MacKenzie wanted an extra desk on which to rest his feet, he could have it. The R.A. observed Keith's unusual depression with concern.

"What's the matter with you?" Rick demanded, scratching

at the place where the desk's arm cut into his ribs. "This is your show. You should be thrilled."

"Rick, maybe I should have talked to you before . . ." Keith was interrupted by another bang from the gavel. He twisted in discomfort, only partially attributable to the design of the desk, the same as the iron maidens in use in the hidden classroom. He wished that he didn't have such a vivid visual reminder of the spot he'd put himself in. The freezing countenance of the Elf Master stayed with him as he concentrated on putting his arguments in the right order.

"Quiet! Please!" Lloyd shouted. "The sooner we can have quiet, the sooner we can finish this meeting." Venita handed him the attendance list and he thanked her formally. She simpered, hair swaying, and sat down. "Before we get on to the reason we're all here, does anyone have any *other* business, old or new?"

There was general pandemonium as the delegates forbore to mention any business, but dragged their seats to the two sides of the room, making it clear that they were interested only in the main event. Lloyd sighed, and banged the desk for order. "Okay, already. I can take a hint."

"Go get 'em, Doyle," Rick whispered. Keith didn't move. Across the room, Carl Mueller had a wide smirk on his face as he got up and walked to the middle of the floor. He looked deeply satisfied for someone who had fewer than a third of the delegates on his side of the room. Rick wondered about his apparent confidence, and stared curiously at Keith, trying to decide if there was a connection.

"Mr. Chairman, I would like to have a vote taken on the proposal whether the administration should build a new Sports Center or a new library building this year."

"Anyone second?" Lloyd asked, looking around the room for raised hands. "Okay, seconded by Woods of Alvin Hall. The chair opens the floor for debate." There was a roar of voices, all trying to make themselves heard at once. "Order! May I remind you that there is a reason why this vote is being taken in full council? This is the first time the administration has ever really asked for our input on a project of this size. Three million bucks! This is your big chance to make your mark on the university. Now shut up unless you want to offer arguments for debate." There was some grumbling, but the roar sank into murmurs.

"Go!" Rick urged Keith. Reluctantly, Keith stood up, hand raised for recognition.

"Doyle, Power Hall?" It was a tentative question. Keith could feel Rick's eyes on his back. He felt cowardly for not taking Rick into his confidence before, but it was too late now. He was about to make a fool of himself by reversing his position without informing anyone in advance.

"Go ahead," said the chair.

"I've been in touch with the National Historical Society in regard to Gillington Library. In view of its age and intrinsic historic interest, they are investigating having it declared an historical landmark. If they decide in favor, the building cannot be torn down, even to make way for a newer structure. Therefore," Keith took a very deep breath, felt his ribs vibrating with nervousness, "I must withdraw my previous proposal, and let it be known that I have no objection to asking for support for the construction of a new Sports Center for Midwestern University." He turned away from the raw triumph on Carl's face, and finished his speech staring down at the floor.

For a moment the room was silent, and then everyone started talking at once. Rick was at Keith's side, yelling at him, but Keith wasn't even aware he was there.

Finally, the R.A.'s voice penetrated his misery. "What's the matter with you? You've just handed him the victory, you moron!"

Keith went back to his desk, and sagged into the seat. "I know. But I had to, Rick. That building turns out to be really pretty important. I didn't think so before, but . . ."

"Terrific. You coulda told me." Rick slammed himself into his seat and kicked his feet up. "I feel like a jerk."

"So do I." Keith buried his head in his hands, and didn't bother to come up for air even during the voting. But that was not the end of his disgrace. To Keith's dismay, in spite of his self-sacrifice the vote came out overwhelmingly in favor of a new library. Keith had done too good a job of promotion. There were cries of glee when the voting results were announced. He felt like drowning himself.

* * *

As the meeting adjourned, Carl came over to him, and spoke to the top of Keith's head. "I really enjoyed that, Doyle, I just wanted you to know. It's too bad you won."

"Lay off, Carl," Rick said in a bored tone, but there was no mistaking the fury blazing behind his eyes. "It doesn't matter. I don't know who put the Historical Society onto Gillington, but I'm sure it wasn't Keith's fault."

Carl puffed up with indignation and pointed at Keith. "What do you mean, who? *He* put them on to it, buddy. You thought it was funny to oppose issues just because I was backing 'em, huh, Doyle?"

"Carl," Keith said, looking up. "Shut up. I still plan to campaign against everything you do for the rest of your life. I blew this one, but it's the only one you'll ever get. I don't like you treating me like a weirdo, and I'm a little tired of you trashing my dorm room, too," Keith added, pugnaciously, rising to his feet. Carl stood a lot taller than he did. He felt like the Chicken Hawk threatening Foghorn Leghorn, but he kept his ground.

"What is going on here?" Rick inquired, uncrossing his running shoes and standing up. "We *won!*"

For once Carl looked honestly surprised. "I didn't touch your room, turkey. I haven't done a thing to you. Yet."

"Not once? Tuesday was the second time." Keith was taken aback. "Then, who?"

Rick looked at one, and then the other, and back again.

"I don't know. Now, blow, punk, or I'll do worse than trash your *room*." Carl leaned forward menacingly.

"Well, okay," Keith shouted, making for the door with a fist raised. "You won't have Keith Doyle to push Carl Mueller around any more. At least until next meeting. I'm going to get that vote overturned." He left with Rick following right behind him.

"Did I miss something? At least you could tell me what's going on, Doyle . . ."

"The next thing I have to do is make sure that the Historical Society doesn't do a basement-to-attic check. It's pretty hard to hide a whole village. I have to get them to declare monument status for Gillington before the committee reports to the dean, or I won't be able to stop the planning commission. The good news is that I get back into the Master's class just before it's time to study for the Soc final. I may even pass, considering how lousy I'm doing on practical social interaction. Marcy?" Keith asked, leaning across her kitchen table and waving a hand in front of her eyes. She was sitting rigid, staring down at a spot. "Hello?"

Marcy blinked. "Sorry."

"Tell old Uncle Keith what's on your mind," he wheedled, patting her hand gently. She endured three pats, then drew away. "I don't like to see my friends miserable. Unless I make them that way myself."

She smiled sadly at that. "No, you didn't do it. The truth is I'm sitting here feeling like a pervert."

Keith did a double take. "Say that again? No, don't. I heard you. Tell me why."

"It started the day you got thrown out of class. Maybe a lot sooner, I don't know. Carl said something insulting to me. I really hate him. He's got such an ego. Enoch jumped on him for it. I think he would've hit him if Carl hadn't backed off. Carl was really surprised. I was, too. He's been . . . protective of me, lately. Enoch, not Carl." She was having to fight to get the words out. "I . . . I feel, I don't know . . ."

". . . Like you've got something going for him?" Keith finished, a little light going on in his mind. "That's why you've been sort of backing off on me?"

Marcy nodded, miserably.

"Great!" Keith exclaimed.

"But I feel like I'm cradle-robbing, or something."

Keith's eyes went wide. "What? Is this the author of the Marcy Collier paper on the sociological stresses of racial dwarfism? The person who stood up to Dr. Freleng when he suggested that there wasn't enough statistical evidence to make a sociological premise out of it? You are treating short people like children." He pointed a finger toward her nose. "*You're doing it*. Enoch is *forty-six* years old. He told me so himself! If anything, you're a little young for him. *He's* cradle-robbing."

Marcy's mouth fell open. Her tongue felt dry, and she swallowed. "He is?"

"Scout's honor," Keith held three fingers up. "That's a fact. Would you like to have *me* play carrier pigeon for a change and find out how he feels about you? Although I can guess already, from what you just told me."

Marcy flushed at his last words, the red suffusing her fair skin to the hairline. "I'm sorry I said that to you about carrier pigeons."

"I'm sorry I didn't tell you everything right away."

"And I'm sorry, because I think you like me, too."

"I do," said Keith, standing up and taking her hand. This time she didn't pull away. "Enough to want you to be happy. So, are we sorry enough? Shall I go?"

"Yes!" Marcy squeezed his hand, and her eyes were bright.

"Miles Standish to the rescue!" Keith assumed a heroic pose and strode out the door. The hallway rang with his triumph.

"What a weirdo," observed one of Marcy's roommates from the living room.

▪ Chapter 20 ▪

Something seemed different about the hidden entrance in the block in the library wall. There seemed to have been some kind of erosion, or a more minor disturbance of surface dirt. "Sandblasting?" Keith asked himself. Apparently, it had caused some internal disturbance as well, because the passage wouldn't open up to him. It took some time before someone heard his pounding and let him in. Marm appeared, peering cautiously around outside before he shut the heavy facade.

"There was scratching on the wall last night," Marm told Keith, guiding him by lantern-light down the ladder inside. "We listened, but decided it couldn't be you. You'd just have come in the other door, then. The Old Ones were pretty worked up."

Keith was disturbed by the news. "You don't think someone else knows you're here?"

The bearded elf spat. "O' course they do. You know, and pretty Marcy knows, and fair Teri knows, and staunch Lee knows. All those do."

"I meant strangers. None of the other students know about this door. Not from me."

Marm looked very worried. "Perhaps from one of us, then. There's been a bit of coming and going of late. More than in past years, I can tell you. Are you going to want the same kind of wood for my boxes, or do I use what I can get?"

"Use whatever you want, Marm," Keith said, absently.

Marm shrugged. "What I want is not what I have. Our supplies are not great. Our stockpiles are gleaned slowly, at night and secretly. You must know that the old ones consider you to be wasting our time and our precious resources."

"I don't think it's a waste."

"Neither do us younger ones," Marm declared. "But we don't speak for the clans."

"Just have to use my salesmanship on them, too," Keith said glumly. "Don't worry. It'll all work out one day." He spotted Holl walking by the hydroponic garden and waved. The stocky blond elf nodded and came over.

"Good day to you, Keith Doyle," Holl said. "You're a bit out of color today. Are you not feeling well?"

Keith found it impossible to meet his friend's eyes, and spoke to his feet. "They took the vote. They're going to tear down this library."

Holl nodded sympathetically. "I know. It's almost an anticlimax after that day in class, isn't it? Very brave of you to come and break the news."

Keith was taken aback. "How did you know? I was coming down here to tell you."

The Maven took a piece of folded newsprint out of a pocket. "We all read newspapers. It was in *The Midwesterner*. Here, 'Student Makes Plea for Historic Gillington.' We're all most happy about it though it went so against you. You did try. That was enough even for some of the oldsters."

"The vote was pretty lopsided. I felt like an idiot," Keith admitted, and thought for a minute. "For once I did something well. Too well. The truth is that I have no idea now when the axe will fall. The Historical Society may not come through for us in enough time. I'll understand it if you decide you never want me to come down here again." He grimaced. "I *may* be able to pass the Sociology final on my own."

"No need," Holl said, grinning. "You're still welcome, and in the class as well. For the first time in forty years, they're stirred up. And the first time ever, by a Big Person. They've decided to follow your idea to stockpile against the future, since we have no pots of gold. We may not be able to avert disaster so neatly if we haven't our able champion. It's an elegant solution, I must admit, to make us work for our own salvation." Keith kicked the pavement uncomfortably, and Holl chuckled. "There's a second reason as well, and it, too, is your fault. They're beginning to see what they've been missing in new goods. We can earn proper raw materials for daily living, and a few luxuries, too, while we save to buy a home. Lee brings some things in with the supplies. I don't mind at all."

"Seeing as you catalyzed them into it," Keith pointed out.

"I just see a bit further ahead than the others. Never having lived anywhere else, I'm not burdened with memories of the 'good old days.' Though I find it hard to picture my home in another place, I can be . . . more objective. But to the point," Holl finished, rubbing his palms together, "your two dozen lanterns will be ready in a week or so. I'll let you know. We're wrapping everything in newspaper. The librarians microfilm all editions of the daily press and then discard them. Such a waste. But we could use a bit of string or tape."

"No problem. You guys are doing terrific," said Keith, elated in spite of himself.

"May I return the compliment?" Holl smiled. "I do not judge success by the results, but by the attempt."

"You sound like the Master." Over Holl's shoulder, Keith spotted Enoch between two of the small houses. The black-haired elf was sawing wood, scowling at each cut piece as it fell between the sawhorses. " 'Scuse me."

"Hi, there," he said gently, so as not to startle Enoch into having an accident. "Can I talk to you a minute?"

The elf's black eyes rose and bored into him. "You're talk-ing. Go ahead. I need not listen if I don't want to," Enoch said curtly, and went back to cutting wood. He had on a carpenter's smock with tools poking out of the many front pockets. There was a heap of small tile-shapes, which Keith recognized as the bases for the elf's own specialty, puzzle boxes. The oddly shaped pieces that made up the rest of the wooden conundrums had been sorted into a neat line of baskets beside the squares. It was a tidy assembly-line.

"Well." Keith sat down on the packed-earth floor with his back against one of the houses. From the eaves, a spider meandered down on a thread and hovered in front of his face, as though pondering his capture. He wondered where it would be best to begin his appeal. "It's about Marcy."

Without looking up again, Enoch snapped, "What about her?" In an instant, his face and ears had turned dark red with anger.

"Well, I only really met her a few months ago. I like her a lot. I think she's a great person. She's intelligent, she's pretty, and she's fun to be with. More than a little secretive," Keith smiled, looking around at the village, "but otherwise what else could a guy want?"

"I know all of these things."

"Oh, I know you do. I just wanted to let you know . . ."

"Aye, you don't have to go on," Enoch said, hostilely. "That it's she and you, and you want me to keep my hands off, isn't that it?"

"No," Keith contradicted him. "You're half-right. It's she, but it's not me. It's you. I am here to ask you, as a friend, just how interested you are in her. *I* think you are very interested."

"How would you know?"

"Well, right now, it's written on your forehead in boldface print. Right under 'Doyle go home,' " Keith quipped wryly. "But mostly, it was your standing up to Carl the day I got thrown out of the Master's class. She noticed it then, too."

"It's none of your business." Enoch gestured sharply at him.

"True," Keith conceded, gritting the words through his front teeth. His back teeth had unaccountably grown together, holding his jaw shut, and he couldn't wrench them apart. He ran his tongue around to determine the cause of the phenomenon. Nothing there. It must be something Enoch was doing to him, but he hadn't sealed Keith's lips, so it wasn't enough to shut him up. "But is it doing either of you any good as just *your* business?"

"Go away!" A slice of wood slipped off the end of the block he was sawing, quickly followed by another, and another. Keith watched in fascination as they clonked to the floor. Each section was dead-even. Sweat beaded on Enoch's forehead. He wiped it away with the back of his free hand without ceasing work, and left a sawdusty stripe over one eye.

Keith cleared his throat to project his voice over the saw. "I can't; I'm not through. Would it help if I said Marcy and I just had a talk, and she admitted she doesn't want to go out with me anymore because she can't stop thinking of you?" Keith inquired, ramming the sentences out so that Enoch couldn't interrupt him. The color faded from Enoch's face until it was as pale as it had been red. He stared at Keith, who concentrated on looking innocent and helpful.

"Is this true?"

Keith's jaws unlocked suddenly. He worked his mandibular muscles stiffly. It must have been a variation on the cohesiveness spell Holl had once described to him. Whew! he thought, I'd hate to get the little guy *really* mad. "Trust me. I'm a carrier pigeon, to coin a phrase. A go-between. Western Union. Cyrano de Bergerac."

"I've read the book," Enoch said, considering. The beginnings of hope shone in his eyes. He picked up another piece of wood, put the saw to it, then carefully set block and saw down on the ground and looked up at Keith. "Why did she not speak to me herself?"

Keith decided not to mention details of his conversation with Marcy. "She's old-fashioned," he said instead. "And she's shy. You understand."

"That's uncommonly good of you, if you care for her yourself." Enoch eyed him suspiciously.

"I do. You know. It's because I care that I'm talking to you," Keith said. "I'm happy to be her friend. I've decided that's enough for me. I guess I haven't found Miss Right for Keith Doyle yet. If Marcy isn't the one, why should I ruin it for other people?"

Enoch nodded, squinting thoughtfully at Keith, and then he smiled. The expression changed his whole face from that of a sullen little boy to an open, mature man. It was so startling that Keith barely stopped himself from gaping at the transformation. "Ach, aye, well. Maybe it's time I talked to her myself, then."

He stripped off the smock and laid it over the sawhorses. With a friendly nod to Keith, he disappeared into his little house, reappeared, buttoned up a coat with a cap over his ears, and walked purposefully toward the wall's entrance tunnel.

"Wait," Keith said, catching up with him. "It's broad daylight out there. They'll see you."

There was determination in the dark elf's eyes, making him look one last time like the headstrong boy who had sized Keith up that first day in class. "They'll get used to it," Enoch said.

A few days later, Keith reached for the phone without looking up from his *Sociology for the Masses* textbook. With the receiver between thumb and forefinger, he punched out Marcy's number using his pinky. One of her roommates answered, and, over the blare of heavy metal music roaring in the background, deigned to inform Marcy she had a call. She seemed a little amused by something. In a moment Marcy answered, sounding breathless.

"Hello?"

"Hi, it's Keith."

"Oh, hi," she said, more casually. "I was doing laundry."

"I was doing homework. I thought you might like to come over and help?" Keith said hopefully. "The final exam is coming up, and all."

"Oh, I can't. I haven't got anything clean to wear that's dry."

"How about tonight, then?"

There was a pause. "No. I'm going out. With Enoch . . . Keith? I'm happy. Really happy."

"I'm happy for ya, dollface." Humphrey Bogart was back. "Don't let him get fresh. But where are you going? You're going to attract a lot of attention."

"Well," Marcy paused, embarrassed. "I thought about that, too; so we're going to the movies."

"What's playing?"

There was a mumble on the other end of the phone, the only words of which Keith could distinguish were "double feature."

"What was that?" he asked, pressing his ear into the receiver. "I couldn't hear you."

"It's a double feature," Marcy announced, louder than necessary. There was a very long pause. He prompted her to repeat, and then laughed until he was out of breath when she said, almost in an undertone, "*Labyrinth* and *The Dark Crystal*."

"That's wonderful!" Keith hooted. "They'll think you're dating the star . . . Marcy? Marcy? . . . Hello?"

▪ Chapter 21 ▪

"I feel like I've been brought home to meet the folks," Marcy said, holding herself bolt upright in the overstuffed armchair in Ludmilla Hempert's living room, squeezing her hands together uncomfortably. She unclenched them to accept a cup of coffee and a plate of cake.

"I suppose I am considering myself to be family." Ludmilla smiled, serving Keith from her rolling tea-tray. Keith took his plate and sank happily into the upholstery of the wide couch. He scooped up a large forkful of cake and disposed of it with a blissful sigh. Ludmilla regarded him indulgently and turned to Marcy. "Are you comfortable, my dear? A cushion, perhaps?" The old woman swept down on Marcy with a pair of ornate pillows and tucked them in behind her.

"Thank you." Marcy smiled timidly, settling back.

Keith was content to sit and eat cake and watch Ludmilla handle getting Marcy to relax. She was a good hostess, and it wasn't long before the girl was talking more freely, asking and answering questions as if she had known the old woman all her life. Keith already felt that way. He'd dropped by to see Ludmilla a few times since Hollow Tree got rolling.

Marcy obviously felt shy about discussing her new relationship, but Ludmilla drew her out naturally, reassuring her. She had stories to tell about Enoch as a child that made Keith gape in disbelief, comparing them to the taciturn adult he knew now. "He has always been most loyal and loving," Ludmilla insisted. "I am the vun he confides in. He comes to visit me frequently. He vas so jealous when he saw you two out together. I was vorried he might do something bad. His feelings were most strong."

"When was that?" Marcy asked.

"He visited me that one rainy day," Ludmilla smiled, "vhen I had baked for them. He came to bring my cakes and breads away. He wished to talk to me, the only person he knew apart from his family and people. About you, my dear. We talked so long he went home after dark."

"Yeah," said Keith, nodding. "That boy with the grocery bag a few weeks ago, after *Attack of the Killer Tomatoes*. When he made a face at me yesterday, I remembered where I had seen that expression before."

Marcy smiled shyly. "I recognized him, but I didn't know then why he was so angry. We've talked a lot over the last few days. I love hearing about how he grew up. He learned all sorts of skills—" Marcy took off the necklace she was wearing and showed it to Ludmilla. "See? The end beads stick together without a clasp. I don't know if there's magnets in it, or what?"

"Amazing," Keith said, peering at the string of wooden beads between Ludmilla's hands. He accepted it from her and played with the end beads, putting them together and drawing them apart. "It doesn't have to be magnets. You know. What's it made of? Um, professional curiosity," he said apologetically, noticing Marcy's perturbed glare.

"If you must know, it's applewood. Do you know, he had to take care of his sister Maura when she was little, while the village was being built. She and Holl were the first ones born after they got here. The bigger children had to keep the babies quiet until they sealed off that part of the basement."

"This I know," Ludmilla nodded, remembering, with a little smile on her lips.

"Boy, wait 'til I bring that one up to Holl," Keith said, filing it for later teasing. "He thinks *I* make noise."

"And he told me how his father came to be sort of the

village headman," Marcy went on, ignoring Keith. "Everyone respects Enoch's father. They're all so opinionated, and they still listen to his decisions. Enoch wants to earn that kind of respect for himself."

"Who's his father?" asked Keith, trying to place an older Enoch.

"Didn't you guess, Keith, even after telling me Mrs. Hempert's story? I'm surprised. He's the Master's son."

"It figures," Keith groaned, striking the side of his head as realization dawned. "They've got a lot in common. Especially the temperaments."

"But Enoch admires Keith a lot for being gutsy enough to confront him," Marcy turned to Ludmilla, "and for not letting it get to him when Enoch was rude."

"So," Ludmilla twinkled, "I am sorry you are deprived of a girlfriend, but I am happy."

"I'm happy about it, too," Keith admitted. "Really."

"And I am proud of you, too, Keith," the old woman said, reaching forward to pat him on the arm. "You haf done a great thing for my little ones. I am pleased."

Keith beamed. "It's nice to hear you say that. I need a reality check every so often."

"In the light of my reality, you are deserving of appreciation."

"Oh, Keith, you are a doll," Marcy insisted, kissing him.

Keith glowed. "Just don't do that in front of Enoch," he told her. "He said he'd paste me one. He's worse than Carl."

"If you are yet admitting that you are talking to me," Ludmilla told them as she escorted them to the door, "give my old friends my greetings."

"Not yet," Keith told her, bending down to kiss her lightly on the cheek. "But I will."

In the dark of night, Keith pulled his ancient midnight blue Ford Mustang around to the side of Gillington Library, and waited anxiously as the Little Folk stole in and out of the wall, carrying newspaper-wrapped bundles piled high in their arms. He worried that passersby might hear them, but their footsteps made less noise than the fallen leaves whispering over the ground. A haze of snowflakes speckled the beam from the streetlight. The trunk was nearly filled to capacity when Holl signalled that the last of the cargo was inside; Keith jumped quickly out and slammed it down. He kept an eye out for patrols. As the last of the elves disappeared back into their home, he flicked on the headlights, and idled quietly forward, his tires crunching gently on the freezing pavement. The security patrol passed by him, shining its searchlamp into his window for the college sticker. Keith let out a long sigh of relief when it drove away from him.

He hurried back to the dormitory lots. The shipments to the local shops he intended to deliver in the morning before classes, and the others that had been promised to out-of-town shops for tomorrow he would drop off after lunch, before Sociology class in the library basement. Hollow Tree Industries was at last underway.

When Keith's car had gone, a single figure slunk out of the bushes where it had been watching the entire operation, and tried to catch the sliding chunk of facade before it closed all the way. Under its clawing fingers, the masonry ground back into place, leaving no sign it had ever moved. Listening to make sure no one was approaching, the figure threw its shoulder against the block, but it held firm. It tried again. No movement. With a growl, the watcher pulled a pointed chisel out of a pocket, and began to pry at the stone block. The tool's blade hopped out of the long groove and screeched across its stone face. With another glance around, the figure continued to scrape and dig with the chisel, attempting to force open the elves' back door.

Under the "Would You Believe" column in the holiday ad edition of the *Midwestern Gazette*, a little girl was quoted as having seen one of Santa's elves. "He smiled at me," she said. "I been a good girl all year, and Santa knows." The columnist didn't appear to take her too seriously, but Catra did. She knew instantly who the source of the little girl's apparition had been. When she brought it to the attention of the Elders, they asked Enoch to be more circumspect on his outings to see Marcy.

"We still don't know where the other articles are coming from," Catra told him, "but this one we do. Stay low!"

Enoch agreed somewhat reluctantly to comply. "Perhaps I should have grown a mustache," he said, ruefully.

• Chapter 22 •

Ms. Voordman recognized Keith right away when he called at her gift shop. "Hello, Hollow Tree," she said, appraising the stacked packages in his arms. Her thin black eyebrows climbed halfway up her forehead. "Right this way. I'll be in the office, Diane," she called. "Watch the door."

"Yes, Ms. Voordman," came a voice from between the shelves near the front of the shop. Keith looked over that way. He couldn't see anybody. Whoever had spoken must be on her knees. Or an elf. He grinned to himself as he followed the shop owner. The porcelain figures smiled blithely at him as he went by.

"Good," Ms. Voordman said, gesturing to him to put down his packages. "Let's see 'em." She began to unwind newspaper and drop it on the floor.

When all of the bundles were unwrapped, she pounced on the lanterns, and held them up one at a time. "These three are mine," she announced, separating her choices from the others. Keith couldn't see that there was much to choose between, but he did notice that wherever a section called for a piece of wood larger than five inches square, two or more smaller bits had been neatly joined together somehow.

All of the items had a semiparquet appearance. He didn't understand why the elves had made them that way, but the effect was kind of pretty. The ones Ms. Voordman had latched onto were the nicest. "I like the way the filigree pattern works with the various grains in the panel. Real artistry. I'll see that the right people get a look at these, and I'll talk to you about another order when I know how they sell. Ah!'' she cried with a pleased expression, snatching up a couple of small items. ''My cookie cutters!''

On his way out, Keith heard the bump and scrape of items being set on the metal shelves, and craned his neck around the corner to see who was doing the stocking. A slender girl blinked up at him from her seat on the floor, flipping back fine blond locks of shoulder-length hair. She wouldn't quite have qualified for Aristotle's Ideal of Beauty, but she was beautiful. The bright blue-green eyes and well-molded cheekbones of her triangular face were appealing and attractive. Keith blinked stupidly, trying to find his tongue, and finally stammered out, ''Hello.''

Her lips curved up at the corners. ''Hi.'' The dustcloth she held in one hand dropped softly to the floor.

''New here?'' Keith couldn't believe how much trouble he was having speaking.

''Oh, no,'' she said. ''I've been working here all semester. I think I know you from somewhere.''

Keith gave up trying to find his tongue and whipped one of his new business cards from his wallet instead.

''Yes,'' the girl nodded, reading the card. ''Wooden handcrafts. Keith Doyle. Ms. Voordman mentioned you.'' She smiled at him, handed the card back. She had a delightful smile. He liked the way she said his name. They looked at each other, waiting for the other to break the silence.

''Well,'' Keith swallowed. ''I'll see you.'' He started for the door.

''My name's Diane,'' the girl called out. Keith looked back at her, but didn't halt his forward momentum, and he and the door met with a bang. He staggered back, looking surprised. The bell jingled indignantly, and Diane laughed out loud.

''Nice to meet you,'' Keith said, gathering himself together, and pulled the door open. ''Can't think what that door was doing there.'' Still grinning, Diane waggled her fingers at him and bent her head to her work. He made it out the door this time, feeling a deep exhilaration.

He had a bounce in his step the rest of the day. His awareness that his car was badly in need of a tune-up brought no more than a resigned, ''Oh, well.'' The steadily worsening weather affected him not at all. There was no good reason for his high mood. There had been no declaration of undying love between them, no vows of friendship . . . not even a promise to have lunch together, and yet he knew that he had just met someone wonderful, and he wanted to see more of her.

* * *

In Sociology class, Carl found that he was being entirely isolated. That weirdo Doyle was back, and he was deep in conversation with Holl. The two of them were excitedly pushing pieces of paper back and forth between them. It looked like one of the notes was a check. Where would he get a *check*? There was something strange going on here, and he couldn't hear well enough to tell what it was.

Goodman and Eisley were into another debate about politics. Teri and those elf girls were giggling about something while waiting for class to start. He noticed that the Little Ones were starting to dress differently than before. Their new clothes resembled the kind of styles he was used to seeing outside. More changes had taken place over the last few weeks than in the whole year and a half he had been coming down here. Marcy seemed more odd than ever. She had given up her seat next to him in favor of one beside the black-haired boy. Their heads were close together, and Marcy was gazing at the kid with a sort of hero-worship in her eyes. If there were no other explanation for it, he'd say that they were . . . involved. Child molesting. That was too sick for Carl to contemplate. He turned away from them. But now he was facing Keith again. With a growl, he stared down at his books.

He was frustrated. There wasn't any facet of his life that hadn't been polluted by Keith Doyle. The dorm, Student Senate—even though Doyle had conceded the victory on the library, it still showed Carl that Doyle could ruin anything he wanted to, and there wasn't anything he could do to stop him—and Marcy. He wasn't sure how Doyle was involved in making him lose his girlfriend, but he was positive there was a connection. Pat Morgan felt the nerd was harmless, but Carl could have given him plenty of examples of his potential for destruction.

And now, the Little People were doing something mysterious, and his rival was a part of it. He had seen them together twice now, late at night. How they could trust him, Carl couldn't understand. He was making money off of them, if that was really a check he had just seen. He almost voiced his question, but the only person in the room not engaged in another conversation was Marm, and he had been ignoring Carl firmly for the last four weeks after their argument. Instead, the bearded elf sat with his nose deep in a textbook, making notes on a scrap of paper. Final exams were only a few weeks away, and the Master liked to keep his class ahead of the university schedule.

Lee Eisley looked around him with suspicion. He watched the little ones hungrily, feeling even more than before that they might vanish before his eyes. When he heard Teri inviting Maura and the others to get together with her outside of class, he started to protest violently. If they left the library, they would disappear, and he would never see them again. He felt almost proprietary toward them, and he resented Keith for his easy familiarity, since it was difficult for Lee to conceive of making them his friends. He still hadn't forgiven Keith for the Student Senate debacle. It was working its way through the back of his mind that he might do something about the worry that Keith caused him.

Holl stopped Keith in the middle of his fourteenth description of Diane, and asked, "What am I supposed to do with all the papers you handed me last night?"

Keith, unaware of the ire simmering about him, snapped out of his reverie and got back to business. "As treasurer of Hollow Tree Industries, you need to fill those out so we can send them in. The I.R.S. requires that we have an Employer I.D. number. And we'll need a resale number, too."

"But these are corporation forms, slow child," Holl explained patiently. "I read all those booklets from the Small Business Administration. We decided that it would be a better plan to make you a sole proprietorship, in case you don't remember my mentioning it. We cannot be employees since we do not have Social Security Numbers or verifiable addresses."

"Oh, yeah," Keith said, hitting himself in the side of the head. "I've got other things on my mind."

"You've mentioned her."

Keith grinned. "Well, I'll get the right forms. Sorry.

Thanks for the check, by the way. It takes a big bite out of the advance money, but I really do need it.'' Keith patted his breast pocket happily. ''Is there anything else you need? All tax deductible as business expenses. More tape? Sharpening stones? Glue?''

''Wood,'' said Holl promptly. ''We need wood.''

• Chapter 23 •

Saturday morning, Keith drove his car to the rear of Gillington Library, reached behind him to undo the look, and kept lookout until the rear door opened and slammed shut and the car sagged slightly on its elderly springs. He had company. ''Stay down until I'm off campus,'' he commanded.

''Just as you say,'' came a muffled voice from behind him.

When he was well out of Midwestern's environs, he called, ''Okay.'' Two faces popped up from under the tarpaulin in his rearview mirror: Holl's and Enoch's.

''Hi, Enoch,'' Keith said, surprised. ''I was only expecting Holl. To what do I owe the pleasure?''

''He's the hardwoods expert,'' Holl explained. ''So long as we were shopping, I brought him along. I didn't think you'd mind.''

''Not at all,'' Keith assured him mildly. ''Strap in, okay? This state has a seat-belt law.''

He drove along the narrow country roads as Holl explained the object of their quest. ''We've used firewood, old furniture the university has discarded, scraps of lumber from the woodshop, but at last we've run out of stock, and there're orders yet to fill. There isn't time to cure cut wood, though we have some aging. We're about out of anything larger than sawdust.'' His voice died away as his head turned from side to side, catching all he could of the scenery. Keith didn't think he had blinked since they left.

''I noticed,'' Keith said, remembering the patchwork lanterns. "Although I wasn't sure you weren't making things that way on purpose. They looked pretty."

"There's far more work in little bits," Enoch said.

"True. Wood's the one thing you can't do without in a woodcraft business," Keith acknowledged.

"Yer a master of the obvious," the black-haired elf complained.

"Yup. We needed a real source anyway. What we want is a lumberyard that sells cheap, or one that won't mind selling to us wholesale. What kinds of woods are you interested in? Enoch? Hey!" He shouted to gain the black-haired elf's attention. Enoch was staring out the window with a look of concentration. "Is something the matter?"

"First time in an automobile," Enoch said, hoarsely, watching the telephone poles flick by with alarming speed. His hand clutched the armrest tightly.

"Mine, too," put in Holl, though he didn't look nervous, only excited. He watched a field full of seated cows go by, his eyes as round as theirs.

"Does it bother you?" Keith asked, concerned.

The two elves' eyes met. "We don't travel much," Holl told Keith. "In fact, this is my first time outside town."

"Ever?"

The blond elf nodded.

"Why don't you travel?" Keith asked curiously.

"Well, why should we?" Holl countered. "Everything I love or want is right there in the compound. There's no need for me to stray far beyond it. The school has kindly supplied experimental farmfields from which we can . . . borrow . . . without going too far. I can't speak for anyone else, though."

"I don't mind travelling," Enoch mused, looking up at the tracery of tree branches on the overcast sky. "So long as I can go home again afterwards."

"There was another break-in attempt," Holl told Keith. "The stonework is marked where our burglar tried to chisel his way in. The old ones are half-panicked."

"I don't blame 'em," Keith said, concerned. "It sounds like someone has seen you guys going in or out. Whoever it is might be watching us. You have to be more security-conscious for a while. Especially until the Historical Society comes through."

Enoch forgot his nervousness, and scowled. "I'll come and go as I please."

Instead of looking alarmed, Keith smiled indulgently. He felt like a collegiate Cupid. "How're things going with Marcy?"

"Oh, well, well. We get along just fine." Noticing Keith's wry look, Enoch asked, "Is there anything wrong with that?"

"No, nothing, nothing," said Keith, a grin spreading across his face, as he swung the car around a corner. Wet gravel rattled under the tires. "Just looks to her roommates like she's dating her little brother's best friend."

"Hmm," said Enoch thoughtfully, studying his reflection in the car window. "Think I should grow a mustache? I've considered it anon."

Keith imagined a big black handlebar mustache on Enoch's face, and sputtered helplessly. He didn't want to hurt the little guy's feelings. Their detente was too recent to stand a fresh breach. But his imagination was too much for him, and he burst out with a hearty laugh. To his surprise and joy, Enoch joined in.

"It is a funny picture," Enoch admitted. "But what do you think?"

"No," Keith decided firmly. "Let 'em talk."

"Aye, I'll do that." Enoch grunted, satisfied.

It took them several tries before they found a lumberyard in which the elves considered the wood to be suitable, and which was also willing to sell wholesale to an unestablished and undocumented company. Keith waited only long enough in each one to let the other two browse. If they gave him a signal of approval, he'd approach the owner. Many times, Enoch would give the place one sniff and stalk back outside to the car. Keith had to admit that he couldn't tell what it was the little guy sensed, but *they* were the ones who would work with whatever it was he bought.

They reached Barn Door Lumber when the watery sun was at the top of the winter sky. Enoch and Holl fell to examining this place with alacrity, so Keith sought out the owner, Fred

Orr, about a discount. Mr. Orr was a burly man, a couple of inches over six feet tall, and almost that much width-wise, with his belly trying to make it six and a half. Keith, with a good deal of diplomacy that was aided by his natural enthusiasm, described the project the wood was needed for, and managed to negotiate a small cut in price. He promised they would present a resale number the next time they stopped in. "We really need the wood right away," he explained, plaintively.

"Well . . . okay," the owner said. While they were talking, Holl and Enoch, both respectably hatted, wove between skids of boards and panels, picking out the best of the raw materials. The man watched them running their hands over the timber and smelling the wood closely to determine its age. He rocked back on his heels and gave a thoughtful sniff. "Okay," he said, squinting meditatively at Keith. "You look honest enough. But no credit. Cash now, and you've got a deal."

"Will you take a check?" Keith asked, relieved.

"Uh-huh. If you've got some I.D."

The pleasantly fresh smell of sawn wood made Keith breathe in again deeply. The dust tickled his nose, threatening to make him sneeze. He followed the proprietor to the rolling metal cart on which the two "boys" had stacked their choices. The bill was calculated, and Keith wrote out a check, cringing at the amount, which brought the balance for Hollow Tree Industries very close to zero. Holl watched closely, his head at Keith's elbow, doing the mathematics in his head and pointing out where he made mistakes in addition. Mr. Orr grinned at them, and held the door as they carried their purchase outside.

"Couple of smart kids you've got there," he told Keith.

"You bet," Keith said. "Sometimes they act about four times their age." Enoch stepped on his foot passing through to the parking lot. "Ouch!"

With the wood secured under the sheet of oilcloth, Keith felt more relaxed, but hollow inside. A glance at his watch surprised him. It was already after one o'clock. He hadn't eaten in hours. "How about some lunch?" Keith asked the others, now seated next to him, as he started the car. The elves again exchanged glances.

"We didn't bring any with us," Holl said, apologetically.

"No." Keith studied their faces curiously. "I meant we could stop in a restaurant. Personally, I'm starving. Yes?"

"Yes!"

They rolled away from Barn Door Lumber, and started looking for a good place to eat.

They pulled into the parking lot of Grandma's Kitchen, a franchise family-restaurant that Keith favored, about fifteen miles outside of town. It was the perfect place for college students, who tended to use it as a distant rendezvous, or a way-station on long trips back and forth to school. It was clean, well lit, open twenty-four hours a day, and fairly cheap, despite the high quality of food it served. There were a few snickers from the back seat when he drove in. The place was a study in plastic quaintness. It was built to draw potential diners to it by oozing wholesomeness. In point of fact, it looked silly. The green-and-yellow building facade, visible from a considerable distance, resembled a bastard cross between a Swiss chalet and a thatched cottage.

Keith recognized no other students from Midwestern there. He wondered what he would have done if Carl or Lee, or any other members of the "I Hate Keith Society," had been eating there that day. Probably spun on his heel and walked out again. If no one stopped him. He was grateful that he didn't have to find out. The last thing he wanted to do was give the elves their first experience in dining out at a McDonald's.

"Kind of a nice clientele we're building up," Keith said in an undertone, while they were waiting to be seated. "Eleven customers, and six or seven others that are possibles, with five more who said they'd wait and see if we died or not. Not shabby for amateurs, huh?" He felt a small surge of pride as the two elves exchanged approving glances. He unzipped his jacket but kept his hat on, to keep the restaurant staff from particularly noticing that the "boys" hadn't removed theirs. They fumbled with the wooden buttons on the front of their coats, looking around curiously at their surroundings.

"So, the charm worked," Enoch said to Holl, also keeping his voice low. Holl nodded agreement.

"Charm? What charm?" Keith asked. The elves looked guilty, but finally Enoch spoke up.

"Well . . . it enhances the attractiveness of things, if you know what I mean."

"Is that why everyone made orders so quickly?" Keith exclaimed, disappointed. "I thought it was because they liked the products."

"Well, I'm sure they did, but we wanted to make certain," Holl said. "We have a strong stake in the success of this venture. Have we done anything wrong?"

"Mmm—" Keith squirmed. "Well . . . not *really*. But it isn't *completely* ethical. I think."

"According to the marketing studies, most companies use a form of suggested selling for their products," Enoch pointed out. "Doyle Dane Bernbach uses images considered to be unexpec—"

"Shall we stop it?" Holl asked, interrupting his friend. "We meant only to help."

Keith sighed. "How strong is this charm?"

"Not very. By definition, it's a compulsion, though not a strong one. What it does is persuade one to drop the inhibitions against seeing the true beauty and usefulness of a thing. More of a simplification than anything else."

"Doesn't falsely enhance the item, does it?" Keith asked. "They call that fraud, you know."

"Oh, not at all. An enhancement would make a shortbread mold more profoundly a shortbread mold, but not a more attractive one."

Keith thought about it for a moment. "I guess you can keep doing it. Those things wouldn't be yours if they didn't have a little magic in 'em."

The hostess signalled to them, and showed them to a table by the window. The two elves gazed around them with avid interest, taking in the brightly colored vinyl-upholstered benches in the booths, the glass-roofed salad bar, and the six-foot-high glassed-in carousel of desserts that spun under lights in the center of the restaurant.

"Look at that," Holl nudged his friend. "Vardin would eat himself sick."

"Aye, he would," Enoch said, trying to contain feelings of panic. This place was stuffed full with more Big Ones than he had ever seen together in one place. He stuck close to Keith, whom he trusted, and slid into the deepest part of the semicircular booth by which the hostess was waiting. She beamed down at him, seeing a shy twelve-year-old boy. He managed a sickly smile in return, and accepted the tall plastic-coated menu she handed him. It was like a picture-book of food. The number of choices was overwhelming.

Holl was already perusing his, appearing to compare the appearance of Grandma's Kitchen's food favorably over that of the Power Hall cafeteria. Keith didn't blame him.

On the way over to their table, Keith had observed the size of the portions being served to other customers. They were enormous. He remembered suddenly how little his two guests ate. A little self-consciously, he thought of his favorite meal at Grandma's Kitchen: a broad ring of thick-cut french fries surrounding a hamburger covered in cheese and bacon strips that was almost the size of a 45-rpm record. To him or one of his other friends, that would be a decent snack. To Holl or Enoch, it might be a little daunting. When the waitress came by, a tall woman with bleached hair and a dark vestigial mustache, Keith appealed to her to bring a couple of kiddie menus. "They're growing boys," he said, amiably, "but not that fast." The waitress smiled maternally down at them, and departed.

Enoch let out an opened-mouth squawk, but Holl burst out laughing. Abashed, Keith pointed surreptitiously to the tables around them, and both had to agree he had a point.

"Any of those'd be a week's food in the village," Holl calculated. "We've never had a bought meal before."

"Great," Keith said, passing them the smaller children's menus. "Order whatever you want. Try something new. How about chocolate chip pancakes?" He looked up to find both of them studying him uncomfortably. "What's the matter?"

"We don't know how we'll repay you for all your help," Holl said seriously. Keith didn't think he meant just the meal.

"Repay me?" he scoffed, deliberately misconstruing Holl's meaning and keeping his tone light. "What's with these 'pay me backs'? I'm not laying anything out but some time. Look," he said, pouncing on an inspiration, "this lunch is a business meeting, so it qualifies as an expense. As such, it comes out of the company treasury. And, since you own the company, you're really taking me out. Can the company afford it? Shall I pay *you* back later?" The two elves frowned at one another.

Enoch said gravely, "We would be most honored if you would join us for lunch. Please order anything you want. You may use the big menu. You growing boys need to eat."

"Thank you." Keith smiled with equal gravity. The waitress reappeared as soon as they closed the menus, and took their orders to the kitchen.

"We haven't heard lately about the famous paper you had to write or die, Keith Doyle," Holl chided him. "The one about legendary peoples, specifically ourselves."

"Oh, yeah." Keith laughed self-consciously, caught off guard. "I guess I haven't thought about it too much lately. It's more fun to rub elbows with the real thing. I may write it one day. Maybe," he said dreamily, "as a series of reminiscences. My memoirs." He snapped out of his daydream when Holl blew him the raspberry.

"You missed a lot in your research," Enoch pointed out. "There're a lot of articles in old magazines. All rubbish, of course, but scholars consider it to be proper research only if it's written."

"Of course," Keith agreed politely. "Just like Dr. Freleng, my other Sociology professor. But I'm too busy to write right now. Business, you know." The waitress arrived and plunked platters of food down before them.

Over their lunch, they chatted about the class and their classmates. Keith listened with interest as the two elves discussed facets of his fellow students that filled him with admiration for their perception. Teri acted shallow, but it was all for show. She actually had a fine brain for spatial mathematics. Barry was afraid of women, probably because of his family life. Lee used the class as a sort of security blanket, and the Little Folk were worried about his dependency, seeing as how he was supposed to graduate in June.

Around a mouthful of hamburger, Keith inquired, "Why isn't the class bigger? I can think of dozens of kids who need tutoring as badly as I do, but there's only the privileged 'we.' "

"Because those of us in it stand a chance of actually learning something from what we're told. Would you assimilate as much if the class were big?" Holl asked.

"Probably not," Keith admitted frankly. "I always go to sleep in lecture halls. I meant, why haven't the *students* brought in more students?"

Enoch scratched the back of his neck uncomfortably, and looked out of the window. Holl studied his sandwich for inspiration. "It's got to do with the same sort of . . . compulsion that's on the shortbread molds," he explained. "One comes in, and he asks the next one, and that one invites the one after that."

"Oh," said Keith. "Like a chain letter. You're invited, and you eventually invite one person to join the class, and then *they* ask one person. How do you know who to choose? And how do you keep from asking more than one person?"

"Well, it sort of happens to you," Enoch explained, making sure no one was in earshot. "When the need is greatest, the newest of you gravitates toward the student in need, and then *that one* comes in. Marcy fought asking you, partly because she is . . . as inhibited as she is. One day, you'll find someone who needs us. Whether or not you know they need help.

"The Master accepts only serious students. We have had a bad one or two, but the ones who come to gape never stay long. Their memory fades away, until they don't really believe that they've seen us."

"They might remember a discussion group, but to them, it was taught by a short man with red hair who brought his kids with him to class." Holl indicated Enoch and himself. "Not very interesting."

"Ah," Keith nodded, comprehending some of it. "A *geas*. I read about those. This magic stuff is complicated. But interesting. I want to know all about it. Can you grant wishes?"

Enoch sputtered. "Do we look like genii?"

"Nope," said Keith gaily. "Leprechauns."

By the time they left the restaurant the sky had cleared. Keith calculated there would still be two or three hours of sunlight. "If you're not in a hurry to get back, I could just drive you around the countryside for a while. Since this is your first look-see at the world outside Midwestern, that is." He gestured invitingly at the road ahead.

"Yes," said Holl, without hesitation. "Absolutely." Enoch nodded enthusiastic agreement.

At random, they took a road leading west, and turned corners when it pleased them. For the most part, Keith followed his nose, keeping track of the route only enough to be able to find his way back. Some snow had already fallen hereabout, but it remained only in gullies and hillsides sheltered from the sun. In the cold wind, the countryside looked lonely, but there was an occasional house set far back from the road with cheery yellow lights showing through the curtained windows. Cats watched them from comfortable sconces atop gateposts and mailboxes, or folded into gaps in the bare, black flowerbeds. Dogs barked at them from fenced yards, and one bold collie, smiling, with his tongue hanging out of his mouth, paced the car along one long slow stretch. On more than a few properties, "For Sale" signs quivered hopefully in the wind over fields cleared of crops. Barns with paint peeling off their walls appeared unexpectedly over the rise, and a few cold cows huddled together on the ground in the corner of a fenced meadow.

A few miles after passing through a small town with only two traffic signals and one strip of stores on its main street, they took a sharp right turn onto a half-paved county road that led them up a low hill past leafless trees. Keith spotted a narrow track leading off to the left that wound around, diving into the crease between two high fields where the cornstalks lay in broken rows. They crossed a bridge over a shallow brown river, and watched a tributary flowing diagonally away from them the length of the heavily wooded lot on their right. Lights winked from the windows of a big house, standing on its own hill deep within the boundaries, almost invisible behind the trees. There was a "For Sale" sign next to the road there, too. Holl, Enoch, and Keith sighed in unison.

"Nice place," Keith decided, pulling over to study it.

"That'd be a perfect place to live," Enoch said longingly.

"It would," Holl agreed. "It has good spirit about it."

"Yeah, but it's probably fifteen hundred dollars an acre, and we don't know how big the parcel is. Land isn't cheap, especially with buildings on it."

They travelled further as the light began to disappear, perusing Keith's Illinois road-map with interest by the light of a hastily twisted wick Enoch made from the rag Keith used to check his oil. Keith watched the process with interest. "It looks so easy," he said wistfully.

"It is easy," Enoch assured him. "A matter of practice, natural, much like your driving this car."

"Want to swap lessons?" Keith offered hopefully.

"One day, when there is more time," Enoch considered.

"Go on," Holl urged his friend, with a twinkle in his eye. "I'll get you a box to sit on."

They looked at several more large farms with "For Sale" signs on them, especially those on lots with heavy forestation. The two elves looked at the farms speculatively. The real estate idea had been firmly planted by Keith, and it was germinating.

When the sky was nearly dark, the Mustang turned back toward town. "The others might like to have a drive around to look at things," Holl said. Enoch nodded.

"Sure," Keith said, pulling into campus. "Happy to oblige. Doyle Tours, Limited, a division of Hollow Tree Industries. We cater to Legendary Beings."

▪ Chapter 24 ▪

When Keith turned the corner to drop them off at Gillington, he spotted a crowd milling in the common outside the building. "Gack!" he exclaimed, and slammed on the brakes. The elves were thrown forward, but Keith was too distracted to apologize. A huge crowd of students and a bunch of police cars, with their blue lights revolving, were clustered around the corner of the building near the elves' back door. Campus security was there, too, keeping the curious onlookers out of the way of the police.

"What is it?" Holl demanded. "What's happening?"

"Did they get in? Is the doorway open?" Enoch barked worriedly.

Keith signalled to them to lie down flat, and got out of the car. He boosted himself up on top of the hood and squinted through the revolving lights at the building. "There're a bunch of people at the wall," he called down to them. "They're looking at the stonework. It looks like it's damaged. But I don't think it's broken through. All surface damage, but it's really extensive." One of the men in gray overalls felt around inside a crater about the size of Keith's head that had been blasted out of the masonry.

"Hey, you!" A security guard in a green uniform came striding over and glared up at Keith. "What are you doing here? There's no parking!"

"I'm, um . . ." Keith said glibly, scrambling down.

"What's all this back here?" the security officer snapped out, yanking up the bulky tarpaulin in the back seat of the car. Keith's heart stopped. "*Wood*?"

"I'm taking it to the woodshop, officer," he croaked out. "It's for a project."

The man nodded, waved a dismissive hand at him. "Good. Then take it over there. Move your car out of this vicinity. Say," he said abruptly, with a searching look at Keith and his Mustang, "do you live on campus? I think I've seen that vehicle . . ."

"Yes, sir," Keith said immediately, interrupting him. "Thank you, sir. I'm going." He jumped back into the car and backed it away from the officer, who was still studying him. "Why didn't he see you?" he asked the back seat in astonishment.

"He wasn't looking for us," Holl explained.

"Magic?"

"Park the car," said Enoch's voice, tiredly. "We'll have to hide."

Keith followed the two elves across the Student Common to a manhole cover well-hidden behind a clump of bushes. There was still enough of a crowd to put Keith in panic. He was afraid that someone would spot them, but the mob's attention was still on the library wall. Now, men in coveralls were bringing forward a wheelbarrow containing a bag of cement. It looked like they were going to fix the break on the spot. A minicam crew from the local news station positioned itself near the damaged wall and began rolling tape. A commentator placed herself in plain sight, and spoke earnestly into her microphone. The crowd moved in closer.

It took the combined strength of both elves to pry up the heavy steel cover. Keith kept a lookout as they slid down into the dark hole. He let the lid down as gently over his head as he could, and felt his way down an iron ladder made of staples hammered into the wall. When he reached the bottom, he discovered that it was not entirely dark down there. They were in a portion of a steam tunnel.

"The way is blocked," Holl explained, pointing along a spotlighted walkway toward the distant end of the tunnel, "but at least we can let them know that we are all right. I will signal."

"They're sealing that block of wall up there with cement," Keith told him. "Someone was definitely trying to get in. He did a lot of damage. You won't be able to use that door."

Holl looked worried. "That means that someone else *was* spying upon us. There's no mistake now. I thought so. Wait here." He strode down the hall through the patches of light and darkness, his figure strobing in and out of existence.

Enoch looked around him with a sort of nostalgia. "This is my earliest memory of Midwestern University. We found this place. I stole food from maintenance workers so we could live."

"I know," Keith said absently, surveying the place curiously. "Ludmilla told me about it." He realized what he had just said, and froze. He glanced at Enoch, and the elf had stopped in place, too, with open shock on his face.

The pose broke, and the brows drew down over Enoch's nose. "You know about her."

It was an accusation. Enoch's hands closed into fists, and Keith wondered if the elf was going to hit him. He considered, uncomfortably, that he probably deserved it. Never could keep a secret from birth, he chided himself.

"How did you find her?" the elf demanded.

"Lee told me," Keith admitted, meekly. "I needed to know things. I've taken Marcy there, too. Ludmilla asked to see her."

"Ah," Enoch said. He pursed his lips thoughtfully and the fists unballed. "I would suppose it is all right, then."

"She said to say 'hi' to her oldest friend."

The elf nodded, friendly again. "I say 'hi' back to her, then."

"Maybe you'd better say it yourself," Keith said, looking around him. "There's no way you can get back into the library through the main door with all this ruckus going on. And it's closed tomorrow, Sunday. This place doesn't look too comfortable. Maybe you should stay with her overnight."

"That is an idea with merit."

"So it is," said Holl, coming back through the lights. "We are accounted for. The Elders were worried to death when they heard the scratching on the stone. It must have been a hammer and chisel that did all that damage. But no one broke through." He examined his knuckles. "I've never tapped so long a message. My hand is scraped sore."

"We will stay here until later, and then go. It is a fortunate thing that we had such a good midday meal. We may have a long wait."

"Well, I'd better get out of here. They'll be keeping a close watch on anyone wandering around after dark, and I've got something to hide."

"Leave me the keys to your car, Keith Doyle," Holl said. "We've still got to get the wood out when the way is clear. We've a business to run."

As Keith started to shinny up the ladder, Enoch looked up at him. "By the way, Keith Doyle, I'm sorry I made a mess of your dormitory room. You're a good fellow after all."

Keith did a double take. "It was you?" he demanded, dumbfounded. "Both times?"

"Well, certainly," Enoch said, with asperity. "Perfectly understandable under the circumstances. Don't you agree?"

Holl chuckled. "It's a good thing there's peace between you now."

Two men in green security uniforms stood up as Keith entered the foyer of Power Hall. He recognized the shorter of the two as the guard who stopped him outside Gillington Library. "Keith Doyle?" one of them asked.

"That's me."

The bigger man behaved as if he was uncomfortable. "We're here because we received information . . . You understand we're not accusing you, but we have to check every lead on something like this."

Keith felt his throat go tight. "On something like what?"

The other guard felt it was time to speak up. "I saw you over by the library. In fact, I've seen you there a lot. You know what was going on there?"

"It looked like someone bashed a hole in the wall."

"Right. Know anything about it?"

"No, sir. I've been out all day."

The big guard jumped on his phrase. "And how did you know it happened today?"

Keith swallowed. "Well, I meet my . . . girl there. A lot. That's . . . where we meet."

"Very sweet," the guard said, unsympathetically. He'd broken up a lot of necking couples in his time, and enjoyed it. "Our source said he saw you hiding around there this morning, around dawn."

"What? Who?" Keith demanded. "Who was hanging around at dawn? Why?"

"Jogging," the guard said, glaring at Keith. "And we're not identifying him to you at this time. I'm asking you again: what were you doing?"

Keith got away somehow, leaving the guards only marginally convinced of his innocence, and fled to his dorm room. Pat was there, lying on his back reading with the stereo headphones on. Setting the book down on his chest, he looked down his long nose at Keith. "The cops were up here looking for you. Where'd you hide the body? I told 'em I didn't know when you'd be back."

"They were waiting for me in the lobby."

"What have you done? Stolen the kiddies' milk money?"

"Nothing." Keith scowled, shucking off his jacket.

Pat levered himself up onto an elbow. "Doyle, I don't believe you. What is going on? Carl told me about the senate thing and the Historical Society. What is there about the library and you, anyway?"

"Nothing I can explain right now. I would if I could. I will, as soon as I can."

Pat raised his eyebrows into a thin, dark arch. "Don't do me any favors."

Keith shrugged, flopping into a chair. "I don't know how, but I'm sure that Carl helped set me up for the security guards."

His roommate threw back his head and groaned. "Will you lay off Carl? You must think he's really out to get you. It bugs him. And he's still pissed at you because you accused him of trashing the room."

Keith considered. "Maybe I should apologize to him for that. I found out who did it."

"Oh? Who?"

"A guy who thought I was trying to steal his girlfriend."

"Is this the girl from Sociology class?" Keith nodded. "Does he live on campus?"

Keith shot Pat an enigmatic look. "Yes."

"Well, then you can return the favor sometime. I'll help," Pat offered. "Gladly. I think we got ants from the last Coke spill."

"We've come to an agreement. Besides, I'm not interested in her any more."

"What, after all semester of dreaming and bellyaching?"

"I've found this wonderful girl . . ."

Pat raised a hand to halt the babble. "Don't tell me. I've got better things to do."

Keith grinned at him, and reached for his homework.

His anxiety over the anonymous informer made him sleep badly. He was sure in the back of his mind that the vandal and the informer were the same person. Security would have noticed if the damage had been done later in the day. Surely it was just one person. Whoever it was, *was* serious or desperate enough to draw the attention of the whole world to the elves' retreat. His nervousness was compounded by his concern for Enoch and Holl, but a call from Ludmilla Hempert early the next morning helped to assuage his guilty feelings.

The local newspaper's headline announced "Vandals Deface Historic Gillington." Keith went through the story a dozen times, and walked as near as he dared to the building, itching to get inside. He felt frustrated because the way was blocked, and he knew he was being watched. He was still concerned about the two elves, but it was a needless worry. They knew their way around the campus better than he did, and ought to have no trouble staying out of sight. He could be their biggest hazard.

▪ Chapter 25 ▪

It wasn't until Tuesday evening that he managed to get down to the village through the classroom passage. To his relief, Holl and Enoch were both there, no worse for their adventure, and had somehow managed to transport the supply of wood inside without attracting notice. When Keith pressed them for details, Holl would say only, "Old skills," his favorite and Keith's least favorite answer.

They had discussed all of their sightseeing with the others in their clans, and most of them were keen to take a tour themselves, with Keith's fellow students wanting first go. He promised to figure out some way to do it, as soon as it was safe.

"I don't think it'll be a good idea for a few weeks," he insisted. "There's somebody out there who knows you're here, and just wants to cause trouble."

"No. The sooner the better," Catra insisted. "We can't find a new home by inspiration. We need to see what is available to us."

"What I'm concerned about is the break-in. Who was it? Did anybody see him? Whoever it was must have been hammering on that stone for a good long time."

"Of course we heard it," Tay snapped, tugging distractedly at his beard. "Short of going up to ask who it was, there was nothing else to do."

"I think you ought to have an evacuation plan, or something."

"I think," said the Elf Master, coming up to the little group, "that ve can take care of ourselfs, and perhaps you should think about the examination that vill soon take place."

With a twinge of guilt, Keith and the others followed the red-haired teacher up the tunnel to the schoolroom.

* * *

If the other Big Folk students were surprised to see Keith emerging from the little door behind the elves, they didn't show it. If anything, most of them took it in stride as a natural occurrence, based on what they'd come to know about him. Keith exchanged smiles and greetings, and made his way to the desk between Holl's and Enoch's.

In spite of his anxieties about Hollow Tree and the attempted invasion, Keith relaxed when he read the essay questions that the Elf Master scratched on the upright slate. Though he had been too busy to study over the weekend, he found the answers forming themselves in his mind almost quicker than he could write them down. As his confidence grew, inspiration took over, and he wrote faster. Even with the greater part of his mind involved with the test, he was aware of how the clarity of the teaching affected the amount of information he was able to retain. Holl was right: a smaller class gave the students an advantage in learning.

The Master promised to evaluate their papers right away. Keith felt smug. After this test, Freleng's final would be no big deal.

Thursday afternoon, he sailed blithely past the librarian on duty, carrying a plastic bag that seemed to be very light for its immense size and kept trying to get away from him, and a box which he took great care to keep balanced. The woman waved away his explanations, obviously tired of hearing them, and watched him ring for the elevator.

Keith shifted from foot to foot with excitement. Even if he had blown the test completely, which he doubted, the end of such a stimulating semester was deserving of some kind of celebration. The doors finally opened, and he maneuvered the cake and his bag of helium-filled balloons and party hats inside.

The classroom looked a little bizarre with balloons floating drunkenly all over the ceiling and bumping into each other where they were tethered to the backs of chairs. Keith presented the cake to the Elf Master with a little speech he had prepared ahead of time and thoroughly rehearsed, remembering his usual incoherence.

"I want to express how grateful I am for being allowed to join this class. I think I've learned a lot more about sociology than I thought I could. Shock does a lot for opening the mind to new experiences." The others snickered, glancing sideways at the Master.

"It has not been one-sided," the Master said, "but I am surprised you did not submit to me your thesis on interplanetary relations."

"I thought about it," Keith admitted. "Only I figured that the next time I opened a door in the library, I might find a lot of little green men and bug-eyed monsters."

"I know of none here," the Master assured him, over the class's laughter.

"Well, all I have to say is thank you for drumming the subject into my head . . . and I'll be happy with any grade I get—so long as it's an A." The rest of the class clapped and cheered. Keith bowed and sat down. The Elf Master got up, shaking his head in mock despair, and handed the papers out to the students one by one.

Beaming at the teacher, Keith took his, and looked it over. "But there's no grade on it," he protested.

"Meester Doyle," the master sighed, rapping him on the head with the roll of exams. "I do not understand vhy you are trying so hard to impress me. You haf demonstrated ample knowledge of your subject. If all you vish is a letter by which you can compare your attainment with that of others, then you haf learned little."

Keith turned red. Sometimes the Master reminded him of Professor Kingsfield from the *Paper Chase*. "I'm sorry. Maybe I should have asked what your method of grading was." Carl and the other male students regarded him smugly.

"I vould be happy to explain. I have marked on your test papers vere your theory is false, or vere your argument fails to support your premise."

Abashed, Keith turned his paper over, and went through the pages. "Well, you didn't mark anything on this at all."

"Then you demonstrated no false theories, and defended those you did propose well."

"Oh," Keith said in a very small voice. "I guess I got an A."

The Master sighed, this time in exasperation. "If you must express it in that limited fashion."

"Yahoo!" Keith cheered. The others joined in.

"I vish only that I could be assured you were as delighted vith having accomplished learning as you seem to be vith a transitory symbol."

"How about it?" Keith asked Marcy, as the cake went around. "Can you take this one home to your parents?"

"Yes," she said happily, displaying pages free of marginal comments.

"I meant the test," Keith chided her mischievously, taking a fingerful of icing from her plate of cake. She blushed. It made her look prettier than before.

"Yes, that too." Marcy glanced over at Enoch. The black-haired elf smiled back at her.

As the other human students drifted out, Holl beckoned Keith into the passageway for a private talk.

"There's a problem. I didn't want to bring it up in front of the others. We've the rest of that order to finish before you leave for the winter break, and there just isn't any way it can be done in that little time."

Keith made a wry face. "So how can you speed it up?"

"I don't know. We just cannot make our hands move any faster. I phoned in a query to a company that makes power tools, but they ask payment in advance, and we have no reserves in the account. Also, all are concerned about losing what money we have made so soon."

"I know where you can get jobs," Keith said, grinning, making points of his own ears with his forefingers, "with Christmas coming so soon. The work's seasonal, but at least it's high visibility, and the pay is good." Holl groaned at him, smacking him on the arm with an open hand.

"Will you stay with the matter at hand and stop recruiting for Santa Claus, you widdy?"

"I am. I'm thinking. Power tools . . . ?" The tall student snapped his fingers suddenly, the sound echoing down the hall. "I know where there are some we can borrow."

"I don't know about this, Keith. The school is fussy about insurance, and things like that."

"Don't worry about it, Mr. Scherer," Keith said, reassuringly. He patted the woodshop teacher on the back. "We'll give you a 'hold harmless' letter of agreement, if anyone asks. But since it's the end of semester, no one will pay any attention anyway.''

Scherer looked around his workshop. He was a middle-sized, middle-aged man who had a bald spot beginning in the midst of his black hair and pretensions toward a pot belly. His usually good-natured face showed an uncharacteristic expression of worry, as he watched a whole busload of little kids messing around with his power tools.

It had taken a large dose of the famous Doyle diplomacy to arrange it, but half the habitants of the elf village were occupying the school woodshop. They had acceded grumpily to Keith's insistence that only females and beardless males should go with him, even though Keith acknowledged that he would be leaving behind some of the top craftsmen. That still left him with fifteen or more workers. With admirable presence of mind, Keith taped a square of paper over the door's window so that passersby couldn't see in. Mr. Scherer, eager to avoid trouble with the administration, not only allowed him to block the window, but locked the door for him as well.

''So what's this all for?'' the teacher asked curiously, walking among the behatted youngsters. The crease between his brows deepened as he watched his precious table-saws run under the hands of a couple of pre-teenage girls, but a few moments convinced him he had nothing to worry about. He was impressed with their deftness. Keith was right. These kids really knew how to behave around dangerous equipment. And fast! He never saw anyone so quick to learn before. It had only taken one demonstration with the punch press, and the black-haired kid was handling it like he had lessons from nursery school on. Too bad he never got students like this for his classes. He averaged about one accident a week with the usual gang of idiots who took woodshop.

''Junior Achievements,'' Keith said, gesturing broadly at the roomful of boys and girls. ''I got involved last fall.''

''Oh, yeah?'' Scherer replied. ''I used to be the adult advisor for a J.A. group. Only mine sold toilet-roll covers and towel racks and easy stuff like that. So, how much is your stock selling for?''

''Stock?'' Keith echoed blankly. ''Right, stock.''

"Yeah, stock. The way they establish a company."

"Oh, yes, of course, stock. I know that. Well, we haven't printed the certificates yet, because we haven't raised the money for the printer. That's what you're helping us to do right now. We sell these, and we're on our way."

"Awright," the teacher said, approvingly. "And what's this? Ornamental lantern, huh? Nice, simple design: pierced screens, four pillars, peaked roof." Candlepat smiled politely at him as she took the frame out of his hands and put the wooden candle into its socket inside. She gave the teacher a coy wink. "Pretty."

"Uh, they're children's night-lights," Keith explained, over the buzz of the table saws. "Their own design."

"Oh," Scherer said, looking admiringly at Candlepat. She raised a hand, delicately flicked her long, golden hair back over her shoulder, and gave him a big, wide-eyed gaze. Catra hissed a warning at her from the next table where she was attaching hinges to boxes. "Yeah, very pretty." The man didn't notice that the other "children" were moving in more closely around him and the girl, prepared to defend her with their lives, no matter if it was her own fault. It always was.

Keith, who knew how little they trusted Big People, leaped in to disarm the situation, and did his best to distract the teacher. He waved the others away with a hand behind his back. It occurred to him that they might have knives. He didn't want one of Candlepat's flirtations to turn into disaster.

"Mr. Scherer. *Mr. Scherer*," Keith said, getting the teacher's attention and dragging him away from Candlepat, with whom Keith exchanged black looks. She pouted after her admirer, but went back to work. "Sir, she's twelve years old!" The teacher blanched, realizing how close he might have come to a fatal indiscretion. The administration frowned on statutory deviance. He didn't look at her again. With the threat allayed, the defenders eased back into their places. Keith took a deep breath.

"Stupid!" her sister growled under her breath. Candlepat put her nose in the air and pretended not to hear.

"Didn't mean nothin' by it," Scherer grumbled, hoping Keith wouldn't misjudge him. "Twelve, huh? Regular little siren. Wow! Think what she'll look like when she's eighteen."

"Huh! She'll never see eighteen again," Catra growled into her work.

"You gotta promise to let me know when you're ready to do business, Keith," the teacher urged him as they finished cleaning up and prepared to leave. "I've never seen such good, fast work in my life. It's almost magic."

"Sure is, Mr. Scherer."

"They look like Santa's little helpers in their little caps," the teacher chuckled heartily, patting one of the blond boys on the head. The kid wielding the broom turned and gave him a dirty look. Scherer shook hands with Keith and smiled at the others as they marched out into the snow. "Merry Christmas, kids. And good luck."

▪ Chapter 26 ▪

"He didn't mean any harm by it," Keith said, following the elves back toward the village. The bags of wooden toys and knickknacks were already in the trunk of his car, and he was planning out a route map for the next day in his head. Holl pulled out a glowing blue key to open the side entrance to Gillington. They stayed on the cleared path as far out of the streetlights as possible, avoiding the scanty new fall of snow on the grass.

Keith was still a little alarmed at their reaction to the woodshop teacher. It hadn't struck him before, but he'd been underestimating them. Now, he saw them as he should have, with a full range of feelings, defenses, worries. And there was nothing wrong with their sense of self-preservation. They might look like kids, but they weren't; not just cute mini-humans, but adults older than he was. And he of all their acquaintances should have known better. He wanted to kick himself for falling into the trap of anthropomorphic association. Wasn't it just a little while ago he'd called Marcy out for doing the same thing?

"I know," Holl said at last, making a face. "Ach, that man. I hate stereotypes!"

"Just call me Santa," Keith chuckled, feeling relieved. "You weren't really putting a spell on him, were you, siren?"

Candlepat was still offended. "*You'll* never know."

The door closed behind them just before the security patrol passed by on its hourly cruise of the Campus Common area.

"Well," Keith said, a little wistfully, "I guess I won't be seeing you guys again until January. Holl, will you stop by and pick up my mail every day? I am still waiting for our Employer's I.D. number, and things like that. We're not official yet."

"Of course," Holl assured him. "But don't be in such a hurry. We've got a custom of present-giving in this season, too. The most of us feel that we owe you something. Not that a small present would pay you back, but call it on-account."

"Thanks," Keith said, flattered, "but you don't owe me anything. When I was a little kid, I believed in brownies and gnomes. I never found any, but it was just because I convinced myself I was looking in the wrong places. Now I know: I check the basements of libraries every time. I feel that I owe *you* for my dream becoming real."

Enoch wasn't satisfied. "That's not much of a gift."

"It is to me," Keith said. "I don't know what else I'd want."

"Name it," Holl insisted. "We'd feel better."

"Well," Keith thought for a long moment. "Some of the things you make have obviously got some sort of magic. Would you do a little magic for me?"

"Little is what it would be," Catra told him. "There's just not enough energy to make a great working last a long time."

"It requires concentration beyond the simple existing life force of the spell's creator," Holl explained, but Keith still looked blank. "Look, it's like this: Sion here could make his ears look rounded, and they would always look so if he wanted them to, without his concentrating, because his mere existing would supply the necessary energy for the spell to continue."

"I wouldn't do it, though," Sion protested, fingering the points of his ears. "It's a matter of pride."

Holl nodded agreement. "Same with us all. Now, if Enoch wanted big fluffy wings . . ."

"Go on!" Enoch scoffed, putting aside the notion.

". . . We'd all have to concentrate, and they wouldn't last too long when we stopped. His own force isn't enough to maintain that kind of circuit. Think of electricity. We're all little batteries. Even you."

"Wow," Keith said. "Can you do something for me that would last?"

"What would you like?"

"Oh, I don't know. Well, my mom always said I was so curious I should have had cat's whiskers."

"Visible or invisible?" asked Dever.

"Invisible, of course," Keith answered flippantly. "I'd never get another date otherwise. But you're not serious."

"Sure, we're serious," Holl said. "You wanted a little magic. Sit down here." The blond elf stood facing Keith, his face eerily half-shaded in the light from the streetlamp coming in through the crack between the door and lintel. One eye socket looked empty in the shadow, with a glint of silver deep under his brow. Keith felt a shiver go down his spine as Holl touched forefingers to his cheeks just an inch or so from the nose, and drew invisible lines outward. The fingers touched again, a little higher up and further out, then moved again, out of the line of Keith's peripheral vision. He felt a third touch, below the second set. The others were gathered around, watching with interest, giggling.

"That's it," said Holl, dropping his hands to his side and shaking his wrists to relax them. "You can't see them, but we can, and there they are."

"Come on," said Keith, reaching up to touch his face. "Without any magic words? Nothing happened, right?" He twitched his nose. Something tickled his palm. He tried the other side, and his look of bewilderment made the young ones laugh even more. He felt around the sides of his nose, and discovered two sets of thin, stiff wires, about the same diameter and texture as broom bristles. He bent one upward to get a look at it. There was nothing to be seen, but he felt the pull on the skin near his nose. "There *is* something . . ." There was an impression in his fingers where the whiskers pressed, but whatever was causing it was definitely invisible. He was delighted. "How long will they last?"

"Only until you can convince yourself that they don't, ' Holl said. "Maybe all your life. It wasn't a difficult request."

Keith wiggled his nose again, laughed with joy. "Well, I couldn't have done it." The headlights passed by again, drawing a long ribbon of light through the gap in the doorframe and sweeping it across the floor. Keith looked up, and glanced at his watch. "Uh-oh. I'll have to sneak back. Thanks for everything, all of you," he said, his eyes going around to each of the elves.

"Save the soap," Enoch said, brusquely. "We're in your debt."

Keith twitched his whiskers, and with a salute to the elves, slipped out of the door. They were gone into the darkness before the door boomed shut behind him.

The periodical librarian at Gillington had a secret magazine subscription that was charged to the library budget, but never actually appeared in the archives. Since she had total charge of the mail, no one knew about it. So, every week on Wednesday, she would open and carefully abstract her copy of the *National Informer* and secrete her illicit "research digest" in her locker until she took time off for lunch. After lunch every Wednesday, she would hide the magazine again among her things, and go about her business. Within minutes after it was placed under her coat, it would be removed by careful elfin fingers and carried off to be perused by other eyes.

The librarian was aware that her magazine was being borrowed, but she never dared to say anything. For all she knew, it was Mrs. Hansen herself reading up on what it was inquiring minds wanted to know. Best not to rock the boat and have to pay for her own subscription.

Holl took it out of the locker on his way back from Keith's mailbox in the second week of winter vacation. The collection in the box included a host of get-rich-quick schemes, ads, and three brown legal-sized envelopes with a box number in the corner and "Penalty for Improper Use, $300" printed on each one. "I.R.S., eh?" Those would have to be answered, with his new supply of postage stamps and his hasty lessons from Keith on the workings of the U.S. Postal System. He tucked the mail under one arm, and thumbed through the digest on his way back home. There was a funny story on the second page about an actress who believed she was going to have alien twins, and the stacks of Gillington rang with ghostly laughter that sank into the lowest levels and then became silent as Holl passed through the hidden door. The librarian returning from her lunch heard the last echoes, and decided that she would be best employed spending the afternoon sorting the card catalog in the main lobby.

Usually, the village had a good laugh over the illustrated adventures of the spoiled and the gullible, but Orchadia, Enoch's mother, was the first to notice one small article on page five. "Sightings of Small Alien Humanoids Rock College Town." In spite of the reporter's vague style, there was no mistaking whom he must have meant. "Now they're appearing in a national magazine!" Catra wailed to the Master, showing him the photocopied story, which she kept in her folder with the other clippings.

Holl begged her to be calm. "It's a guess," he assured her. "One of those jokers at the *Informer* picked up on that little girl's story and improved on it, that's all. Just another literary echo."

"It's that Doyle," the elders agreed, and nothing Holl said could shake their opinion.

"It must be," Curran said. "Who else ha' seen us so close?"

After that, there was a careful perusal of every periodical that came into the library. Anyone leaving the village had to make doubly sure he or she was unobserved. The craftsmen were still working on reopening the back door, so they had to exit by way of the library stacks. It was more difficult during the holiday break with fewer bodies on campus. Any movement was notable. "We have no choice," Curran said at last to his gathered clan. "We canna live on vegetables for three weeks. If the snow comes again, we'd be too easy to track."

"I don't want my children taking the risk of being carried off," Shelogh said, indignantly. Her brown hair had a thread of grey at the temples, but her face, in spite of its set expression, was as smooth as a child's.

Catra sighed at her. "Mother!"

"When he gets back, we can have Keith Doyle look into

that story," Holl told them confidently. "I've heard nothing on radio or television. Could be someone caught a glimpse of one of us without a hat on and had a 'hallucination.' "

"No one vould be dot careless," Aylmer insisted.

"I hope not," Candlepat said, alarmed. "When we three visited Teri Knox, we were all most careful. Swore to her companions it was too cold to uncover our heads."

"Were they not suspicious?" Keva asked.

"No," the blond girl giggled. "We're her old summer campers, she tells them. Big Folk don't look for difficult explanations. They're so simple. She dined us on pizza, served from a flat box. It was very tasty, though untidy. May we make pizza sometime for supper? The Big Ones would never know it wasn't some of theirs. I can get a box."

"No," said Shelogh firmly.

"What kind of pizza was it?" demanded Dola, Tay's only daughter, and Keva's great-granddaughter. She was ten, and had a crush on Keith Doyle. Anything the Big Folk did fascinated her.

"*Carryout* pizza."

"Oooh."

"I dinna like having adults masquerading as children," Curran complained. "And as for Keith Doyle, who's to say 'tisn't he spreading the story himself." The old elf snorted. "By purpose or no. He's a fool."

"And all from one unsubstantiated story," Holl sighed. The Anti-Keithites were unappeased. "I wonder if he's the only fool." He put away Keith's letters in a box in his hut.

▪ Chapter 27 ▪

"I got your Christmas card," Keith told Marcy.

"I got yours, too," she said. "Did you have a nice holiday?"

"You bet. Everyone was home, so it was a nonstop parade with brass band."

"With your family, I'm not surprised."

"Playing in seven different keys, I'll wager," put in Holl, stepping over to greet them both.

"Hello, Teri Knox." Maura left Holl to touch her friend gently on the sleeve. "It is good to see you."

"Maura! Hi! God, what a wonderful dress!" The blond girl stepped back to admire the little elf as she twirled, billowing out the skirts of a parti-colored dress, white on one side, and red with tiny stars on the other. "That's more of Keith's weird Christmas materials, but wow! I love what you did with 'em. I ought to have you make my clothes."

"Hey, Barry!"

"Hey, Carl, how was the vacation?"

"Great. Went cross-country skiing. My mother broke her leg, so we went out for Christmas dinner. My folks gave me a color mini-TV for the dorm."

"*Hand*-sewn?" Teri squealed. "My fingers would fall off!"

"If you please?" the Master said, coming into the room from the tunnel and holding his hands up.

Nobody heard him.

"Mom tried roasting a goose this year. It wasn't done for hours. I thought we'd starve."

"Got a new snowmobile. It does zero to—"

"If you please!" The Master raised his voice over the din, banging a pointer against the easel chalkboard for emphasis. "The hour is long past vhen ve vere to begin the class."

There was more socializing and good cheer before the Elf Master was able to call the class to order. Nobody mentioned the wall outside that had been damaged and repaired, and Keith didn't want to voice any suspicions in class about the vandal. The spring semester was just beginning at Midwestern, and everyone was fresh and full of new energy from the vacation. Most of the human students were laden down with new books from their other courses. The Master was starting a new course, too.

"The topic is biology," the Master announced. "The science of the life of plants and animals."

Keith was nonplussed. As a Business major, biology had

limited application for him, unless he went into selling medical equipment, or something. He had done all right in high school biology, but it hadn't thrilled him much. Still, anything the Elf Master taught was likely to be interesting, whether or not he had any use for it. It was clear that other humans had different feelings about the change in subject. Teri was happy. She had a new Bio textbook already under her desk. Barry looked queasy and ambivalent.

"Do you mean we'll be dissecting things?" Barry asked, raising a hand for attention.

"No. Ve haf not the laboratory facilities for practical study, though microscopes and prepared slides are available to us in the science department. Ve vill be exploring the theory only."

"Oh. Good."

"Um, Master?" Keith raised his hand.

"Ye-es, Meester Doyle?"

"Will we be examining elf biology, too?"

The teacher looked at him over the top of his gold-wire glasses. "In theory only, Meester Doyle. Haf you any specific questions?"

"Uh, no, sir." Keith subsided. "Just general curiosity." Holl elbowed him in the ribs with a snicker.

"Gut. There is nothing random about the accrual of knowledge. There is always a purpose to vhich research can be put. Curiosity can be a useful tool. If you think of your questions, ask them."

"Keith Doyle!" Holl leaned out the door. Keith turned back. The elf waved a rubber-banded bundle at him. "Your mail, saved faithfully throughout the vacation. There are some letters here that look important."

"Thanks for taking care of it while I was gone," Keith said.

"My pleasure," Holl assured him, letting the door swing closed behind him. As the light vanished, Keith dashed along the aisle toward the elevator. In the darkness ahead, he could hear Barry exclaiming over his good luck. "I'm really weak in science. I'm going to see if I can drop into a basic biology course for the credit." Keith remembered that Barry was a Liberal Arts major, and had to have one lab science to graduate.

"We'll help you out, too, won't we, Carl?" Teri asked.

"Sure," Carl agreed amiably.

"See if you can get into my class," Teri went on. "I'm registered in BIO 202, Tuesdays and Thursdays at 11 A.M., Dr. Mitchell. He's a doll."

"I think I have that free," Barry said.

"That's what I like about this group," Keith declared, joining them just as the elevator rolled down. "Teamwork."

Teri took him aside on the steps of Gillington as the group dispersed. "I just wanted to tell you how much I appreciate what you're doing, Keith. I saw the wooden stuff in the gift shop in town. I knew it came from . . . there." She tossed her head meaningfully in the general direction of the stacks.

"You did? How?"

Teri leaned close to him, lifted the wave of hair away from the side of her face. Attached to a scented earlobe by a hinged wooden clasp was a small ring and carved bead of the same shade of wood. "Maura gave me these earrings for Christmas. I love them so much I wear them all the time. The design is of a style that's kind of hard to miss. And if there's one thing I do know, it's style." Keith recognized the twisting ivy pattern Holl favored, and acknowledged that it appeared on a lot of the Hollow Tree merchandise.

"I'd never deny that," Keith said, giving her an appreciative up-and-down glance. "I didn't think that anyone would really notice things in gift shops."

"Why? Your customers have to come from somewhere," Teri pointed out. "Not everyone goes to Chicago to shop. Can I suggest adding jewelry to your inventory? These are nicer than anything I've ever bought in a store. I was interested, so I did a little detective work." Teri smiled. "I know Diane Londen over at Country Crafts. When I asked her where the great boxes and things came from, she described you." Teri paused, her head cocked to one side. "Why don't you ask her out?"

"I don't know." Keith was enchanted, the bundle of mail clutched forgotten under his arm. "What makes you think she'd want to go out with me?"

Teri dimpled. "Just call it a little more detective work."

* * *

"Hi, Ms. Voordman," Keith sang, in tune with the jingling doorbell the next day. He stamped the snow off his shoes with a happy little one-two dance step.

"Oh, Mr. Doyle," the shop owner said, straightening up from a shelf she was arranging. She pushed aside a metal cart with discarded price stickers stuck all over it, and came over to shake hands with him. "I was just thinking about you."

"Keith, please. Only teachers who hate me call me by my last name," Keith assured her with a smile.

"Keith. Do you want to know why I was thinking about you?"

"Yes, ma'am!"

"Come this way." He walked behind the black-haired woman to a small end-cap of shelves. "This. This is where I had the Hollow Tree display all through the Christmas season." It was empty, except for a porcelain statue. Keith grinned at it. It was the elf-in-a-tree that had inspired him to name the company. She waved a hand through the space between the shelves. "I have never seen anything go out the door so fast. It was like magic! The customers loved everything. How quickly can I get another shipment?"

Keith considered. "I'll have to ask my craftspeople, but it shouldn't take too long. I hope."

"And I'm sure you want the balance on my account." Ms. Voordman led him to her office, took out her checkbook and a pen, and wrote the date on a long blue check. "It's been sixty days. I presume that's why you're here." She noticed Keith's attention had wandered out toward the main room of the shop. "Or is it?"

"Is Diane here today?" he asked, accepting the check with an absent little grin.

Ms. Voordman smiled back at him. "Two birds with one stone, eh? She's doing inventory, but I suppose she can take her break. If she wants to."

"Thanks," said Keith.

"Hi, there," Diane said, coming into the back room. Seeing her boss, she flipped her hair back over her shoulder, looking studiously nonchalant. "Ms. Voordman, may I . . . ?"

"Yes, of course," the shop owner smiled, and turned to Keith. "I would say she wants to."

* * *

"I hope orange juice is all right with you," Diane asked, opening the refrigerator behind the shelves in the stock room and drawing out a plastic quart-bottle. "I get so sick of sugary stuff I could barf. And the water here is too mineral-heavy to drink." She set the bottle and a couple of Styrofoam cups onto a low, battered coffee table and plumped onto an ancient brown satin-upholstered couch. Dust flew up from the cushions and they both coughed. "So, what are you doing selling handcrafts door-to-door?"

"Helping out some friends. And the commission doesn't hurt," Keith admitted, sitting down next to her on the couch. Dust flew up from the cushions and they both coughed.

"Sorry. This thing smells mouldy, but it was free. We're going to re-cover it one day," Diane apologized, fluttering an annoyed hand under her nose. "Your merchandise is great. It has class. Believe me, you see the height of tacky come through a gift store. You should have seen what the last salesman wanted to sell Ms. Voordman: ashtrays made of little seashells glued together and shaped like houses. Yuck!"

"My friends couldn't picture their work in the same shop with that sort of thing, but it makes a great contrast, though. So," he asked, toasting her with his cup of juice, "how about . . ."

"Diane!" Ms. Voordman's voice out him off. "Customers!"

"Sorry," she said, gulping down her juice and shoving the bottle back into the refrigerator. "I've got to take care of them. Coming, Ms. Voordman!"

"Hey, wait!" Keith pleaded. "Would you like to have dinner with me at Frankie's tonight? I just got my commission check. The sky's the limit. Anything up to three bucks apiece."

"I can't. Busy tonight."

"Tomorrow?"

Diane laughed. "Yes, that's fine. I'd like that. I get off at six every day."

"I'll be here," Keith promised.

"Diane!"

"Aargh!" Diane cried in exasperation. She gave him a friendly smile and ran out to the front of the store. Keith threw her a silent toast with the last of his juice.

▪ Chapter 28 ▪

Keith's cheerful mood lasted until he returned to his dorm room, when he discovered that his bed had vanished. In its place lay a ton of announcement flyers circulated by the Power Hall management, telephone books, and a variety of notebooks, plays, and drama digests.

"Hey," Keith protested, pointing. It all belonged to Pat, who was piling more possessions on his own bed.

"Sorry," Pat said, dropping the stack of books. "Ungh! Rick came by, said the administration lost all record of our damage deposit, and wants to collect it again."

"What? Why?" Keith joined in and helped him move everything off his desk.

"Your pal, the one who trashed our room twice? He owes us. The rug is ruined under where the Coke dripped off the wall. They want us to pay again to replace it. I'm trying to find the receipt. You know, you're expensive to live with. You could funnel some of your new business profits back to deserving folk like me."

"No way," Keith asserted. "Are they sure the rug's ruined? I know you can get soda stains out of carpeting. My mother does it all the time. Wait a minute, here it is." He brandished a flimsy piece of paper stamped with the university seal.

"Than-kew!" Pat plucked it out of his fingers and stalked out of the room to find Rick.

Keith bent to clear his bed off. Pat hadn't started with his own desk. Under the first layer of papers was the detritus from Keith's. In the midst of a heap of books, he found the bundle of mail Holl had set aside for him.

Ignoring the rest of the mess, he slumped down on the floor to go through his mail. The package contained the usual mix of junk mail and advertisements aimed at the college community. "Students—earn up to $6.00 per hour!" "Typist,

$1.00 per page." Holl had been right, though. Keith noticed a few unfamiliar and very official-looking envelopes with official-looking return addresses in amongst the others. They were addressed to Keith Doyle, D.B.A. Hollow Tree Industries. He tore them open, letting the remainder of his mail drop to the bed. Two of them contained copies of I.R.S. tax forms; one for paying in quarterly income taxes, and one that informed him he had been granted an Employer's I.D. number. Attached to these by a paperclip was a note in Holl's perfect handwriting that the originals had been filled in and sent out.

The third contained a computer-generated form letter, checkmarked in ink on the third possible clause, advising him of penalties he owed for not submitting a quarterly return for the fourth quarter of last year. These penalties were being levied because of an administrative crackdown on small businesses. An immediate reply was requested. A pre-addressed envelope was enclosed for his convenience.

There was a phone number for the local I.R.S. office on the letter. Hurriedly, he grabbed for the phone and dialled it. The I.R.S. wasn't in a hurry to hear from him. He sat through an endless prerecorded message, before there was a click, and a nasal female voice from very far away said, "Internal Revenue."

With panic rising in his belly, Keith explained that he had received the letter and needed to talk to someone about it. With a "just a moment, sir," the voice clicked off. Keith sat on hold for another eternity half-listening to another prerecorded message advising him to file his 1040 early while he fought down mental pictures of anonymous men in dark, narrow-lapeled suits and sunglasses taking the elves away in handcuffs. Another click came. A dry voice informed him, "This is Mr. Durrow."

Keith swallowed. He hadn't realized before how terrified he was of the I.R.S. His voice came out in a squeak as he introduced himself. "Mr. Durrow, I got this letter, telling me I'm liable for a tax penalty for not filing a fourth quarter quarterly return. My associate filed that while I was home for spring break. Can't you check to make sure that you have received the form?"

"Who is your 'associate'?" the dry voice wanted to know. "You have filed as a sole proprietorship."

"Just a matter of speaking, uh, sir. It's a sort of wholesale manufacturing operation, and we haven't brought in any profits yet. I take things on consignment. You see, I had to . . . in the beginning it was necessary to give away a lot of merchandise . . . you know, woodcrafts . . . so I'm in the hole. All expenses, but no profit. I live in a college dorm," he explained. "I only just got back to school today."

Durrow's tone told him he'd heard those excuses before. "I see, Mr. Doyle. You must understand that we cannot afford to make exemptions. Except the standard one per person, of course." It was a joke, and Durrow let out a little snake's hiss of a laugh at his own wit. "It is admirable that you have started your own company, but you are responsible for your debts as much as for your successes."

"Yes, sir. Just send the forms again," Keith pleaded, "I'll be more careful."

"See that you are. The first quarter estimated tax is due April 15th."

"I'll know that, sir. I'm doing better," Keith promised him, eager to sound as if he knew what he was doing. "Lately, business has been improving. Black ink is actually appearing on my books."

"Fine," said Durrow, his tone indicating it was nothing of the kind. "We like to see small businesses doing well. You will need to file a 2210 stating you had no income during the last quarter, and make sure you keep up with the tax payments over this fiscal year."

"Yessir, I won't make that mistake again," he vowed. Then Keith hung up the phone and dashed off to find a 2210 before going to Voordman's to pick up Diane for dinner.

"Haven't I seen you before?" Diane asked Keith, putting down her soup spoon and looking at him closely across the restaurant table.

"Sure, yesterday," Keith insisted playfully. "Remember?"

"No, I'm sure . . ." She studied his face. Keith gazed at her, wiggling his eyebrows. "I know. You rescued my term paper. That day in the street."

Keith's facial contortions stopped as his jaw fell slack. "You're right. The girl in the pink jacket. How could I not remember someone as beautiful as you?"

"You must have had something else on your mind," Diane said gravely. "I could tell by the look on your face. Of course, it could have been pain. Your ears were sort of a dull red."

Keith grinned at the memory: standing outside Marcy's apartment in the wind and the blowing leaves, waiting for her to lead him into the library basement, and finding what he found there . . . It could have been a million years since he had met the elves, seeing how completely his life had changed. In fact, he had been sitting at this same table in this same restaurant with Marcy.

It felt different with Diane, though. He liked Marcy, but she had never been his girlfriend. She had deliberately avoided having him think of her as one, first because of Carl, and later, Enoch. He was glad she had. The look on Enoch's face when he told him what the score was . . . *Those two really do belong together.* Now Diane was sitting here, waiting to hear what he was going to say next. She was interested in him. He twitched his invisible whiskers happily.

Diane watched his face with amusement. "Doing a spell?" she inquired, imitating him.

"Nope. Just checking the results." She noticed things easily, Keith observed. *Better be careful not to lead her unintentionally to the elf village*, he thought, *if we're going to spend a lot of time together*. He rather hoped they would. He understood very well how Marcy had felt that evening, trying to decide whether or not to tell him about the class. "What year are you?"

"Freshman," Diane grimaced. "Before you say it, I know: 'There's nothing lower than a freshman.' Except pledges," she finished, with satisfaction.

"Not joining the Greek tradition?" Keith teased.

Diane waved sororities away. "No time," she stated. "I've got to hustle if I want to stay at Midwestern."

"Is that why *you're* selling handcrafts?"

Diane shrugged. "It's a job. I suppose you're from Illinois?" Keith nodded. "Well, I'm from Michigan. It costs a lot more for me to go here than for you. I have to pay out-of-state tuition. And I really wanted to come here. They have the best Health Sciences school in the country. I'm going to be a dietician. I'm on a grant from a local merit scholar's association, and the National Merit Scholarship Program, but it is really tough to pull it all together without outside income. Even with it, it's tough. I may have to go home to a Michigan school, where I can afford the tuition, and maybe live at home.'' She made another face. ''But I don't want to. I like it here. It's the first real privacy I've ever had. I have three sisters.''

''I have two. I hope your folks have got more than one bathroom,'' Keith said sympathetically.

''Well, no. We fight about it a lot. I pleaded with my father to build another. You know what he said? 'It's too expensive. Next fall you go to college. Why bother?' I really don't want to have to go home.''

''I'd hate to see you leave, now that I've found you. Maybe we can get in some of the same courses. What are you taking?''

''Oh, English, European History, Biology, Mythology 248—''

''No kidding!'' Keith exclaimed. ''Me, too.''

''Terrific,'' Diane said eagerly. ''Want to study together?''

''You took the words out of my mouth, gorgeous.'' He regarded Diane with growing affection. The thought of having her vanish next year was too much for him. He put two and two together and came up with an interesting sum. In seconds, his imagination formulated a shiningly brilliant idea to keep her at Midwestern. The obvious solution. ''If you're having trouble making it financially, what about other grants?''

''I've tried. There's no such thing as a grant for Nutritional Sciences.''

''You're a Mythology student.'' Keith took a deep breath. ''Why not apply for the Alfheim Scholarship?''

''Alfheim, like the Norse myth?'' she asked. ''I've never heard of it before.''

''No,'' said Keith, though it had been that which inspired the name. She *was* quick. ''Frederick Alfheim is a renowned scholar of mythology. It's a national grant. If you get a recommendation from the Myth professor and apply, you could get it.''

''That would be great,'' Diane said, her blue eyes brimming with hope. ''How much do they offer?''

''Oh,'' said Keith airily, ''full tuition. You still have to pay for your books and room and board, but it helps.''

''It sure would! Where can I find an application?''

"I'll bring you one when I see you tomorrow."

Diane tilted her head and peered at him through her eye-lashes. "Who said we were getting together tomorrow?" she asked, tossing her hair back. The gesture reminded him of Candlepat. He clamped down instantly against any thoughts of the elves as if he believed she was a mindreader.

"I did, just now. Any objections?"

"None at all. Uh-oh," she caught sight of his watch and grabbed his wrist to get a better look. "My God, ten-thirty! I've got to get out of here. I'll turn into a pumpkin if I don't." Noticing the worried look on Keith's face she sputtered, "I'm just kidding!"

"I hope so," Keith said, recovering. " 'There are more things on heaven and earth than are dreamed of in your phi-losophy, Horatio.' "

"You're weird, Keith, but I could get to like you." Diane chuckled. She pushed back from the table and let Keith help her on with her coat. Blowing him a kiss, she whisked out into the darkness. He glowed for a long while after she left. Then he started to worry how he would approach the Little Folk about what he had just done.

"This is vun of your more disastrous feats of inspiration, Meester Doyle," the Elf Master said, when Keith went to see him the next day. Holl was already in possession of the whole story, but even he had to admit that Keith's imagination might have taken him too far. "Creating a mock scholarship, tch! The resources of this infant company vill not be able to bear many of your ideas, if they are like this. Have you so easily forgotten your concern over the taxes?"

Keith hastened to explain. "Of course I haven't, but we don't have to give her the money right away. It can wait until the fall when tuition is due. I'll buckle down. I'm sure we can bring in enough extra by then. She's a good student. She deserves a break, and I couldn't think of anything else except inventing a phony scholarship." The Master didn't look con-vinced of the idea's value. "She works for one of the stores selling our stuff. You wouldn't be wasting money. It'd be just like paying another employee. And," he played a card he hoped would be a trump, "you told me that I could reasonably expect

30 to 40 percent of the profits from Hollow Tree, and I only took ten. Out-of-state tuition doesn't come anywhere near the other 20 to 30 percent.''

"I can add, Meester Doyle."

"He could be right. He is working hard enough, Master," Holl put in. "Widdy, are you sure? Did you have to promise this girl? You've only just met her."

"You haf only just met her?" the Master echoed, aghast.

"No, wait," Keith insisted. "She's special."

"You are infatuated."

"It's not like that. I thought about it. I just, uh, talked before I thought." Keith appealed to the Master, who stonily shook his head.

"I cannot consider it. You must take back your promise."

Keith sighed. "I didn't promise her anything. I just said she could apply to you for a grant. And she really does need the money." The Elf Master looked him up and down, and Keith fidgeted, ashamed of being so greedy. "I'm sorry. It was an impulse. It was only that I didn't want to lose her after just one semester."

"Your feelings are that strong?" the Master leaned back in his chair to study Keith's face.

"I didn't know, Keith Doyle," Holl added, softening.

Keith waved their sympathy away. "You'll need all the capital you can get to move out of here. Forget it. I know I shouldn't ask."

"Since vhen haf you not asked vhen you vanted something? Very well." The Master waved a hand to forestall interruption. "You haf done a foolish thing, but you mean vell. Certainly if ve can be imposed upon by your generosity, ve need not suffer alone. She may haf her scholarship, if I meet her and I like her."

"You will," Keith promised. "You will."

▪ Chapter 29 ▪

Jubilant, Keith set out the next morning with his head full of plans for legitimizing the Alfheim Scholarship. The Elf Master would surely like Diane, and then she wouldn't have to leave the university next year. It was an ideal solution. He whistled a tune to the birds perched in the thornbushes. What a perfect day. If it hadn't been for his problems with the I.R.S., Carl, and the Historical Society, the world itself would have seemed perfect to Keith.

He crossed the campus, cutting behind the cafeteria annex of Power Hall, and headed for the entrance. Absently, Keith ducked a fast Frisbee game taking place in the sunshine right under the windows of the Food Service office. His mind was deeply concerned about how to sell enough Hollow Tree merchandise to make up for the hole in the bank account that Diane's tuition would leave. They needed another good idea for a new product. Keith knew there was a goodly balance of cash building up, but a bad month could kill their advantage. Catra still complained that they weren't making money fast enough. For a people who never used money, the Little Folk sure took to the concept in a hurry.

"Keith Doyle?" asked a man's voice from behind him. "Keith Doyle of Hollow Tree Industries?"

"Yeah?" Keith answered, turning around.

He caught a brief glimpse of huge meaty arms just before his back was slammed painfully into a shadowed corner of the dorm wall.

Keith looked wildly at the two burly thugs holding him and at the mustachioed man in the neatly tailored spring suit behind them. Standing away at a respectful distance was a middle-aged policeman in uniform. "Who are you? What do you want?" Neither of his guards spoke. The tailored suit gave him a fierce white-toothed smile that made Keith very uneasy.

"I'm Victor Lewandowski. I'm the president of the Local Number 541. I've seen your goods. Nice stuff. But there's something missing from your stock. No union label."

"Union?" Keith asked. "I don't have to put union labels on merchandise to sell it."

"If it's made in this state you do. This is a closed-shop state. That means your employees have to belong to a union. I want a list of your workers so we can make sure they're getting fair representation."

"No! I mean, I don't have any employees. I make some of it and I sell stuff on consignment for friends." Keith squirmed uncomfortably in the grip of the two men and watched hopefully over their shoulders for anyone he knew. Maybe he could telegraph S.O.S. with his eyebrows or something. The cop, who was standing with his thumbs hooked into his belt, looked sympathetic but stayed neutral.

"I don't believe you. You got stuff in maybe twenty stores. You restock quickly. Nobody's got that many friends." The man nodded to his henchmen, who dragged Keith a few inches away from the brickwork and then dashed him back against it. Keith wheezed, the air knocked painfully out of him. Lewandowski waved the policeman over, who unbuttoned the upper right-hand breast pocket on his uniform shirt and drew from it a paper that he unfolded and handed to Keith.

The man on Keith's left let go of his arm enough for him to bend it toward the policeman and take the paper.

"This is a court notice signed by Judge Arendson, ordering you to release to me a list of the names and addresses of all persons working for you, doing business under the name Hollow Tree Industries," Lewandowski said. "If you refuse, you will be considered in contempt of court. You understand?"

Keith nodded weakly.

"Good." The union boss raised an eyebrow and the two men let go of Keith. "I'll expect to hear from you. My people will be keeping an eye on you. Just remember that. You look worried." Lewandowski smiled his shark's grin again. "You shouldn't be. Just cooperate with us, and we'll cooperate with you."

They left him clutching the paper in the shadows.

Keith spent a good part of the day in the college computer center studying the Illinois Business Statutes on unions, and coaxing the school's mainframe computer through its graphics program. He wondered if he should tell anyone about the union men. The Little Folk were already worried about the proposed demolition and the mysterious magazine articles being published. The thought of anyone else snooping around would likely be too much for them.

"I've gotta tell Holl anyway," Keith resolved, typing furiously. "And the Master. They'll have some ideas on how to deal with it."

After a few hours work, he was able to produce some realistic-looking forms on a laser printer that bore a reasonable resemblance to the handful of scholarship applications he had picked up that morning at the Guidance Center. "ALFHEIM SCHOLARSHIP," the letterhead announced proudly. Keith blew the computer a kiss and tucked two copies of each page into his briefcase.

Diane met him that afternoon in a classroom on the tenth level of the library and filled them out. She was excited about meeting the mysterious Mr. Alfheim. "It's such a great scholarship I wonder why I never heard of it before."

"You're not a Mythology major," Keith pointed out. While she was writing he read over her shoulder. "Londen, Diane G. What's the *G* for?"

"Grace," she explained, "and boy, were my parents wrong."

"No," Keith assured her. "They were right. You're beautiful. And graceful."

"But look at me," she said, with a nervous giggle. "I'm so nervous I'm trembling. Look at my hand." She held it up for Keith's inspection.

"You'll be fine," Keith assured her, sidling around the table and sitting down across from her. He kissed the hand, unsuccessfully avoiding the point of her pen. "Mr. Alfheim will like you, I'm positive. You have the recommendation?"

She giggled, and leaned over to wipe his face with a Kleenex. "You have a blue spot on your cheek. Yes, I've got it right here. Mr. Frazier didn't know what I was talking about, but he gave it to me. You're sure you have your facts right? Mr. Alfheim is coming here? Today?"

Keith nodded. "Absolutely."

"But *why* is he here? I haven't even applied yet."

"Oh, he's here to interview me," Keith said, watching out the door for the Master. "I'm an applicant too. You'll have to hurry. I don't know when he'll get here."

Diane slapped her pen down. "*You're* applying? Then I won't. I'm sure you need the money as badly as I do."

"*No!*" Keith whirled back to her. "If you don't get it you won't be back next fall. It's okay, I'm really in better shape." For several seconds they just stood there.

Diane blushed and reached out to touch his hand. "I didn't know it meant that much to you."

"Um . . . I guess it does." He squeezed her fingers and leaned across the table to kiss her. She didn't protest, but she did lean forward, eyes closing, until their lips touched, joined. Keith felt skyrockets going off in his head.

After a little while, Diane giggled. "Your mustache tickles." She opened her eyes, fingers tracing his upper lip. "That's funny. You don't have one. Must have been your hair . . ."

"Ahem!" said a voice from behind him. Surprised, Keith jumped to his feet. Diane did the same. The Elf Master stood in the doorway, looking as uncomfortable as Keith had ever seen him. The little teacher was wearing a grey pin-striped suit, white shirt, tie, shiny black shoes, and a fedora. His lips were pressed together. Keith stared, his own lips quivering with amusement.

"Mr. Alfheim, I presume?" he said with the utmost control, when he recovered his voice. If I laugh, he thought, he'll kill me.

"Zo, Mees Londen, tell me about yourzelf." The Master was making himself comfortable. With his air of confidence, it didn't matter that his feet couldn't quite touch the ground from the seat of the old padded armchair. Diane didn't notice. Her eyes were fixed on his.

"Well, I'm from Michigan. I'm the eldest of four children, all girls. My father works for Ford. I'm majoring in the Health Sciences. I have a GPA of 3.47 on a 4-point scale." At that point, her confidence broke down, and she appealed to the Master. "I don't know what else you want to know."

"What do you think?"

"Well . . . I was fascinated by the customs that evolve in

people of primitive cultures which bring out their hopes of life after death, and how little a person changes, even though he no longer has a corporeal body.''

"Yes, although it is said . . .'' The Master began, but Diane never slowed down enough to let him speak.

"And the Hawaiian myth of the tree with fragile branches, which says that only an old spirit can attain the journey's end, obviously shows that they didn't believe death brings wisdom except to those who died of old age.''

"I do not believe so. In *The Masks of God* by . . .''

"Joseph Campbell. Yes, that's where I read it. It's really deep stuff. And I've read Bulfinch, and all the Avenel books, but my . . .'' It was the little teacher's turn to interrupt.

"How interesting that you haf gone into so much depth,'' he said gently, "but I am asking about you.''

Diane seemed flummoxed by his question, and Keith came to the rescue.

"I think, Mr. Alfheim, that she is demonstrating her knowledge of the subject. For the mythology scholarship. Isn't that what you want to hear?'' Keith prompted him.

"No.'' The Elf Master coolly stared Keith down. "I vish to hear about her, personally. Mythology does not change over the centuries. It is only added to and interpreted. Your turn to speak will come next.'' He turned back to Diane.

"Well, I've filled out the forms. And here's the recommendation from my Mythology professor.'' She handed them over to the Elf Master who gave them a cursory glance, and laid them aside.

"What brings you to Midvestern?'' he inquired.

"It is the best school in the country for my major. I love to cook, and I was good in chemistry. It seemed logical to combine the two in my career.''

"Yes, that smacks of logic,'' the Master nodded, approvingly. "To combine vocation with avocation. But how do you plan to extend your education through the study of mythology?''

Diane noticed Keith watching her, and was suddenly conscience-stricken. "Look here, Mr. Alfheim, I feel bad. I've been talking about myself, and Keith is really the applicant. I just found out about the scholarship yesterday. It's him you should concentrate on.''

"You are qvite right, Mees Londen. But soon. Meester Doyle, von't you excuse us?"

Keith didn't want to go, but the Elf Master peered at him over the rims of his gold glasses, and he remembered that this was supposed to be the first time they had met. Clearing his throat, Keith stood up. "I'll be in the next room if you want me."

Forty-five minutes later, the door opened.

"Meester Doyle, come in here, please?" The Elf Master gestured him in. "No, don't leave, Mees Londen. You may find this interesting and instructive."

"Yes, sir." Obediently, she sat, hands folded nervously before her while the Elf Master enjoyed himself, grilling Keith on his fund of mythical knowledge.

Keith spent the next half hour having his brain turned inside out on every facet of mythology that he had ever heard of, and a lot that he hadn't. The Elf Master solemnly corrected him on minor points, shook his head sadly at mistakes on major ones, and pencilled little notes on the back of Keith's carefully forged forms. Keith was frustrated, because he wanted to be alone with the Elf Master long enough to tell him about the union organizers and ask his advice.

At last, after Keith had reached a state of unbearable discomfort, the impromptu oral exam came to an end.

"I haf heard enough!" the Elf Master announced, folding the papers and putting them in his pocket. "Meester Doyle, it vas most enjoyable talking to you. Mees Londen," he stood up and took her hand, "you are a charming young lady. I approve you."

"Does that mean you're giving me the scholarship?" Diane asked, hopefully, standing up to shake hands, and finding herself towering substantially above the head of her benefactor. He appeared not to observe the discrepancy in their heights. Keith stood up, too, towering over them both.

"Yes. That is precisely vhat I do mean."

"Oh, thank you! . . . Oh, Keith, I'm so sorry!" Diane rushed over to condole with him, and turned back to the Master to explain. "I mean I'm grateful, but I'm sorry for him, too."

Keith made a show of looking disappointed. "Uh, yeah, that's too bad," as Diane expended sympathy on him, but inwardly he was cheering. The Elf Master humphed to himself as he went out the door. "Caught in your own net," he said over his shoulder to the room at large. Diane threw her arms around Keith and the door closed on them.

▪ Chapter 30 ▪

When at last Keith was able to seek the Master out to ask his advice, the red-haired teacher nodded solemnly at his student's caution.

"You vere correct not to announce this generally. Very vise. Mit care, it should not become necessary to alarm the others."

"But vhat . . . I mean what do I do?" Keith pleaded.

"My suggestion is that you obtain legal advice. There is nothing you can do to discourage them by yourself. Call a counsellor. Yours is not an isolated case. There must be legal recourse."

The ad in the *Yellow Pages* pinpointed attorney Clint Orczas as a labor relations specialist. Keith had no trouble getting an appointment to discuss his problem.

"No fee for consultation," Orczas said cheerfully, showing Keith into a handsome walnut-panelled room lined with thick books. He had smooth dark hair slicked back over his forehead, and smooth, swarthy skin. "I don't start charging until after we decide if you need me." He gestured to a deep leather chair and sat down at a shiny black onyx-topped desk, tenting his fingers.

"Thanks," Keith said. "Because I don't have a whole lot of money."

Orczas spread his hands. "Who does? Please, tell me your story."

Keith described his encounter with the union organizers and handed him the court order. Orczas examined the signature closely and put the paper down with a sigh.

"That's Arendson, all right. I've seen a lot of these in my day. What they're doing is considered legally questionable, but it takes a long time and a lot of courtroom gymnastics to fight."

"That isn't fair."

"I know," the lawyer said solemnly. "But there's a loophole that keeps allowing such abuses to go on. Ideally, you know, these unions defend the rights of their members."

"Can you help me?" Keith asked.

"Well, probably not. Some of these cases take up to three years to resolve. By then, a lot of the businesses go under. I would have to ask you for a $5,000 retainer just to get going. It could cost as much as ten to twenty thousand dollars more."

Keith blanched. "I can't afford that, not in a million years. So what can I do?"

"Free advice," Orczas said, handing back the court order. "You have two choices: beat 'em or join 'em. I'm sorry."

"It's not my day," Keith complained to Rick as they sat in the first Inter-Hall Council meeting of the new year. "Well, it started out being my day, but it isn't now."

"Probably someone else's day. Try the Lost-and-Found," Rick said offhandedly while taking a huge handful of potato chips out of a bag they were sharing. "No, it's Groundhog Day. *That's* your trouble." He stuffed the chips into his mouth and reached for more.

The council was engaged in a huge fight over the parking lot distribution. Keith and Rick weren't interested, and watched the bloodshed with glee. To Keith's relief, Rick had forgiven him for turning his coat at the fall meeting, and now offered to back him up on reversing the vote. "You understand it's because I don't really care, don't you? 'Cause if I cared a damn about the library or the gym, I'd probably have broken your nose for screwing around like that." Keith took a handful of chips and crunched them one by one.

Carl, as usual, was in the thick of the argument. Keith hadn't seen much of him since Marcy had started going out with Enoch, which suited him fine. Nothing new was being proposed during the debate by either side. It seemed to go nowhere. To Keith, it confirmed all the worst and most humorous theories about committees. Instead, he sat back in his desk and thought about Diane. He called up before him her face and figure, the sound of her voice, and her laugh as he had bashed himself against the door.

"Thank you, delegates," Lloyd Patterson said, finally getting the contenders back to their sides of the room. "We'll take a vote on that. Now, all in favor . . . ?"

More arguing. Keith wondered what he should do about the list the union man had demanded. The last thing he wanted was to have attention drawn to the elves in any way. They were paranoid, and with reason. He was very proud of the trust they had in him. He liked them all, even the ones that didn't like him. They had so much character, if that was the word he meant. They seemed more real than the other people with whom he interacted every day. He wished that the first thing he had ever done that they'd heard about wasn't a speech advocating the tearing down of their house.

"Okay," the chairman said, standing up. "The vote is about evenly split. No clear majority. We'll have to get votes from the members in absentia. You know who they are. Tell 'em to get in touch with me. Any other old business?"

Keith was on his feet, arm in the air. "Doyle, Power Hall."

"Chair recognizes Doyle."

"Regarding the new library project?"

Patterson raised an eyebrow at him. "Something new, I hope, Doyle?"

"I would like to move that the previous ballot be set aside and a vote taken again on the measure."

"On what grounds?"

"Well," Keith urged, as if it was obvious. "In light of the interest shown in Gillington Library by the Historical Society, I think we have to hold off on any action for when they come through. Nobody's interested in preserving the old gym building, so we could approve that one right away."

"I see. Has the Society sent any guarantee of its protected status yet? We don't want the old dud standing in place of progress if there isn't a guarantee that they want to declare it a monument."

"No," Keith admitted. "I've been phoning, but they haven't returned my calls." The last time he had tried, he'd been handed the runaround by a secretary who tried to convince him the director was in a meeting, when Keith was sure the guy must only be out to lunch. The delegates weren't impressed. A few of them heckled Keith, calling for him to sit down. He tried again to make them see sense. "Look, wouldn't you feel really stupid if we tore down Gillington just as they declared protected status for it?"

Lloyd asked him in a bored voice, "Do you move for a second vote?"

"Yes."

"Seconded," said Carl Mueller, standing up. Keith was gratified until he saw the look in Carl's eye. The big student wasn't doing it for him. He wondered who Carl was doing it for, and why.

"Fine. Venita, call the roll."

In a few moments, it was all over, again. The Inter-Hall Council, with the exception of Rick, now loudly in favor of the new gym along with Keith, voted precisely the same way it had the last time. Keith felt cast down. Lloyd Patterson acknowledged the count, and ordered it noted for the minutes.

"You might also be interested to know that the other voting bodies in the university are split on the subject," Lloyd said. "I'm proud to say that we will cast the tie-breaking vote when our delegation joins the Administrative Council this spring. Movement to adjourn?"

Keith left feeling lower than before. That week, apart from his classes, he spent his time canvassing the rest of his customers for February orders and picking up the January receipts. Diane was working, so it seemed the most useful thing he could do.

Among the Little Folk, the real estate frenzy was on. Over the weekend Keith took out three tours of Little People, and all of them insisted he pass by the same piece of property he and the other two elves had found: the forested plot with the house on the hill and the stream flowing through. The place just cried out "privacy," surrounded as it was by fields with pale blond rows of winter wheat and a nature preserve on one side, the river on another, and more forests and hilly fields all around. There was a tinkling little cascade from the tributary as it fell into the icy waterway, sort of a miniature waterfall, and everyone stopped for a longing stare. Keith had to admit that it would be a perfect place for the elves to live. They never saw anyone in the house or on the road, so there was no one to remark upon Keith's repeated presence.

A few of the older ones, openly enjoying their trip and mellowed by the wintry sunshine, forgave Keith for his recklessness, understanding now that he had acted from ignorance, and that he was trying to amend his mistake. The collie was back during his third run, panting at them in red-tongued good humor, his breath clouding in the cold air. Keith waved out the window at the dog, who barked playfully at him.

Curran, Keva, and a few of the others sat huddled in the back seat for the last trip on Sunday. They had issued bitter complaints to Keith about having to hide under the tarpaulin on the trip out of town. Wisely, he put their ire down to nervousness at riding in an automobile and ignored it. Other than gripes, they were stonily silent all the way out to the rural roads, until he began to drive past the farms. Some of the Old Ones, who remembered having their own animals and fields, chatted among themselves in wistful undertones, too low for Keith to overhear. They never spoke directly to him.

At odd moments, he called out a sort of running travelogue, telling his passengers where they were, how many people lived in this or that town, and inquired whether or not anyone needed him to stop. There were no replies to his pleasantries. He felt as though he was talking to himself. He resented that he was no more than a taxi driver until he looked in the rearview mirror at the back seat. All of the oldsters were quiet, and one of the old ladies was weeping into a corner of her apron. Keith was touched and a little embarrassed for his now-evaporated ire. Turning back toward home, he found that he was feeling sorry for the people who had lived for forty years in a concrete cellar.

Holl was waiting just outside the wall when Keith rolled up. The Old Ones debarked, and Holl rode with Keith to the parking lot. "You look as though some conversation would be welcome," he told Keith.

"Hello!" Keith said, rubbing his ears. "Is that a voice? I just wanted to make sure I wasn't going deaf. I haven't heard so much silent disapproval since I was in fifth grade math class."

With a nod, Holl studied the snow-covered street, pawed the puddled slush with his toe. "Those others can be trying. Come back with me. We'll have a drink. There's something I wish you to see."

"Oh, no," Keith said, remembering the little old lady and her quiet tears. He didn't feel equipped to deal with more emotions. "Thanks anyway."

"I insist," Holl stated. "You need one."

In a short while, they were seated around one of the long tables in the dining chamber with cups of spiced cider. Keith was pleased to accept one that held about eight ounces, and had evidently been made particularly with him in mind, being about half-again larger than the one Holl held. He fingered the carving, which showed Holl's favorite ivy pattern.

"It's a gift to you," Holl asserted. "It will wait in a place of honor until each time you come to drink with us. You're popular. They talk about nothing else than their outings, leaving us younger ones to work on woodcrafts. I thought this last group would be the hardest, but there's those of us who don't want you to go away with a sour taste."

"Not after this stuff." Keith turned the cup around approvingly. "It's very smooth. Not too strong, is it?"

"It's between weak and strong," Holl admitted. "Home-pressed. You've been past that place again?"

Keith knew which one he meant. "Three times today."

"We've kept up with the real estate news. The very size of the numbers in each advertisement have us all scared."

"I know." Keith sipped his cider. "Me, too. I haven't got a hope to get a mortgage for you while I'm still in college. I don't know what else to do."

"That's for later. For now, we have an order for power tools that needs to be made," Holl said. "How shall we get them?"

"Where are you ordering them from?" Keith asked.

"Martin Tools. The address is Little Falls."

"That's just down the street," Keith told him. "It's a suburb of this town. Why don't I just pick them up?"

"That will do nicely," Holl nodded, refilling their cups. "You are very good to us. The Master has told me about the nosy men from the union. If we can do anything to help you avoid them, let us know.''

''I will,'' Keith said fervently, remembering the rough hands of the president's henchmen.

''I have a theoretical case to put to you,'' Holl continued. ''What would you do if you liked something that was plainly out of your financial reach?'' Holl peered at him. ''Speaking theoretically, that is.''

''Oh, I don't know. If it was that far away, I'd kiss it good-bye.''

''But if you truly wanted to have it, come what may?'' Holl pressed him. ''A very attractive purchase, one that many people would want to possess as well. If it meant everything to you.''

''I'd see if the owner would take a down-payment,'' Keith said promptly, joining in the spirit of Holl's question, and trying to imagine a *thing* of his dreams, something that would tempt even the thrifty Holl, ''before anyone else could sweep it out from under me. I could secure it that way, and then I'd figure out some way to take out a loan. Sell the family jewels. Steal candy from babies.''

''Ah,'' Holl said, meditatively. ''The Elders think down-payments are too modern. In their day, as they are so fond of telling me, you bought only what you could pay for on the spot with cash, truck, or hard work.''

''Things were cheaper in their day,'' Keith moaned. ''Now, trying to pay up all at once takes a miracle.''

The phone rang and rang at the Historical Society office. Keith counted sixteen burrs before the secretary picked it up. ''Hello, Historical Society.''

''Hello? My name's Keith Doyle, and I just want to know . . .''

''Just a moment please,'' she said pleasantly, and put her hand over the phone. Her mouth twisted sourly. ''Chuck, it's that kid again.''

Charles Eddy, director of the Midwestern Illinois Historical Society, barely looked up from the *Chicago Tribune* crossword puzzle he was doing. ''He must think this office is full of self-righteous little old ladies running around inspecting houses. We haven't made the decision yet. I don't know when we're making the inspection on which the decision will be based. Other matters take priority.'' What Eddy meant was when the inspector came back from vacation, and when the departmental Buick was back from the shop, but the secretary couldn't say that, and she knew it.

"I'm sorry, Mr. Doyle," she told the receiver. "We will most certainly be in touch with you when anything is happening. Yes. Thank you for calling." She put down the receiver. "Whew!"

Eddy smiled, filling *chronicle* in six-down for "historical account." "Perhaps we should hire him. I don't have the energy to make that sort of fuss anymore."

February and most of March passed by. Keith was busy, sandwiching his schoolwork and the Master's classes with sales sweeps to increase the Hollow Tree customer list. He had the uncomfortable feeling that he was being followed on his rounds, but he said nothing of his suspicions to anyone but Holl and the Elf Master. All the rest of his available time was spent with Diane.

He would have considered the rest of the school year perfect, if it hadn't been for his worries about time running out on the library. The Historical Society, after much pursuit by Keith, had promised to take the matter up no later than early May, and with that Keith had to be content. He knew he was pushing it with them, but profits weren't rolling in as quickly for Hollow Tree as he hoped. The elves who were making the merchandise began to look tired, and Keith avoided asking them to hurry anymore.

On the profit-side of the ledger, there were more of them making things. After Keith's spate of tour-guiding, a substantial number of the oldsters began to participate. Holl had reported to him that they were still talking as if the Big Person was selling them out, but they were working harder than any of the youths, and with more experience. In some cases, centuries more, Keith suspected. He was delighted. And the union seemed to have backed off from harassing him.

The semester broke for Easter vacation, and the students vanished from campus like smoke in the wind. In spite of their concern for their home, the elves still insisted on presenting Keith with his commission check before he left for the holiday break. A glance at it assured him that it was enough to pay for next semester's books and fees. "Say, we did really well this month."

"It's not enough," Catra said sadly, looking over Holl's shoulder as he showed Keith the ledger books. "It takes such a long time for the balance to grow."

"Wow! I didn't know we were making so much!" Keith exclaimed with pleasure, whistling at the total.

"You don't know what you're collecting?" Enoch was scornful.

Keith shrugged, stroking his whiskers with a bemused forefinger. "Well, picking up the checks one at a time, I don't really notice. By the way, Teri Knox suggested an idea to me for some new merchandise that would probably just walk out the doors. I wanted to ask what you thought of producing jewelry." He smiled at Enoch, inviting him to speak up. "I've seen the necklace you made Marcy. It's terrific."

"It'd be easy enough to make more," Enoch admitted. "But I'd make none as special. That's for her alone."

"A new idea wouldn't go amiss," Sion agreed. "Something to catch the eye. It is a concern that we do not want to reach market-saturation. I was reading in the *Journal* . . ."

"As to that," Catra said, turning to Keith, "I want to ask if you'd read . . ."

"By the way, I might be nosy, but are you ever going to bring Marcy down here to meet the folks?" Keith asked, unaware that he was interrupting.

"Ye're being nosy," Enoch asserted, "but the answer is, not until all you Big Folk have cleared out of campus. And the sooner you go, the sooner that'll be."

"I can take a hint," Keith said cheerily, and strode away.

"Wait up, Keith Doyle," Catra called, but he was already out the classroom door.

The phone rang at the home of Clarence Wilkes. The old man was watching television. He had it up loud because he was getting a little deaf, and if it hadn't been for the station break, he would never have heard it ring. He levered himself out of his rocking recliner, as creaky in its joints as he was himself, and answered it. "Hallo-o?"

"Is this 543-2977?"

"Yes. Who's calling, please?" Wilkes asked, trying to place the voice.

"I'm interested in the piece of wooded property you have for sale. I saw your sign out in front. How much are you asking?"

"Wa-al," Clarence calculated. The caller sounded like a city man. He talked clean, no drawl. "Two thousand an acre, twenty acres. You interested in buying, mister?" Might as well throw in a little padding for the years he'd spent farming it.

"I might be. Let me see. Two thousand dollars an acre, eh? . . . Um . . ." The voice became thoughtful. "I'm not that crazy about banks. I do as little with them as I can. How about a contract between just us? I'll pay *you* the interest instead."

This caller was kin to Clarence Wilkes under the skin. Banks had been the source of half his troubles all his adult life, but he had their lingo down pat. "Me neither," he admitted. "Two thousand down. Two hundred a month with 5 percent simple interest after that. You can move in after I've seen the down-payment, and your check don't bounce. Taxes is your problem."

"I'll be getting back to you, then. I'm interested, but there's people I've got to check with."

"Suit yourself," Wilkes said. "By the way, I'm Clarence Wilkes."

"Pleased to know you," said the voice on the phone. "I'm . . . Keith Doyle."

▪ Chapter 31 ▪

"You're crazy," Diane told him as the Mustang hummed along the country roads. "You can't drive me all the way to Michigan. Drop me at the bus station in Joliet, or something."

"Why should I?" Keith glanced away from the road.

"Don't do that!" Diane pointed back at the steering wheel.

"You'll hit something. It's not that I'm ungrateful, but isn't it a silly thing to do? It's six hours out of your way!"

"I'm famous for being silly. How else can I monopolize your company?" he asked, skimming around a file of children on bicycles. "Besides, why go Greyhound? It takes longer than I will, and you can't get all the way home on a bus."

"Oh, all right," Diane grumbled, sitting back in resignation.

"I have a quick detour I want to make. We can catch the highway just north of here."

"You're driving."

Keith steered through the two-signal town and looped around the roads until he was on the wooded stretch near the farm the elves were so crazy about. He liked the place, too. It had a good aura. No . . . good spirit. Who had told him that? Holl. Holl had said it, that beautiful cold day out looking for wood. His car's springs would never be the same. The second trip to Barn Door Lumber had yielded just as heavy a load. He hoped he wouldn't have to buy new shocks too soon.

He pulled up in front of the farm and took a quick look out the car window. It had been several weeks since he had been here last, and now the leaves were bursting on the trees, almost hiding the house on the hill.

"Nice place," Diane said. "Who lives here?"

"I don't know," Keith told her, "but it's for sale. I like it."

"Me, too." Diane thought about it a moment. "You mean you brought me out here to look at a farm?"

Keith looked a little ashamed of himself. "It's my friend's dream house. I'm just . . . making sure it's still here."

"It isn't, you know. It's been sold."

"What?" Diane pointed and Keith stared. The "For Sale by Owner" sign had a sticker across it which clearly stated that the property was "Sold." "Oh, no." Keith collapsed against the steering wheel. "It can't be sold."

"I thought you said it was just a dream. Keith?" Diane shook him. "What's wrong?"

Keith groaned and threw the car into gear. How can I break it to Holl? his mind cried. "Everything," he sighed.

After a few miles, Keith was resigned to losing the chance at that farm, and cheered up enough to be charming to Diane.

She was easy to travel with. She understood that the task of the passenger was to keep the driver from being bored, and told him stories of her life and her sisters and brother, discussed her hopes and plans for the future.

"My dad is really proud of me for winning that scholarship," she said happily. "I called him up right away after we talked to Mr. Alfheim. It takes a lot of pressure off of the family."

"That's great," Keith agreed, pleased at the success of his subterfuge. Unfortunately, the pressure was off for the elves, too. They didn't have to worry about buying that particular piece of property anymore. Well, others would come along, although he was sure they couldn't be as perfect. He hoped that one would, before the sheriff showed up with the eviction notice. Shoving the thought forcefully to one side, he thought of a funny story Diane would like and told it to her. Laughter helped to pass the time on the way to Michigan.

"Diane!" Her mother called to her through the kitchen door. Keith's car was just turning out of sight at the end of the street. With a sigh, Diane left the curb where she had been waving good-bye, and went up the stairs into the white frame house. "Telephone, honey." Her mother was waiting with her hand over the receiver. "Keith gone? He's a fine boy. Your father likes him so much. They had such a nice chat last night."

Diane took the instrument with a little nod and smile. "Hello?"

A male voice, Diane couldn't tell how old or young, asked, "May I speak to Keith Doyle?"

"I'm sorry, but he just left for Chicago. He'll be home in about five hours. Is there an emergency?"

The voice sighed. "No. I'll see him when he gets back. Thank you so much."

"You're welcome," Diane acknowledged, puzzled. "Goodbye."

The receiver on the other end clicked off.

▪ Chapter 32 ▪

The first piece of mail waiting for Keith in his pigeonhole at Power Hall after he returned from spring break was another of the brown envelopes with the warning notice in the corner. Keith shuddered before opening it. All of those envelopes had so far brought him bad news. This one was like its predecessors.

The Internal Revenue Service invited him to call the office to arrange an appointment for an audit of his account. Keith read the letter over and over on the way up to his dorm room, and tore at his hair in dismay.

The letter reminded him that he also had quarterly taxes coming due, and those would have to be paid promptly by the deadline. He made a whirlwind search of his dorm room, desperate to find the new estimated tax forms, but he couldn't remember seeing or receiving them, though the letter made clear mention that they had been sent to him.

Keith sweated over the mathematics, trying to remember exactly how much Hollow Tree had made before the end of the year as he ran downstairs to the dormitory office, hoping to track down the papers.

"Don't know nothin' about it," Anton Jackson said defensively. He was the permanent dorm supervisor of Power and nearby Gibbs Hall, and lived on campus all year round. He aimed a long brown finger at Keith. "This little blond kid picked up your mail every day. He had a letter signed by you. You telling me he was a phony?"

"Oh!" Keith exclaimed, recognizing the description. "Um, no, sorry. He's all right. I forgot all about him. Thanks." Keith shot out into the sunny street.

The sunlight in the elf village matched that upstairs with amazing faith to detail. Keith had to blink, passing through the darkness of the stone stairs and into the clan precinct. He found Holl sitting in the classroom, whittling, and distractedly throwing the shavings on the floor. "Hi. I'm back."

"I can see that," Holl said, without glancing up.

"Have you got my mail? I just got another love letter from the I.R.S. We are in deep trouble. They want to do an audit on us for last year. Did you send in my tax return late or something? That's going to get us nailed, you know."

"No. I sent it in plenty of time." Holl turned toward him, finally letting Keith see his face. He looked worried and unhappy. "Follow me, but wait in the tunnel. Big Folk are not popular today."

All around them, there were signs of activity. Some of the minute elf children were wrapping individual wooden items in newspaper, and carrying them to bigger children, who packed them in boxes or paper bags. The young adults wielded carefully muffled power saws and drills in clouds of sawdust. Others, obviously detailed as caterers, coughed and waved hands before stinging eyes as they brought baskets of food to the workers. The oldsters, eschewing modern equipment, put delicate fragments of wood together with glue. "God, it's Santa's workshop," Keith observed, trying to cheer Holl up. He didn't have the heart to get excited about the missing forms when his friend looked so low. "Where's the reindeer?" he asked under his breath.

"More alien oddities?" Holl sighed. Keith noticed a deep line furrowing between the blond elf's eyebrows.

"What's that mean?"

"Shhh! Here. I've carried a copy with me since it appeared." He handed Keith a sheet on which two slips of newsprint had been reproduced. Keith read them quickly and scoffed.

"The *National Informer*? Holl, this is a load of crap. Nobody believes them."

"Why then do they have a circulation of over two million? There are the gullible out there."

"Oh, come on," Keith scoffed. "I admit it sounds like a thinly disguised Midwestern, but still!"

"It isn't the only one," Holl corrected him. "There are several others, and have been more since. Catra has them all. Most are revises of this same one, with the words changed around. I keep this one to remind me of the date on which it first appeared. But it's the most recent one," he pointed to the second story on the page, "that worries us the most. It all but identifies Gillington as our base! The others are all but ready for decamping tonight."

"What do you want me to do?"

Holl considered Keith's offer for a moment. "I thought you could approach the *Informer* to discover from whom this story comes. The articles were written by someone who is personally familiar with us."

"I bet it was Lee," Keith said, speculatively. "He's a Journalism major, you know."

Holl shook his head. "I doubt that as much as I doubt that it was you who did it, which is what the Elders are saying."

"What?"

"They're desperate," Holl offered, turning up his palms in appeal. "They have no other explanation. Will you find out for us, so we can put a stop to it?"

"I'll try," Keith promised, "but first, can we solve *my* little problem? What about the I.R.S.?"

"Your pardon," Holl apologized, embarrassed. "What do you need?"

"Records. Estimated tax forms," Keith replied. "Can you help me? I've been trying to figure out everything we've done, and I'm confusing myself."

"You're good at that. I'm pleased to see you're not immune to your own skill," Holl said wryly, sounding more like himself. He walked to his hut, emerged with a box of letters, and beckoned Keith back up the tunnel to the classroom. "Come with me, and we'll see what we can see."

The editor to whom Keith spoke at the *National Informer* was smugly pleased to inform him that they always protected their sources. "The First Amendment, you know," he cackled. "Threats and pleas have no effect on me." He refused to give Keith the name of the anonymous source.

"Well," Keith offered, "what if I said I could get you another article, but I had to make sure I wasn't intruding on your writer's territory? I mean, he might want to send you more, right? But if we're not in the same town, it would be poor journalism to let a corroborating story go . . ."

"Hmmmmm . . ." the editor mused. "Mr. Doyle, you're

very persuasive, but I still can't give you our source's name. I will tell you he filed the story from Midwestern University.''

"Oh," said Keith, not surprised, "that's where I am. I mean, I suppose that you can't give me any other information . . . ?" he inquired hopefully.

"Nope, sorry," he was told. "That will have to do you, son. Can you provide us with corroborating evidence? We pay free-lancers well. Your byline on a national gazette . . ." the editor said temptingly.

"Um, no. I, uh, only heard a story from a guy. I'd be a lousy writer. Thanks."

"Okay," the editor said before he hung up. "But if you change your mind, gimme a call."

"Here you are, sir. From November to now," Keith said, spreading his receipts and papers out on a table in the I.R.S. office. He gave one last, longing glance out the storefront-style window at the deep blue spring sky, dotted with fluffy cumulus clouds, before the door of Agent Durrow's cubicle swung shut, cutting off the view. He plumped his briefcase from his lap to the floor, heard the unmuffled *clack* of unwrapped samples banging together. With a quick glance to make sure nothing was broken, he gave all his attention to the I.R.S. agent across the table from him.

When he called to make an appeal for help, it was suggested that he come in to talk to Agent Durrow, who had Keith's file in his possession. That way, it was explained, he wouldn't need to give all the facts of his case all over again. It made him nervous that an I.R.S. agent knew all about him, but he tried to conceal his apprehensions. He turned the slim envelope upside down and shook it to ensure that it was empty. "Like I said, I didn't open until late last year."

"Why didn't you file for a different fiscal year? Say, November to October?" Durrow asked, sifting through the papers. He was a thin-faced, thin-voiced man in a black suit with lapels sharp enough to cut fingers. "You would not have had to send in a 1040 until next year."

"I'm used to filing in a January to December fiscal year, sir. I didn't really think of it as an option."

"Few do," Durrow admitted. "Very well, I will help you with the papers just this once, but I suggest you send for these forms." He opened a drawer in his desk and withdrew a gray pamphlet on which he circled several numbers. "They will assist you in figuring your estimated tax. I regret to say we do not have extra forms here at this time. We are waiting for a shipment. New tax laws. Beyond that, I suggest you find yourself an accountant."

While the agent noted down the figures from Keith's receipts on a legal sheet in his quick, neat hand, he went on with his suggestions. "You should concentrate on keeping track of your expenditures in a ledger . . . My, my, isn't that a tidy sum. What did you say are the goods you manufacture?"

"Woodcrafts," Keith said.

"Average price?"

"Oh, five to twenty dollars or so."

Durrow turned a razor-edged glance on him. "How can you have generated so much income by yourself? You are certain you are not using employees to supply your inventory?"

"Why do you ask, sir?" Keith asked.

"Information received," Durrow said austerely. "Well?"

"I make 'em myself, during spring break, Christmas break, you know," Keith said firmly. "Except for things I take on consignment from friends, but they're not working for me. I get 10 percent."

"You have income from commissions, then." Durrow jotted that down.

"Yes, sir," Keith said, watching the pencil fly down the page in bewildered concern. "My 1040's there."

"Out of curiosity, I wonder if you know the zoning laws for this town, young man." Durrow acknowledged a shake of Keith's head. "Aha. That school is not zoned for cottage industry. You could be fined for violations if the zoning commission cared to make a fuss."

Keith held out his hands in protest. "Oh, I don't make anything here, sir. I use a . . . friend's house. And . . . is there any problem with my finishing things in the school woodshop?"

"No," Durrow allowed, somewhat reluctantly. He looked askance at Keith, having developed skepticism about student businesses in general. "Very well. Based on the income so far this year, you will need to pay in this much per quarter," he jotted down another number, "and if there are increases, you will divide up by the remaining quarters and pay them in that way. Providing there are no irregularities, your account will be entered in our computer files. Your next quarterly payment will be due by the quarter ending on April 15th.''

That gave him a couple of weeks to work it out. Keith agreed, and Durrow went back to the papers. The thin pen scratched out more numbers, adding up the accounts receivable, then the expenses, which he divided into several categories, with remarkable speed. To Keith's eye, it was working out very well. He began to think he might get out of that stifling office and back into the fragrant air, perhaps to take a walk later with Diane, when the approving ''um-hmm's'' ceased abruptly. ''What's this?'' Durrow asked, going through the cancelled checks in the latest bank statement, and holding one out to him. ''This is a check for $2,000, made out to Cash, and the memo line says only 'down-payment.' And another check, 'property tax escrow'?''

Keith goggled at it, forgetting all about the air, the sunshine, or Diane. Two thousand dollars? That was nearly the whole balance! ''I don't know.''

''It's signed Holland Doyle. Who is Holland Doyle?''

''My nephew, sir.'' Keith swallowed miserably. ''He must have bought something with the company money . . . a machine, or a car, or something . . .'' He took the check. There were two signatures on the back, and he could read neither of them.

''How old is your nephew?''

''Um . . . twelve. Almost thirteen.''

Durrow's thin eyebrow raised, wrinkling the hairless forehead in precisely two places. ''Why do you allow him to sign on *your* checkbook?''

''In case of emergency,'' Keith said. ''He's got more common sense than I have.''

''I see.'' Durrow was amused. A tiny crease appeared at the corner of his mouth. That meant he was smiling. ''I strongly suggest that you find out what it was he spent your funds on, so you can submit quarterly taxes. If it is not an appropriate expense, you must pay tax on it as income. That is all for now. You may go. We will be in touch with you.''

''Yes, sir.'' Keith gathered up his papers and fled.

* * *

"They must have paid out Diane's scholarship already!" Keith exclaimed out loud, going over the papers again and again on the way back to campus. "Well, I can't ask *her* about it." The fact that worried him most was the huge discrepancy between the tax which was about to fall due, and the size of the remaining balance in the checking account. The two sums weren't even close. The elves certainly wouldn't have any reserves, and his own checking account balance contained only the remains of the commission check he had received before vacation. He thought of calling his father and asking for a loan, but put that aside, recalling a discussion about money his family had had while he was home on break. Any savings in expenditure would be appreciated, Mr. Doyle had said, since Keith's sister Karen would begin college that fall.

"I don't have any choice," he said, resolutely turning the car away from campus. "I've got to save my own skin. The Little Folk are counting on me." It sounded very heroic in his own ears, but he was aware how much of a long shot it would be for him to raise that much money in so little time.

The signs leading up to Matt's Cheese Chalet and Snack Bar mentioned that it sold gifts, so Keith followed an impulse and stopped in. The place, an obvious tourist trap, was made up to look like a Swiss gingerbread building, and screamed "tacky" at the top of its lungs, but it did indeed sell knick-knacks of every description. Keith began to admire the taste and forbearance of shop owners such as Ms. Voordman, who showed restraint in her choice of merchandise, if garbage like this was available wholesale. Idiotic little cedar boxes held together by tin hinges and varnish, and stamped with "Matt's, Illinois," lay between iron trivets shaped like Pennsylvania Dutch hex symbols and porcelain spoon holders with calico geese painted on the bowls. He sighed, but Matt's was the only new prospect he had been able to turn up all afternoon, and it was already getting close to evening. He had some new ideas, but nothing would bring in cash right now except orders.

"Think of how items like this would jazz up a display," he told Matt, who looked like an ex-truck driver now gone more to fat than muscle, and who liked cheap cigars. Keith smelled the stale smoke in the air when he came in. There was no way he would ever eat a meal in a place like this. He had already lost his enthusiasm for the sale, and was wishing that he hadn't come in. But since he had begun, he might as well finish. "It's for a good cause."

"Nah," Matt said, rubbing his cigar out on the snack counter, narrowly missing one of Maura's precious cookie cutters. Keith cringed, and moved everything subtly away from the restaurateur. "This kinda stuff doesn't *sell*, ya know what I mean? I got troubles with the merchandise I've got, and it's all good stuff. Didja take a look around?"

"Yeah, I did. I don't see how I could compete with what you've got out already." Matt's line featured the very ugliest in junky little gifts. Keith figured he was about a hundred classes above it.

Matt rolled his belly to one side, scratched at his ribs with satisfaction. "Right. So, what's the good cause you were talking about?"

"Oh, nothing," Keith said, preoccupied, starting to put his samples away. There was no hope of a sale here. He had wasted time, and the I.R.S. was getting impatient. He could feel the hot breath of the auditing computer on his back at this moment. "Junior Achievements."

"Oh, yeah?" Matt stopped scratching. "Where from?"

"Local," Keith said, preparing to trot out his now well-rehearsed tale. "I'm at Midwestern."

Matt's face lost all semblance of joviality. "Really? I think that's interesting. It so happens I am the local president of the Junior Achievements chapter for the last twelve years, and I know everyone, every single senior advisor, every single kid in the whole organization, and I have never seen you before in my life." He plunged a forefinger against Keith's chest, punctuating every syllable with a stab. "They call that fraud, when some guy tries to make money off the kids. How would you like it if I called the cops, huh?"

"Uh, please don't do that," Keith said, frantically, picturing the officer who had accompanied the union thugs. "Uh, really . . . my group picked up the skills in a Junior Achievement group in the Chicago area. I buy things from them on consignment. Here," he thrust one of the charmed cookie cutters into the man's hands. "Nice workmanship, isn't it? And if it had not been for good old J.A., we'd never have gotten anywhere."

Tension eased out from between the man's thick gray brows as the cookie cutter did its magic. Keith breathed again, pulling air into his constricted lungs. "Okay," Matt growled. "But I don't ever want to hear that you're representing yourself as J.A. again, or I'll wanna have a talk with you face-to-face, get it?" He brandished the cutter in Keith's face.

"Got it," Keith said. Matt slammed the wooden mold down on the counter, heaved himself off the pink plastic stool, and waddled away.

Keith snatched up the cutter and hurried out into the clean spring air. He was happy to have escaped, but he was still without money to pay the quarterly taxes.

▪ Chapter 33 ▪

He let himself into the village by way of the classroom. The hallway seemed more remote than usual. It wore an air of forboding, and Keith felt more than once a compulsion to turn around and leave.

"Security measures," he decided, since there was actually nothing more threatening in the passage. It was protective magic; no, a charm, he corrected himself. He was glad the Little Folk had finally taken his advice.

"Hi, Enoch," he said, seeing the black-haired elf reading at a table in the dining hall. "I had a great idea I wanted to talk to everyone about. I figure we can increase our sales, without it costing a penny. All we need to do is get grass-root papers to do write-ups on the merchandise. They don't have to focus on the 'factory' at all. They can wrap us by doing the story on the shops we sell to. Ms. Voordman would probably go for it like a shot. Can you tell me where . . ." His voice faded away as Enoch regarded him in open-mouthed shock.

"Your nerve, Keith Doyle!" Without another word, the elf rose and walked out without letting him finish his question.

"Enoch? Something wrong?"

There certainly must have been. He followed into the sloping passage that led to the clan enclosure. Faces turned toward the entrance when he emerged, to see who was coming down, and turned away again, as if they had all been on one control, as soon as they saw him. He was puzzled and hurt. "Dola? Hey, honey," he began, approaching the child, who he knew liked him. She was jumping rope and counting out loud near her mother's hut. He bent down to her eye-level, his hands on his knees to speak to her. "What's going on down here?" Dola went wide-eyed at his question, pressed her lips together, and kicked him solidly in the shin. While he hopped up and down clutching his bruise, she fled inside, shutting the door on him.

Keith was beginning to get frightened. He hurried over to Curran's clan, and tapped on Holl's door. "Hello? Anyone home?"

"He'll no' be in. Ye may go away now."

Whirling, Keith found himself face-to-face, or rather, shirt button-to-face with Curran himself. The tiny clan chief had never quite gotten over his dislike of the Big Man, and he wore his jaw in a set that brooked no argument.

"Will he be back soon?" Keith asked, backing away.

"No' soon enow for ye to be waitin' fer him. Go." Keith started to speak, but the elf turned his white-maned head away, refusing to hear Keith's questions.

Keith kept moving, hoping to find Holl or the Elf Master, to ask them what was going on. He needed to find out about the missing two thousand dollars, and fast, but it looked like he wasn't even going to get the time of day. The usually effusive villagers were taciturn and quiet. Conversation stilled as soon as he got near. The only face he saw that didn't blanch on sighting him was Marm's. The bearded elf stood in front of his clan houses, sweeping the pounded walkway with a wisp of straw.

Keith went over to talk to him, willing him to stay where he was until he got to him. "Hi there."

"Greetings, Keith Doyle," Marm replied, resting his broom on his bent arm. Keith almost fainted with relief to get a friendly response.

"Nice day, isn't it?" he asked. Marm grunted, his usual reply to questions about the weather. Keith pressed on. "You know, I just came down to talk about income taxes, and a great idea I had for publicity, but everyone is acting like I have the plague!"

"What great idea is this one?" Marm asked, friendly as usual, but there was strain in his voice. Whatever was bothering Enoch and Curran seemed to have rubbed off on everyone. Keith swallowed his discomfort.

"Free publicity. What we need are write-ups in the local paper," Keith began again with as much enthusiasm in his voice as he could muster, but as he continued, Marm's face turned the color of a boiled beet.

"There you go, and aren't you ashamed of yourself?" Marm demanded, and tossed the broom aside. It clattered on the packed-earth floor.

"What?" Keith asked, agog. "Nobody is talking sense today."

"You made the local press. I expect you'll have a hundred copies of your own. Here!" Marm rummaged through one of the huts and emerged with a beechwood stick with a long slit in it, which he thrust into the human's hands.

Keith recognized it as the kind of stick libraries thread through the daily papers, so that no one will steal them and save a quarter. In this case, it had never left the library, so it really hadn't been stolen. "This page, here!" Marm pointed to an article entitled fantastically: "Elves Discovered Living in Downstate Illinois!" Keith stared at it, his astonishment growing. This one was just like the stories Holl had shown him, but it was in the city newspaper. Alarmed, he began to read.

A source, who had asked not to be identified, had told the syndicated press that there was proof that a colony of heretofore-believed-mythical creatures was living somewhere in one of the buildings on the Midwestern University campus. And, more damning still was the description of their cottages. There was even an artist's sketch with the article of a small wooden hut, which Keith had to admit did look like one of the clan homes. Marm pointed to a paragraph. " 'Witness the wonderful "nightlights" being sold in the gift shops. No known science can duplicate such things. Surely they are evidence of magic?' No other has seen our homes. You did it, did you not, you fool? Do you think if they know that, that they'll be satisfied with toys? No, no, grant me a wish, it'll be! Three wishes! Aren't we under enough pressure already, having to leave our home?''

Keith was dumbfounded. "*I* didn't do this," he protested.

"Then who did? They are saying things here that only you would know. The other stories might have been guesswork, I grant, but you're the one who began to call us elves!"

"I didn't write that article. Look, it mentions the date it was submitted. That was over spring break. I was somewhere between Chicago and Michigan all vacation."

"Ye could have *mailed* it," Marm said darkly. He had never written a letter, and clearly hoped he never would. "I should have believed Carl Mueller the first time when he called you treacherous."

"I swear, this has nothing to do with me!"

"Can ye prove it?" the little man demanded.

"Well, no. Newspapers won't tell who their sources are. You just have to take my word for it. I swear I'd never jeopardize you guys like that. You're my friends."

"So you can't prove it?" Marm picked up his broom. "Well, no one else will talk to you, but I will tell you what they say. They think you are guilty. Until and unless you can prove you are innocent of this mischief, we will fulfill no more orders."

"But wait! You promised," Keith protested. "We have contracts to fulfill. Customers are waiting!" He had visions of Mr. Durrow cranking the wheel on the rack to which a screaming Keith Doyle was tied.

"It is no good," Marm assured him. "You promised, too. You promised us security. Now we will take care of ourselves." The elf went back to sweeping the walk and ignored Keith until he went away.

"Needs work, but it's in pretty good shape," Lee Eisley said, pounding on the walls of the farmhouse. "You're going to have to do something pretty quick about the ceiling in the back, there. There was a lot of leaking."

Holl walked in wonder around the place. "Hard to believe it is ours, eh?" he asked softly, more to himself than any of the others. His voice echoed in the empty rooms. Dust mice rolled away from his feet on the polished wood floors. "Ours. Our home."

"How bad is it?" the Elf Master asked, looking over the blueprints.

"Well, if it's drywall, no problem. That's cheap. If it's plaster, that's cheaper, but it takes a lot of patience to get right."

"Ve haf much patience," the Elf Master assured him. "Vhat ve do not haf is much time."

"I've got some tools outside in my station wagon."

"No need," said the Elf Master dryly. "I vill test it for you in a moment."

"Has Ludmilla seen this place yet?" Lee asked. "She'll love it."

"No. No time haf ve had to inform her. You may, if you like." The Elf Master put his nose back into the plans.

"Nine large rooms. One clan will have to share if we are to keep the biggest room as a meeting place," Maura reported, showing them her notes. "The cellar will make a good workshop, since we have no need to place the garden there. Of course, the attic is habitable. The kitchen is of a good size, with a flame stove, but everything is so high."

"Our crafters will take care of that," Holl assured her, taking her hand. "But will they give up their own roofs after such a long time?"

"Before ve came here, it vas all one roof," the Elf Master assured him. "And in time before that, many roofs. Ve vill adapt. As always ve haf."

Holl peered out the window down the slope of the hill behind the house. Among the weeds were useful herbs and blooming tulips and hyacinths. "There's no reason we can't build if we need more room. I for one would like to see the workshop in the old barn. I don't like sawdust in the bed, nor listening to power tools while I sleep."

"You are correct," the Elf Master nodded, his lips pursed. "It is time ve lived mit confidence, and less like refugees."

"We ought to start moving some of the Folk here right away," Holl suggested. "If we want our own vegetables, we need to plant immediately. And the leak in the roof along with weak flooring upstairs won't wait long."

"Very vell. I vill ask for volunteers to come out right away to begin vork and set up their homes. If you vill oblige us mit more taxi service, Mr. Eisley?''

''Sure. I'd be happy to. 'Old Farmhouse Becomes Model Craft Community.' It'd make a great magazine story.'' Lee grinned, looking over the plans and calculating the amount of work the old place would need. ''Too bad I can never write it.''

Keith slunk out of the library so engrossed in his depression that he walked past without seeing Diane. Clouds were gathering from all corners of the sky, threatening to rain.

Diane ran up to kiss him, her cheeks flushed red in the brisk spring air. ''Hello there, stranger! How about helping me study for Biology? Would you like to have dinner with me tonight, and go on from there? With Biology, I mean?'' She gave him a slow wink. ''Since it's going to be rotten outside.''

''Oh, yeah, sure,'' Keith accepted with a grin. ''I think I could eat a horse. At least I think that's what they're serving tonight.''

Diane laughed. ''You're funny. It's buzzard on Wednesdays.''

''You're absolutely right,'' he said, taking her books and sticking out an elbow for her to grasp.

''I really need help. I think I'm failing the stupid course. Can you believe that? It's no different than high school bio as far as I can tell. What were you doing in the library today?'' Diane asked, as they walked toward the dorm.

''Oh, studying.'' But something in his voice didn't convince her.

''Studying? Studying what?'' she asked, sharply.

''Marketing . . . and a little Sociology,'' he said sadly. He had a faraway look that puzzled Diane, and she pressed him for more information.

''Keith, I thought we agreed we were always going to be honest with each other.'' There was a long pause. ''Keith?''

''Really, I was just studying,'' he protested.

''Sure. In the deepest part of the stacks? Come on. You must think I'm really stupid.'' Diane was annoyed. ''*I* know what goes on down there. I was on Level Twelve and I saw you come up the stairs. You never spoke to me, so I followed you out here.''

"Diane, I—I wasn't doing anything you would disapprove of, I promise."

"So what were you doing?" she demanded, but before Keith spoke, she held up a hand. "Never mind. I don't want to hear anything you'd say. I'm sure it would all be bullshit. I thought you really cared for me." She snatched her books out of his hands and stormed away.

"Diane!" he called after her, but she shook her head and kept moving. Keith watched her go with resignation. "I wish a car would hit me right now and end my misery," he said morosely. "There's nothing more that could happen to me."

There was no answer at the office of the Historical Society. Keith spent the evening with his thoughts racing between the quarterly taxes, the mysterious articles, and the elves' unfriendliness. On top of that was Holl's unexplained absence, and his frustration in not being able to explain to Diane what was really going on in the library. He sighed, gazing from where he lay out the window, watching lightning sear the clouds. Maybe if it rained hard enough, he could drown himself without ever getting out of bed.

It was raining the next day, too. Keith dashed between his classes with his head down, as much from unhappiness as from the cold wet wind. He spent most of Mythology class with sad, soulful eyes watching Diane, who sat four rows ahead of him. She noticed his gaze, but turned away with her eyes down. It reminded him of the mass-shun in the village, and depressed him further.

"Keith?" Diane followed him out of the classroom when it was over, and drew him close to the wall. "I just wanted to apologize."

"You don't have to apologize," Keith said, steeling himself to tell her the true story.

"No, I do." She held her hands over his mouth. "I'm sorry. I should believe you. You're a lousy liar. I wouldn't get so upset if . . . I weren't so involved. I do trust you. If you say there's nothing to be worried about, I'll believe you." She threw her arms around him and kissed him soundly.

Shedding his gloomy mood all at once, Keith got enthusiastically behind the concept of kissing. "You know," he breathed when they came up for air, "this is the first decent thing that has happened to me all day. Maybe all week."

Diane pouted. "Only decent?"

"Well . . ." Keith took another sample of longer endurance. "A lot more than that." A further kiss assured him it was the best possible anywhere. "Look," he said. "The rain is stopping."

The door at the bottom of the fourteenth level of the stacks creaked open, and Carl hid his key so the distinctive green light wouldn't give him away. He left the classroom door propped open for a quick getaway. It was Wednesday, so there wasn't supposed to be anyone in there. If Doyle or anyone was here, Carl could just say that he forgot something. He was sure that he could explain his way out of any situation.

He felt his way in, hands out for the iron maidens. The room seemed much wider in the dark. After he touched the wall, he eased first one way, then the other, feeling for the low door. His fingers showed him the lip of the entrance, and he crouched down and walked hunched over along the tunnel's rough cement floor. His soft-soled shoes made a tiny *tok* each time he set down a foot, but he congratulated himself that he wasn't making any noise.

Down at the tunnel's far end, Dola and two of her friends, Moira and Borget, were playing in the empty dining hall. They had already detected a presence and reported it to the Elf Master down in the village, who was giving a lesson in map reading to a group of volunteers who had offered to be the first to move out to the farmhouse.

"It's not Keith Doyle," Dola said. She still had a minor crush on the tall Big One. She was sorry she was not allowed to talk to him anymore, but he hadn't come back since that day she had kicked him.

"Zo?" inquired the Master, setting down his atlas and looking at them over the tops of his glasses. "Go and ask whoever it is vhat he vants." His eyes twinkled. "But quietly. Other people do not vish to be disturbed."

The young ones looked at each other gleefully and dashed back to the passage.

Dola waited by the entrance to the village, concentrating hard on a linen cloth woven by her mother, while the other two silently sneaked up on Carl in the passage. Though she was young, Dola's talent of weaving illusions was one that the Elders insisted she begin developing immediately. She was rather proud of it herself, but as yet couldn't design anything in mid-air. She still needed a "canvas" on which to draw her magical pictures. Dola preferred to create beautiful designs, but the Elders had decreed that for distracting intruders, she had to make an ugly, boring image. As Carl turned the corner and looked the rest of the way down the passage, Dola held up the cloth.

Looking straight at her, all Carl could see was a storeroom, dimly lit by bare bulbs hanging on cords. Scattered on the floor were elderly cardboard cartons festooned with cobwebs and dust. Concentrating very hard, Dola made the image of a great, black spider walk across the floor.

"Huh?" Carl gasped; then, realizing he had spoken, he clapped his hand over his mouth, willing the sound to come back. He knew he must have missed the entrance. It was somewhere behind him. He turned and began to feel his way back up the corridor. Moira and Borget were huddled together against the wall behind him, holding hands. As soon as Carl passed them, Moira squeezed Borget's hand.

"Eeeeeeeeeaah!" shrieked Moira at the top of her voice.

"Hmmhmmhmmhmmmmhahahahaha . . ." laughed Borget, in as sinister a tone as he could manage.

In spite of himself, Carl straightened up to his full height, and bashed his head on the ceiling. There was another burst of ghostly laughter. Clutching his head with one hand, he felt his way out of the tunnel and schoolroom, hotly pursued by his banshees. He screamed curses back at them, but they only laughed. An elfish trick!

"I'll get you, too," he swore, as he ran up the stairs. He wasn't going to get his evidence this way, that was sure. The two young elves laughed and ran back to Dola to share the joke.

The Elf Master was thoughtful as they reported their guest's identity and actions. "This one will bear watching," he said. "A burglar is the only guest who does not knock."

"But what would be here to steal?" Moira asked. "We have no fancy possessions."

The elder elf shrugged. "Our privacy is very valuable," he said, with a sigh.

▪ Chapter 34 ▪

Something of great importance was definitely going on in the village, but Keith was being kept in the dark. Worse yet, he hadn't been able to catch Holl outside of class. Every time he tried to strike up a conversation, one of the others would head off the blond elf and lead him away from Keith. The tall student felt it was important that the two of them should talk. Quarterly income taxes would be due soon, and by Keith's calculations, the amount would far exceed the balance presently in the checkbook that Holl held. Though to be fair, Holl had the forms in hand, too, and he had been faithful about sending them in on time. If it got too close to the deadline, Keith would simply swallow his pride and ask the Elf Master for intervention.

Since he was deprived of his friends in the village, he had been spending more time with Diane, but as his anxiety increased, Diane complained that he was becoming distant.

"You've got something on your mind. Is it the craft business?" she demanded as he walked her home from Mythology class one evening. "How's it doing?"

"I'm not too sure," Keith replied, running a mental inventory of his available merchandise and groaning over the total. He wished he could ask someone if everything would be ready when needed. Diane studied him, and he flashed her a quick smile. She shook her head.

"Now I know something is wrong. You used to have every single fact at the tip of your tongue. It's a sign that you're probably doing too much." She leaned down from the steps and kissed him. "If you want to talk, or if there's anything I can do, just let me know."

"Mmm." Keith reached for another kiss. "That helped a lot. Good night."

"Good night. Oh, I just remembered. Ms. Voordman wants you to stop by. She wants to talk to you. Good night again."

228

Diane disappeared behind the frosted glass of the front door and Keith turned away into the twilight.

The evening was quiet, with the hint of scent in the air that proved Spring had arrived and she meant business. A few late birds chorused with the crickets that lived in the cellars of the ancient brownstones. Keith thought of stopping in to see Ludmilla and telling her his troubles. Her kindness and warm sympathy were very soothing to miserable souls. She didn't live far from Diane's. He smiled. The two of them would probably get along very well. They were both strong and caring women.

A few early bicyclists whizzed past him along the curb. Keith heard the whirr of spokes and a burst of swearing as one of them accidentally flashed in front of a pedestrian in the crosswalk. He glanced back. There were two men at the intersection about half a block behind him. One of them was still swearing, and his buddy was holding him back from giving chase. It would have been pointless. The bicyclist was probably half a mile away already.

Keith had expected more foot-traffic on a nice night in a campus town, but he figured it was his indoctrination to the elves that now made him walk more than he ever had before he met them. Most of his Big Folk classmates still drove wherever they could. Self-locomotion was only used when nothing else was available. He thought it was weird that these same students would jog or run eight miles every morning before dawn, but they'd rather die than walk to the movies. He turned a corner onto Ludmilla's street.

After a while, he began to have a funny feeling between his shoulder blades. He looked back. The two men were still walking about half a block behind him. They weren't exactly casual strollers. There was purpose in their stride. He thought that he recognized their forms: they looked like the union president's men.

It could have been a coincidence. Keith walked past Ludmilla's brownstone and turned left on the next street, reluctant to lead them to his friend. The men kept pace. He turned another corner, and another, and still his shadows stayed the same distance behind him. The streetlamps sprang alight high over his head. It was growing darker, and Keith found that he was nearly back to the Midwestern campus. The buildings were closer together here. He could hide. Closing the distance between him and them, the two thugs passed under a light and Keith caught a glimpse of their faces. It was the union men.

Keith panicked and started for the alleyway between the Science Building and the faculty garage. His only thought was to find a security guard who would drive his pursuers away. There was a cry behind him. He threw a glance over his shoulder. The men had seen him break into a run and were sprinting after him.

Keith ran down the ornamental paths on the other side of the Science Building and leaped over a marble bench onto the lawn next to the library, avoiding the thornbushes that flanked it. He could open the stone facade and escape into the elves' village—if he was fast enough. He didn't know how far behind him the men were. Safety was getting closer. He ducked around the side of the thorn hedge, and swung past the sycamore tree by the boulder. There was rustling in the shrubbery to either side of him. To his dismay, the thugs had separated. One was bounding toward him across the grass, and one was heading off his other escape route, past the main entrance to Gillington. He couldn't open the facade now; he'd give the elves' secret away.

Rough hands caught him from behind and held his arms as he turned back into the thornbushes. Keith cried out and kicked, striking his captor in the kneecap. The man swore and kicked back a few times, staggering Keith to his knees with the angry blows to his calves and buttocks.

The other thug moved in slowly, like a boxer under water. He smacked one gigantic fist into the other. It sounded like a pistol shot. Keith winced. "Mr. Lewandowski has been waiting for your list. It is bad business to keep him waiting."

"Sorry," Keith grimaced. "I haven't gotten around to it yet."

"Wrong answer," the man told him, and the giant fist took Keith in the stomach. He folded over, gasping, seeing black stars against the darkness.

One of the ham-hands clutched his hair and his face was dragged up, away from the agony in his midsection. "You get that list, or you're going to have real trouble, you hear me?" Keith nodded weakly. The man let go, and Keith sagged down against the thug behind him. He stared at the ground, trying to gather enough strength to say something, when he noticed that the thornbushes were moving.

For a moment, he was so fascinated he forgot about his pain. Thin switches of thorn, with the buds of new leaves gleaming at alternating intervals along their lengths, were weaving out of the hedges, along the ground, and twining themselves up around the legs of the man in front of him. And the man behind as well. The vines pulled taut.

"Didn't you hear me, punk?" The man grabbed Keith's hair again. When his face came up, Keith could see two pairs of bright eyes behind the bushes. Or rather, one pair of eyes, and one pair of spectacles. The Master, and possibly Holl. "We mean business."

"Yeah," Keith grated out, not recognizing his own breathless voice. "I see what you're doing." The spectacles in the shrubbery glinted. Message received. With a heroic effort Keith straightened up. "No sale. Tell him I'm not interested."

"I'm warning you, punk," the man growled. He reached for Keith with both hands.

With a swift jerk, Keith pulled both arms free from the grasp of the gorilla's assistant and jumped to the side. Both men twisted to grab him, and ended up flailing their arms wildly in the air for balance. They fell forward, emitting ululations of pain and obscenities; the dormant thornbushes had no leaves to conceal or pad the inch-and-a-half-long thorns as sharp as roofing nails that grew between the buds.

Keith was not going to wait around for them to get free. He took to his heels and fled, searching for the security patrol. A mighty wrenching and ripping of cloth, accompanied by much swearing, suggested to him that one of the thugs was abandoning modesty and stripping off his trousers to come after Keith.

While they struggled, he dodged between the hedges and pelted down the ornamental path to the street. To his everlasting gratitude, a patrol car rolled into view as he rounded the corner of the library building. He leaped into the street to flag it down. The car screeched over to the curb. He dashed over to it.

"Help!" Keith yelled in the window at the two security guards, waving back toward the library. "Officer, two flashers out there near the library! Muggers! *Perverts*!" Steadying riot clubs and flashlights on their belts, the uniformed officers followed Keith's energetic pointing, and were just in time to intercept the union men as they appeared around the angle of the building clad in jackets, socks, shoes and undershorts.

Spotlighting their captives with flashlights, the guards shoved the men against the wall of the library and started to frisk them. The senior guard shone his flashlight on the torn backside of one man's peacock blue shorts. "You a streaker, bud? I don't think your butt's so pretty that you ought to show it. I wanna see some I.D. What are you doing on this campus without authorization?" He noticed Keith hanging around behind him, and shone his flashlight into Keith's face. "What's your name, son?"

"Keith Doyle, sir. Power Hall."

"Okay, Doyle. We'll want a statement from you in the morning. In the meantime, get out of here. Thanks for alerting us."

"Sure thing!" Keith waved a jaunty salute, half to the security officers, half to the invisible figures in the bushes. "Thanks again."

"I'm gonna get you, kid!" the muscular thug shouted. "Now it's personal!"

"Up against the wall, you," the guard growled, shoving him back into place.

▪ Chapter 35 ▪

"Keith!" Marcy came running up to him as he walked Diane toward the Science Building for her biology class. "Oh, Keith, I'm so glad to see you!"

"Hi, Marcy," Keith greeted her warmly, and turned to Diane. "Diane Londen, this is Marcy Collier. We're former fellow sufferers from Sociology class last semester. Marcy, Diane."

"Hi," Marcy said, a little offhandedly. It was clear she had something on her mind, but didn't know how to convey it to Keith.

"Pleased to meet you," Diane returned, somewhat suspiciously.

Keith saw the danger signals flaring in Diane's eyes, and hastened to ask Marcy, "So how's Enoch?"

There was nothing false about the glow that lit Marcy's face. "Wonderful. I had the most marvelous time over the break. My mother didn't understand why I didn't come home, but . . ." She smiled again, and blushed. Beside Keith, Diane relaxed.

"So, how's everything else?" Keith asked, meaningfully. "I haven't seen the Folks lately. Most of them aren't speaking to me."

Marcy nodded her comprehension. "Keith, I think Carl is planning to do something horrible. He wrote an article, a lot of unsubstantiated rumors . . . ?"

Keith nodded. "I know someone did. They thought it was me." Diane, puzzled, looked from one to the other, but didn't interrupt.

"Well, it was Carl! There are going to be more. Lots more. Says he's got *evidence* to support his case. If it wasn't about *family*, you might almost call it an exposé."

"Oh, no!"

"He's got an investigative reporter coming, Keith. Steven Arnold. You've heard of him?"

"Yes, I have! Have you told the family?"

"You must have some strange family," Diane commented to Marcy. "This Carl your cousin?" They both looked at her. "Sorry. Just an impression."

"I can't. They wouldn't believe me." Marcy sounded desperate.

"Well, don't worry. I'll take care of it. And Carl, too," Keith promised, with a glint in his eye. "I'll upset all of his plans."

"Good evening, Keith Doyle," Holl said quietly from the doorway.

Keith looked up from his books and beckoned the young elf into the room. "Hi! I'm glad to see you. You weren't home last time I dropped in."

"No. We have business to straighten out." His manner was stiff and strained, and Keith felt instantly uncomfortable.

"May I offer you something to drink?" he asked, formally, gesturing Holl to a chair.

"No, thank you," just as formally.

"Holl, you can't honestly believe that I'd do anything . . ."

The elf held up a hand. "I know what I believe, but I must side with my folk. No other way would I be allowed to come here." He brought out a handful of papers from his jacket pocket. "We have work to do."

Keith struggled to keep his voice level and reasonable. "We have a problem. There are a lot of people we promised merchandise to, they're going to get upset if we don't deliver."

"They are only in contact with you. It doesn't concern us directly. I have brought these papers by to do you a favor, as it's your name on them."

He tried again. "Marcy stopped me today. She told me that Carl was working on exposing the village."

"Do you wish me to carry this tale back, so the pressure will be taken from your back?" Holl asked angrily. "Do you have any proof?"

"There's no pressure on my back," Keith shouted, "except the I.R.S. and a bunch of shortsighted short people!"

"Do you imagine that is funny?" Holl demanded.

"Look, I wanted you to come by today so I could give you the proof."

"If you could do that," Holl said, hope brimming in his eyes. "You'd restore their faith. How?"

"I've got a plan." Keith pricked up his ears. "Carl's going to stop by. We'll let him hang himself. You hide in there." He pointed to his closet.

"Not for you or any other Big—"

"Shh! I hear—"

Holl promptly interrupted him. "I want to hear more—"

"Shh!" Keith swept Holl up and shoved him into the closet. The next second, as he pushed the double doors shut, there was a rap on the door. Keith swung it open. Carl strode in, suspiciously looking this way and that. Keith wondered if he was looking for contraband legends.

"Yo, Carl," he said, running a hand through his hair and

hoping Holl hadn't left any recognizable possessions in the room.

"Hello, Doyle," Carl said, eyeing him with amusement. "You left me a note. You say you've got something for me?"

"Started any good rumors lately?" Keith asked, with his best village idiot expression.

"Nothing I can't handle," Carl replied smugly. "Thanks for bringing out the Hollow Tree stuff, Doyle. The best thing that ever happened to me."

"Like it, huh?"

"Yep. Just the sort of thing successful news articles are made of. Proof."

"So you DID do those articles I read, huh?" Keith asked, his voice full of surprise and admiration.

"Yeah," Carl admitted proudly. "And there'll be more. I called Steve Arnold, the investigative reporter from the paper, to come and interview me on Friday about legends and stuff."

There was a gasp from the closet. Keith's smile widened. There was his proof, right from the horse's mouth.

"I'd sure like to come and hear what you have to say to the guy," Keith gloated, rubbing his hands together. "You were certainly around there a long time."

Carl was clearly preening. "I figure I know enough. I tried to get into the other part of their complex twice without their knowledge, once through the classroom and once through the wall, but I muffed it." He gave a shamefaced little laugh. "I nearly blew myself up with a couple of M-80's. That wall must be really strong. They have got to have a really powerful mechanism. I bet the construction industry would like to know about it." He eyed Keith. "If you help me find out, I'll cut you in for 10 percent of my profits. I'd get you into the article, too."

"Hey, thanks. I've always wanted to have my name in the papers."

"No problem. It's a piece of cake. Those elves are going to make me a lot of money. And they don't even know it. They're so dumb. Every time they wander around town and someone sees 'em I can sell another story to the papers. No wonder fairies are extinct."

Behind Keith, the doors gave a convulsive shove. Keith

threw himself backwards, dislodging Holl who, judging by the sounds, sat down backwards on Keith's boots. There was some muffled swearing, and Holl started pounding on the doors from the inside. "Stop it," he hissed.

Carl blinked at the closet Keith was guarding. "Is someone in there?"

"Yes," said Keith, thinking quickly. "It's my girl, Diane, and um, we were interrupted . . . So if you wouldn't mind?" He gestured toward the hall. "You know, nice talking to you and all."

Carl smirked. "Try a rubber band next time, Keith. This being-subtle stuff just gets you in trouble. See you on the front page."

"Whew!" Keith turned the lock, and opened the closet. A furious Holl sprang out into the room and reached for the doorknob.

"We'll get him!" he vowed, starting after Carl. "It was him all the time. I'll take care of him, the traitor! I'll make him stink!"

"No, you won't," Keith cautioned, hauling him back. "That'll blow everything. He wants you to be seen. It'll give credence to his newspaper stories. If that happens, it'll never stop. Help me, and we'll destroy his credibility."

Holl regarded him with shame. "You knew, Keith Doyle. Why didn't I voice my trust in you, as I have before? I knew you were honest. On behalf of myself and my folk, I apologize."

"Save it," Keith said flippantly. "I might need a real apology some day."

There was a cautious tap at the door. "Come in," Keith called out without thinking. Pat pushed in.

"Yo. Oh, hi, kid. I met Carl in the hallway. He said he was just by here. Where's the girl?"

"Um, she went home," Keith babbled out.

"Oh. Minute-man, huh? You know, Carl is starting to sound just like you," Pat told him, putting his books on the floor and stretching out full-length on the bed. "Legends and fairy tales. Too bad he doesn't like you. You could babble at each other, and leave me in peace. Giving me all this razzmatazz about legendary elves. In fact, he claims the campus is crawling with the little suckers."

"Do tell," Holl inquired blandly.

There was something about the way the boy spoke that made Pat really look at him. Something about the boy was different from the last time the dark-haired student had seen him. New haircut? No. He wasn't wearing a hat now, so you could see his ears. Boy, what big ears the kid had . . . ! "Those ears!" Pat gasped, sitting up. "Doyle, what on earth? I've been thinking all this time that your nephew here . . ."

"Holl," said Holl.

". . . Yeah, *Holl*, is just a kid with a Trek complex, but you're one of 'em, aren't you?" he asked, taking in Holl's appearance carefully for the first time. "Carl's right. You're not a kid at all." Pat got up and looked closely at the side of Holl's head, tugging on the point of one ear.

"Ouch," Holl said distinctly. "They're attached, you know."

"They're real," Pat breathed. "God damn."

"Yup," Keith told him. "Holl's one of the 'legendary elves' Carl was writing about. At least I call 'em elves," he finished, doubtfully. "Can't seem to get any confirmation from them on a scientific classification."

"It's all empirical anyhow," Holl said casually.

"Wow," sighed Pat, sitting down on the coffee table. "I suppose he isn't really your nephew, after all."

"Nope," Keith said, regretfully.

"Fear not. We're most likely distant kin," Holl assured him. "Ten thousand research books can't be all wrong."

"Hey, great," Keith crowed, diving for pen and notepad. "Can I quote you on that?"

"How's it feel?" Pat wanted to know.

"Never a problem to me," said Holl. "I was born normal, same as you. Oh, no," he held up his hands, palms out, seeing that Pat was misinterpreting his words. "Not an oversized babe like yourself. A normal, healthy squaller who drinks milk and pulls hair."

"Keith," Pat said faintly, "I take back almost everything I ever said about you."

"Carl is causing Holl and his family a lot of trouble."

"Who's his family?" Pat looked at him in amazement. "You mean the stuff with the investigative reporter? And the Inter-Hall Council?"

"They live in the basement of the library. For forty years now," Keith added. "Their village chief is the reason I passed Sociology last semester."

"Jeezus!"

Holl nodded. "It's not easy finding housing for eighty. We must be able to escape notice."

Pat eyed Keith. "So what's your role in all this?"

"I went into business to raise money so they could buy a place to live."

"You're the ones he was going to teach to fish."

Holl bowed to Pat. "I understand we owe the suggestion to you. It's a good one, and perhaps Keith Doyle would never have come to it himself."

"Much obliged. You know," Pat said thoughtfully, "if Carl had told you what was going on in the beginning, you would never have come out in favor of tearing the library down."

"That's just one score of many we need to settle with him," Holl said seriously. "You see how *you* react to encountering me, and Keith trusts you. I've no wish to be the object of gapers."

Pat was still overwhelmed. "After living with Keith for two years, I should be better prepared to deal with you guys. Although this is the first time he's actually brought home a research project. What can I do to help?"

"We're planning," Keith said. "But now that I think of it, you can help out if you want to. I'm happy that I can ask you openly. Meantime, there's a few more people we ought to get involved with this. We need to call a council of war." They sat down to conspire.

"Why'd we have to meet down here?" Teri said, hugging herself and looking around nervously at the steam tunnel. "Brr! I got dirt on my new toreador pants coming down that ladder. I bet it's all grease. I'll *never* get it out."

"Shh!" Barry hissed. "These tunnels echo. We had beer parties down here my freshman year."

"Mine, too," Pat said. He was still watching Holl and the other Little Folk with open fascination. "That was normal. *This* is freaky."

The elves stood away from the humans in a knot under the

light of a hanging bulb. Maura, Holl, and Keith conversed quietly with the other students near the entrance. Marcy and Enoch stood off on the side between the two groups.

"May ve know vhy ve are assembled in this place?" the Elf Master requested in a quiet voice.

"Just a moment," Keith said. "Are we all here?"

"Two more coming." Lee's voice sounded from above them. They all looked up, expecting to see the big student backing down the ladder, but to everyone's surprise, including Keith's, a small elderly lady descended first.

"Mrs. Hempert!" Keith exclaimed, his voice echoing in the lonely hall. Lee came down next, grinning.

"She didn't want to be left out."

"But naturally," Ludmilla said, smiling at Keith. She walked over to Marcy, kissed her on the cheek, and gathered her protectively under her arm. "Hello, my dear."

Keith gestured to them all, gathering them closer. "Here's the problem," he said. "The elf village is about to have its cover blown." He had to hold his hands up to silence comment. "But not by me, or anything I'm doing. You'll notice that Carl isn't here. He's the one causing all the trouble. Just recently, he published a few articles." Keith nodded to Catra, who held up a folder of news clippings from her archives.

"I heard him confess it," Holl called out.

The murmuring grew louder. Keith raised his voice just a little to be heard. "And on Friday, he's going to talk to a reporter whose job is to ferret out facts and make a big deal about them. They call him an exposé writer."

There was a lot of muttering as the two groups, still separate, mulled over the information. Keith waited a moment for them to digest it, and then went on. "Now, there's been a lot of hard feelings lately, with everybody suspecting everybody else. The only way we can fix that is with cooperation. In fact, that just happens to be the only way we can get Carl to back off."

"What can we do?" Teri asked, concern in her eyes.

"I thought, between the bunch of us, we could come up with a creative way to queer it with this reporter. It's important to me to make it go wrong for him."

"I intend to help," Ludmilla said immediately. "I *know* it is important. You haf but to ask me."

"Me, too," Lee told him, and turned to the others, unconsciously echoing Holl. "I apologize for Carl on behalf of my species."

From the isolated group of elves, the Master stood forth. "It is our species, too," he said. He took Ludmilla's hand and bowed over it. "Danke shoen, mine old friend."

She put her other hand on top of his. "It is gut to see you again."

"They talk alike," Teri said, amused.

"I think we should all have a chance to help," Barry said, making the accord unanimous. The elves drew closer, mixing again with their friends. The girls hugged Teri and Marcy, and the men all shook hands.

"There is a time limit, you realize," Holl said. "We don't have as much time as we'd hoped, and we can't move while there is a watch out for us."

"Move? Where?" everyone asked at once.

"To a place. Keith knows."

Keith realized he did. "You bought the farmstead! I was really worried when I saw the 'Sold' sign. So that's where that money went."

The elves were visibly ashamed. "Of all folk, it is you we should have trusted." Candlepat put an appealing hand on his arm. He smiled down at her.

"You would have found out sooner or later," Holl put in apologetically. "I tried to call you after the sale was agreed, but you were in transit. After that, I was prevented from meeting with you."

"I took 'em there the other day," Lee grunted approvingly. "Nice choice. Needs work, though. I'm going to help out, too. If you don't mind, that is. It's all 'Keith Doyle this,' and 'Keith Doyle that' to them." He made a face, drawing his voice up into a falsetto.

"I'm sorry for the things I thought about you, Keith Doyle," Marm said, slapping him on the back, reaching high enough to hit between Keith's shoulder blades. "I'll pass it to the others to begin production once again. We have commitments to meet." There was a wholehearted murmur of agreement.

"Good," Keith said. "Now, here's what I have in mind. A few little surprises, that's all."

* * *

On the way back to campus, Holl looked up the street, and blanched. "Uh-oh." He stuck his hand into Keith's.

Keith looked down in surprise. "What's this?" he asked playfully. "I thought you had a thing for Maura."

"There's a security officer down there, you had-a-thing," Holl growled out of the side of his mouth. "At least in this twilight he can't see me clearly. Now escort me safely across the street, Uncle Keith."

"Naturally, Holl, my dear boy," Keith said indulgently. "Look both ways."

"We do," Holl muttered in an undertone. "I look uncomfortable, and you look like a fool. As usual."

▪ Chapter 36 ▪

As promised, the elves had geared up to full production again, and reported to Keith through Marcy that they would have all orders filled within the week. Keith was pleased, because he was able to reply to a mayday call from Ms. Voordman, pleading for her shipment. "It's gift season, Keith. If I wait too long I'll miss the window."

"I'll get it to you today, Ms. Voordman," Keith vowed, smiling at Diane, who disappeared into the back room to put away her purse. Ms. Voordman was his best customer, and he felt bad about letting her down.

"And by the way, Keith, there was a man in here last week looking at your merchandise. I would call him a snappy dresser. He made a fuss about union labels." Ms. Voordman's eyes grew cold, and Keith swallowed, suspecting that Lewandowski hadn't forgotten about him. "He didn't say anything openly, or I would have gotten a restraining order, but he suggested if I kept buying non-union goods I might have a fire."

"What?" Keith squawked.

"Oh, I've heard it before, but this is the first time at Country Crafts. He particularly wanted me to pass it on to you."

Keith nodded, his mouth in a grim set. "Don't you worry, Ms. Voordman. I'll do something about it." He turned and strode purposefully toward the door.

"My shipment!" she called out to him.

"Oh, yeah!" Keith swung around and kept moving toward the street. "This afternoon, Ms. Voordman. I promise!"

Holl's estimate on completion of the orders was right on the money. Just after Mythology class on Wednesday, Keith picked up a colossal bag of newspaper-wrapped bundles from the elves' newly opened back door and started for his car.

Suddenly, he spotted a broad figure in a black suit. He turned around on his heel and pushed himself and his bag back through the doors of the building.

"Hey!" Diane squawked, all but knocked off her feet. "You sure know how to impress a girl."

Keith dropped the bag and helped steady her. "I'm sorry. I owe a guy some money, and I'm trying to avoid him."

"A lot of money? I could lend you some."

"No, thanks," Keith assured her. "I don't think you'd have enough." He peered out the window, but the man in the black suit turned out to be a Jesuit theology teacher walking to class. He panted a sigh of relief.

"It's because of me, isn't it?" Diane asked woefully. "I've impoverished you forever by taking that scholarship away from you."

"It's okay, really," he assured her. "An investment of mine will pay off in a few days. I just have to wait for it, and everything will be okay. I just want to avoid some people 'til then."

"Are they looking for you? Do you need to hide out?" she asked anxiously, fearing for his safety. She moved protectively closer to him.

"No," Keith said appreciatively, slipping an arm around her waist. "I can handle it. But there is something you can do for me."

"Anything."

Keith shifted the bag into her arms. "Keep your boss from wringing my neck."

"Why not? Count on me," Diane said, moving out the door Keith opened for her. "Don't let 'em get you."

Leaning around the bag, he kissed her on the cheek, and started out the door behind her. Suddenly, he spotted another burly figure on the common, coming toward the classroom building. The union man whom he'd gotten arrested for indecent exposure. It was clear the thug had seen him, too, for he had quickened his pace. He was back here to make it "personal."

Keith could hear the man's promise of revenge ringing in his ears as he fled back into the building and began to look for some place to hide. There was nothing on this floor but classrooms and storage rooms. Behind him, the man opened the door and stepped in, stopping at the top of the hall to let his eyes adjust to the dimness. Keith picked a door at random and pulled the door open.

A class was in session. "Yes, young man?" a thin, elderly professor asked him. "Can I help you?"

"Sorry," Keith said. "I guess not."

The union man walked swiftly up the hall toward him, an expression on his face which Keith equated with murder, but his pace was even, as if he belonged here.

Keith swallowed. He had to find a place to hide. He thought hopefully of finding a security officer, but they rarely patrolled the classroom buildings.

Glancing frequently over his shoulder, he walked rapidly away from the union man, trying to seem nonchalant. He ducked among a crowd of students who emerged suddenly from a study room, and then he started running down the hall.

His pursuer dropped pretense and ran after him, roughly shoving the other students out of his way. Books flew out of arms, and the girls shrilled protests.

Keith flew down the corridor. There was one solid wood door near the end of the hall that he believed led to a storeroom in which he could hide. Reaching it only a few feet in front of his assailant, he flung open the door and shot inside, slamming it closed behind him.

It was filled with filing cabinets and boxes. There didn't appear to be anywhere he could stay out of sight that he would fit, as thin as he was. He heard footsteps in the hall, and willed himself to come up with an idea fast. There was a lot of dust in here, and his eyes watered. He knew just a moment too late that he was going to sneeze.

"Aa-choo!" His whiskers twitched, tickling his ears.

The footsteps outside stopped, and the door creaked open. "All right, Doyle. I saw you come in here. Come out and I'll make it quick."

Keith plunged between a pair of filing cabinets. His whiskers extended the width of the space, dusting long lines in the grime on either side. It had looked like he wouldn't fit, but no, it was just wide enough for Keith, who was of no great bulk, to move through. He reached the back, and poked his nose into first one and then other possible hiding places, measuring each with his whiskers, which were exactly as wide as his narrowest dimension. He flattened himself in the niche made by one of the files and an upended metal-topped desk into which his whiskers fit snugly, if not comfortably.

Malcolm was used to clients being reluctant to cooperate with Mr. Lewandowski, but never had a reluctant client managed to get Malcolm and his partner thrown in jail for the night, either. Mr. Lewandowski had been justly pissed off to hear that the two of them had gone down for a simple scare-visit and ended up bare-assed before the night magistrate. Malcolm's pride was bruised. That kid had to pay.

He'd had no trouble finding where Keith was going, either, thanks to a large young man with a brown crewcut in Power Hall who was happy to give him Keith's schedule. Sure enough, he'd spotted the red-haired kid leaving the big building. Too bad the kid had seen him so soon.

With a quick lookout to make sure there were no nosy security guards walking around, Malcolm slowly pulled open the door to the storeroom and put an eye against the edge. The room was dim and full of tall, blocky shadows surrounded by darker striped platforms. Creepy. A glance to the left showed him the light switch, and Malcolm reached in to flip it upward. In the light, the tall figures became stacks of desks and tables ringed with filing cabinets. To Malcolm's eye, there wasn't room to fit a playing card between 'em, let alone a teenager.

He heard the rasp of a shoe on the floor somewhere in the back of the room behind a row of folding chairs. With a malicious smile, he flexed his shoulders and moved in on the chairs, picking them up by the dozen and depositing them behind him, like John Henry forcing his way through the mountain. If the way out was blocked, Doyle would have to come past him to escape.

"I'm gonna get you, kid," Malcolm whispered. The hiss of soles brushed the floor again. Must be the kid shaking in his shoes. "I'm gonna tear you apart."

At the back of the row was a dead end. Filing cabinets had been laid in a column all the way to the ceiling. Malcolm looked around, wiping his dusty nose on the back of an arm. No Doyle. There wasn't room to hide a rat among the heaps of furniture. Angrily, he flung the chairs back to fill in the gap. The ringing of metal on metal echoed deafeningly in the room, and Malcolm remembered too late he shouldn't attract any more attention. He didn't want the security force to find him before he taught that Doyle some manners. Leaving the remaining chairs in a heap, he slunk through the door and out of the building as casually as he could.

Keith heard the door slam behind him, and let go the breath he was holding. When the thug had started to push between the rows of chairs, he had passed right by Keith. Only the most incredible kind of luck kept him from looking to the right, straight into Keith's cramped niche. There would have been no escape, and that man would have torn him into little pieces. He vowed to do something about the union men, just as soon as he could get back to his dorm in one piece.

He counted up to a hundred before squeezing out between the cabinets, just in case the union man came back. Cautiously, slowly, he eased out of his hiding place with the ease, if not the grace, of a cat. "Thanks, guys," he said fervently, fingering his invisible whiskers and sending the elves grateful thoughts. "They worked!"

"So, kid? You called me yesterday for a meeting. You wanted to meet in a neutral location. So here we are. What do you want?"

Sherman Park was virtually deserted during business hours on a Thursday. And yet, Keith figured, if Lewandowski's two hoods started to beat him up, the chances were better that someone would come to his rescue here than in some secluded alleyway.

"I asked you to meet me because I want you to leave my friends alone," Keith said furiously, standing before the union boss, his arms crossed firmly over his chest.

Lewandowski ate some peanuts out of a cellophane bag and threw a few to the squirrels who surrounded the park bench under the brilliant green of the maple trees. He seemed unimpressed with Keith's bluster. After all, the skinny kid wasn't likely to try to pick him up and deck him with the two union enforcers standing so close. If he could pick him up at all, which Lewandowski doubted. "Where's my list?"

"You threatened one of my customers with a fire if she continued to carry my goods. And one of your goons there," he pointed to Malcolm, who still wore the scabs from the thorns in the hedge, "chased me around the campus in his underwear. Why should I cooperate? I thought you were going to do this legally."

"Chased you around the campus—? Wait a minute," the union president held up a hand, glaring at his employee. "Is he wired? Did anybody search him? He could be recording this."

"No, sir," said Malcolm, avoiding Lewandowski's eyes. Nodding to his fellow, they went over to Keith, patting down his windbreaker and jeans.

"I got something," the other thug said, unzipping Keith's jacket and stiff-arming the student in the face when he tried to get his property back. "A camera." He pulled the woven strap from around Keith's neck and dangled the object before Lewandowski.

"It's not real. It's a toy," the union president complained, poking at the small wooden carving with the circular cloth window where the lens should be. "You think you're funny or something?"

"That's one of my samples," Keith said. "I call it a magic lantern. Can I have it back?"

Lewandowski sighed and nodded to his man. Keith looped the strap around his neck and sat down next to the union president.

"So, where's my list?"

"I don't have one," Keith said. "I don't have any employees."

"Oh, yeah? Where do you get your merchandise, then?"

"They're made by elves," Keith stated. "Look, Mr. Lewandowski, I don't like the way you do things. I can't afford to fight you in court. I'm too small for you to bother with. Why don't you just leave me alone?"

"It's in the interests of the members of the union. They've got families to feed. Scabs like you take sales away from them. That's what we protect them from. Listen, kid," the union boss got suddenly bored with the smart-assed college student defying him. "You had just better play along with me. I've got police and judges and elected officials on my payroll who could see to it that you won't get a job in this state for the rest of your life, let alone a lousy diploma. Judge Arendson gets plenty from me every month to sign court orders, and, well, he sees that the court cases go my way. I got insurance adjusters who never settle arson claims for the insured, not if they cross me, so warn your lady friend. Even a stooge with the police, so it won't do you no good to call them."

"I'm impressed," Keith said.

"You ought to be. If I don't get that list from you pretty soon, you'd better never get a traffic ticket in this city, or my man on the force will write up every ordinance they can find on that blue eggbeater you call a car. You may as well let yourself get organized. Save yourself a lot of trouble."

"Well . . . I didn't know what I was dealing with before," the boy admitted. "I'm awfully busy right now. Let me have a couple of days to decide. Okay?"

Lewandowski crumpled up the cellophane and tossed it aside. "Sure. I can wait that long. I'll be waiting to hear from you."

▪ Chapter 37 ▪

The next day, Friday afternoon, Keith tripped into Carl's room, ignoring the death-dealing looks with which the other student burned him. Pat had given him the tip-off that Steven Arnold had already arrived, and gone back to the dorm room to help with his part of the "surprises." There was a man sitting on the edge of Carl's desk, jotting things down on a legal pad, who Keith guessed must be Arnold. He was about thirty, with dishwater brown hair beginning to creep backwards from his forehead; he wore a skeptical expression that went well with his slightly slanted eyebrows.

"Hi, Carl," Keith said cheerfully. "Heard you had company." Keith carried a glass flask, containing a potently stinking liquid (Holl's inspiration) with a long piece of white cotton twine coiled up in the bottom, which he waved at the reporter in greeting. Some of the liquid sloshed up, creating a miniature miasma. Keith coughed. "Hi. Keith Doyle. Fellow student of Carl's."

"Steven Arnold. Nice to meet you." The reporter gagged and pointed to the flask. "What's that?"

"Oh, lantern wicks." He cocked an eye at Carl to see if the big athlete caught the hint. The fish went right for the bait; not even a fight. Carl caught him by the upper arm and dragged him over.

"Doyle here knows the Little Folk. Tell Mr. Arnold about the elves. We're both in the class taught by one."

"Well," Keith said brightly, "Mrs. Depuis is really short, but you couldn't call her an elf." He wrinkled his nose. "Maybe a dwarf."

"No," Carl urged. "The group in the library."

"Well, yeah, we were in a group for a while. But it was a sort of encounter group," Keith told the reporter. "The stuff we talked about is private. I mean, what did *you* dream about when you were thirteen?"

"No, it wasn't," stormed Carl, finally deducing that Keith was making fun of him. That was the end of any 10 percent of merchandising profits for Keith. "It was the Little Folk. Look!" He reached in a drawer and produced one of the Hollow Tree lanterns. He blew on the wick and it lit. Another puff and the flame went out.

"Lemme see that," the reporter said, fascinated.

"Do you like that?" Keith asked, full of pride. "I make 'em."

"You what?" Carl interrupted him incredulously.

"Yeah. I sell them to the gift shops around town. The string is treated with a chemical. Look, I was just whipping up some more. Got the raw materials for the wicks right here in this bottle.'' With a long pair of tweezers, he fished an end of the cord out of the liquid. Exposed to air, the chemical compound was horribly pungent. Both Carl and the reporter choked and backed away. Keith, even though he was prepared for it, felt a little faint. One of Teri's little concoctions. All he knew about it was that it contained nail polish remover and vinegar. What else, he had no idea. For all he knew, she'd cornered a skunk and persuaded it to contribute to the cause.

''Sorry,'' he said. ''Brings tears to your eyes, doesn't it? It doesn't stink when it's dry. Here. I'll show you.'' He picked up Carl's blow dryer and turned it on the cord full blast. Hot, the smell was close to unbearable. Over the roar of the motor, he told the reporter, ''It's 99 percent cotton and 1 percent I can't tell you, because that's what makes the magic work, so to speak. It's nitrogen/carbon-dioxide sensitive, but perfectly safe.''

''Doyle!'' shouted Carl. ''Get out of here!''

''Wait a minute, Mr. Mueller,'' said the reporter, pointing his pen at Carl. ''I'd like to see what he's got there.''

Keith beamed at him. When it was dry, he picked up the tweezers and held the long piece of twine out to Carl. ''Blow on it,'' he suggested to the reporter. Doubtfully, the reporter obliged. He puffed at it. The whole length caught fire. With a curse, Carl jerked his hand back, dropping it, and stamped on it to put the fire out. ''Don't do that,'' Keith admonished him. He knelt and blew on it. The rug was unscorched where the burning cord had fallen. Carl studied his unburned hand and regarded Keith with enmity.

''That's wonderful,'' gasped the reporter, both eyebrows reaching for the ceiling. ''Can I have a piece of that?''

''Sure,'' said Keith magnanimously, cutting off a few inches of the cord with a pocket knife. ''But please don't try to duplicate it. My patent is pending. They last for a decent while before the chemical is all used up.''

''Thanks. I might like to order some of your merchandise,'' the reporter said, carefully putting the string away in an envelope. ''I've heard of you, now that I think of it. My editor will love this. You could get a science award for that fluid.''

"Nope. I'm in it for the money. My card." Keith flourished it, with a dramatic expression. "Hollow Tree Industries. Woodcrafts and wonders."

"Nice name," the reporter said. "How'd you like to talk to me a little later? It'd be some free publicity for you."

"Sure." Keith beamed. "Always happy to meet a member of the legitimate press." Arnold beamed back.

"Damn you to hell," Carl snarled, hating Keith for casting doubt on his story. "Well, come on, Mr. Arnold. I'll show you where the Little Folk meet for those classes."

"What sort of classes?" the reporter wanted to know.

"Biology, Philosophy, uh . . . Sociology."

"Interesting curriculum," Arnold said. "Who teaches this class?"

"One of the older ones. He's called the Master."

The reporter scribbled that down on his pad. "Uh-huh. Humans and, uh, elves both, in the class?"

Carl scowled, suspecting he was not being taken seriously. "Yes."

Keith was delighted: the reporter was a skeptic. He made Keith's job a thousand times easier. With an air of ennui, Keith announced that he wanted to come along for the ride. "I have to see this," he insisted, a mischievous grin on his face. "Never heard of elves associating with college students."

Carl was about to retort, but he noticed the questioning expression in the reporter's eye. His credibility was already on the line. Doyle, he could take care of later.

"Uncle Keith?" Holl tapped on the door, right on cue.

"Oh, wait," said Keith. "I'm babysitting for my nephew. He's a Trekkie. You don't mind if he comes, too, do you?"

"No, not at all," the reporter assured him.

Holl came in, hatless, casually dressed in a new pair of jeans made by Maura and a windbreaker borrowed from Keith's younger brother. He could easily have been a member of the Doyle clan. There was theatrical latex smeared all over his ears, courtesy of Pat, which made them look larger than usual. Holl scratched fitfully at the rubber goo, which was dried to a matte finish. "Uncle Keith, can I have a can of pop?"

Carl jumped to his feet and pointed. "That's one of them. That's not a kid. He's an elf."

"He's a Trekkie," Keith explained. He gestured at Carl, then made a spinning motion at his temple with a finger.

"Oh, I see," the reporter nodded.

"Fascinating," Holl intoned.

"For God's sake, his ears! Look at his ears!" Carl dragged Holl over to the reluctant reporter, and turned the elf's face sideways. Holl put on a convincing demonstration as the uncooperative adolescent. "Lemme go!" He struggled and kicked at Carl until Keith interceded.

"Look, you'll pull them off. Watch it," Keith said, moving Holl away. "They're expensive."

"I shall have to stun you," Holl threatened in what was obviously an excited child's attempt at a Vulcan monotone, pulling a toy phaser from the pocket of his borrowed windbreaker. Keith pushed the barrel of the toy gun toward the floor.

"Never point guns at anyone, Holl," he admonished his 'nephew' solemnly. "Not even toys."

"They're latex and rubber," the reporter said to Carl coldly, after examining the plastic coating with Holl's grudging cooperation. "You'll have to do better than that to convince me you've got something, Mr. Mueller. Two articles in the *National Informer* do not constitute proof to me. The library, I think you said?"

"After you," Keith said, courteously bowing Arnold and Carl out before him. He hung back until he was sure they were well on their way down the hall. With a maniacal chuckle, he tilted the flask at eye level, and very carefully poured about an ounce of skunk cocktail into each of Carl's track shoes. Holl gave him a wink as they pulled the door closed.

A guest pass was secured for Arnold in the office of the library. The plump administrative assistant on duty recognized the name when she stamped the card with the date and hour. "Steven Arnold?" she asked almost flirtatiously, smoothing her flowered print dress. "I've read everything you've published. You have a fine mind."

"Thank you, ma'am," Arnold said politely. "Takes one to know one."

She blushed and giggled, for a moment looking far younger

than her fifty or so years. "Are you going to write a piece about our library, young man?"

"I sincerely hope so," Arnold said. "I've been promised a special exclusive." He gave Carl a this-had-better-be-worth-it look.

"Come on," Carl said, impatient with protocol and all librarians. "This way."

As they reached the checkpoint for the stacks, the librarian on duty stopped them. "Just a moment," she said.

"They're with me," Arnold said, flashing his pass and a big smile. The librarian perused them indifferently and let them by. Holl lifted an eyebrow at her as he passed.

"Fascinating." Holl was really catching on to the Trek jargon, Keith thought approvingly.

"My nephew," Keith said, as he went in behind Holl.

They took the elevator to the twelfth level, and walked down the stairs from there. There was no screech or struggle as they entered Level Fourteen. Carl had obviously set it up beforehand; the security door had been left propped open and the hinges oiled. The lights were on, but the place still had an air of eeriness.

Arnold scribbled on his legal pad, having no need of illumination to write, a talent forged over long years of experience. He looked around at the tall shelves of books looming over him forbiddingly, like giant librarians. After a moment, he noted the image in his pad. It would make good copy for the sensationalist editor to whom his work was frequently assigned.

The corners of the chamber were dark in spite of the fluorescent lighting, which was inadequate for the expanse it had to cover. Arnold had to admit that willing suspension of disbelief would be easy to accomplish in such a spooky location, but he was still waiting to be shown.

Carl marched his little train proudly down the aisle to the wall that separated the classroom from the rest of the library. It was his moment, and he was going to enjoy it. Doyle and the elf kid with the stupid glue on his ears were in the back watching him, looking like they might laugh. Doyle was a jerk to miss out on bringing the Little Folk to the attention of the world. Now it was Carl Mueller who would get all the kudos. And all the rewards.

"Now, watch." The reporter leaned in as Carl gestured them

to come closer. The burly student took out his green glowing key, and felt the invisible door in the wall for the smooth metal scratchplate. It was still too dark in this corner to see what he was doing, but never mind. He'd been doing it without light for years. With a deep breath, he put the key to the keyhole.

There was a blinding green flash, and the green light around the key went out like a birthday candle. Keith, the reporter, and Carl all rocked backward as they were momentarily dazzled into shocked blindness. They scrubbed at their eyes, seeing red flashes that faded slowly back to normal vision. Holl, who knew what to expect, merely looked Vulcan and imperturbable. He had had his eyes closed.

When Carl could see again, he looked for the keyhole. He scrabbled at the wall. The doorplate had vanished completely. "What happened? Where did it go?" He looked down at his key. It was cold and dead again, just a piece of metal with nothing special about it but the shape.

"Where did what go, Mr. Mueller?" Arnold asked, watching the big student's antics with an air of displeasure.

"Phasers on stun," intoned Holl, from behind Keith. He resheathed his toy gun, which he had drawn when they boldly went where no man had gone before. "Request permission to beam up."

"Sorry," said Keith plaintively. "I shouldn't buy him toys his mother hates. She always gets even with me. I've got him for a whole week."

"What the hell happened?" demanded the reporter. "Is this some kind of elaborate college prank? My editor is going to be furious. You promised him an exclusive on alien beings living on this college campus. I don't waste my time on student rookery. If you got me down here on a false pretense, I'm going to report it to your dean. I don't work for the *National Informer*, you know!"

"Where's the door?" Carl felt the wall wildly, sounding desperate. He was nearly sobbing with frustration. "You did this, Doyle. Somehow I know you did." His voice reverberated hollowly in the concrete room, but the echoes sounded like the voices of children laughing.

"There's no door here. This is the oldest part of the stacks," Keith explained, patiently. "The walls are solid." He knocked on one, and it gave out with a flat *thonk*. "Everybody is always blaming me for things I haven't done." He turned back to the reporter, who was putting his pencil away in his breast pocket. "Did you know that the Historical Society has declared Gillington a historical monument? I have been in touch with them over the past months, and they have finally reached their decision. We're looking forward to the restoration committee's recommendations."

"I'd heard," Arnold said, taking the pencil out again. "Well, since I won't be getting the story that I came out for, I might as well hear about your library."

"Well, we're proud of it. Built in 1863 during the Civil War . . ." With an arm around the reporter's shoulders, Keith led him and Holl back up the stairs to the ground floor. Carl didn't follow immediately. There was a wild yell and a thud as the burly student hit the dusty floor facefirst. From somewhere behind the American History section, Enoch had thrown a minor cohesiveness whammy, and stuck Carl's shoes to the floor.

On the way out of the stacks, Keith gave Steve Arnold a quick rundown on the history of the library. They parted with a friendly handshake before the disapproving eyes of the stack librarian. "I think you can count on seeing this Gillington article some time next week, Keith. And I'll be sending you an order for Hollow Tree pretty soon. Sure you can't spare free samples for the press?" Arnold asked persuasively, putting his notebook away.

Behind them, the elevator door opened. Carl emerged, red-faced and fuming, and stalked across the floor to just behind where the three others stood. He had to walk with some care because he was shod only in sweat socks, but they helped him to move with greater stealth. His shoes still lay stuck to the floor on Fourteen as though by industrial-strength Crazy Glue. He didn't know how he was going to blame Doyle for that, but it had to be his fault, just like the way Doyle made a fool of him in front of Steven Arnold.

"I would if I could, but I have a really high overhead and a loan to pay back," Keith said, regretfully. He liked Steven Arnold. "The best I can do is a discount."

Arnold shrugged. "It was worth a try. No hard feelings. Good-bye, kid." The reporter waved to Doyle's nephew.

Holl raised his hand in the Vulcan salute, in which he had been carefully schooled by Keith. "Live long and prosper."

Arnold left the library with Keith waving him a friendly farewell from the entryway to the stacks. Carl waited until Arnold was out of sight, then he sprang out and grabbed Keith by the front of his shirt. He had recovered from the shock he'd received downstairs, and now he was going to get even with the person responsible for ruining his plans. The satisfied look fled from the red-haired youth's face as his air was cut off.

"Ulp!" Keith protested, trying to free his collar. He glanced over at the fire door.

Carl followed his gaze, then glared back at Keith. "You've got a heck of a lot of nerve," Carl said, shaking him roughly. "It took me forever to set up that interview. I'm going to beat the funny stuff out of you. Yeah. Come on." He dragged Keith back into the stairwell and let the door whine closed. Carl pushed him to the wall. "It's just you and me."

"Wrong," said Lee, stepping out of the corner and dragging Carl away from Keith with the ease of a man used to flipping around fifty-pound sacks of flour. "It's you and all of us. We've been waiting for you."

Carl stared at him in disbelief. "Where . . . ?"

"I'm disappointed in you," Teri said, appearing from behind him and shaking her head. "I'm the one who brought you in. I'm so ashamed. I thought he'd ruin it because he's such a nut," she pointed at Keith. "But *you* tried to do it. You know what this means to the rest of us. How could you?"

Carl goggled like a fish. A sentence forced its way out. "I didn't think anyone would care. It was my chance . . ."

"You're crazy," a voice grunted from the other side. Barry stood there in the shadows with an arm around Marcy, holding her, keeping her from springing out at Carl. She looked ready to explode, and Barry seemed dubious about his ability to keep her where she was much longer. "Mister Hotstuff," Barry spat. "As if you don't owe them, the same as the rest of us."

"We do care." Teri tossed her head. "In fact, we care more than we really knew. When it looked like we might lose our friends and teachers, it tore us to pieces. We blamed the wrong man because you *accused* him. And we believed you! You won't ever be able to betray the Little Folk again, because you won't know where they are."

"No one will believe you when you talk about 'em. And none of us will back you up." Lee punctuated his statement with another push.

"From now on, the Little Folk will just be a legend as far as you're concerned," Marcy said, throwing off Barry's arm, her eyes glowing fire as she stepped right up to Carl. She drew back her hand and slapped him ringingly across the face. He was so surprised he backed up a pace. *"That's* for that day in class. Maybe you'd better study up on it, big man. Come on, Keith."

Rubbing his shoulder, Keith turned out the door, side by side with Marcy. As one, the students walked out behind them, leaving Carl stunned on the landing, rubbing his cheek. "Hey!" he called.

The hinges squeaked faintly as the door sagged shut behind the other students, drawing the attention of Mrs. Hansen, who was discussing changes of assignment with the librarian on duty at the front of the stacks. "Oh, no," she said, catching a glimpse of the fire door swinging closed. "Not again." She shot through the chamber, pulled the door open, seized Carl by the shoulder and marched him out into the lobby. "If I have told you students once, I have told you a thousand times. That stairwell is OFF LIMITS! Come with me. I want to talk to your student advisor!"

Surreptitiously, Keith examined his own key. It was still glowing.

"Don't worry," Holl said, peeling at his latex disguise. "Yours will still work, always. We'll just be opening a new door. Here." He handed him the phaser. "I do not need this anymore."

Keith twitched his invisible whiskers in satisfaction. "By the way, I have a present for you," he told Holl. Digging into a pocket, he came up with a small piece of beige paper. "It took a little conniving, but I pointed out you have got a bank account and a job, however nepotistic." It was a Social Security Card made out to Holland Doyle.

"Thanks, Uncle Keith," Holl said, reverently handling the card as if it was printed on crystal.

"Don't mention it, nephew," Keith replied, knowing that the breach between them was completely healed now.

▪ Chapter 38 ▪

Five after three. The union president waited in the middle of the Sears television department for Keith to appear. It wouldn't have been such a bad wait if there was any place to sit and watch the thirty or forty sets on display. Besides, with ten of 'em tuned to each of the four local stations, the place sounded like a zoo anyway. The manager had recognized him and was getting nervous. Sears employees were represented by a different union, but you never knew: they might be thinking of a change of organization. The wait didn't bother him, because he knew he was going to win. Hollow Tree would join the happy membership roll of Lewandowski's union.

Ten after. His bodyguards were watching two different soap operas on the most expensive receivers in the place. Lewandowski casually leaned against a big cabinet set as Keith came running up to him.

"Sorry I'm late. I couldn't find a place to park."

"No problem, kid. Well, what can I do for you? We're private." No one could hear a thing over the racket.

"Well, I just wanted you to know that there's no hard feelings," Keith began, removing the toy camera from around his neck, "but I'm not going to join your union."

Lewandowski's blood pressure went up twenty points. "Are you nuts? Didn't I tell you what I can do to you?"

"Sure you did," Keith agreed. He set the toy down on top of the nearest console television. Suddenly, all forty sets showed the same scene. It was a man on a park bench under a maple tree with pigeons and squirrels all around him. Lewandowski glanced down curiously. The man on TV was himself. And he was talking, on every set in the store.

". . . I've got police and judges and elected officials on my payroll who could see to it that you won't get a job in this state for the rest of your life, let alone a lousy diploma. Judge

Arendson gets plenty from me every month to sign court orders, and, well, he sees that the court cases go my way. I got insurance adjusters who never settle arson claims for the insured, not if they cross me . . ."

Lewandowski's bodyguards looked up with shock as their programs were interrupted by their boss's confession. They noticed Keith and started toward him.

The manager of the television section was beginning to get interested in the sudden change of programming on his sets, and was coming over to ask Mr. Lewandowski what was going on. The union boss grabbed Keith's arm.

"Stop it! Shut it off!"

"Sure, Mr. Lewandowski." The kid moved the camera away, and the taped confession was immediately replaced again by the soap operas. "See? I remember *everything* you said."

Lewandowski narrowed his eyes at Keith, who still looked innocent and stupid to him. He waved away the bodyguards, who were within inches of grabbing the college student. "All right. You win. You're not worth it. I'm a businessman, too. I know when I've lost. Gimme that tape."

"I can't," Keith said firmly. "I think I'll always keep it to remind me of you. But you'll never hear from it again if you leave my customers alone." The union man nodded reluctantly and Keith smiled. "Just one more thing," he pointed out. "Please keep your gorillas off campus. We have an ordinance against wild animals in the streets, leash laws, you know."

Keith watched the thugs' faces turn red.

"Nice doing business with you," he said cheerfully. "Excuse me. I've got another appointment to make." The union boss was still staring at the bank of television sets as Doyle went out the door.

"You wanted to know where I was studying down in the library," Keith said, guiding Diane down the stairs to Level Fourteen on that Tuesday afternoon. "So, I'm showing you."

"What's this got to do with my failing Biology?" Diane wanted to know. She looked around anxiously for any library personnel. They could get in trouble for being down here. The level was restricted, but Keith seemed to be pretty well at home.

"Well," Keith began, "that just happens to be what I'm studying this term. The very thing."

"Uh, Keith," Diane babbled uncomfortably, clutching his arm as they crossed the dark floor. "I don't think that, um, *practical* instruction in biology is what I need."

"Don't worry," Keith said. "It's not what you think. Trust me. Please." He walked her through the stacks and took out the glowing key. Diane stared at it disbelievingly. Keith put the key in the lock and turned it.

"What *is* this? This is just to scare me, right? It's a make-out corner," she determined pugnaciously.

"Nope," Keith said, pausing. "I want to present you to the greatest teacher in the world on *any* subject, *including* biology."

"You mean you?" Diane asked, with mock skepticism, turning into the bright room. "Hi, there, Mr. Alfheim," she called. "How nice to see you. What are you doing down here?" Then her eye took in the unique characteristics of the room's inhabitants. Her jaw trembled and fell open. "Oh, my," Diane said. Keith gently propelled her inside and closed the door.

"Good afternoon, Mees Londen. Von't you sit down?" the Elf Master suggested, pointing to an empty desk next to Marcy. It was Carl's.

"If it's all the same to you, Master, I can move," Enoch volunteered, lifting his books and leaving the desk next to Keith's vacant. Keith winked at him. Enoch smiled as he settled down between Marcy and Lee.

Diane's eyes followed the child-sized figures with wondering fascination. "I don't believe it."

"You'd better," Keith informed her. "These are my best friends."

"I know what she's thinking," Marm complained. "Those ears."

"They all do that," Holl chuckled as the Master rapped on his easel for order.

To Keith's delight, Diane fit in with the current class as if she had always been there. Teri gave him a silent thumbs-up behind her back, and he grinned. When the session broke up for the day, Holl suggested that she would be welcome to help box and wrap orders, since extra hands would be useful. Keith was delighted. Holl always voiced the others' opinions, and their opinion seemed to be that they were happy to have Diane with them.

Keith was pleased to have gotten his secret off of his chest to Diane, but he was equally pleased as to how well she was handling getting to know everyone. She had an easy facility for making friends, and it didn't take long before she stopped noticing the differences between the Big Folk and the Little. Within an hour, she was chatting as freely as she would anywhere else. Maura and Candlepat liked her immediately, and involved her in a passionate talk about fashion that made Keith want to flee the room. The look on Holl's face told him probably he'd have company.

Diane instantly agreed to help pack up Hollow Tree's merchandise, "to make things move more quickly," she said. "Ms. Voordman'll have a fit if the Hollow Tree shelf drops empty again." She went through the new items with careful, awed hands. "Ms. Voordman's going to love this jewelry," she said, holding a necklace of tubular beads up to her throat, and then reading the tag. "She won't be able to keep it in stock." She paused and stared. "Diane Teri Designs? What's this?"

"Well," Keith admitted sheepishly. "Teri gave me the idea, but they thought they should put your name on them, because you're my lady. In the end we compromised."

"Take it," Maura said, thrusting the necklace on her. "We'd be pleased if you accepted it as a gift."

"Oh, I can't," Diane protested, admiring the tiny lady timidly, almost afraid that by looking at her she might break her. "What about you? You'd look beautiful in something like this. You should have it instead."

"My man is the one who makes them," Maura said, proudly glancing at Holl. "I can get others."

"So," Diane asked Holl over a packing crate full of bundles, "why do they call you the Maven?"

The next morning, Wednesday the 15th, Keith and Diane cut all their classes, and spent the day taking the parcels around to his many clients. They waited impatiently at each stop for the owners to write out checks. "I don't know why you're in such a hurry," one shopkeeper admonished him, looking up at the two nervous faces across her counter. "I always pay within thirty days."

"Taxes, Mrs. Geer," Keith answered pathetically. "They'll skin me and hang me out to dry if I don't get in a quarterly payment."

"Of course. I understand perfectly." She bent her head over the checkbook and plucked the pink slip away from its perforations. "Many happy returns of the season."

It took them hours to get around to all of Keith's scattered customers. Most of them were as understanding as Mrs. Geer had been, but others had passed over tart remarks about economy along with their checks. Only a few were unsympathetic enough to insist on the standard thirty days, but in the end, there was enough in their hands to make the payment. At five minutes to five, Keith roared up to the front door of the Midwestern Trust Bank, and leaped out. "Sit in the driver's seat, will you?" he shouted to Diane as he ran inside, not waiting to see if she moved.

There was a long line for the tellers' windows, and Keith nearly died of impatience before a teller beckoned him over. He drummed on the counter while the girl counted the checks and then added up the total on her machine, until she stopped and looked annoyed at him. He flashed her a toothy smile, and put his hands behind his back. She went back to her addition.

At last, all the paperwork was finished. Keith stopped at one of the convenience tables and wrote out his checks to the I.R.S. and the Illinois Department of Revenue and sealed them with the appropriate forms into stamped envelopes. He saluted the guard who opened the door to let him out into the street, and heard the click of the deadbolt lock behind him. Throwing an OK sign to Diane, he trotted over to the mailbox, yanked down the handle, and threw the envelopes inside.

"Good evening, Mr. Doyle," a thin voice said from practically next to him.

"Yaah!" Keith jumped in surprise. Mr. Durrow stood there, his lips pursed in a tiny smile. This was the sort of effect I.R.S. agents lived for. He was pleased.

"I just mailed the check, honest to God," Keith wailed in protest.

"I know," Durrow said, austerely. "Your next payment is

due June 15th.'' And he walked away without changing expression.

The Historical Society met with the press on campus. Director Charles Eddy was pleased to announce to the newspaper-reading and television-watching public that: "Gillington Library has attained monument status, and it will be cared for in perpetuity. It is my honor to have discovered this worthy structure in our midst and brought it to the attention of those who care about the history of America.''

There was some scattered applause. Eddy smiled fatuously, posing with a broad gesture to the high doorway. Several cameras flashed in his face. "We are proud to have such a fine example of Civil War-era architecture in our own little town, and we want to make sure it will be available for our children to appreciate.'' There was much cheering and confetti-throwing as Eddy presented a small plaque to Mrs. Hansen, and they shook hands for the cameras. Eddy was pleased to note that he would have his picture in several papers by morning.

Brushing confetti out of his hair, Keith went to announce the good news to the Little Folk.

"That's a blessing,'' Holl told him. "Now, there is no need to hurry up to get to the farm. It will take quite a lot of work before it is habitable to our standards.''

It hadn't struck Keith until that moment that his friends would be moving just that much further out of reach. His heart sank in his chest. "How much time before you go?'' he asked with a long face.

Holl chucked him on the shoulder. "Cheer up, widdy. The Master won't leave the students while the course is in session. Perhaps we'll go in the summer. We'll be staying a good while yet.''

"Just as well,'' Diane put in, coming over to them with a handful of flowers from the village garden and a paper-covered bundle, "since I need to finish the Biology course. Don't fail me now, just when I think I could pass!''

The Master regarded her. "Ve keep our responsibilities in mind, Mees Londen.''

"We can't do without you in any case, Keith Doyle,'' Holl

continued. "We'll need help getting there and moving all our things, and finding sources for wood and plaster and the like."

"You bet." Keith got a dreamy look on his face and studied the glowing ceiling. "I've been formulating a plan to help with that. I have these friends . . ."

"My dad drives a big van," Diane interrupted eagerly. "I'm sure he'd lend it to me if I tell him I'm helping some friends move house."

"Uh-huh, and I think I can get a deal on bulk plas—"

Listening to Keith and Diane exchanging enthusiastic plans, Holl searched the heavens in exasperation. "We didn't know when we were well off. Now we have *two* like Keith Doyle."

"Now how bad could that be?" Marm inquired, frowning at his neighbor. He flipped a hand out and enumerated the blessings of Keith Doyle on his fingers. "Look at all the good he's done us. Found us a new home and the means to acquire it. Been a good friend."

"I agree," the Elf Master added. "I do like him, but I must admit he drives me mad."

"Me, too, but I like him anyway," Diane said, agreeably. The Elf Master didn't seem to intimidate her. "I have a present for you, Keith. From Ms. Voordman and me." She handed him the bundle, and he stripped the paper off of it. "This is thanks for everything, including the scholarship. Even though I know now it was phony." She looked at the others regretfully.

"You may still haf it at least for this year," the Master stated graciously, sketching a little bow to her. "I haf not changed my opinion of you, though I know not how finances will fall out in the years to come."

"Thank you," Diane said gratefully, turning to him. "I didn't know how I was going to break the news to my father." Behind them, Keith let out an exclamation.

Underneath the wrappings was the original ceramic elf-in-a-tree from the Country Crafts shop. "Now that I've seen the original, I know where he got the logo for your company. It wasn't just a fantastic myth." Diane grinned, winking at the Elf Master. He gave her a stern look, which made her smile more.

· Keith hugged her. "Thanks, Diane. Listen, I have to tell you. Wait 'til you hear about my project for next year," Keith said enthusiastically, holding the figurine carefully. "I'm going to be taking archaeology, you know. There are still reported sightings of the Fair Folk that no one's ever been able to disprove. Maybe I can find historic traces. *You* know——and, Holl, you haven't heard this one yet. I figure, if I can get up high enough in a hot air balloon——an airplane is too noisy, you'd scare 'em off——I can find out if there really are air sprites up in the clouds. There's much more atmosphere than there is surface on this planet, and I'm sure Nature never wasted it. But if I don't find anything *there* . . . Wait, Master! Where are you going?" The Elf Master turned and walked away, shaking his head as if it hurt.

"Progressive," Aylmer stated, teeth clenched around the stem of his pipe. "You are too progressive."

"Perhaps we should make statues of you, Keith Doyle," Holl said wryly, "as a fantastic myth."

"Yeah," Diane agreed. "But it shouldn't be an elf for you, Mr. Keith Doyle. I looked it up. It ought to be a gremlin. I found it when I was researching my Mythology paper. There you were, right in the dictionary. 'Gremlin: Mythical creature. Meddling spirit.' "

With a mischievous grin on his face, Keith bowed to them. "That's me," he said.